The
Naani
Diaries

Celebrating
30 Years of Publishing
in India

The Naani Diaries

RIVA RAZDAN

HarperCollins *Publishers* India

First published in India by HarperCollins *Publishers* 2023
4th Floor, Tower A, Building No. 10, DLF Cyber City,
DLF Phase II, Gurugram, Haryana – 122002
www.harpercollins.co.in

2 4 6 8 10 9 7 5 3 1

P-ISBN: 978-93-5629-160-7
E-ISBN: 978-93-5629-162-1

Typeset in 11.5/15.7 Minion Pro at
Manipal Technologies Limited, Manipal

Printed and bound at
Thomson Press (India) Ltd

The
Naani
Diaries

Contents

1.	Performance	1
2.	Proposals	31
3.	Dignity and Decisions	50
4.	Beginning	75
5.	Secrets	91
6.	Arranged	109
7.	Apology	135
8.	Children	164
9.	The Court Dance	189
10.	A Matter of Taste	210
11.	A Song for the Sehgals	227
12.	Heat	259
13.	Safety	274
14.	Delhi	284

15.	Cards	294
16.	Home	303
17.	Invitation	322
18.	Business	332
19.	Venture	355
20.	Decoration	366
21.	Planning	382
22.	Conversation	419
23.	Fabric	448
24.	Memory	465
25.	Tangled	476
26.	Fortune	488
27.	The Wedding	515
28.	Marriage	536

1

Performance

*M*y eyes burned because of the sugar, but they mistook it for wild curiosity. They always did, my colleagues and clients at McKinley Global Consulting, and they were impressed at how eager I was even at 9 p.m. on a Friday, closeted in a conference room with data sets and spreadsheets while New Yorkers around us returned home to loving partners and pets.

'Your account means that much to us, Mr Goldenblatt,' I cajoled the portly old man who had been trying hard not to look at my legs while I presented his quarterly profits. 'We're here because we believe in your laptops. We'll ensure your profit margins remain intact, despite the reforms.'

I considered reiterating the facts of the US–China trade war, which had led to an increase in the price of Mr Goldenblatt's China-made laptops and reduced his profits, but his attention seemed to be wavering. I didn't want to confuse him with any more with numbers; I just wanted to get him out of here so that he could sleep on our strategy and return on Monday, fresh-faced and ready to accept my proposal.

'You're saying our share price will fall further …' he said finally, keeping his eyes determinedly fixed on my face.

'If you don't take precautionary measures, yes.'

Goldenblatt's lawyer whispered in his ear. The CEO nodded once and studied the files again. His gaze slipped downwards slightly, towards my ankles. I cleared my throat and he looked up immediately, embarrassed at having been caught out.

Perhaps I shouldn't have worn the pencil skirt to work. It always unnerves the older male clients. The situation was unnerving enough as it is: having a twenty-nine-year-old girl pronounce the worth of your thirty-year-old company in a pie chart.

Men, I've noticed, like feedback from women in conference rooms as much as they like it in the bedroom. So, I try to dress it up as well as I can. The feedback, I mean.

When a company is failing to meet its targets, I make it my business to promise a more profitable outcome. I give them hope and encouragement and make it seem as though their failures have nothing to do with them and everything to do with 'subdued market conditions'. This strategy applies to the bedroom, too.

My greatest hope in that moment was that Mr Goldenblatt would go to his grave without ever discovering that his 'affordable laptops' were of such deplorable quality that they were not worth their cost price.

Mr Goldenblatt looked past me, at my boss. 'Rich,' he said, 'are these figures accurate?'

I bit my lip so hard that it started to bleed. Rich Stevens didn't know anything about this account. I had dealt with the figures for the last three months. Rich had only stayed at the office this long because his wife had told him not to come home tonight, after she had found out that he had cheated on her with Lisé at the Fourth of July office barbecue last weekend.

'Radhika knows what she's doing, Mr Goldenblatt,' Rich reassured him. 'She's put together three different proposals for your consideration.'

Oh God, I prayed, *please don't make me launch into each proposal now.*

I had a dinner reservation with Siddhant in thirty minutes. It was the only reason I wore this pencil skirt. And dragged poor Rajni to SoulCycle for the 1,000-calorie-burn workout at 7 a.m. this morning.

I could sense all my colleagues stiffening with a similar fear as Mr Goldenblatt raised the iPad to look at the proposals. Oh dear, this was it.

The minute he swiped left, the presentation would be on the big screen and I would be *on* again.

Fine. I will just make a quick trip to the bathroom, cancel on Siddhant, take another hit of sugar—

'I think we're good,' Mr Goldenblatt said. 'We can work it out on Monday.'

The team and I didn't dare look at each other for fear of breaking into grins of relief as Rich escorted the clients out. A bead of sweat ran down my collarbone.

Goldenblatt turned, and looked at my legs one last time.

❦

I have mastered the art of getting ready in a bathroom cubicle. Someday, I will have a cabin with its own en-suite bathroom, where I will beautify myself in solitude instead of sitting on a closed toilet lid to smear the hundred-dollar Clinique foundation on my bumpy skin while squinting into my Lancôme compact's mirror.

For now, however, I had mascaraed my eyes, spritzed myself with more perfume (J'adore by Dior) and swapped out my clumpy platforms for strappy high heels. I was contemplating putting some rouge on my cheeks to brighten up my face when there was a knock on the door.

'Occupied,' I yelled. Who was still here? Everyone else in Equity went home as soon as Goldenblatt's limo left Lexington.

'It's me-e-e.'

I swung open the door to see Rajni Dutt, my closest friend, named after the night sky, in her usual bronzed splendour. Rajni was perhaps the only woman on the planet who could make a shapeless grey shirt look sexy. Unlike me, she had never doubted her own desirability, at least not long enough to buy anything more than a lipstick at Bobbi Brown. She said it was because they didn't make cosmetics to suit her skin tone, but I suspected a deep-seated self-confidence that she was too modest to flaunt.

'You look gorgeous,' she said, as I brushed the ends of my hair quickly. 'But we're going to have to cut short the dolling-up. Rich wants to talk to you.'

What? Why now?

'Shit,' I said, immediately opening a sachet of brown sugar and pouring it into my mouth under Rajni's disapproving gaze.

'That is a disgusting, disgusting habit, and I'm going to send you to a detox camp soon.'

I ignored her as I swallowed the sugar. Now I could face the speed bumps. 'Do me a favour—'

But Rajni knew the drill. She took the empty sachet and flushed it down the toilet. 'I've already texted Siddhant. It's all right; he's having a drink at the bar with the other guys from Legal.'

'I love you,' I said and kissed Rajni quickly on the cheek, before power-walking as quickly as I could to my boss's cabin, trying my best not to let my ankles twist in the stilettos. The sugar rush helped. It helped me speed forward just when I was ready to collapse from the exhaustion of this never-ending day.

I really wished Rich hadn't slept with that silly Lisé from the French vineyard account. For one thing, his wife, Sheila, was a sweetheart who baked date cookies for the employees every month. Also, it would mean that Rich would be going home at a normal time instead of waiting around here, thinking it was okay to dump work on us to keep his evenings busy.

'Good work on Goldenblatt's computers,' he said as soon as I walked in.

'Thanks,' I smiled and sat down reluctantly.

'Radhika, you've outdone most of our senior analysts, both on Provence Wines and Ka-Ching Computers. I didn't think you'd be able to lead two projects with such a short turnaround time, but you've really pushed yourself and your team in the last two months to get the best results.'

'My review isn't due for another two months,' I joked.

Rich smiled and looked down. His eyes widened with understanding as he noticed my electric blue heels. 'I won't keep you longer,' he said, 'but I thought you deserved to hear good news after a job well done.'

'Thank you,' I said, slowly getting up, thinking the meeting was over. Siddhant was probably getting drunk on martinis by now. His jerk lawyer friends must have shown up at the bar to keep him company. Ugh. I needed him to be sober to have the discussion I had planned for tonight. I know it's only been a year, but I think we're ready to move in together.

'Lisé's team has asked if you can visit their bottling set-up next week to help them implement the efficiency changes your team came up with,' Rich droned on, but

I was faraway now, having cutesy arguments about rose-patterned duvet covers with Siddhant in Pottery Barn.

'They want you to go to Provence,' he said.

I broke out of my reverie of Siddhant and I decorating a Christmas tree together.

'You mean …' I nearly laughed, 'in the south of France?'

When was the last time a holiday fell into my lap like this? Never. Not since the freshman year of college at least.

'Yes, they've invited you to stay at their chateau on the vineyard. Along with a guest of your choice. Lisé's idea.'

I took back every nasty thought I had about Lisé. Everyone has their reasons for infidelity. As it is, 45 per cent of marriages in America failed. Who were we to judge?

'Yes, but—'

My face fell immediately. He shouldn't do that; he shouldn't offer me the lavender fields of Provence and then add a conjunction so casually.

'Oh, don't look so concerned,' Rich grinned. 'It's good news. In fact, it's an embarrassment of riches for you tonight.'

'So, what is it?'

'Mr Goldenblatt has already decided to approve one of your strategies.'

'Oh,' I sat back down, surprised. That was quick. 'Which one?'

'He chose the strategy that partners with a firm in India to create parts for his computers, instead of the one in Chengdu province.'

Oh yay. I had inadvertently created business for the mothership. Not bad, Radhika. Naani would be proud.

'That's a profitable option,' I said, smiling and already imagining the silk sundresses I'd be slipping into in France.

'Yes, but it has to be handled correctly.'

'Our offices in Mumbai can do that,' I pointed out. Rich, however, didn't look convinced.

'Radhika, Mr Goldenblatt was impressed by your work on his account. He wants you to personally handle the transfer of operations to the India office. It's the same week as the Provence Wines supervision. So, it's a toss-up between India and France.'

The ready response died on my rose-tinted lips.

'It's up to you, of course. But Mr Goldenblatt has offered a considerable compensation for the time you spend on his account in India. The number is …' Rich paused. 'Well let's just say there's a reason Lisé is inviting you and a friend on an all-expenses-paid trip to Provence.'

Rich wrote a figure on a paper and slid it over to me. But I didn't look at it. I already knew in my bones what I was going to do.

I thought neither of cheques nor chateaus when I made my decision.

❦

'Why?' Rajni screeched again, as I spooned yoghurt into her cereal bowl. 'Why would you do that?'

'Shh. Siddhant's asleep.'

As I had predicted, Siddhant and his friends had got blackout drunk on Manhattans, not martinis, celebrating the takeover of some Japanese doll-making firm. They had been comparing pictures of the inflatable dolls they would order with their bonuses when I had arrived at the most testosterone-fuelled part of the night, to drag him away to dinner. Jake, his annoying friend from law school, had tried to put up a fight, but Siddhant had yanked his arm away and said, 'Why would I spend the night looking at plastic when I have a real, live doll here?'

I forgave him the inebriation immediately and even let him sleep over instead of insisting upon making it to our dinner reservation. I didn't mind really, even though I'd been on the waitlist for two weeks to get a table at Wasabi-Masabi, the new Japanese–Iranian restaurant on 21st Street. Sometimes, it was just about being around the person you love, watching an episode of *Dating Around* while your partner slept peacefully next to you.

'Still, I don't understand why you would pick Bombay over Provence.' Rajni angrily crushed Weetabix into her cereal bowl. 'Radhika, you can go to Bombay any time. Your grandmother lives there. But does she have a chateau in the south of France? Can she invite you on an all-expenses-paid trip to a vineyard whenever you want?'

I smiled. Rajni was a contract lawyer. She was always trying to negotiate the best deal, to look for loopholes and to leverage a little more out of life. But she didn't understand, at least not yet.

'Rajni,' I whispered. 'Siddhant's parents live in Bombay.'

Her eyes widened in realization and then closed in irritation. 'Radhika,' she began in a warning tone, but I cut her off.

'I know what you're going to say, but I don't care. We've had a wonderful year together, and it's his thirtieth birthday this month. He's growing up. And he will feel differently, I can tell.'

Rajni looked like she wanted to hit me. She had never been too fond of Siddhant, even when we were all in college together at Yale. She always thought he was a rich Indian brat trying too hard to be white. But honestly, all of the Indians at Yale were the same breed. Secretly, I thought that they had the right to be. After all, they hadn't paid the seventy thousand-dollar-a-year admission price *just* for the Ivy league education. It made sense to want to pretend to be part of a superpower for a while if you had paid the exorbitant fee to be there.

Rajni and I were exceptions—she was a scholarship student, and I was, am, a professor's daughter, with the added advantage of being an American citizen by birth (New Haven, born and raised). We were never part of the (rich) Brown Gang, or the BGs as they called themselves. Siddhant, however, was their unspoken leader.

Our circles being so different, Siddhant and I barely interacted at Yale. I was always running—from the track to class to business society meetings. He was always in the courtyard, looking cute and drinking coffee with a large group of friends under the big oak. He hosted toga parties on the weekend and *The Great Gatsby*–themed dinners. I didn't even think he knew my name till he turned up at McKinley two years ago, fresh out of law school, asking me if I wanted to 'hang out' after work, given that we were fellow Yalies and all.

After a year of 'hanging out', he finally started calling me his girlfriend on 6 January 2017. (It had been a perfect Sunday; we had had a late breakfast of crepes and mimosas at Le Pain Quotidiene, the cute one on 96th Street.)

I am his first girlfriend. Before me, there were just a string of hook-ups. Just girls that he could never talk to beyond a few dates. Nobody with substance and purpose.

Nobody like me.

Which was why I thought it was time for me to meet his parents. And more importantly, for him to meet Naani.

'Do you remember what he got you for your birthday?' Rajni asked softly.

I recoiled. I wish I'd never told her.

'Who the fuck gifts *lube* to their girlfriend on her twenty-ninth birthday?' Rajni looked livid on my behalf. 'That's not someone who's ready to get married, Radhika.'

'SHH!' I practically yelled. She couldn't just scream the M-word around the apartment with Siddhant asleep in the next room. She could set me back months of progress! I glanced into the bedroom, but he was fast asleep—thank God—with that adorable dopey expression on his face.

'Rajni, look,' I told my best friend in a low, desperate whisper, 'I know this seems crazy to you, and I'm grateful to you for looking out for me, but I love him. And I know that Bombay will make him realize that he feels the same way about me.'

She looked at me with complete exasperation. '*Why?*' she demanded, picking up the contracts Goldenblatt had sent over and shaking them emphatically. '*What* is so magical about Bombay?'

Perhaps it was time to show her. I smiled as I pulled out the diary. Her irreverence wasn't going to last a minute longer.

❧

Personal Diary of Gayatri Khurana, Indian Administrative Service (IAS) officer, Delhi Division.

5 January 1960

Bombay

I was sure I'd fall in love here, but I didn't think it would be so soon.

Alighting on Bombay's railway platform was like arriving at a party. All the passengers in first class shed their woollen sweaters as soon as they stepped out to reveal smart suits and silk saris. It felt like we were all shaking off the dreary Delhi winter. The knotty knits were no longer needed here in this cool, cool city. Porters came up to us immediately, asking permission to string flower garlands around our necks like party favours. I paid one a few annas and wound it around my braid, breathing in the fresh scent of jasmine, wishing I could bottle it forever.

'Shall we call a taxi?' Birdy asked as he picked up my bags.

I nodded, forcing a quick, tight smile. I really didn't see why Yashwant Saab had to send him along with me. Birdy was a fine friend, and he had been a compassionate mentor, but I had hoped to have this one adventure alone, to be a traveller among travellers. The passengers in my cabin were lovely and had been quite happy to chat about their favourite discos in Bombay, but they fell silent when Birdy sat down opposite me and glared at anyone who tried to make conversation. Apparently, Bauji had given him strict instructions to ensure that I don't get duped by strangers in Bombay. Well, so far nobody had tried to snatch my chain, nor had they tried to steal my tiffin of parathas. Birdy said it was because he was around and keeping an eye on things, but I failed to see how a string bean like him could scare off thieves and suchlike.

Fortunately, once we reached our accommodation, I finally got rid of Birdy.

The Central Telegraph Office has allotted me a nice and airy little flat on Peddar Road. I have it all to myself since there are no other women in the Bombay IAS division to share it with. Although it is flattering to be the first of my kind here, I hope more women qualify for Bombay's state jobs soon. I would like to have a roommate, one to share grocery lists and reading recommendations with.

I didn't have time to do more than stare at my little sliver of the sea from the balcony before Birdy was back again. This time, however, he had a reason.

'You're wanted at the headquarters,' he said, 'The chief of the States Reorganization Committee has asked to see you.'

I smiled, revelling in my self-importance. 'We can't keep him waiting then, can we?' I sang and ran downstairs. A white Fiat was waiting to take us to the Central Telegraph Office at Kala Ghoda.

I despise the British for many reasons, but I found myself grinning with gratitude when the fantastic Victorian building rose from behind a row of Gulmohar trees. I couldn't believe that this Cathedral-like structure was going to be my office for the next six months.

'Ah! Our cartographer,' Mr Sinha said as soon as I walked into the large wood- panelled room filled with men and their moustaches. All of them were uniformed in warm three-piece suits despite the oppressive heat of the city.

'Officer Gayatri Khurana, reporting, sir,' I said, shaking his hand.

'The floor is all yours,' he said and moved away, allowing me to preside over the large wooden table. A large map of the Bombay Presidency was spread out on it, patiently awaiting dissection. I promised to be gentle.

'Gentlemen,' I began, tucking the pallu of my sari away so it didn't sway about as I spoke. 'We're here to reorganize the boundaries of the great state of Bombay. To divide it into Gujarat and Maharashtra, according to the languages spoken in each part.'

There was a slight murmur to my left, from the Gujarati field officers, I realized, who hated losing Bombay city to the new state of Maharashtra. They didn't look happy.

I leaned slightly towards them as I spoke. 'It may seem like a grievous task to you, but I ask you to remember the great man of Gujarat, the esteemed Sardar Vallabhbhai Patel who made it his life's mission to unify our states into a robust, independent India.'

The murmurs stopped.

I could tell from the respectful expression in their eyes that the tremendous form of Sardar Patel had conjured in their minds. Now, not I, but their deceased idol would command their support.

Mr Sinha smirked. He knew what I was doing.

'Sardar Patel believed that the Indian states had to work together to make our country powerful again. As officers of the IAS, it is up to us to continue his legacy—to create two strong states with rich economies, instead of one Bombay in which everyone is fighting for space and opportunity.'

The men on the left seemed less suspicious now. I continued, my voice soaring with conviction. 'Let us not mourn the division of Bombay. Instead, let's celebrate the creation of Gujarat and Maharashtra, which will give

Gujarati speakers and Marathi speakers a government that responds to them in their own language.'

The men weren't smiling yet, but they were not frowning either. The tension was about to break, I was sure of it. Birdy's eyes were twinkling at the back, proud already.

'I am confident, given the calibre of the men in this room—'

'That's a fine speech,' a low British accent drawled through the room, cutting me off. I turned to see a tall young man at the door, his handsome face furrowed by a frown. 'But are you sure the boundaries you have drawn up to divide Bombay into Gujarat and Maharashtra will actually divide it into Gujarati-speaking and Marathi-speaking parts?'

The men fell silent and turned to the newcomer. I glared at him. *How dare he interrupt the lead officer without permission?* I was sure that if I was in a suit, and not in a sari, he wouldn't have dared to interrupt.

'And you are?'

'A lawyer who is wondering if all the people you're about to shove into Gujarat actually speak Gujarati.'

Who was this man who was turning down his aquiline nose at my maps and hours of research? I paused for a moment, wondering if I should ask him to wait till the question hour had begun. But the men were all looking at him, at his Oxford suit and polished shoes, in awe. I had to answer immediately or risk appearing weak.

'My proposals are based on language and demographic data from the national census,' I replied crisply.

He laughed. 'The national census was done by the British in 1930.'

I flinched.

'Aside from the three decades that have passed since the data collection, are you really going to trust the *British's* understanding of the difference between Gujarati- and Marathi-speaking people? You trust English officers to know the difference between "*su chhe*"[1] and "*kashe aahe*"?'[2]

Low chuckles emanated from the left of the room. The Gujarati officers clearly loved him. The rest of the officers were looking at me dubiously, wondering if I was capable of leading this assignment. I wanted to say something cutting to the young lawyer, to chastise him for his arrogance in speaking out of turn with the lead officer—as I had seen Birdy do so many times—but I didn't think that was the solution.

He did have a point. My data was from the wrong sources. And I was absolutely wrong-footed. Fortunately for me, Mr Sinha stood up just then.

'Team, this is Jairaj Anand,' he said, shaking hands with the young man, as though nothing dramatic just happened. 'He's the lawyer appointed by the state to constitutionally supervise the reorganization of the Bombay Presidency.'

Mr Sinha then gave me the briefest of nods before turning to Jairaj Anand. 'Jai, you're absolutely right. We

---

1 'What do you want?' in Gujarati.
2 'How are you?' in Marathi.

shouldn't be working based on the information collected by the British about our citizens.'

I followed Mr Sinha's lead and shook hands with Mr Anand myself. He grinned in amusement as I snatched my hand back. I pretended not to notice. I straightened my sari and turned to the officers.

'I will issue a new census collection,' I said in my most diplomatic voice, even though I was seething inwardly at Jairaj's sarcasm, at his unbridled arrogance.

'Good,' Jairaj said and turned his back to me.

It is not a defeat, I reminded myself as I folded up the map, *but a more thorough plan to ensure the welfare of our citizens. It is not a defeat. It is not.*

But Jairaj walked around the room and made jokes with the officers, as though it had indeed been his triumph.

The party tonight was delightful enough for me to forget the vexations of the day. Mr Sinha had organized a welcome dinner for our team in the assembly hall of Bombay University. Birdy and I were having a grand time chatting with the officers and their wives. All of whom were sophisticated women with discreet diamond studs in their ears and finely embroidered kurtas. I was glad I wore the lightly crushed gold sari Bauji had given me for my last birthday. If I am to survive in this stylish city, I will have to go shopping at some point.

But what I lacked in ornamentation, I tried to make up for in conversation. I had been doing well enough for my colleague, Mr Bawa, and his wife to invite me to their home for tea the following weekend. We were joking about a faux pas committed by the chief minister of Punjab when Birdy came up to me with a goblet of wine. 'Mr Cambridge is here,' he whispered.

We turned to see Jairaj enter, late again, but this time with a glamorous girl on his arm. She had done up her face and hair like Helen, the actor and dancer. Her cat eyes and large bouffant made her tower over the other women. Gold hung from her ears. Rubies rested on her wrist.

I turned back to my friends, hoping nobody had noticed my eyes roll, but Shanti had caught it. She grinned at me and asked, 'Quite inappropriate, isn't she?'

'It's not her fault,' I said with a shrug. 'He should have informed her that government events aren't so ostentatious.'

Mr Bawa smiled at his wife. 'Jairaj didn't make a good first impression on Gayatriji.'

'Oh yes, I heard about the incident,' Mrs Bawa said eagerly. Now Manohar and his wife were listening in, too. 'So, what's the verdict? You don't like him?'

'She has good reason not to,' Birdy began, furious.

'I have no opinion of him,' I cut him off coolly. I was determined that there be no office gossip about me. Birdy should have known better.

'How is that possible?' Manohar's wife narrowed her eyes, not letting up. 'Surely after today—'

I shrugged. 'I don't think of people who have no manners.'

They burst into laughter, satisfied at having extracted some kind of vitriol.

I stayed away from Jairaj all through the first half of the evening. He caught my eye once, while I was standing by the large window at the end of the room, but I looked away immediately and stared instead at the city of Bombay sprawled out before me. At its buildings and trees washed in a pink and purple palette by the stained glass of the banquet hall. And then I thought I heard him whisper my name to Mr Sinha, while we were settling down in our seats for dinner. I pretended not to hear and began folding the red table napkin into a swan for Birdy's amusement.

But then Birdy was called away by a waiter under the most peculiar circumstances.

'Sir, there is a phone call for you.'

'A phone call?' Birdy was as flummoxed as I was. Nobody in Delhi could have known where we were tonight. 'It must be a mistake.'

'It's no mistake, sir,' the waiter insisted. 'It is your wife, and it is urgent.' Birdy looked so thoroughly gobsmacked that I couldn't help but giggle.

'I have no wife!' he spluttered, causing officers from across the table to shoot curious glances at us.

'You better go see what the issue is, Birdy,' I said, trying to keep my voice even. I didn't like how much attention we were attracting. Bauji would have cautioned against it.

Birdy looked at me with such sincere embarrassment that I had to make a serious effort to rein in a horse laugh. I didn't want to hurt Birdy's feelings, but sometimes he looked like such a jellyfish that it was impossible not to laugh.

'All right,' he said and rose reluctantly, following the waiter out of the banquet hall.

Moments later, his seat was filled, by none other than my first nemesis in Bombay. Jairaj Anand.

'I have offended you,' were the first words out of his mouth.

'You have not,' I said and turned to study the menu of the evening. We were having saffron rice and—

He flicked the menu out of my hand in an easy swipe. 'Excuse me—'

'Mr Sinha says I embarrassed you by pointing out your mistake in front of our colleagues,' Jairaj took the table napkin from my hand, unfolding it on his lap. I quelled the urge to snatch it back. It would mean placing my hand on his lap.

'May I have my napkin back, please?'

Jairaj grinned. 'You will have to accept my apology first.'

How dare he dictate my actions! In my most frigid tone I said, 'There is nothing to—'

'I apologize regardless. I should have recommended the census collection in private. You're only a twenty-three-year-old girl after all. It will take you a while to figure out how all this works.'

I glared at him. His impertinence was astounding.

'How long will it take *you* to figure out "how all this works"? You've reached the ripe age of twenty-eight without grasping the basic courtesy of letting a speaker finish her sentence.'

'I knew you were offended.' He was grinning openly now, his eyes dancing with amusement.

I had had enough. 'Mr Anand—' I rose.

'This is the last time I interrupt you, I promise,' he began. 'Let me apologize properly before you confirm your bad opinion of me.'

Not wanting to be too dramatic, I sat back down. The Bawas were looking at us intently from across the table. I could wait till his apology ended and then switch seats surreptitiously.

He leaned closer to whisper fervently into my ear. 'Officer Khurana, I'm sorry for my bad behaviour earlier today. When it comes to anything to do with our country, I often get so impassioned that I ... I fail to pay attention to the people before me—'

He broke off, his eyes intent on my face. 'I'm glad I get to pay attention now.'

I blushed, despite myself. I was furious, but I was also ... something else. Something as powerful as fury. There was something about Jairaj Anand that was intense and confusing. I imagine standing under a burning chandelier must feel the same way. But I wasn't sure if this was another power play of his, to flatter the lead officer only to set her up for a fall again.

'You aren't the only one who cares about our country, Mr Anand. Some of us have even *lived* through the British Raj and are determined to improve conditions for all citizens.'

Jairaj's eyes widened with surprise. 'Ah, whereas I've escaped oppression, because I was born in London and went to school at Oxford ...'

I shrugged coolly. 'It's hard to understand Indians when you've grown up playing in the lap of the British.'

His eyes widened. 'Gayatri Devi—'

I glowered at him, but he continued unaffected.

'Growing up "in the lap of the British" doesn't make a person any less of an Indian. If anything, you're reminded of your inferior status every day, when you spend your childhood with people who believe you are good enough to walk on the same road as them, but not on the same side.'

Bauji had similar memories of England, but I never thought a wealthy fellow like Jairaj would be treated as badly as a scholarship student from India. My anger began to dissipate, transfixed as I always was by stories from the British Raj.

It was why I had joined the IAS in the first place. I was determined to be involved in the creation of policy for Indians. No Indian would ever be treated as a second-class citizen again if I could help it.

'You have a dimple in your cheek, even when you're frowning,' he said. 'It's very interesting.'

I ignored this observation. 'Was it bad?' I asked. 'My father was terribly ostracized in London—but that was a public university ...'

Jairaj waved a hand, dismissing my question. 'Let's not play victim all evening. It is such a bore. Tell me all about yourself. I'm sure it's a dazzling history. Did you grow up here, or in some ashram where only beauties are raised, like Shakuntala?

I raised an eyebrow at him. 'Is that where your companion for the evening was raised?'

I looked at the glamorous Helen-esque girl who was now seated alone at the opposite end of the table. 'You know, it's rather rude to invite someone to dinner and then leave them to eat by themselves.'

He shook his head at me, disappointed. 'Sinha was right. You are ridiculously well-brought-up.'

'This is your chance to be ridiculously well-brought-up,' I said. 'Please join your dinner companion. Don't worry about me.'

But Jairaj stayed rooted to the spot. 'She doesn't want to have dinner with me. She wants to have me for dinner,' he whispered.

The gorgeous girl was staring at him with such a starved expression that, suddenly, I was giggling uncontrollably.

'Not that well-mannered then,' Jairaj said, grinning.

Just then, Birdy reappeared, looking harrowed. I imagine his phone call hadn't gone too well. His expression grew even more disgruntled at finding me chortling away with Jairaj.

'Excuse me, Mr Anand. You're in my seat,' he said with restrained politeness. Jairaj was unfazed. 'I'm so sorry, Badrinath. I have some urgent business to discuss with Ms Khurana regarding the census collection. Would you please do me the favour of switching seats just up to dessert?'

Birdy looked at me questioningly. I nodded in agreement with Jairaj. *Why?* I can't say for sure.

Jairaj smiled at me and turned back to Birdy genially. 'You can sit with my dinner companion over there,' he said, directing Birdy towards the Helen lookalike.

'Very well,' Birdy said coldly and left.

Honestly, I was quite glad to be rid of Birdy for a while. His attention, in the past few days, had become near claustrophobic. How was one to have adventures and lead things when someone was always hovering around you, like a mother hen?

'Problem solved,' Jairaj said, but neither Helen nor Birdy looked quite pleased with the new seating arrangement.

'He'll be back by dessert, trust me,' I said, shaking my head.

Jairaj looked at me curiously. 'Is he your—?'

'Oh God, no,' I protested, perhaps too eagerly. 'Birdy and I have been friends since he studied under my father for the IAS examinations, that's all.'

Jairaj's eyes twinkled. 'Well, if you call him Birdy, I'm not worried.'

'And why would you have cause to worry in any case?' I asked, arching my eyebrow.

I was flirting, I admit. Jairaj had loosened my tongue and unfastened my guard as expertly as a rogue with a petticoat. I blushed as the thought of him with a petticoat in his hand crossed my mind. I should have stopped at the first goblet of wine.

But he was smiling at me, and I was enjoying it. I could be Officer Khurana tomorrow. Tonight, I wanted to be Gayatri. I wanted to bask in the attention of the most handsome, most arrogant man I had ever met.

'Let's not wait till dessert,' he said suddenly.

Jairaj got up and buttoned his coat before I could respond or ask him to elaborate. 'Follow me in two minutes,' he ordered.

I stared at his retreating figure, striding out of the banquet hall, shocked. I had no idea what he meant by that, or how I was supposed to react. I turned back to the table of officers. Everyone was exclaiming about the feast before them, inhaling the steam wafting off the biryani and helping themselves to cool raita. But I had no appetite, neither for the food nor the conversation of my colleagues.

Suddenly, as though on a dare, I rose and left the table as quickly as my feet would allow. I glanced over my shoulder at the door to see if anyone had noticed. Only one pair of eyes had followed me, distraught.

I pretended as though I hadn't seen Birdy.

Jairaj was waiting by the phone booths. He grinned as I emerged at the top of the staircase. 'Shall we?' he proffered his elbow. I must have been absolutely drunk on flattery because I happily took the arm of the man who had nearly cost me my reputation that day.

The cool January air rushed past us as we ran across the courtyard of Bombay University. I had no idea where we were going, but curiously I felt safe with him. Jairaj, I knew instinctively, was both a rake and a gentleman. He was probably one of those men who took as much as life would let him have. It was up to me to decide how much he could have.

'Where to?' his chauffeur asked. Jairaj's eyes were lit up with mischief as he turned to me.

'I'm going to take you to have the best meal in Bombay this evening,' he said. Then he turned to his driver and commanded, 'Hotel please, driver.'

I stiffened and leaned away from him slightly. *Had my instincts been incorrect? Was he not a gentleman at all?*

I knew I would find out soon enough.

The Taj Mahal hotel in Bombay is nearly as impressive as the iconic monument it is named after. I tried not to appear daunted as Jairaj escorted me through the glittering lobby, filled with glittering people and foreboding concierges.

'This is where they put you up?' I whispered, trying to keep the awe out of my voice as I absorbed the rich upholstery, the forests of carnations, roses and lilies on every table.

Jairaj shrugged. 'It is not unusual,' he said, guiding me into the restaurant we were to dine in.

The Sea Lounge—the title had a playful shell at the end of its name, possibly the only thing that was playful about the imperious restaurant with all its distinguished guests. I think I even spotted our prime minister by the cigar-smoking section, but I was trying so hard not to stare that I can't be sure.

We sank into a booth by the window, with a view of the ferry boats docked in the Arabian Sea glinting in the moonlight. Jairaj smiled and handed me a menu.

'Are you ready to order, Mr Anand?' the waiter, dressed as a butler, asked in lightly accented English. I wonder if they had trained all their staff to sound faintly British to impress the guests.

'Whatever the lady wants, Peter.'

Peter turned to me, unsmiling. The menu was as intimidating as he was. But I was determined neither to be bullied by Jairaj's butler nor by his fancy hotel.

'A bowl of strawberries, please,' I said.

Jai and Peter stared at me, confused. I'd obviously done it wrong. I was supposed to pick some awfully fancy shellfish. But I didn't have the stomach for it, and I wasn't going to pretend.

'Is that all?' Peter asked.

'I don't mind a little cream on the side, if you can manage that,' I said with my most winning smile.

Jairaj leaned forward and I followed suit.

'Gayatri, I'd like you to have whatever your heart desires. Price is no problem.'

'I have simple desires, Jairaj. Strawberries are fine.'

Jairaj looked at me and emitted a low chuckle. 'All right then,' he signalled to Peter. 'Two bowls of strawberries, please.'

'You don't have to ...' I began, but Peter had disappeared already.

'I can order my choice of food any time. This will tell me what your taste is like. Whether it's up to standard.' He was grinning challengingly.

'Is everything a test with you?'

'Yes, but don't worry, you're doing tremendously well.'

I should have slapped his face and left. But there was something magnetic about his self-importance. I wanted to stay, to take on his challenges and pose my own.

Peter reappeared with our order. I spooned out two dollops of cream on to the ripe, red fruits and emptied a packet of sugar over them. Jairaj watched me carefully as I mixed the concoction together before putting a large strawberry, coated in cream, into my mouth. Juice spilled out from the corner of my mouth. He grinned. I patted my lips daintily with the edge of the table napkin.

'May I try that?' he asked. I shouldn't have offered him my spoon. Bauji would have a heart attack if he learned that I did. But it felt very natural to lift my spoon to his mouth. He smiled as he chewed, his eyes set intently on mine.

'Delicious,' he said, gazing at my face. There was something about the way he said it, his voice low and nearly guttural as he lingered on the last 's' of the word—it broke the spell.

The imprudence of it all crashed upon me like a wave. It suddenly struck me that Jairaj had concluded that I would spend the night with him. Of course he had. I had been behaving like a harlot. *What was I thinking?* Feeding strawberries to a strange man at midnight! Bauji had ignored my aunts when they had advised him to marry me off to a Bombay man, so that I would have a husband here to keep me from going astray. He had trusted me.

'I should leave,' I said, rising with as much dignity as I could command.

Jairaj seemed confused. 'No, please, stay—' he began, but this time I was moving too quickly for him.

'Thank you for a lovely evening,' I said and left.

My manner had resumed the stiff civility that my father had disciplined me with. I knew Jairaj would not follow, and nobody would stop me as I made my way to the entrance, hailed a taxi and gave the driver directions to my new home.

Now, safe under the covers of my bed, I can re-examine the evening and see why I fled. It is better not to fool myself, so that he cannot catch me unawares again.

What a curious effect he had on me! He made me forget twenty-two years of rearing and start acting out the funny dreams borne out of reading too many Jane Austen novels.

I must stay well out of Jairaj's reach if I am to get any work done.

Jai. The Victor.

I'm sure he thinks of himself that way, too. Just as long as I can remember that *I* am a victor too. Not just the spoils.

2
Proposals

'What are you girls looking at?'

Rajni and I turned so sharply that we nearly fell off the futon.

Siddhant had appeared out of nowhere and was regarding us curiously. I didn't blame him. We were hunched over a lace-bound diary and Rajni's eyes were crazed with curiosity. Siddhant's gaze landed on the open journal in my hand, peering hard to get a good look at the writing on the page.

'Nothing,' I said, closing Naani's diary with a snap, and turned to give him a light kiss on the cheek, which somehow smelled divine even after a whole night of debauchery. 'It's a special, handwritten edition of *Little Women* that Rajni found at the Strand …'

'Oh, nice.' Siddhant's eyes glazed over, totally losing interest, just as I had expected.

'There's French toast for you in the kitchen,' I said, giving him another quick kiss. Rajni made a slight face, but I couldn't help it. He was adorable in the morning.

'You're the best, babe,' he grinned and disappeared.

I turned back to see Rajni reaching for the diary. 'You know, I wish I had met your grandfather,' she said. 'He sounds like a total heart-throb.'

'He was. But you should have seen Naani. She was a babe. All this long black hair and creamy, smooth skin. Not like mine.'

I started to rub the freckles on my cheeks and Rajni immediately swatted my hand away.

'Yes, well, you survive on a diet of brown sugar and caffeine. You know that the spots on your face will disappear as soon as you start eating actual meals.'

I waved Rajni's lecture away. 'The point is, Bombay is the city for real romance. More so than Paris or Provence. Those places are just departures from real life. I'm done with passionate relationships that only last a holiday. I want a lasting attachment like the one my grandparents had.'

I lowered my voice so it didn't carry to the kitchen. 'And Bombay is still old-fashioned enough that most people get married by thirty.'

Rajni let out a big laugh and then clapped a hand over her mouth. 'Oh my God!' she said, shocked. 'So, you're hoping that the patriarchy pressures your boyfriend into doing things your way?'

'Absolutely,' I grinned. 'I think he'll get his priorities straight once he's distanced from this crappy Western culture of optional commitment.'

'You sound fabulously progressive right now.' Rajni shook her head in disbelief, but then she bit her lip and asked, 'Can I read the rest of it?'

I stuck my tongue out at her. 'It's much too regressive for you.'

She tried to make a grab for it, but I held it above our heads, just out of her reach. She jumped again and nearly knocked over Siddhant, who had entered the room holding a glass of milk.

'Hey, hey!' he said, grabbing a tissue to wipe the milk that has spilled on his T- shirt. 'Rajni, you're a menace.'

'I'll leave then; let you two enjoy your Saturday,' she said with a pointed look at me.

'Thank God,' Siddhant whispered in my ear as the door clicked shut.

I turned to Siddhant, mock-annoyance on my face and my hands on my hips. 'Be nice to my best friend,' I said, but he was taking his shirt off already and snaking his arms around my waist.

We didn't speak much for the rest of the day.

❧

At dinner, however, I was adamant that 'The Subject' be broached. We finally made reservations at Bar Pitti, a chic Italian place on Sixth Avenue that I had wanted to visit with Siddhant for weeks now. (The staff at Wasabi-Masabi had just laughed when I asked if they had a table available for that night.) But neither the excitement of being at this buzzing restaurant nor the hunger from not having eaten all day could distract me from my purpose. As soon as the wine was poured, I raised my glass and said, 'I have a proposal to make.'

Siddhant nearly spluttered out his Cabernet Sauvignon. 'Proposal?'

Oh dear. That couldn't be a good sign. This trip to Bombay couldn't come a minute too soon. The boy obviously needed to be exposed to some good, old-fashioned desi family values.

I laughed lightly.

'Don't be ridiculous,' I said breezily. 'It's just a holiday I'm suggesting.'

'Oh,' his jaw relaxed. 'Thank God,' he said and chuckled before taking another sip of his wine.

Thank God? Really? Was not being engaged to me something to thank God for?

I was about to ask him this, but in a nice way. In a way that was ha-ha-what-is-that-about rather than *HEY*-what are-you-saying-asshole.A happy middle.

'Are we ready to order?' The waiter appeared and launched into the specials before I could say anything more. 'We have this fantastic braised veal with garlic potatoes and an exquisite truffle fettucine with a white wine reduction—'

'The truffle thing sounds really good,' Siddhant nodded along.

'It is. I'd recommend a peach sorbet for dessert—'

'Actually, could you give us a moment, please?' I said to the waiter a bit abruptly. He retreated with a hurt expression. Siddhant gave me an odd look, too, but I was unapologetic. I didn't want him to be thinking about food right now. I had waited all of last night, and all of today, to bring this up with him. I couldn't wait any longer.

'I'm sorry. I was in the middle of propos—of suggesting something.' I smiled brightly at him.

'All right,' Siddhant leaned back, letting an easy smile spread across his face.

I nearly lost my nerve. Siddhant had the most alluring smile in the world. It could relax you into forgetting all the things you thought were so important to communicate only moments ago. I was tempted for a moment to let it go, to enjoy our dinner, and continue our carefree existence.

But I couldn't. I wanted more for us. I cleared my throat and lifted my glass again.

'I propose that we spend six of your twelve vacation days in Bombay this year.'

I handed him the boarding passes I had printed out earlier in the day.

'McKinley is sending me to Bombay to supervise a deal in October and I managed to wrangle an extra ticket. We can stay with my naani! And I know you haven't seen

your parents in a while …' I trailed off as I realized that
Siddhant's grin had frozen as he read the boarding passes.

He dropped the tickets down on the table, took a sip of
the wine and laughed.

But there was an edge to his laughter. His eyes, which
were eager with intrigue a moment ago, were now receding
into a removed wariness. I hadn't seen this expression since
our year of 'hanging out', when I would mention something
that came on too strong for him.

It would take me weeks of pretending to be 'cool' and
'down for anything' to get him to answer my calls again.
But I had managed. We had graduated from 'hanging out'
to actually being in a relationship.

*Then what was the problem? Why couldn't we go on a
holiday together?*

'Is something wrong?'

'Not at all,' he said, gesturing for the waiter like a
drowning man waving for help. 'Shall we order?'

The waiter reappeared eagerly. 'Hello, sir, so have we
decided on the fettucine?'

I couldn't believe Siddhant just cut off our conversation.
I refused to be cut off.

'Just a second,' I was grinning so hard at the waiter that
he probably thought I was manic. I turned to Siddhant, with
the same ferocious level of joy, and said, 'So, are the dates
okay? It is 20th to the 27th. We will be there for Diwali.
Isn't that exciting?'

I was aware that my voice was high-pitched and tense. Even the waiter knew something was wrong and retreated into the kitchen. Now, it was just Siddhant and me at our table by the window. I was trying my best to remain patient, but he looked at me like a hunted deer caught in the headlights of blinding affection.

'This isn't a vacation, Radhika,' he said finally.

'Yes, it is,' I argued. 'We're vacating ourselves from our actual lives to go to—'

'Bombay,' he said, deadpan. Siddhant was no fool. 'That means we'll be meeting each other's families.'

I shrugged, not backing down. So what if we met each other's families? It had been a year of dating, a year of 'hanging out' and four years of knowing each other at college. Wasn't it about fucking time?

I said none of this though. Instead I smiled sweetly. 'I don't see what's so wrong with that. I mean, I think it will be kind of nice to be back in India with my naani and your parents for Diwali. That's how it's meant to be celebrated anyway. With family.'

Siddhant put a hand over mine and said, 'Radhika, October is six months away. You've already planned our weekends for the next six weeks. Can't we just …' his voice trailed off, looking around the table as though the salt shaker would have an answer.

'Can't we just *what*?' I was done pretending.

Siddhant exhaled, exhausted. He was done pretending, too. 'Why do you have to plan every single thing?'

I looked at him in disbelief. He should be grateful that I made reservations, scoured eventsnyc.com for jazz evenings and made the calls that brought our friends together for weekend dinners. If it were up to him, we'd spend every single night off eating stale pizza and watching Netflix reruns in unwashed Yale hoodies. But I couldn't tell him this, of course. I was still holding on to some ridiculous hope that we would get past this argument and be engaged by October, and maybe married by December.

I shrugged sweetly and tried to sound apologetic. 'I've planned our weekends because we have high-stress jobs, babe. If I didn't schedule it, we would never have any fun—'

'Scheduled fun. Jesus!' Siddhant was shaking his head, looking more tired than ever.

It's because of the hangover from last night, I told myself. *And the lack of nourishment.* I should have let him eat a couple of breadsticks before launching into this.

'Babe, it's all right,' I said shaking my head and letting out a light-hearted laugh. 'We can talk about this later—'

'Later? At 9 p.m. *sharp?*'

I recoiled. He was imitating the way I talked to my colleagues on the phone.

'Sorry. Sorry,' he said, but his expression was still tight. Siddhant removed his hand from over mine and looked at me apologetically.

'Radhika,' he said. 'I don't know if I can do scheduled fun for the rest of my life.'

'W-what,' I needed to keep my voice from wobbling, 'do you mean?'

'I don't want to do this any more.' The alluring smile had vanished. There was a finality in his voice that I hadn't heard before.

'Siddhant, you're just hungover,' my voice was low with desperation. If I heard myself, I'd probably cry.

He shook his head resolutely. 'I've been thinking about this for some time, Radhika.'

My stomach suddenly felt hollow. While I had been planning to introduce him to my grandmother, while I had been cooking him breakfast, and laying my body on top of his, he had been thinking of escape strategies. I was to be enjoyed, and then left at his convenience. I had never felt like such a fool before.

The waiter noticed a lull in our conversation and approached us, this time with a plate of pasta. 'Excuse me, just a minute, ma'am, sir. The chef has sent over a sample of his fettucine for you to try—'

Siddhant was looking at me with a concerned expression. He was worried that I was going to make a scene. He thought I would burst into hysterics because he was depriving me of his companionship.

'You may want to come back later,' Siddhant said, with an apologetic smile.

But I picked up my fork and coolly twisted the long strips of pasta along the twines. I popped it into my mouth, chewed and swallowed as Siddhant watched, surprised.

'It's a bit undercooked,' I said. Then I got up and left, with the most even expression on my face.

❧

'YES, YES, YES! Do it! BE YOUR BEST SELF TODAY!'

The SoulCycle instructor was screaming in my face. I was nodding with her as I pedalled my bike furiously. I believed the fit girl standing under the purple lights, and so did all the other perspiring women in that room of blasting music and spinning stationary bikes. We were all thinking: *Damn right. I will be my best self today.*

I let out a little groan as Beyoncé reached her musical crescendo. Sweat was pouring down my face, dripping on to my collarbones and snaking into my sports bra, but it felt triumphant instead of uncomfortable. I was a warrior, who would emerge stronger.

It had been a month since I had been mouthing off similar motivational aphorisms to myself. Break-ups were like my improvement–detox periods. I worked harder, worked out harder and sang pop songs to myself; I tried to be the most upbeat version of Radhika that there was. Even though she had no man!

I felt a little bad for Rajni, who always did these bootcamps with me out of solidarity. Right now, she was panting heavily on the white bench of a blindingly white locker room and gulping from the bottle of mint-infused water they gave us at the end of the session. She hadn't complained once all month, but now, after the mandatory post-workout cold shower, she seemed at the end of her tether.

'Sometimes,' she said, putting the water bottle down, 'I wish you'd deal with heartbreak by just eating some chocolate.'

I smiled at her and turned back to the mirror, patting concealer over the bumps on my face.

'Nothing says "He won" like a plump ex-girlfriend,' I said, giving my nose an extra rub of powder.

'He lost, babe,' she said automatically. I nodded, still smiling. Rajni shot me another one of her concerned glances, but I ignored it and moved on to perfecting my eyeliner.

'It's all right to not be okay, you know?' she offered. 'You dated for nearly two years, and you thought he was going to propose—'

'I was an idiot,' I said sharply. 'And I refuse to waste any more time on him.'

I finished the wings of my eyes and leaned back to assess my work.

Rajni looked at my face and nodded. 'You know what, you're right,' she said. 'I admire how strong and proactive you're being by dating other men already. You've handled this really well, and I'm proud of you.'

I felt a slight twinge in my stomach, but I didn't say anything. I couldn't tell her. She wouldn't understand.

'Thanks, Rajj,' I kissed her cheek and walked out of the locker room before I lied to her any more.

'Sneak a picture of him if you can!' she yelled.

'I'll try,' I said, laughing lightly as I disappeared out the door.

I knew I won't be sending any pictures to Rajni tonight. And I would have to come up with a whole story about an imaginary date who was cute but not 'right' for me. I would say I forgot his last name, so she would be unable to undertake a Facebook search. I hated lying to my best friend, but I couldn't possibly tell her the truth. For one thing, she'd lose respect for me, and for another, she'd try to stop me.

And I was not going to be stopped.

I walked into the bar in my sexiest LBD with my head aloft and my shoulders thrown back. A power pose meant to 'attract' success.

'Can I buy you a drink?' a guy in a shirt and chinos asked me. He was quite attractive and had a nice, deep voice. But I had another goal in mind tonight.

'Sorry,' I said. 'I'm expecting someone.'

'No worries.' He melted away into the crowd of Friday night revellers at Belfry's. I sipped my Manhattan and swayed to the music, trying to appear as casual as possible.

It was not totally untrue, what I had told the stranger. I was expecting someone.

I knew I shouldn't be at this bar. In fact, when the email chain first popped into my inbox, I even deleted it. But it was committed to my memory by then.

TO: siddhantlodha@legal.mckinley.com
FROM: jiaK@nyu.edu
Error! Hyperlink reference not valid.Error! Hyperlink reference not valid.
SUBJECT: Tonight!
Hey,
Sorry, can't get thru to your phone, so I thought I'd try here. LOVED running into you the other night—what a crazy subway ride, wasn't it? I've told all my friends about the hot dog-man already. ;)
Anyhoo, would you like to do The Belfry tonight at 8? LMK
Jia K.

His reply had dinged back within seconds.

TO: jiaK@nyu.edu
FROM: siddhantlodha@legal.mckinley.com
SUBJECT: RE: Tonight!
Belfry at 8 sounds good to me. See you.
PS: I'll be the one with the napkin ring this time. ;)
Siddhant

It was nauseating watching these two email back and forth like a couple of teenagers, sharing inside jokes and making plans. I knew I should have logged out of Siddhant's email ID on my laptop the minute we broke up, but it had been such a comfort to open my browser and know that we were still linked in some way. He had never left anything at my apartment—not even a toothbrush. So, when we broke up and he disappeared, it had almost felt like he had never been a part of my life. Like the last two years had meant nothing.

His inbox open on my laptop was like the drawer of important letters that Naani kept in her dresser. It was proof that we were intimate enough, that he trusted me enough to share his important correspondence with me. It was proof that I wasn't crazy for imagining that we had a future together. For two years, I'd been a good girlfriend, who had earned and respected his trust. I had never snooped through his inbox or stalked the people on his contact list.

Until now.

Jia K., it appeared, was a graduate student at New York University (NYU) who 'loooved' performance art and Shakespeare in the park. Her profile picture showed a round-faced smiling girl with blonde highlights in a mass of curly hair.

I straightened up to get a good look at her as she walked into The Belfry, her curvy frame accentuated by a figure-hugging pink dress. She swung her hips into a booth by the window and gurgled with laughter at a joke the waiter made. Her hair bounced as she laughed. Everything about her bounced. She was bustier and bubblier than me. My suspicions were confirmed. She was basically the physical opposite of me.

I had never felt so old and thin and haggard.

Siddhant sauntered in a few minutes later and smiled lazily at her, apologizing but barely as he hugged her. He did it well, I realized. From the beginning, he had got this pretty, hippie girl feeling like *she* was eager to see him.

I watched as he ordered her a drink. They started to laugh and he grazed her hand while gazing at her fresh face appreciatively. I didn't think there was even a trace of make-up on Jia's face. He whispered something into her ear and she gazed up in silence.

Okay, this was excruciating, not being able to hear them. I was going to need some audio.

I took the earpiece out of my clutch and screwed it into my ear.

'*Connected,*' an automated voice said. I could see the red light under Siddhant's table light up in response.

Yes, I had found out which table Siddhant had reserved, picked up a cheap spy-transmission device from Best Buy and bugged the table. Whatever. At least I was not stuffing my face with chocolate at home. It was still proactive because this was a kind of closure.

I am not crazy. I am curious.

'… we're doing a production of *A Midsummer Night's Dream*. It's ballet, actually,' Jia said, her voice fresh with excitement.

'That sounds exciting,' Siddhant said.

Liar. He wasn't the slightest bit interested in ballet.

'So do you dance?' he asked. There was a suggestive note in his voice. It was disgusting, but Jia giggled.

'I do,' she said. 'I'm playing one of the Fairy Queen's minions. It's a lot of fun, but it's hard work.'

Siddhant nodded, as though empathizing. 'Do you wear those little shoes? Pointes?'

Jia laughed. 'Yes.'

'With the straps that go all the way up?'

'Yep.'

Siddhant grinned.

'I can even stand on my toes now.'

'You'll have to give me a private performance some time.'

I nearly retched. *How was I ever into this guy?* I looked at his date. She couldn't be older than twenty-one. His behaviour was near predatory.

He did me a favour, I realized with shattering clarity. This was what he wanted. A cute young girl who'd dance to his tune. And I was so ecstatic about the fact that the college jock had chosen me that I had been purposefully blind to it. I was glad that he broke up with me, or I would have held on for many more months hoping he'd change. Maybe even changing bits of myself in the process to fit his mould.

I had got the closure I needed. I was about to take the earpiece off, pay for my Manhattan, and leave when I heard her say—

'So … have you ever been in a serious relationship?'

I screwed the earpiece back in quickly.

Siddhant took a moment, as if mulling. He took a sip of his drink and I waited with bated breath.

'Not really.'

The hollow in my stomach, which had just begun to close, swung open again like a chasm with wind whooshing past, corroding my insides.

What. An. Asshole.

'Didn't you say you dated your ex for two years?' Jia asked. Her eyebrows were raised and her voice was challenging.

I liked this girl. She was asking the right questions.

Siddhant, unfazed, took a sip of his martini. 'Yeah, we dated for a while,' he said slowly, 'but I don't think the duration signifies the seriousness, you know?'

'Doesn't it?' Jia asked.

'You're young, so you don't know yet.' Siddhant said in an all-knowing manner, and then he continued, 'You can know a person all your life and never have that … connection. And then with some people, it's just instant.'

Siddhant looked intently into Jia's eyes for emphasis. It was so melodramatic that I was sure she was going to tell him off. She was going to stand up for women everywhere by telling him he was full of bull.

But to my dismay she was nodding along. 'I know what you mean. My ex was like that,' she said. 'He was sweet and all, but I never felt that … spark.'

Goddamn theatre majors.

'Exactly,' Siddhant said and took her hand in his. 'That's what I've always wanted! I've been looking for that spark for so long.'

What? You've been look—? We had spark!

'WE HAD SPARK, GODDAMIT! We could set your fucking house on fire.'

The entire restaurant turned to look in my direction. *Shit!* I didn't realize I said that last part out loud. I was just hoping it hadn't carried all the way to the entrance.

Sadly, it had. Siddhant was looking directly at me.

'Radhika?' he yelled. My earpiece exploded in my ear.

'Ow!' I screamed and took it out. His eyes widened even more in surprise.

Oh, well. Shit.

The DJ had chosen that very moment to take a bathroom break, so it was totally silent in the bar and I was the entertainment of choice. A blonde girl was looking at me and whispering something to her friend. Jia was whispering confusedly to Siddhant.

I could leave, but I felt responsible now. So I did the only thing that occurred to me. I walked up to his table.

'Jia K.,' I said, knowing that Siddhant was probably going to get a restraining order against me. 'You deserve better than a commitment-phobe.'

Siddhant looked at me horrified, but I was not paying any attention to him. My gaze was fixed on the young girl. She should be saved from wasting her twenties on insensitive men. I was expecting her to stand up and walk out on him with me.

How stupid would he look, sitting there alone.

But Jia just looked up at me with a pitiful smile.

'I'm kind of a commitment-phobe, too, to be honest,' she said. Then she gazed back at Siddhant and grinned at him. 'No strings attached?'

'Fantastic,' he laughed.

What the hell?

3
Dignity and Decisions

I should be awarded star employee of the year. I should get the Provence trip and the Bombay trip, and my name should be on the door. It should be Radhika Anand Global Consulting Services.

I hadn't gone home in five days. Not since The Belfry incident. That was what it was being called by the guys down in Legal, according to Rajni. It didn't matter. I didn't care what a bunch of lawyerly leeches had to say about me. I made more than most of them.

And now I had been given a bonus for volunteering to spend each evening working on a new client's account—a multinational soda conglomerate that I couldn't name till all the i's had been dotted and the t's had been crossed.

Rich thought I had shown a 'single-minded drive' this month that deserved to be recognized. So, he offered to let me out of the Goldenblatt–Bombay agreement and put me on this very high-profile company's account full-time.

It was a fantastic offer, one that would only be reserved for a head of department and not a twenty-nine-year-old consultant who was only three accounts old at McKinley.

I was chuffed, obviously. But if I was being completely honest, I was a little concerned about sustaining this work ethic.

I didn't mind spending every night sleeping in my office. In fact, I had made a nice little bed out of the couch in my cabin, by covering it with fur throws from Bed, Bath & Beyond. And I had stocked my desk with cereal bars and nuts for a variety of meal options. So, all in all, it was not a bad existence.

But I did miss having a real shower. The office ones were perfunctory. They blasted cold water and only lasted a few seconds, so you couldn't wash your hair under it. And I could feel the grease collecting in my roots now.

I knew I had to go home tonight. And I would. As soon as I finished re-reading the agreement, just to make sure it was all in order.

'I have someone on the line for you!' Rajni burst into my office. I turned my face up to see her holding a laptop, from which Dr Mangala Anand's blurred face was looking down at me, bespectacled and concerned.

I rolled my eyes. 'You called my mother?'

'It's past midnight,' Rajni said. 'Everyone else has gone home.'

'You're still here,' I pointed out.

'I went home, had dinner and returned because I knew you wouldn't have left despite all your promises.'

I was about to make a wisecrack, but Mum was gesturing on the screen, trying to get us to pay attention. Rajni looked at Mum apologetically and disconnected her AirPods. My mother's sharp, confident voice filled the room.

'Radhika, what is this I hear about you not sleeping at home anymore?' she asked.

I tried to sound as reasonable as possible. 'Mum, I've been put in charge of a major soda conglomerate's account. I can't leave anything to chance. This could be my path to eventually becoming a partner.'

Rajni snorted and I shot her a look. 'What? I could be a partner,' I said, annoyed.

'Radhika, I think we both know that this has nothing to do with your ambitions,' my mother pronounced, 'and everything to do with your deep-rooted fear of being alone.'

This was the problem with being raised by an Ivy League professor of Freudian psychology. Every emotion had to be analysed and linked to one's parents. Other kids watched *The Price Is Right* with their parents after dinner. Mum and I sat and discussed all my potential feelings of abandonment because my father left us shortly after my birth. Christmas was never roast chicken and presents; it was soggy sandwiches and cognitive behavioural therapy.

Needless to say, I moved out as soon as I got into college, despite living in the same town and sharing the same commute with my mother. Kids at Yale often came up to me, raving about Mum's gender and psychology class. *'Dr Anand blew my mind. She can just parse the human subconscious in such a ...'* they would say, but I never waited for the rest of it. As long as she wasn't parsing my subconscious, things were fine.

I couldn't believe Rajni had actually called her. *Traitor!*

'I'm not afraid of being alone, Mum. I enjoy my own company.'

'I'm not denying that Radhika,' she said. 'But you've craved companionship since a young age. In fact, Steve and I were discussing that maybe you should come home for a while.'

Oh God. No. Steve used to be my mother's graduate assistant. When I was growing up, he was always hanging around the house, 'working on citations' for Mum's research papers. When I left for college, he moved in. It was still 'casual' though, because my mum's the one with abandonment issues, not me.

I didn't mind Steve at all. He was a sweet guy and he seemed to truly love Mum, but he was always trying to be oddly paternal with me. And one just couldn't think of Steve-the-citations-guy as a paternal figure, especially since he was only ten years older to me. Of course, Mum had tried to talk to me about this, continually assuring me that I had no reason to feel threatened because Steve and she were 'just colleagues who cohabit together', but I had made an oath not to discuss my feelings with Mum after

I discovered journaling—it had been an upward journey ever since.

'I don't need to come to New Haven, Mum. I'm perfectly all right,' I promised, putting on my most confident smile. 'I was actually on my way back to the apartment right now.'

'Really?'

Rajni looked at me with renewed hope.

'Yes,' I nodded. Anything to end this conversation. I got up and prepared to leave, unbreakably confident.

But I felt less confident when I was standing in my large living room on 42nd Street, wondering what to do next.

Rajni watched me from the door, worried. 'Babe?'

I didn't want to move. I didn't know why I was being so dramatic. I was fine for weeks after the break-up, until I went and made a fool of myself at The Belfry.

Mum had hit upon a truth and a nerve. Ever since that horrific evening, spending time on my own had become a frightening thought.

I could change into my pyjamas, put a face mask on and watch *Under the Tuscan Sun*, but in the time I would watch the film Siddhant would be out there, building a relationship with someone pretty and fresh-faced and passionate. And not just Siddhant. It seemed like all of New York City's men were looking for someone like Jia K. Someone young. Someone fun. 'Unscheduled fun'.

'I just don't understand,' I turned to Rajni, annoyed. 'If he knew there was no spark, why didn't he tell me? We could have worked on it. I could make the spark—'

Rajni screwed up her face in apology. 'Radhu, you can't make a spark. You have to feel it.'

'I FELT IT. And I swear he felt it, too.'

She looked at me with such a doubtful expression that I yelled, 'I have PROOF!'

'Proof?'

I blushed and quickly went into the kitchen. But she followed me, relentless.

'What do you mean "proof"?' she asked, as I started to rifle through the fridge, ignoring her. But Rajni shut the fridge door and forced me to look at her.

'Radhika,' she said, sounding worried. 'What did you do?'

Oh dear. It was time to come clean. I reopened the fridge door and took out the tub of chocolate ice cream. She would need soothing dairy to digest what I was about to show her.

For the next hour, Rajni said nothing as she sat on the bar stool in my living room and stared at my laptop, riveted. I was watching her more than the tapes. Anyway, I had seen them enough for review purposes. As Siddhant's moans grew louder, reaching climax for the umpteenth time, I lowered the volume. Rajni turned to me, shock apparent on her face.

'I told you he felt it,' I whispered in a small voice.

'Did he know?'

I flushed.

'Radhika!' she exclaimed in horror. But I refused to apologize.

'I did it for our benefit!' I retorted, pulling out the Excel sheets that would serve as my defence.

Rajni looked even more shocked. 'What is this?'

'Look, in the beginning it just wasn't working between us, physically,' I said, trying to sound as reasonable as possible. 'And Siddhant refused to talk about it, so I had to do some … field research and analysis of my own.'

To be honest, I was quite proud of my scientific approach. I taped us every Saturday night and reviewed the footage on Sunday evenings to make notes about the pleasure points and most successful manoeuvres. In the last few months, we had reached our sexual peak because of my careful recordings. The Excel sheets were proof.

Radhika and Siddhant's performance for 2018–19

Date	Mood	Place	Music	Pleasure Level (moans at climax)
1/4/2018	Siddhant hungry, not had dinner	Rad's bedroom	John Mayer playlist	1.5 screams
8/4/2018	Siddhant tipsy, two glasses of wine	Sid's bedroom	Post Malone playlist	2 screams

Date	Mood	Place	Music	Pleasure Level (moans at climax)
13/4/2018	Pleasant mood, post-dinner and Netflix	Rad's couch	Bruno Major playlist	3 screams
20/4/2018	Post-dinner, pre-Netflix	Rad's bedroom	Bruno Major playlist	3 screams
22/4/2018	Post-workout, no dinner	Rad's bedroom	John Mayer playlist	3 screams
2/5/2018	Post-workout, post-dinner	Rad's bedroom	Bruno Major playlist	3 screams
9/5/2018	Post-workout, no dinner	Rad's bedroom	Bruno Major playlist	6 screams
23/5/2018	Post-workout, no dinner	Rad's bedroom	Bruno Major playlist	6 screams
3/6/2018	Post-workout, no dinner	Rad's bedroom	Bruno Major playlist	6 screams
12/6/2018	Post-workout, no dinner	Rad's bedroom	Bruno Major playlist	5 screams
21/8/2018	Post-workout, no dinner	Rad's bedroom	Bruno Major playlist	7 screams
24/9/2018	Post-workout, no dinner	Rad's bedroom	Bruno Major playlist	7 screams

I had accounted for all the variables and found a perfect combination for sexual success. After his workout, but before dinner, he would be on an endorphin rush that left him hungry but not ravenous. And with Bruno Major playing softly in the background, we were sure to reach some form of mutual satisfaction.

Of course, Siddhant thought it was all down to his intuitive way with women; I let him think that. Now I had half a mind to fling my Excel sheets at him and destroy his delusions.

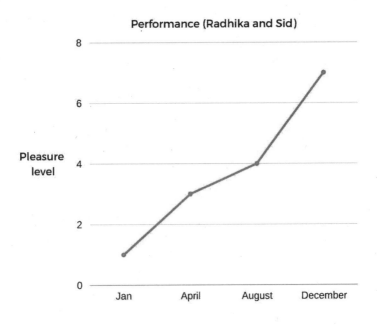

'Radhika, you made ... data sets for sex?'

'I know it's weird, but it worked!' I showed Rajni my graph. 'Look, it's *exponential growth*.'

I expected her to be impressed by our progress, but she was looking at me with such a mixture of pity and horror that I could feel my cheeks starting to burn.

'I was just trying to keep … the graph … up.'

Rajni's eyes bugged.

I felt quite pathetic now. I wished I'd never showed her any of this.

'You don't have to try this hard,' Rajni said softly. 'It should be natural.'

'Maybe I shouldn't be trying at all,' I snapped. 'Maybe I should just sit back and accept a life of spin classes and spinsterhood.'

I was almost about to add 'like you', but I bit my tongue just in time. It wasn't Rajni's fault that I didn't share the 'cool girl' attitude that she and Mum possessed. Things like commitment didn't concern them at all. In fact, they seemed to enjoy the tease of never knowing whether they were in a casual or real relationship. It was not my thing. I had to know for sure whether my emotional investment was going to yield a corresponding return or not. I wanted to go grocery shopping with the same person every week and spend lazy evenings in comfortable silence. It was exhausting to keep meeting men at dimly lit bars and pretend to be bright and interesting and wildly passionate after thirteen hours of working and one hour of working out every day.

I could not tell another man that my favourite film was *Sleepless in Seattle*, only to have him disappear with a theatre graduate from NYU right after we streamed it together.

Later, after Rajni was gone, I did the only thing that could bring me comfort on a lonely Thursday night, when Siddhant was, in all likelihood, introducing his new girlfriend to his lads from Legal.

I lay down on my large bed. And I read.

❦

The Personal Diary of Gayatri Khurana, IAS officer, Delhi Division.

21 January 1960

Bombay

My first fortnight in Bombay was uneventful because I kept away from Jairaj. In contrast to that first evening of imprudence and adventure, the rest of my time in Bombay was spent very sensibly in settling into my new home and office. I can't afford to act girlishly when I am trying to win respect in a new city.

Negotiating boundaries and infrastructure divisions has taken up all my time and energy. It is just as well, because it has ensured that I remained unavailable despite Jairaj's many attempts at conversation. After being politely refused by my secretary four times, he seemed to have finally understood that I was not the kind of woman who was willing to be paraded on the arm of a strange man at fancy hotels across the town.

Though he has given up harassing my secretary, I think she quite misses the attention. I, however, couldn't be more grateful.

Bauji wrote to ask if I am lonely. But despite living alone for the first time, I am not. I love my independent routine of working at the office during the day and listening to the gramophone as I cook for myself at night. By evening, I am glad for the solitude. I revel in the certainty that anyone who is a native of Bombay must feel the same way.

After all, during the day, everyone here seems immersed in a rhythm of relentless life that resembles a jazz melody. It is slow and lilting in the beginning, like the scribbling of my files and ledgers early morning, which abruptly erupts in a burst of saxophone-like excitement at noon when I open the wide windows of my musty cabin, overlooking the colourful street of Kala Ghoda bustling under the bright Bombay sun.

On some days, during my lunch break, I join the music. I step out to see the paintings at Jehangir Art Gallery, or to browse the book stands by Flora Fountain, or to buy fresh lilies for the flat. There is also a sugarcane juice seller there, by the High Court, who has eavesdropped on lawyers' conversations for the last forty years and has the most interesting stories to tell.

It was here, as I was chatting with the juice vendor about the confidential cases that had been discussed at his stall and sipping a large mug of sugarcane juice, that Jairaj emerged from the High Court, his black lawyer's robe flowing behind him. He burst into boyish laughter as soon as he spotted me.

'So, this is why I haven't been able to pin you down during a lunch break?' he asked, bounding up to the vendor and I. 'Your secretary lied to me. She said you had gone out for lunch with an associate!'

'Dayapal has become an associate,' I said, smiling and turning to the juice vendor. 'He has taught me more about Bombay than any of my guidebooks.'

Jairaj flicked a cursory glance at the vendor before turning back to me, one eyebrow raised. 'I hope you haven't been walking around the city alone?'

I smiled. Jairaj, for all his British modernisms, was just as old-fashioned as Bauji.

'Why not?' I raised my eyebrow in turn.

'Well, for one thing, it's rather boring, isn't it? Much better to do things by twos,' he said and handed Dayapal a ten-rupee note, adding, 'Keep the change.'

My eyes widened, as did the vendor's, who quickly began churning a sugarcane for this generous lawyer.

I lowered my voice. 'Jairaj, it's only twenty-five paise.' He had paid several times the amount for a glass of juice. But Jairaj shrugged, unconcerned.

'Any friend of yours is a friend of mine,' he said and drained his glass in one go.

Dayapal, who was looking at Jairaj with deference, suddenly looked at me with a new, leering glint of understanding in his eyes. It made my face flush. I shook my head, embarrassed, and began walking away from both the juice vendor and Jairaj.

He caught up with me easily. 'Where are you going?' he sounded genuinely confused.

'Jairaj,' I said, sighing and turning to him, 'we can't be seen together.'

'Why not?'

'Because this isn't London. It's Bombay.'

'I'm aware of our location, Gayatri Devi,' his eyes laughed.

I gave up on euphemisms. He was going to make me say it.

'And because I'm not the type of woman you're used to!'

I flushed immediately and fell silent. We weren't supposed to actually *talk* about flirtation or courtship with men. I was keenly aware of the dangerously unchaste neighbourhood I was suddenly crossing into.

'I know.' He lowered his voice and added, 'But I'm hoping to get used to you.'

I was rendered speechless. No man had ever confessed his affection for me, so candidly before. *This was practically a proposal, wasn't it?* I certainly didn't expect it to happen on a Tuesday afternoon, in the midst of traffic at Kala Ghoda, with taxi drivers honking at each other.

'You needn't look so shocked,' Jairaj said coolly as he stuck his hand out to hail a taxi. 'I'm just hoping for your respectability to rub off on me. I figure it will help my career.'

His mouth was twitching, and now mine was filled with fire. Was this all a great joke to him? He thought he could keep flirting to see if I took the bait?

'Hop in,' he said, and flung open the door of a taxi.

'I will not "hop" to anything, thank you.' And I swung around and walked away.

'The office is in the other direction,' he yelled.

'I know.'

He let the taxi go and joined me in my trot on the pavement. For someone who only wanted me around to increase his respectability, he certainly was eager. I smiled inwardly. Outwardly, I glared at him.

'Don't you have somewhere else to be?' I asked in my most imperious tone.

'I am accompanying my lead officer on her private assignment for the benefit of our state,' he said, eyes wide with innocence. 'What could be more important?'

'How do you know that my assignment is for the benefit of our state? I could be playing truant and wasting time.'

Jairaj smiled. For the first time since that dinner, his smile seemed genuine and devoid of mockery.

'It is the end of your lunch break, Officer Khurana. And, according to office legend, you haven't wasted a single productive moment in your life.'

'You've been asking about me then?' I asked, feeling triumphant.

Jairaj shrugged. 'If you were indeed playing truant, I'd think it would have something to do with the dizzying effect of meeting me.'

I rolled my eyes, but he continued, unaffected, 'And in that special case, I would consider it my duty to join you in whatever misadventure you are taking me on.'

'I am not taking you anywhere,' I said, pointedly. 'May I remind you that I haven't requested your company. *You* have imposed upon me. And as far as misadventures are concerned, I believe we have had enough of those already.'

I caught a twinkle in his eye as we strode into the David Sassoon Library.

'I knew you had been avoiding me since that evening!'

The librarian looked at us, curious. I put a finger over my lips to hush Jairaj, but he continued in a flippant tone, regardless. 'Have you been thinking of it every night? Has it been driving you mad?'

I glared at him. 'It has driven me to remorse and nothing else,' I said, signing my name into the librarian's ledger, slightly annoyed. 'Fortunately, there will be no more such evenings in the future to regret.'

'And why not?' he leaned lazily against the ledger, dangerously close to me. I moved away from him to begin the business for which I had come to the library.

'Gayatri Khurana,' I said to the old librarian who was gazing at Jairaj in girlish awe. 'I'm here to read the Bombay Province population records—'

A glimmer of shrewd curiosity appeared in Jairaj's eyes. 'What is this about?

'Are they ready?' I asked the librarian again, forcing her to stop looking at Jairaj.

'Of course, Madam Khurana. I've kept the files out on the first chair for you,' she said, reluctantly tearing her gaze away from Jairaj's perfect jawline.

Before Jairaj could launch into an interrogation, I began climbing the winding wooden staircase to the Archives section.

Jairaj tried to follow, but the librarian stopped him, much to my glee.

'Only members,' she said, finally remembering her official duties.

'But ma'am—' he turned on his most charming, sahab-ish tone, but she shook her head firmly and gave him a resolute 'no'.

I started to grin, imagining his expression. He, who had never been refused by anybody.

'GAYATRI!' Jairaj yelled out suddenly, 'What is it about that night that you regret?'

I stopped, halfway up the stairs. I could hear the mirth in his voice, but I could also feel the eyes of the librarian and the clerks boring into my back with scandalous censure. I turned to see him looking at me, a malevolent smile spread across his face, enjoying the spot he had put me in.

I was about to ignore him and keep going when he spread his hands out dramatically. 'I'm sorry if I offended you that evening at my hotel, OFFICER KHURANA,' he yelled again, his voice thick with false sentiment. 'I know you're a lady. I never expected you to spend the—'

At this point, I rushed down the stairs, grabbed his hand and yanked him upstairs, quickly mumbling to the librarian, 'He's with me, I'll sign him in later.'

The librarian, whose cotton blouse seemed like it was about to rip from the excitement of the moment, nodded. She was as shocked as I was. Jairaj and I continued our ascent to the third floor of the building, with him laughing the entire way. I tried hard not to trip over the trail of my sari in all my frustration.

'Now that we're here, please let me work,' I said to him as I collected the files laid out for me. He mimed zipping his mouth shut and picked up a newspaper from the shelf, while I examined the records I had come for.

They were just what I had expected them to be.

I retrieved some carbon paper from my little leather bag and began copying out the data I needed, delighted in having my predictions confirmed. Jairaj watched me, intrigued.

'Your dimples are back,' he noted from his position by the Classics shelves. I ignored him and went on writing, careful not to get the carbon ink on the soft cotton of my lilac sari.

'What are these figures?' he asked, suddenly shutting his paper and towering over my shoulder.

'They're population breakdowns of Bombay Province from the last census.'

Jairaj's expression changed from jocular to imperious. He frowned at me with irritation. 'I thought we weren't using these!' his voice was stern. 'These were taken under the British Raj. Gayatri, just because the census will take time—'

'Mr Cambridge. Who do you think was working for the British?'

Jairaj fell silent. A little victory.

'I looked into it. The census collectors in 1930 were Indians. The British don't sink so low as to knock on the doors of the Indians to find out what languages they spoke.'

Jairaj's eyes grew wide with every sentence I spoke. I must confess that I relished the feeling. It led me to be bolder than usual. I looked into his eyes and smirked as I spoke.

'The data was physically collected by Indian men *who did know* the difference between "*su che*" and "*kashe aahe*".'

Jairaj's surprise turned into a grin. 'And when did you find this out?' he asked.

'The idea struck me during our welcome dinner.'

'Why didn't you say something then?'

'I was waiting to check the records to confirm it. Which they just did,' I said and pointed at the Devanagari script in which the data was recorded and raised an eyebrow at Jairaj. 'I doubt a British census collector wrote this in क ख ग घ.'

Jairaj let out a low laugh, but this time it didn't seem like he was laughing at me, but at himself. He was conceding defeat, and this self-deprecatory chuckle was a white flag. It made me smile, despite myself.

'You're good, Officer Khurana.'

'I know,' I smiled and turned the page to copy the next list of data, but he touched the bangle on my hand lightly and I stopped.

'Then you should also know that I wasn't expecting you to go to bed with me that night,' his voice dropped to a whisper.

I was so appalled that I didn't know how to react.

'I would never treat you with anything less than the utmost dignity. No matter how undignified my thoughts may be,' he said.

I could feel the colour rising to my cheeks. I should have slapped him and walked away, but his expression held not a trace of its usual taunting. In fact, he was looking at me with such a flattering sincerity that I felt my breath get stuck in my throat. Far from slapping him, I felt a wild desire to reach out and touch his hand, as naturally as he had touched mine. I quickly shut the files and stood up to leave.

'My father would shoot you if I told him the things you say to me,' I said before heading down the stairs.

He smiled; his eyes seemed gentle. 'It will be worth it, especially after seeing the colour of your cheeks, pink as they are now.'

'Good day, Jairaj.' I turned and left, taking care that he didn't see my grin on the way home.

Everything about Jairaj is fun as long as it lasts. But with men like him, one never knows. I was wary of this tug and tease that had lent a new colour to my day but drained my evenings of their easy pleasure. Even Rafi Sahab's most beautiful melodies seemed sparse in my flat now. They seemed to be calling out for me to have someone to hum them with. Someone with laughing eyes and a crisp British accent.

I wish I wasn't losing my heart to a trifling. And I wish I wasn't enjoying it quite as much.

✎

I licked the spoon hungrily, my eyes intent on the page when the phone rang. Reluctantly, I put the tub of chocolate ice cream down and answered it, without glancing at the caller ID. That was a mistake, I realized, as my mother's face popped up on the screen.

She was at the kitchen counter of her house in New Haven, making a sandwich. Most people feel a tug of nostalgia when they see pictures of their home, but I only felt a fresh wave of gratitude at not having to live there anymore and eat those awful tomato sandwiches that always found their way to the dinner table. Mum didn't care much about taste, she ate only to be fuelled enough for the day, so that she could lock herself in her study and work on whatever cognitive psychology paper she had before her at the time. If it weren't for me (and now for Steve), she probably wouldn't even remember to stop for lunch; she would keep going till the knotty human mind was fully examined in her paragraphs and completely unravelled in her sentences.

'You have chocolate on your face, Radhika,' was the first thing she said to me. Politely corrective as usual, while I was standoffishly obstinate. That had been our relationship ever since I could remember, and no amount of Freudian psychoanalysis would be able to change it.

I wiped the ice cream away slowly. Then I took the tub of Halo and emptied its contents into my mouth. The last dregs of chocolate dripped on to my tongue. I licked my lips, satisfied.

Mum smiled tightly, a knowing look in her eyes. She thought I was acting out. She thought she knew all my reasons and motivations. After all, she had literally written the textbook on female psychology.

'Radhika,' she said. 'Just because a boy left you doesn't mean you can fall to pieces like this.'

I flinched, but she didn't apologize.

'I'm allowed to be in pieces for a while, Mum. I loved him and I got dumped. I'm allowed to be sad.'

She nearly rolled her eyes. 'You did not love him.'

'I did!'

'Radhika, that boy was the most shallow of all your boyfriends. He had no opinions and no principles—'

'But he said he loved me!' I sounded like a child, but I always did when I spoke to my mother. 'I'm twenty-nine years old, Mum. I don't want to be alone forever.'

'What does age have to do with—'

'You know it does, Mum. I don't want to get stuck with some younger white toy boy.'

Mum's mouth pressed into a thin line. It was obvious that I was talking about Steve, but I continued ruthlessly. 'And I don't want to be alone forever either. I want to … I want to be married!'

My mother looked shocked. The comment about Steve took a complete back seat to this confession.

Marriage was a Fraught topic in our family. Mum had written a paper titled '**A Psychology of Servility: The Wife in the Indian Marriage**', which was widely quoted across the world by scholars whenever women and India came up. So, you can guess that I was never taken to my cousins' colourful weddings in Atlanta, or back in Delhi, while I was growing up. Quite a shame, too, because the pictures on Facebook of my cousins bedecked in jewellery, grinning at the camera with henna glittering on their palms looked like great fun. I had saved all the invitations though. They were in a box next to the makeshift temple in my closet. On bad days, I came home and looked at them, lightly touching the golden peacocks and silver calligraphy, dreaming of my own big fat Indian wedding someday. Naani had secretly promised me that if I wanted, I could have it. But she had begged me not to tell Mum.

So, I kept my girlhood longings a secret; but once, while watching a Hindi film that had a particularly elaborate wedding song, I had hinted to Mum that I would like a similar, intricately embroidered lehenga on my wedding day. She went full Dr Mangala Anand on me. I received a lecture that was a more emphatic version of:

A PSYCHOLOGY OF SERVILITY: THE WIFE IN THE INDIAN MARRIAGE.

I hadn't visited the cinema with my Mum since.

'Radhika,' she drew breath now, appalled.

But I held up a hand. 'I've read the abstract, Mum. I know what you're going to say. But I believe that there is a way to be married without being in bondage.'

Her eyes widened with anger. I was a disappointment, I knew. But I had learnt to roll with it ever since I had discovered how fun it was to kiss boys and have them tell you that they loved you. It was a high even greater than winning the business of a billion-dollar soda company.

I looked at my mother, blinking suddenly. Being in love *was* a greater high than winning the business of a billion-dollar soda company, I told myself again. What I must do next was clear to me.

'I've wasted a lot of time,' I said. 'Maybe my entire youth.'

'You haven't "wasted" time, Radhika. You were studying and working and networking. Look how far you've come.'

'I don't want to make any more money, Mum. Not if it means sleeping alone every night.'

My mother looked exasperated. 'Beta, what do you want me to say? Do you want me to apologize for raising you to be independent and successful?'

'No! Of course not.' I shook my head furiously. I was grateful to my mother for raising me to be fiercely ambitious. I was glad to be intelligent and to have pursued my goals. I just thought it was time to shift my perspective, from profit satisfaction to emotional satisfaction, before I ended up withered and locked in my study, eating tomato sandwiches alone with a colleague who cohabited with me. But I didn't tell her that, obviously.

'This isn't your fault. It's mine, Mum. I have to fix it.' There were tears spilling out of my eyes. I couldn't remember the last time I cried in front of my mother.

Mum was confused. She could not believe it, and neither could I. For once, she could not explain my behaviour. This was something her own textbook had not prepared her for. Finally, Mum gave up and did something she had never done before.

'What are you feeling, beta?' She looked desperate. 'What are you thinking?'

'I think ...' I drew some air; my decision was final. 'I think I'm going to live with Naani, in Bombay, for some time.'

4
Beginning

Mr and Mrs Jairaj Anand

Those were the letters emblazoned on the plaque outside Naani's little bungalow on the fourteenth road of Khar, Bombay. Even ten years after Jairaj's death, everything about Gayatri, from her name to her home, belonged to her late husband. She was determined, however, not to let her life belong to him any more.

For the rest of the world, she was the sweet widow of Justice Anand, one of the great chief justices of the Supreme Court of India, but she refused to let this shrouding identity define her.

Gayatri was not one to feel sorry for herself, and so, even today on the tenth death anniversary of her husband, she did not bow her head in remorse. Instead, she bent her head to tie the laces of her pink joggers. And as she prepared for her morning walk, she prayed.

She prayed for her ambitious daughter in New Haven, that she may find peace; and for her beautiful, independent granddaughter in New York, that she may find companionship. She never prayed for their success. They had her spirit. That would ensure success. Happiness, however, did not spring as easily from a work ethic. It must be prayed for.

Having drank her glass of fresh lime juice, Gayatri strode out of the bungalow into the morning, walking past old IAS comrades who also had homes along the same tree-lined avenue. The men paused in their sipping of coconut water to wave at her. Gayatri Anand offered a delightful departure from their usual topics of conversation. Who cared about the somersaulting Sensex or the extortionate new tax regime when such a romantic figure of well-aged beauty and gentility strolled past them, her healthy appearance and bright eyes injecting life into their own cynical irises. Mrs Anand's life had been so interesting that it seemed as though every day they could uncover a little piece of its hidden adventures simply by gossiping about it.

'I wonder if her daughter will be here today,' Mr Shah mused to Mr Agarwal as they paid the coconut vendor his thirty rupees.

'Why? What's special about today?'

'It's the ten-year anniversary of her beauty salon. A big party is being thrown at the club. My wife's been going on about it for weeks.'

'Well, your wife does spend all her time there,' Mr Chavan chipped in. The men guffawed. Mr Shah coloured. His wife, Lata, had been a struggling actress back in the '70s and was still the butt of the more educated IAS wives' jokes.

'She barely has anything done,' Mr Shah insisted, even though he didn't believe it himself. 'She visits mostly to keep Mrs Anand company.'

'I believe Mrs Anand has enough company already,' Mr Fadnavis, the least genteel of the lot, smirked.

Mr Fadnavis wasn't wrong. Gayatri liked to keep busy, which was why she had started a salon with the remainder of the money in their joint account on the day Jairaj had died. She had called it 'Grace', and it had been a success since the day it opened. Initially, women went there to discover the secret to her fair and glowing skin, to have their hair become thick and luscious like hers. They returned, however, not for her beauty treatments but for her empathy.

In a society where women feared other women, Mrs Anand was a rare jewel who harboured no insecurities and freely complimented her clients and nurtured their beauty. It was a comfort to come to Grace after a day of being chastised by one's mother, husband or mother-in-law, and know with certainty that one would be greeted with genuine affection and a cup of creamy coffee, all for the price of a mani-pedi.

Today, the salon was aflutter with excitement. The girls and ladies were getting primped for the evening that lay ahead. They all felt like they were part of Grace's celebration and success. Gayatri was glad they felt that way. After all, she had begun the business not so much for profit as she had for finding friends and purpose. She had been lonely for a long time. Her work at Grace had nourished her heart in a way that her marriage could not.

Bauji would have balked at the idea of his brilliant daughter spending all her time talking to women about their skin and nails, but then he was a man. And his sex and stage of life did not permit him to understand the kind of power wielded by a desirable woman. Gayatri, however, knew what it felt like to be powerless, and she was determined that her clients would never hold a low opinion of themselves. She may begin by working on their roots, but with every oil massage administered by her girls, she was massaging into their heads the idea that they were intelligent, desirable and important.

Gayatri had helped middle-aged women divorce their adulterous husbands and encouraged young girls to study for entrance exams they thought they could never sit for. If this had been advice coming from any other woman, it would have been scoffed at or shrugged off, but Gayatri delivered her encouragement with such sincere investment in the welfare of the listener, and with such an intelligent plan of action, that it was hard not to believe in a better life for oneself. When the judge ruled in the wife's favour and the young doctors graduated from medical school, they all came back to Grace with a bottle of wine or a box of laddoos for Mrs Anand, the lady without whom they might never even have thought any of this possible.

She had been a part of all their celebrations, and now they were glad to be a part of hers.

'Just see, you've ruined it!' a high-pitched voice screeched from the lower floor of the salon.

'Ma—' a young voice whined.

Gayatri descended down the steps to the skin section, where Sangeeta, a plump society wife, was berating her daughter, Preeti.

'What is the problem?' Gayatri asked.

'Just look at her face. I've spent lakhs of rupees on her skin, but these spots won't go away.'

'How is it my fault?' Preeti shot back, pouting. 'They're your genes.'

'Drinking vodka shots every night with those idiot Mehra boys doesn't help matters,' her mother retorted.

Gayatri reined in a smile at Preeti's woebegone expression. She must be a few years younger than Radhika, Gayatri realized. And she was probably on the arranged marriage market, which was why Sangeeta was so tense.

'How old is she?'

'Twenty-six,' Sangeeta said, clicking her tongue. 'But twenty-four, if any nice boy's mother asks.'

'Noted,' Gayatri said before turning to Ferozi, her skin expert.

'Ferozi, mix up the rose uptan for her please.'

'Will you be able to get rid of the marks?' Sangeeta looked at Gayatri, frustrated.

'Ferozi, why don't you make a yogurt and honey mask for Sangeeta?' Gayatri called out.

'It's cooling,' she explained, turning to Sangeeta with a pleasant smile.

When the fretting mother had been escorted to the upper floor for her skin and temper to be soothed, Gayatri turned her focus towards the young girl. 'Preeti, sweetheart,' she began, but Preeti screwed her eyes shut.

'I won't give up drinking,' Preeti said, shaking her head defiantly. 'I like going out with Vicky and Krish. They're ridiculous, but they're fun. And after a whole day of working with Dad at the shop, I *need* the buzz!'

'I'm not asking you to stop,' Gayatri said with a slight shrug.

Preeti's eyes flew open, surprised to see Mrs Anand grinning at her.

'A buzz is indispensable to living,' she said, tying a shocked Preeti's hair into a loose plait. 'But you will be surprised to find that it comes not from the alcohol, but from the moment. Switch to a white wine spritzer. Dilute the wine with soda. The buzz lasts longer and tastes much better.'

Preeti's eyes widened and she smiled. 'I'll try it tonight. Thank you, Gayatri aunty.'

Gayatri smiled and squeezed the girl's shoulder.

'Oh and happy anniversary!' Preeti yelled as she left the room for the rose uptan to be scrubbed into her skin.

For some reason, the young girl's wishes struck Gayatri. She had always thought of Grace as a community, almost a family effort. But really, it was *her* anniversary, wasn't it? She had managed to make a success of this, all on her own. She looked around the blush-coloured walls, the rows upon rows of glossy cosmetics and the Bandra ladies chatting happily in their comfy swivel seats. A song burst in her heart, an old Rafi tune that she used to sing to herself in the kitchen when she lived alone in Bombay. A happier time, before she met—

Never mind. This day wasn't about regret. It was about celebration.

Gayatri sat down in a chair herself and called out to her best beautician. 'Priscilla,' she said, 'I'd like a blow dry please.'

The salon girls looked at each other in surprised delight. It was rare for Mrs Anand to indulge in any pampering herself, no matter how much they insisted.

Gayatri lay back in the chair and let the young girl's expert hands massage shampoo into her scalp. She relished the water, warm and cold, as it ran through her hair that was still thick and strong despite her years and all that she had weathered.

I will look especially beautiful tonight, she thought. It would give her courage to right a past wrong.

❧

Heads turned across the lantern-lit lawn of Otters Club as Gayatri made her way to the front of the party, wearing a light gold sari that matched the glass of Scotch in her hand. Bauji had gifted her this, may his soul rest in peace. She had little occasion to don it, but when she did, she felt he was looking down on his little girl, smiling still at how grown up she was.

She looked like a fairy, shimmering in the soft light of the moon and the lamps, against the green of the garden. Even after all these years, Badrinath 'Birdy' Rajan could not help but admire her.

'Thank you all for coming,' Gayatri began, 'to celebrate this milestone in my life. For me, Grace was not just a business but a rebirth. Not many people know this, but Grace was born on the same day as my husband died. And at a time when I felt very, very lost, this salon gave me a reason to get out of bed and participate in the living, in the decorating of the wonderful women I call my neighbours. All of you, who have gathered here have become part of my family, the reason for my rebirth. Thank you. For being a part of my life, and for letting me be a part of yours.'

Where is her actual family? A few guests wondered as they exchanged knowing glances. Fortunately, out of great respect for Mrs Anand, nothing was said out loud. They could gossip about it later at the buffet. For now, let the elderly lady have her toast.

'To Grace!' Gayatri said and raised her glass. She was gratified to see old friends and neighbours smiling and raising their glasses in response, their faces bright with genuine smiles for Justice Anand's widow.

One man's face, however, wore a look of surprise, a reaction that Gayatri had expected. She sauntered over to him first, politely accepting congratulations from her many guests. He saw her advance and straightened up, wishing there was some place to put his drink down so he could take her hand.

'You've gone pink with shock, Birdy,' Gayatri said as she got to her old friend and comrade. Her eyes had their usual twinkle.

'I thought you would have toasted him.'

'My life has been a toast to him. This decade will be about something else. I've decided.'

Birdy looked at the inviting expression on his friend's face. He wondered if he was letting his imagination run too wild. All his life, he had been in love with the same woman. He had watched her marry the most egoistical man in their office, and he had provided a steadying hand as she had picked up the pieces of her life after his death. But, in all this time, he had never once uttered a word about his true feelings for fear of losing her friendship forever. In the last

year, however, there had been moments—as they played
bridge together at the club or watched a film at Globus
Cinema—when Gayatri looked at him with such fondness
that he had dared to hope of the possibility of ... no, that
would be asking for too much, risking too much.

'Birdy,' she said, taking his palm.

He all but flinched. Her soft, fair palm felt so natural in
his. He hadn't held it since the time he took a splinter out
of her thumb in Professor Khurana's bungalow.

'I'd like for us to spend more time together,' she
whispered.

She seemed oblivious to the fact that Mr Sinha and
Mr Agarwal had turned to look at them, whispering
mischievously. 'It's Badrinath's lucky day,' they said and
laughed amongst themselves, aware that their wives were
already gossiping about the delicious scandal it would cause
amongst the Bandra ladies. Sangeeta said she wouldn't be
surprised if this meant that Mrs Anand would lose a lot of
business and may have to close her salon. Perhaps this was
her retirement party.

'After all,' Mrs Shah quipped, 'Mr Anand left her quite
well off, and Badrinath has pots of money of his own thanks
to his textile business.'

But wasn't that business going to the nephew? They
turned to gawk at Zain Rajan who was sipping a glass
of brandy by the bar. Nobody knew much about the tall
fellow except for the fact that he had returned from the UK

five years ago and become indispensable to his uncle. They knew that his mother, Birdy's sister, had been a flighty young thing who had defied her parents by eloping in London with a Muslim man. He must have been a Pathan, the neighbours guessed. That was probably where Zain got his golden beard and green eyes from. But what had caused him to leave his life and family in London, to come to Bombay and live with his estranged uncle? Nobody knew, but everyone tried to find out. Especially the girls.

Preeti was chatting with him now, drinking her white wine spritzer, but Zain didn't seem to be listening. He was gazing at the couple of the moment, who everyone else had their eyes on, and he was smiling a rare smile.

Birdy glanced at Zain the moment Gayatri took his hand. His nephew raised his glass from a distance.

'Gayatri,' Birdy said, taking her other hand as well, 'I'd like to spend the rest of my life with you.'

A sweet smile was his answer as she continued to look at him expectantly.

'But,' he said, 'I will not ask you here. Will you accompany me to Poona tomorrow? I have a horse in the races, and I have named her Grace. Whether she succeeds or not, I believe we will have something to celebrate by the end of this weekend.'

Gayatri looked at him, her eyes shining. 'I thought you'd never ask.'

They spent the rest of the party by each other's side, accepting congratulations and greeting guests together, as they hoped to be doing for the rest of their lives.

When she floated home that evening, Gayatri held none of the queasy uncertainty that accepting her first proposal had brought with it.

After forty long years, she finally felt a buzz.

❧

When her eyes opened the next morning, Gayatri realized that it was probably her last morning as a widow, as Mrs Jairaj Anand. The thought gave her such a jolt of joy that she practically bounded to her storeroom to take out the old suitcase, which lay unused under a pile of extra mattresses. The last time she had used it was to visit her granddaughter for her graduation in America, nearly a decade ago.

This year, her girls may have to visit a lot sooner than Christmas, Gayatri realized with glee as she headed back to her bedroom. She knew that her daughter, Mangala, who had doted on Birdy all through her childhood, would be delighted to learn of their engagement. It would be the only thing they would have agreed on in the last few years.

Radhika's reaction, on the other hand, could not be predicted. *It may be difficult for her to process, close as she had been to her grandfather*, Gayatri mused, neatly folding her white cotton kurta into the suitcase. After all, he had been her king, her only male role model, whose stern eye only softened when his colt-like granddaughter was sitting cross-legged with him, the two of them reading quietly on the living room sofa.

For Radhika, this wedding would be like reliving her grandfather's devastating death, Gayatri realized.

But Radhika had grown up to be her own woman, and she would want the best for her grandmother. It wasn't like her grandmother's love life would have any impact on her own. Still, the news would have to be broken to her more carefully. She was a sensitive girl, unlike Mangala who rationalized everything and bared her teeth at anyone who couldn't do the same.

The doorbell rang, ripping through Gayatri's daydream of phone calls to New Haven and New York. Her maid ran up the stairs and appeared at the door of her bedroom.

'Memsahib, someone is here to see you.'

'Is it Zain with the car? Tell him I need two minutes. I'm not done packing yet. Make him his usual cold coffee—'

'It's not Zain Baba. It's a girl.'

Gayatri's eyes widened, confused. 'The salon is closed today. I've given them the weekend off—'

'Naani?' a hollow voice wobbled through the bungalow. Gayatri looked over the railing of the first floor, scarcely allowing herself to believe what she saw.

Radhika, her granddaughter from New York, was standing at the foot of the steps with her suitcases, clutching a bar of dark chocolate. When she spotted Gayatri, leaning over to look at her, she nearly burst into tears of relief. Radhika couldn't help it. There was something incredibly reassuring about her grandmother's appearance, vital with excitement as it was that morning.

Abandoning her bags, Radhika ran up the stairs to hug her grandmother, who smelled familiarly of French perfume and freshly ironed cotton.

'Naani, I need your help.' Radhika burrowed her head in her grandmother's soft neck. Gayatri instinctively wrapped her arms around Radhika and stroked her greasy hair. Every other idea vanished from Gayatri's mind.

'Shh, sweetheart,' she said. 'You will be fine. You're here now. It will all be fine.'

❧

'Hello, Birdy?'

'Gayatri?' his voice sounded so eager that Gayatri winced.

She made it quick. 'Birdy, I'm so sorry ... I won't be able to come today.'

There was silence at the other end. She heard Zain's voice ask agitatedly in the background, 'What happened, Mamu? Are you okay? Please sit down. Did she change her mind?'

'I haven't changed my mind, Birdy. Far from it,' Gayatri whispered fervently, trying to imbue as much emotion in her voice as possible without letting Radhika hear it.

'Please don't feel obligated to say these things, Gayatri,' Birdy began, his voice thick with restrained emotion. 'I wouldn't want to force you in any way.'

Oh dear, sweet Birdy, Gayatri thought. The man had spent his entire life making sure that she didn't feel any kind of discomfort. Her heart surged with more love than ever for him.

'Birdy, please listen. Radhika has turned up, out of the blue—'

'From New York?' he asked, confused. 'Is everything all right?'

'I don't know. She seems upset about something. I can't leave now …'

'Of course not. Of course not.'

'I'm really sorry, Birdy.'

'It's all right, Gayatri,' he said. And then, with forced cheer in his voice, he added, 'Family comes first, I understand.'

Gayatri felt awful. She knew that Birdy had always considered her his family. And yet, she had chosen Jairaj over him. Then Mangala had taken precedence, and now Radhika was being prioritized. She wondered if Birdy felt as though every generation, in being given its due prominence, was cheating him out of his.

'Best of luck at at the races,' she added feebly. 'I hope Grace wins.'

Birdy let out a hollow laugh and said nothing more.

Gayatri closed her eyes and whispered 'goodbye' before disconnecting the line. Then she steadied her breathing and turned to her granddaughter, who was pulling out a can of Diet Coke at that very moment. All thoughts of Birdy vanished from Gayatri's mind as she watched, aghast, while Radhika popped open the can at eight in the morning. The fizz ripped through the quiet of the bungalow as Radhika glugged the artificial sugar syrup, as though it were her life force. Gayatri bit back the rebuke that immediately rose to her tongue. Instead, she took in her granddaughter's appearance with the expertise of a beautician and a grandmother.

Radhika's skin was grey and peeling. The ends of her long hair were frayed. Her rosebud mouth, which used to be plump and pink, was chapped, probably from biting it out of frustration, Gayatri realized.

Somehow her beautiful granddaughter, who had inherited all her genes and should have been glowing with the health and vitality of youth, had become this old, skinny … zombie.

What in God's name had happened?

5
Secrets

*P*erhaps I should have called before turning up. Naani seemed more shocked than surprised to see me. I think she was heading out somewhere when I arrived. I shouldn't have been so dramatic, flinging my arms around her and crying on her shoulder like that. After all, I was a fully grown woman and the newly appointed head of American accounts at McKinley India. I couldn't be behaving like a headcase with a broken heart, even if I did spend the last twenty-two hours listening Taylor Swift's 'Dear John', on repeat, and sobbing softly during the interludes as I looked at the clouds passing by. (Pro tip: there is something immensely cathartic about transatlantic crying. It makes grief seem a lot more romantic, and it scares your neighbouring passengers away, giving you a lot more leg space and elbow room.)

I was regretting the sobs a little bit now because twenty-two hours of tears and caffeine had made for the worst under-eye bag situation, one that hadn't been helped even by the pounds of Lancôme concealer I rubbed on them. Naani, who's own face was bereft of make-up and as fresh as the morning, was looking at me horrified. I thought she'd slap my hand away when I pulled out a can of Diet Coke from my Dior tote. Now, her eyes moved from my hair to my nails, abject disappointment lining her face.

'It was a long flight,' I said defensively, putting the bright red can down.

'Of course,' her eyes zipped from the can back to my face, her expression rearranged into a sympathetic smile. 'You should take a nap, sweetheart. And a shower.'

'Naani, I've been promoted,' I said in a pathetic attempt to win some respect. 'That is why I'm here.'

Finally, she smiled a real smile, one that reached all the way up to her eyes. 'Congratulations, beta!'

She got up to kiss me, but then she decided against it, settling instead for holding my hands.

Wow, I wondered if I smelled that bad.

'That's why I'm here, Naani,' I continued, tucking one leg behind the other, trying to appear as in command of myself as possible. 'I've been sent to supervise all the American accounts of my company that are operating in Bombay. At least for the next six months.'

'That's wonderful, sweetheart,' Naani said, but the concern had returned to her eyes. I didn't blame her. My voice was so insistent that it sounded shrill.

'My office offered to put me up in this really posh flat,' I said high-handedly, 'but I thought I'd live with you, help you out …'

My grandmother's eyes narrowed. I stopped. I shouldn't have tried to be cool. Naani didn't take kindly to being considered dependent.

'I'm proud of you, Radhika,' she said. I could tell she was forcing herself to be gentle. 'And I'm happy to have you here. But I think you can drop the act now.'

Naani looked directly into my eyes, raising my hands and looking at my body and face. 'What on earth happened to you?'

Ouch.

✎

Twenty minutes later, we were at Grace. A team of salon girls was looking at me concernedly. I felt like the pauper from *The Princess and the Pauper*, who had wandered into the castle looking for a hug and a hot meal but was met with judgement and eyebrow wax instead.

On the way over, I had told Naani all about my sordid break-up with Siddhant, including the awful Belfry incident. She had looked at me with such an expression of pity and disappointment that I had nearly launched into my 'we had a spark' defence, but that would have involved showing my grandmother my Excel sheets. I hadn't sunk that low yet.

'Sweetheart, stop,' she had said, shaking her head and cutting me off mid-sentence as I had droned on about what an unfair prick Siddhant was. 'Don't talk about this any more.'

I had been confused. She had had no other response to my break-up. No expression of sorrow, not even a measly 'you poor thing', which was really what I was after. I felt cheated. I had seen her consoling all her clients and friends about their love affairs. It was practically part of her job description as the proprietor of a salon for women. But all I got, effectively, was a 'shut up about your feelings, Radhika'.

And now, at the salon, she was whispering in a corner to Priscilla, her chief of staff, while looking at me worriedly. Ferozi, the skin expert, was prodding at my cheekbones, trying to get a better look at the freckles and spots, shaking her head in disappointment.

'Unbelievable,' she muttered at last. 'The same face as Mrs Anand, but ...' she dropped her hand in disbelief. 'Unbelievable,' she said again.

For the love of Christ.

'I work really long hours,' I managed to say.

'So do I,' chimed in a pretty, young girl from the next counter. Her skin glowed like she had just chugged cucumber juice after her vitamin injections. 'I keep telling these girls, too! It's so hard to keep up a beauty regimen, isn't it?'

'It is,' I nodded, trying not to frown at her perfect face. 'Especially since I'm the new head of American accounts at McKinley.' That should shush her up. I picked up a magazine and flipped through it nonchalantly.

'I'm a cardio surgeon,' she said brightly. I stopped mid-flip.

'Dr Parineeti Sadanah. Here, keep this, you may need it,' she said, handing me a business card. I looked at her, confused, as she added chirpily, 'Every high-stress career woman should have a heart specialist's number on hand!'

She squeezed my shoulder and moved away to the blow dry bar.

Bitch.

I was about to throw her card away when Naani appeared with Priscilla by her side. 'Radhika, we're going to change some things, all right?' She had a false cheerful smile pasted on her face, the kind one used with a mentally ill person.

'Just necessary things,' Priscilla reassured me. 'Just your hair and eyebrows.'

'And skin!' Ferozi yelled from across the salon. 'Lots of work to be done on her skin.'

I could see Dr Sadanah smile from the corner of my eye. My cheeks burned with embarrassment.

'Naani,' I said, using my most superior-sounding tone, 'I'm not defined by the way I look. I don't feel the need to change anything. My body is my home; it is a raw reflection of my spirit.' I shot a glance at the doctor whose eyebrows were raised at this sudden feminist tirade. Take that, cardio surgeon.

Naani looked at me, visibly unimpressed. 'Does your spirit have spots?' she asked finally.

Priscilla snorted and hurriedly covered her mouth, camouflaging her laughter as a cough.

I opened my mouth to argue, but then shut it, suddenly exhausted. *Didn't I move here because I wanted a different life?*

'All right,' I said, giving up and sinking back into the chair. 'Do whatever you like.'

Gayatri could not believe her luck. Birdy, who was supposed to be in Poona, was somehow in her living room, holding a box of liquor chocolates in one hand and a bottle of wine in the other.

'I thought you'd be in Poona,' Gayatri smiled as Birdy raised her hand to his lips.

'My horse can race without me. I couldn't resist meeting Radhika. I haven't seen her since Jai's funeral. I've already booked us a table at the club for dinner.'

Radhika descended the stairs just then, thankfully in the new sundress they had bought that afternoon. Gayatri made a mental note to burn all her hideous black sweatshirts.

'Hello, Birdy uncle!' Radhika said, surprised, as she hugged him.

'Radhika, wow!' Birdy said, breaking away from the embrace and chuckling. 'The last time I saw you, you were so young.'

Oh dear, Gayatri thought, looking at the crestfallen expression on her granddaughter's face. Birdy, poor thing, never knew what to say to young women. If he continued in this vein through the evening, Gayatri would have a tough time breaking the news of their marriage to Radhika.

Gayatri quickly shot Birdy a look. Light dawned on his face.

'I mean, not that you're old,' Birdy faltered. 'You were just a college girl then, that's what I meant.'

Radhika's smile froze completely and she nodded along, muttering 'of course, of course' politely.

'Where is Zain?' Gayatri asked, cutting off Birdy's apology. 'Will he be joining us?'

'Of course. He's already at the club.'

There, Gayatri thought, *the evening won't be a total disaster now.* What Radhika needed after her serious relationship and serious job was a little fun. A young friend to bring her colour back. And Zain was Bombay's best candidate for the job.

'Zain Beta, it's so good to see you. I don't think you've met Radhika. Beta, this is Birdy uncle's nephew.'

Naani is good, I'll give her that. Somehow, on my first evening in Bombay, she had managed to wrangle for me the most attractive man at Otters Club. Zain wasn't conventionally handsome, in the pretty-boy sense, like Siddhant, but there was something about his straight-backed posture and golden-bearded grin that commanded the attention of everyone.

You could tell he wasn't shying away, neither from the attention nor from the many young women who glanced in our direction as he shook my hand firmly. But there was a wolfish glint in his eye that immediately put me on guard. I knew his type. And no, I would not be joining his horde of followers.

'Zain, why don't you get Radhika a drink?' Naani suggested. I frowned. She could not be more obvious if she nudged and winked.

'I can get it myself, Naani,' I smiled and began moving to the bar.

'Is this a feminist thing?' Zain grinned as he caught up with me. 'Or a head-of-department thing?' His eyes were twinkling dangerously.

I raised my eyebrows, surprised by the extent of his information. 'Mamu boasts about you like you're his own granddaughter,' he explained. 'Congratulations on the promotion.'

'Thank you,' I said modestly. 'So, what do you do?'

'I work at Mamu's textile factory.'

'Rubbish. He's the boss at this point,' Birdy said as he joined us at the bar and asked for two glasses of wine. Then he turned to us. 'All I do is race horses and play bridge with your Naani.'

The bartender put a bottle of Merlot on the counter. Zain and I smiled at each other as Birdy waited. For a long minute, I was conscious of Zain's eyes absorbing my face over the stream of pouring wine. By the time Birdy left, I noticed that nearly everyone around was watching us with their heads bent together, ready to whisper. In particular, there were two older women in black who kept stealing glances.

Zain followed my gaze and smiled widely. Then he raised his voice to a falsetto and said, '*Gayatri's granddaughter! Turned up from nowhere! Do you think she's pregnant?*'

I looked at him in shock. He nodded in the direction of another aunty I recognized from the parlour. *Lata, her name was*, I thought. She was pretending not to look at us anymore. Zain put on the funny voice again. '*And she's standing with Birdy's nephew. Maybe she's asking him for help? I'm sure he knows a thing or two about unplanned pregnancies.*'

I burst into laughter. Zain nodded at a third pair. A couple of uncles were nursing their whisky and staring blatantly at us. Before he could speak, I put on a gruff voice. '*I wonder if they pay taxes here or abroad,*' I said, in my best uncle imitation. '*These green-card holders have it too good.*'

Zain turned to me with surprised appreciation on his face. 'Shall we take a bottle and disappear?' he asked.

I grinned and grabbed a Cabernet by the neck.

❧

DO NOT TRY THIS AT HOME.

The rest of the club was busy playing Sunday-evening housie, I guessed, which was probably why nobody stopped us as we climbed on to the diving board, three levels above the pool. I was not sure whose idea it was to sit on a springy plank at a dizzying height after guzzling a bottle of wine. Possibly mine. It seemed like the impulsive, fun thing Jia K. would have done. We were walking around the garden, sipping from the bottle and chatting about our jobs, when I spotted the diving board and spun a yarn about how it had always been a secret fantasy of mine to sit on it, without springing forward.

Zain looked at me, eyes twinkling. 'I'm all for realizing fantasies.'

I hadn't expected him to say anything of the kind. I mean, he was the CEO of a textile company, wearing a tie even on a Sunday. If he could be fun enough to agree to this ridiculous plan, I would have to match his daring to follow through. After all, I had come here to be someone else, hadn't I?

Zain and I walked down the green plank with our hands raised horizontally, like the Pirates of Otters Club. As we sat, I let my legs dangle in the air. Zain kept his palm on top of mine to steady me. The butterflies in my stomach darted on the wings of adrenaline, romance and ridiculousness. We had a view of the Arabian Sea before us and a blue pool below us. I continued our conversation, as though nothing bizarre had happened.

'Did you grow up in Bombay?' I asked.

Zain looked at me and chuckled, as though we were both in on a fantastic secret. Then he played along. 'Yes and no. I was born in London, but I came here after college.'

'That's a no, then.'

'I definitely did some growing up after college, too,' Zain said with a broad smile. 'If you ask the girls I go out with, I still haven't grown up.'

Girls. Plural. Interesting. Outwardly, however, I didn't take the bait. 'Why did you move back here?'

'I felt like I could learn more about business from Mamu, at the factory here, than I could at any organization or business school in the UK.'

His tone had become reverential. He probably realized it, too, because he immediately turned flippant. 'Plus, my dad wasn't around much. I like hanging out with Mamu.'

I understood the off-handedness. I used it myself when anyone asked about my father. It was the easiest thing to do to ward off unnecessary interrogation. You feigned indifference.

'I'm sure Birdy appreciates your company,' I said, changing the subject. 'It must be lonely for him since he's a bachelor.'

Zain looked at me so puzzled that I could see all the colours in his eyes. There were flickers of gold in the otherwise light green irises. *Never trust cat-eyes. Wasn't that an old Hindi saying?*

'I don't think he's lonely, Radhika,' Zain said slowly, smiling at me.

I was not paying much attention. His face was close to mine, but it was fuzzy because of the wine. 'No, I know he isn't lonely anymore,' I was slurring, and I knew it. 'Now that he has you, of course,' I swayed a little, trying to get away from his face.

I didn't want him to think I was after him. Especially since every other woman here was. I edged away a little on the board. Besides he was a wolf, it was obvious. I edged even further to the left, but my body swayed to the right and I nearly lost my balance …

Zain caught me. 'Easy, easy,' he said.

I rested against him for a moment before clutching the side of the board. *Whoosh. That was close.* A second late and I would have been floating in the pool below, probably seriously hurt.

'Sorry,' I shrugged, shaking my head a little.

'No problem,' he smiled kindly. 'Can I hold on to your arm, if you don't mind? I think it's safer that way.'

I nodded and he put his arm around my shoulders. I leaned into him, sighing. We were much too comfortable for two people who had just met, one of whom was desperately trying to play it cool and be ladylike at the same time.

'I feel like a bit of a fool,' I whispered.

'Don't worry about it,' he whispered back. And then he did the sweetest thing to reduce my awkwardness. Something very not wolf-like.

He continued the conversation.

'So, what about you? Why did you move back here?'

Oh dear. I wished I hadn't begun twenty questions now. It was hard enough answering this one sober.

'Similar reasons …' I said, smiling up at him. 'A work opportunity and I wanted to spend time with Naani.'

I didn't feel even slightly guilty as the lies tripped off my tongue.

'And you're doing long-distance with your boyfriend?' Zain asked casually. A little too casually.

I sat up straight and grinned. 'How do you know that I have a boyfriend?'

'Gayatri aunty showed us pictures you sent her,' he said quickly.

'I never sent Naani a picture of Siddhant,' I said with a frown.

'I may have googled you a little bit,' Zain admitted, looking away from me and at the sea before us.

'Stalker,' I said, but I was laughing. It was quite flattering to have such a sought-after guy stalking me. *Maybe he wasn't a wolf after all.*

'Maybe a little bit,' he said, half-smiling. He had a good, clean smile. Not like the crooked one Siddhant favoured. 'Mamu keeps talking about you, and somehow we've missed each other every time you've been in town. I suppose I was just curious.'

His smile was so warm and bright that I relaxed the cool-girl facade I had held on to so tenaciously all evening.

'I'm just as guilty.'

'How so?'

'Your favourite colour is blue, for Chelsea Football Club. And you went to LSE for your MBA. You stayed for a year before dropping out.'

In my defence, it was the wine. Zain looked so shocked that I laughed. The sound chimed in the air and reverberated on our diving board. I could feel it ringing in my toes even. I should have been embarrassed, but it was such a relief to not be pretending any longer that I just kept laughing.

'That's more than a little bit of stalking,' he said, but he was laughing as well.

'I never checked to see if you have a girlfriend though,' I teased. 'No impure intentions, just plain curiosity.'

'Okay, well, I guess mine were a little more impure.'

I nearly fell off the board. Zain steadied me again. He looked thoroughly apologetic now.

'Damn. I'm sorry,' he said, sounding quite genuine. 'I shouldn't have said that. You're somebody's girlfriend.'

'I'm not.'

Until now, I had not thought that there could be any advantage to this statement.

✒

'I think the two youngsters are getting along!'

Birdy tore his gaze away from Gayatri to look in the direction her little finger was poking at from under her chin. He saw his nephew walk slowly into the bar, his arm around Radhika's waist. The two of them were whispering and laughing as though they had shared the most delicious joke that nobody else would understand.

Birdy frowned. He had seen Zain assume a similar stance with too many young girls. This was Gayatri Khurana's only granddaughter.

Zain and Radhika stumbled to their table. 'Mamu,' he said, 'I'm going to take the driver to drop Radhika home. I'll send him back for you in an hour.'

'I think it might be better if we all go back together,' Birdy began, but Gayatri cut him off.

'Nonsense!' she said vehemently. 'Zain beta, I think that is a lovely idea. Radhika must be exhausted, and I still want to say hello to a few people. Please drop her home. Thank you so much.'

Gayatri handed Zain the house keys with a beatific smile, as Birdy watched, helpless.

'Thanks, Naani,' Radhika said, slurring slightly. Birdy winced. He could tell that this was not going to end well. He wondered whether he should object. Perhaps he should accompany them home and then return with the car to fetch Gayatri, but before he could come to a decision the young couple had left.

Birdy sent up a silent prayer that Zain would behave himself tonight.

Gentlemen, I've decided, are more fun in books than they are in person.

Zain Rajan was being too much of a gentleman tonight. Twice, I gave him the opportunity to kiss me. Once on the diving board, and once on our way home. Both times, he let it pass. It would have been understandable if he had leaned away. I would have understood that he was either not attracted to me, or that he was gay.

But it was not like he wasn't tempted. He looked at my mouth intently and then looked away forcibly. We were standing on the doorstep of Naani's bungalow now, and it was obvious as to what he should do. It was so obvious that he was smiling at me with an apology in his green-golden eyes as he fumbled around in his pocket for the keys.

I knew he was restraining himself because he looked at me the way I looked at tiramisu. And while I loved being thought of as a particularly decadent dessert that he didn't have the permission to enjoy, I wanted to know whose permission he was seeking. At this point, I was so high on him and the wine and the evening that I didn't even care if he was a commitment-phobe like Siddhant. I just wanted to be kissed.

'Zain,' I said as he inserted Naani's key into the front door. He turned around, businesslike.

'What's up?'

'You said your intentions were impure.'

He let out a laugh and swung the door open. 'I did.'

I looked at him, surprised, and stepped into the house. The bungalow was empty except for us. It felt a bit odd to be standing in my grandmother's living room, trying to seduce a man.

'So,' I cleared my throat, waiting for him to say something. When he didn't, I coughed slightly. I didn't know when I decided that guttural sounds were the way to make him fall in love with me, but I tried again, this time with a 'hem' so rough that I actually started to wheeze.

'Are you okay?' he asked, patting my back with a slightly amused expression.

I looked up at him, annoyed now. This was bullshit. He flirted with me all night and made me do dangerous, feet-dangling things. The least he could do was give me a goodbye kiss so that I would not be frustrated all night about the anticlimax of my undesirability.

'Why won't you kiss me?' I snapped.

He looked at me, stunned for a moment, but then let out a low chuckle. 'Because I think Mamu will kill me if I do.'

I was confused. 'Did he say that?'

'He doesn't have to, Radhika.' Zain grinned. 'I don't date. And I don't think I could not date you.'

I blinked at him. 'That's a double negative.'

Even though I knew he wasn't boyfriend material from the moment I laid eyes on him, I must confess I was disappointed. That disappointment must have shown up on my face because Zain sighed and began to explain himself.

'I can't give a relationship the time and attention it needs,' he sounded rehearsed. 'I work fifteen hours a day—'

'I work the same hours,' I pointed out.

'Look why don't we—' he paused, thinking.

'Yes?' I leaned towards him.

'Can we be friends?'

I nearly laughed. When did my life become a sad Ella Fitzgerald song?

'All right,' I said, tired now.

We shook on it and he left.

6
Arranged

I pulled the drawer open carefully. The wood creaked, as though yawning after a good, long rest, before opening out fully to reveal the treasures I was after. Stacks of photographs lay piled up one on top of the other. Black-and-white and covered in a layer of dust that rose in play and scattered in a sunbeam, as though dancing in celebration of the memories they had captured. I picked the prints up and settled down cross-legged at the foot of my bed. My coffee mug was set down as I rifled through the years; flying back in time—Naanu's appointment as chief justice, Mum's birth, the glory of the Parisian honeymoon, the secret wedding, and finally what I was looking for.

The proposal. A little black-and-white photograph of Naani and Naanu at Bauji's bungalow on the campus of Shri Ram College of Commerce, Delhi.

Ever since last night, I had been thinking about proposals. Zain's offer of friendship seemed to be a proposal of its own kind. It was an invitation to be something more than just a modern couple that flirted for a while, shagged for a week and soon grew completely oblivious to the other person's spirit over hours spent flitting from restaurants to bars until Instagram captions started to demand specificity. Then came the inevitable boredom (because how could you not be bored when you hadn't taken the time to discuss anything other than music and movies with your partner), the roving eye, wondering who-else-was-out-there, chatting them up after work and finally deleting any incriminating social media posts with the previous person.

Friendships, on the other hand, lasted a lifetime. You were both implicitly committed to having coffee and sharing conversations, so long as you were within walking distance of each other. And then that implicit commitment might naturally grow to be a quiet hunger for your friend, so that when she was removed from your society you had to follow her across cities just to be within walking distance of her again.

Naanu always said that he realized he wanted to marry Naani the day he met her. But it became a compulsion the minute she left for Delhi in March 1960.

❦

The Personal Diary of Gayatri Khurana, IAS officer, Delhi Division.

9 March 1960

Delhi

There are few hours as delicious as sitting on the verandah with Bauji, reading Austen in the soft sunlight of spring while Rishi's laughter gurgles up from the lawn beneath us. Bauji shivered a little, and I ran inside to get his shawl.

'What would you do without me?' I teased, wrapping it around his shoulders, which had shrunk in width in just the last week. *At least his colour is back*, I told myself to prevent anxiety.

'I would get along just fine,' he harrumphed. 'You didn't need to come back at all, you know. I have Rishi.'

'Rishi is ten years old.'

'Not that much younger than you.'

I shook my head and settled back down in my chair with Emma and Mr Woodhouse. I refused to engage in this argument again. Bauji harrumphed yet again. He didn't take kindly to being ignored.

'You cannot take holidays like this. You're in charge of a whole presidency.'

'The chief minister himself gave me leave when I told him that you had dengue,' I quipped. Secretly, I was glad to hear the fire returning in Bauji's tone. So far, he had only managed weak protestations. The numbing medications must finally be wearing off.

The moment when I had been telegraphed from the university's clinic had been horrific. It was one thing to read in the newspapers about the hundreds of deaths the infamous mosquito-carried disease was causing in Delhi, but a whole other degree of fear to hear that your own father had contracted it and was battling delirium.

When I had informed Yashwant Saab, Mr Sinha and my fellow officers, they had looked at me with such mournful expressions that I half expected them to begin whispering condolences. Even Jai, who I thought did not have a sympathetic bone in his body, had skipped going to court that day to drop me to the train station, muttering words of helpless encouragement the entire way. If I hadn't been sick with fear, I would have been quite amused. It was a pleasant surprise to see Jai lose command of himself.

Fortunately, Bauji had fought the virus with his usual robust determination and returned home in a record amount of time compared to other patients.

Secretly, I wished the doctors had kept him at the hospital a little longer because Bauji was the worst convalescent when he was not under medical supervision. But I was happy to play nurse in the absence of real ones. I'd rather be here, stubbornly pumping the colour back into his face, than anywhere else in the world.

'Shall I bring your apple juice now?' I asked, noticing that it was nearly noon.

Bauji narrowed his eyes. 'I can get it myself. Don't start to think of me as the pernickety father in that book,' he said, pointing to my copy of *Emma*. 'Dependent old fool.'

'Since when do you read Austen?' I laughed. He was always making fun of my 'romances'.

'I've spent too many hours in the hospital,' he said, defensively. 'Thank God I will be able to return to my students this week. And you will return to Bombay.'

'We will see about that—'

'Gayatri,' he said warningly. 'Khuranas don't quit things—'

'Including life,' I retorted. But before he could launch into an argument, we were distracted by the abrupt silence in the lawn. My baby brother's chortling and his make-believe muttering had stopped. He was talking to someone. Someone who was making him laugh.

Birdy must have returned! Good. Now I have someone who can help me dissuade Bauji from cutting short his period of rest.

I leaned over the railing of the verandah, peeked into the garden and called out to Birdy, but he wasn't there. Instead, Rishi was staring in awe at a broad-shouldered man in an Oxford suit, who was demonstrating to him how to correctly hold a cricket bat.

Jai? I laughed, surprised.

'Who is it?' Bauji asked.

I wasn't sure how to respond. I had barely admitted to myself what Jai had come to mean to me over the three months that we had spent working together. To describe him effectively would require a longer, deeper reading of my thoughts, something I hadn't permitted myself to do.

'A colleague,' I said. 'Jairaj Anand.'

Jai must have heard us, because he looked up and smiled at me. 'Good afternoon, Officer Khurana,' he said.

'Good afternoon, Mr Anand,' I called back, trying not to appear too gleeful.

❦

It was unnerving, having Bauji and Jairaj sit opposite each other. They had the same ramrod straight backs and the same strident tone while speaking. When they laughed together, the sound exploded like machine guns being fired.

'I hope you're here to summon my daughter back to work, Mr Anand,' Bauji joked once the introductions were over. I could tell that he liked Jai and was impressed with his Oxford education. Bauji had been at the University of London himself, but he had travelled to Oxford once for a conference. The place was enshrined in his memory as the cathedral of learning, like no other place in the world. It was my parents dream to send Rishi there.

'Professor Khurana, your daughter's detailed instructions have ensured that our work does not suffer even while she is away,' Jai said. 'Mr Sinha and I often joke that her daily telegraphs are going to cost as much as the entire operation of splitting a state into two.'

'You see?' I turned to Bauji, triumphant. 'I could easily stay another week, at least.'

Jai frowned. 'Is that necessary?'

'It is not,' Bauji said vehemently. 'I do not need a babysitter.'

'That is debatable,' I shrugged.

'This is what you get for educating your daughters,' Bauji complained. 'Back talk and disrespect. Do yourself a favour, Jairaj, and lock your daughters up in the house instead.'

'Yes, learn from Bauji's errors,' I said, equally grave. 'Or you risk having your opinions challenged by intelligence every day. Few men have the wit to endure or enjoy such banter.'

'See, more insolence!' Bauji pinched my nose affectionately.

Jai watched us, smiling. 'You two have a lovely relationship. It's quite different from the one my sister and father share.'

'Where are your parents?' Bauji asked as I poured us some more tea.

'They live in London, Professor. But I have asked them to return immediately.'

Bauji's eyebrows shot up at the urgency of his tone. 'And why is that?'

'I would like them to meet you,' Jai said casually, adding a cube of sugar to the teacup I had handed him.

Bauji's expression was curious. 'For what purpose?'

Jai stopped stirring and looked straight at my father. 'For the purpose of requesting your daughter's hand in marriage.'

I didn't dare to look at Jai for fear of blushing right down to my roots, like some simple village girl with no manners or grace. I couldn't imagine what Bauji must be thinking. No woman in our family had chosen her own partner.

Every trace of familiar jocularity vanished from Bauji's manner. The north Indian in him couldn't allow the marriage of his daughter to be discussed in such a casual fashion. He pinned Jai with a piercing stare and struggled to keep the aggression out of his voice. 'Mr Anand, normally the parents of the boy approach the father of the girl,' he said slowly. 'It is considered a sign of respect.'

I watched Jai's face carefully, praying that he didn't assume a high-handed manner with my father. 'I understand, Professor Saab, but my parents are old and travel from England isn't easy for them. They will be coming at the end of this month, but I couldn't risk waiting so long.'

'You were worried that I may introduce her to someone else during her time at home?' Bauji challenged.

A glint appeared in Jai's eyes, confirming this suspicion. 'Some other man will probably be interested in Gayatri solely for her beauty. I'm not so inconsiderate to her intelligence.'

I could no longer restrain the colour that was fast rising to my cheeks by trying to recite the preamble to the Constitution. I gave in completely to the drama of the moment, hoping with all my heart that Bauji accepted.

But Bauji wasn't looking at Jai with the affection that I was feeling. Instead, his eyes held a dormant, almost defensive, anger.

'I will never marry my daughter to an inconsiderate man,' he said, his voice rising. 'She is my pride and joy!'

I decided to intervene then, before things rolled into unsalvageable territory. 'Bauji, I don't think Mr Anand means to offend you.'

Both men turned to me, surprise clear on their faces. I was not supposed to be speaking at all during a marriage proposal, much less interpreting for them. But I couldn't remain a spectator any longer, now that my heart was involved and every happiness seemed to be hanging in the balance.

'He is just impatient for things to go his way, as usual,' I said.

Jai looked at me, surprised by this taunt. Bauji, however, burst into laughter as I knew he would.

'The matter is important enough, at least to me, to warrant impatience,' Jai said, shooting me an accusatory glance.

Bauji's eyes flitted from Jai's arrogant jaw to my obstinate eyes.

'You are definitely a match for each other,' he declared. 'Mr Anand, I will make no formal promise till I meet your parents. But you are welcome to have your meals with us for as long as you are here.'

Jai was about to protest when Bauji cut him off. 'Don't worry, I won't entertain any other marriage proposals till then. You have my word.'

❧

'What would you like to do Gayatri?' Bauji asked after Jai left. We were taking our evening stroll through the sprawling lawns of the university campus, my arm tucked into Bauji's under his shawl and my face looking directly into the reddening evening sun.

I pretended to think about his question for the sake of propriety. It would not do to appear too eager in Bauji's eyes, even if my heart was thumping so loudly that I thought it would burst out of my chest. I had never experienced such a longing before. So far, my brain had been focused on definite, achievable goals. There was the coming first in the school exams, the BA, the MA, and then finally the IAS exams. All that had involved studying hard, writing papers, practising skills like penmanship and debating and horse riding to eventually reach the level of excellence that had brought me to where I am. I had everything that I had hoped for as a young girl, all as a reward for unforgiving focus and relentless industry.

Jai had neither been dreamt of nor worked towards. *How could I want him so badly then? And how could I possibly be allowed to have him?* I needed more time to be sure, to know that his affection for me wasn't a mirage, before I agreed to marry him. Questions and worries whirled through my mind, rendering me speechless with indecision. Bauji smirked, enjoying my rare moment of confusion.

'I like him, Didi!' Rishi yelled as he cycled past us.

Bauji looked at him, eyes twinkling. 'Well, the men of the house have decided it for you then.'

I looked at Bauji. 'I thought you found him arrogant and brazen.'

Bauji shrugged. 'We're a young country with few resources,' he said. 'We're going to need arrogant and brazen men to lead us through the next few decades.'

Something odd rose within me then. 'And women,' I said, insistently.

'And women,' he agreed. 'But there will be few like you, and even fewer who understand you. Jairaj will be good protection from those who will wish you ill.'

Until then, I had never imagined that I would need protection.

❧

10 March 1960

I was helping our cook stuff the parathas with potatoes when Jai appeared next. He cut such an odd figure; his grey tie and blazer were such an orderly, stark contrast to the busy colours of our kitchen with ripe tomatoes being sliced on one counter and green chutney being churned on another.

'You needn't dress so formally for lunch,' I teased as I turned on the stove and dropped the paratha on to a tawa.

The scent of roasting ghee and potatoes filled the kitchen. Jai inhaled appreciatively.

'Perhaps I should be like you and revisit my childhood,' he said, tugging at the two braids my hair was tied into. The cook laughed and slipped out of the kitchen with the pickles and the peas. I swatted Jai's hand away as it reached for my braids again.

'What do you think you're doing?' I demanded. 'I don't want all the cooks of the college gossiping about me!'

'There can't be any gossip if we're engaged.'

'Which we aren't,' I pointed out, wriggling my hair free from his grasp. No luck. His hands moved to play with the ends of my dupatta instead.

'What did you tell your father?' he asked.

'Nothing yet.'

His eyebrows shot up, annoyed. He pulled at my dupatta, nearly causing it to slip off.

'Jai,' I glared at him warningly, casting a look at the door. 'If the cook was to come in—'

'You would have to marry me to save your reputation.' His eyes gleamed with mischief.

I shot him another look. 'We haven't done anything quite that illicit.'

Jai looked at me, his expression inexplicably cross. 'You're right,' he said gruffly and dropped my dupatta. I didn't pay much attention to it. He was always getting into a huff and getting over it on his own.

I thought the conversation was over. In fact, I was just about to take the paratha off the tawa when he held my face and turned it towards his. My lips were crushed under his hot mouth. I could feel his breath on mine. We stayed that way for long, but not long enough to be discovered. Smoke filled the kitchen.

The paratha, of course, was burnt.

17 March 1960

Nothing was formally decided by the end of the week. But Bauji was speaking to Jai, not me, when he bid us goodbye and wished us a safe journey. A curious shift seemed to have occurred. Jai was now the unspoken warden of my safety, not Professor Motilal Khurana.

It was curious because, for a brief time in Bombay, I hadn't realized that I still belonged to anyone. I didn't realize it until that moment that I would be handed over from one person to another. It was lovely being handed to Jai, the man who had appeared in every one of my dreams since the evening we met, but the feeling was still strange.

I put it out of mind as soon as we sat down next to each other on the train and he opened a newspaper, so that he could hold my hand underneath its sprawling pages.

'I've wanted to do this since I met you,' he whispered, lightly patting my palm with his lips behind *the Indian Express*. 'I just didn't realize how badly till you went away.'

I didn't dare to look at him, conscious as I was of the eyes of the passengers in the berth opposite ours. Instead,

I looked out of the small window, at Bauji on the platform, buying a book from the news stand.

As the train started to move, I felt uneasy. Bauji's figure began to shrink in the distance with the loud chugging of the train. The train suddenly felt like it was going down the track much too quickly. I had a sudden, wild desire to pull the chain, to run back to the comfort of our college campus, of Bauji's study and our never-ending supply of tea.

A cool piece of metal slithered down my palm. When I looked back at Jai, two solid gold bangles were cuffed around my wrist.

'With love from my mother,' he said.

I smiled, putting all inane worries and unfounded anxieties out of my mind. They had only arisen because I was on the verge of so much happiness. I wasn't being married off to a stranger like my mother. I had actually fallen in love over the last three months in Bombay. And what's more, the man I loved, loved me back. And both our families seemed to have blessed the union. Together, we would rise in our administrations, partnering and bolstering each other to triumph. With his help, perhaps I would be home secretary one day, and he would be the chief justice of India. Then we would look back and smile fondly at the memory of stolen kisses in shared train berths.

What a lucky, lucky girl I am.

❦

'Radhika?' Naani yelled out. I put the diary down reluctantly as she entered the room.

'What are you doing?' she asked, surprised to find me in the store room, covered in dust and clutching on to her old diary. Her eyes grew wide with worry.

'Where did you get that from?' she demanded, agitated.

I smiled sheepishly. 'I've had it for a couple of years now.'

The truth was I stole it two Christmases ago, when I was scrounging through the cupboards, looking for something to read to distract me from the fact that Siddhant hadn't replied after I had texted him 'Happy holidays'. I hadn't expected to stumble upon a story so gripping and beautiful and real. It had changed my attitude to dating overnight. Until then, I had been okay with casual flings with no breakfast after, and I had been too proud to ask Siddhant for more.

But then everything had changed. A light seemed to have switched on in my chest after reading Naani's diary. It made me believe that a couple could have a real, lasting romance, mutual adoration and respect outside of a fictional love story. Suddenly, I found myself wanting the same thing. In fact, I found that I had always wanted such constant companionship. I was just too independent to acknowledge it. *After all, acknowledging desire makes you appear weak, doesn't it?*

Well, it doesn't. Not if you are unapologetic about your standards, like Naani and Bauji were. Naanu had to commit to Naani if he wanted to spend time with her. There were no two ways about it.

I decided to break up with Siddhant the minute I finished reading her diary for the first time. I sent him a quick text to this effect. I couldn't afford to waste my time dilly-dallying with a boy who refused to acknowledge me as his girlfriend. Within the day, he had made three frantic, apologetic Skype calls to 'talk things out'. By the time I returned to New York, I was officially his girlfriend. 6 January 2017.

Of course, a year and a half later, he dumped me. But that didn't change the fact that for a while even a selfish brat like him had succumbed to the idea of a relationship— all because my attitude had become less accepting of his selfishness. It was like Naani's diary gave me power. It encouraged me to believe that I was worthy of the love of a good man.

I figured that if a diary could do so much to make me desirable to the opposite sex, living with the author would transform me entirely.

'Sweetheart, I don't want anyone reading that,' Naani said and put her palm up, expecting me to relinquish her journal. But there was no way that I was giving it up.

'Please, Naani, let me keep it? I miss the stories Naanu used to tell. About how much he loved you. I wish someone would love me as much.'

Naani looked at me, concerned. 'I love you as much. More.'

'I mean, a boy,' I said, and then I corrected myself. 'A man, actually.'

Naani shook her head. 'Your Naanu was a boy for as long as he lived. I'll tell you that.'

'He seems like the perfect man here,' I said, brandishing her own diary at her.

'Beta, there's a lot of rubbish I wrote,' she began, her face colouring. 'It's not the whole story.'

'You have no reason to be embarrassed, Naani,' I said, moving the diary out of her reach again. 'Naanu and you are the most romantic couple I know. To approach Bauji like that, without even knowing what your answer would be, just because he had to, because he couldn't bear not being married to you—'

Naani emitted a brisk laugh, cutting me off. 'Sweetheart, everything seems romantic when you're young and foolish,' she said, gathering the photographs and putting them back in their neat stacks in the drawer.

'Things are much better now,' she continued. 'You don't have to get married until you want to. Until you know the person well enough to decide to spend your life with them. It takes years to know a person's character—'

'You knew in just three months,' I pointed out.

Naani paused as she picked up the last stack of photographs. 'I didn't know your grandfather properly till after we were married. The first three months are just the honeymoon phase.'

She shut the drawer with a firm thud. 'I think one should wait till they are absolutely sure of their decision. It's a huge life alteration.'

I took a breath. 'I am absolutely sure.'

Naani turned to me, her fair face wrinkled in surprise. 'What?'

I took my grandmother's soft hands in mine and sat her down next to me. 'This is why I came back, Naani. I want to get married before I turn thirty,' I said and picked out a fluff of cotton from the edge of her sari to avoid looking at her. 'I want something lasting. Like Naanu and you had.'

'Radhika—' Naani was really concerned. I knew what she was going to say. She was going to tell me that I was beautiful and independent and that I didn't need a man to fulfil my life, but I didn't want to hear comforting philosophy any more. I had heard Gloria Steinem and I had read *The Feminine Mystique*. What I wanted now was a strategy.

'Naani,' I cut her off, 'I believe that I deserve to be with someone good. Someone who likes me enough to stick around for more than six months. Don't you?'

'Of course, sweetheart, but there is no need to rush—'

'I don't want to end up like Mum,' I whispered urgently.

Naani fell silent and her brow furrowed in thought. I could tell that I had got through to her now. She still looked concerned, but she was no longer combative. Finally, she straightened up and tucked my hair behind my ear.

'All right, Radhika,' she said in her most businesslike manner. 'We will have you married by the end of this year.'

My grandmother's tone sent a jolt of courage through me. For the first time in weeks, I felt reassured. Elated, I wrapped her in a hug. I knew that I won't be alone as long as I had her in my corner. Naani patted my head, chuckled slightly, and shook her head.

'If you're sure about this—'

'I am,' I insisted, nodding seriously.

'Then you will have to stay away from Zain, beta.'

I broke away from the embrace. This, I hadn't expected. Naani smiled at me, grimacing apologetically.

'He's not the marrying kind, Radhika,' she said. 'And we can't risk your reputation.'

'Reputation?' I laughed. 'Surely, you're joking.'

Naani shook her head. 'There will be quite a lot to adjust to, beta. The boys may be modern, but the system is still old-fashioned … you will have to decide, if you're ready, to make some necessary changes—'

'Changes?' I asked.

Naani looked at me in amusement and pity. Then she nodded. 'I'm afraid so. A few adjustments.'

Adjustments. The word my mother hated more than any other. She had a whole lecture series centred around the pathetic 'adjustments' that women made to accommodate men in countries with strong patriarchal values.

But then, hadn't I purposefully come to a patriarchal country in search of an old-fashioned romance? I knew some compromise would have to be made.

'What kind of adjustments?' I asked timidly.

Naani's expression was unreadable. At last, she said, 'I'll make a list.'

She kissed my forehead and left.

I deleted the friend request I had sent to Zain on Facebook.

꙳

Gayatri waited till the front door had closed and her granddaughter had accelerated out of their neighbourhood in her company's car. Only when she was satisfied that Radhika would not return for a few hours, she rushed into the storeroom and pulled open the drawer they had been rifling through earlier during the day.

There, underneath the photographs, lay the pages she had ripped out of her diary years ago. Fortunately, Radhika hadn't seen them yet. Gayatri picked them up and clutched them to her chest.

Her granddaughter must never know that her wedding was forced and that her marriage a disaster.

꙳

The Personal Diary of Gayatri Khurana, IAS officer, Delhi Division.

12 April 1960

London

The day had begun like any other in Bombay. It had ended in London. Somewhere between morning and noon, between India and Britain, I was married.

Perhaps my surprise was unwarranted. After all, Jai's parents were coming at the end of this month to meet me and formalize our union. Bauji and Rishi were taking the train to Bombay for the engagement as well, because work had become too demanding to allow both Jai and I to make another trip to Delhi. There was only one month left until the partitioning of the state, and my department was working hard to ensure that no communal riots broke out between the Maharashtrians and the Gujaratis. I wanted to meet with representatives from both communities this week and incentivize them to keep the peace.

But my agenda for the week was erased the moment Jai walked into my office, his face ashen. I rose immediately and went to him, responding instinctively to his expression and defeated body language.

'What's wrong?'

He held out the telegram he was holding. 'She's dead.'

I read it carefully, trying to help him into a chair. There wasn't much more to it than what he said. We would get the whole story later. About how his mother had contracted pneumonia a week earlier, but the family hadn't written to Jai at her request. She hadn't wanted to alarm the newly betrothed couple about what was only a passing cold. After all, she had been making steady progress till the day before she died. Later, we would learn that she had been looking forward to meeting her eldest child's bride.

But for now, all we knew was this. His mother was dead.

'Jai, I'm so sorry.'

I held him as he wept, large tears spilling on to the folds of my blouse. The door of my cabin had been shut for a while now. I knew people would start to get suspicious soon. I had to get Jai out of there, and safely home, before anyone started asking questions or saw him crying. He would regret this vulnerability later, I knew.

'Jai, sweetheart,' I said, using the term of endearment for the very first time. 'We have to go home, all right? I'll explain the situation to Yashwant Saab—'

'I'm going,' he hiccupped in broken sentences. 'I'm going ... to the airport ... now. Flight to London this evening. The funeral—'

'Of course.' I nodded. He had responsibilities as per Hindu rites.

'You will come with me,' he said, taking out a long piece of paper from his pocket. It was a ticket with my name on it. To London.

'Jai,' I began in my most soothing tone. 'I can't ... we aren't even engaged properly.'

But he was shaking his head, clutching my hand tight 'We will get married this afternoon then.'

I was so shocked that I snatched my hand from his. I forgot about consoling him entirely as I sank back into my chair. An uncomfortable sweat broke out on the back of my neck. The cabin was suddenly too warm. Jai was too close.

I opened a window and breathed in relief as the sounds of Bombay began to pour in. Out on the streets, people were still living, working and making decisions of their own. I could do it, too.

I went back to Jai and held his hand. 'I can't do that, Jai,' I said. 'I can't do that to Bauji.'

He looked at me with a desperation so helpless that my protestations died on my lips.

'Please, Gayatri. I can't do it without you. I won't be able to bring my mother's ashes back to India. I'll be stuck there forever, wondering what the hell just happened.'

His face was contorted in a frightening sadness, which I believed would consume him if I refused. I immediately knelt down in my sari and took his chin in my hand.

Before I knew what promise I was making, the words were out of my mouth, forming of their own accord like the lyrics of a favourite lullaby. 'Jai, look at me, please. Shh. I'll come. We'll leave right now. Let's go. Come, let's go.'

There was a cluster of orange mogras in one hand and a fistful of ashes in the other. We threw each into the fire as the priest at Siddhivinayak temple instructed us to do. The court marriage was wrapped up in a matter of minutes. My surname was changed indefinitely, in an expedited process that would take a normal citizen a prior appointment and at least a couple of hours. I suppose I was already enjoying the perks of having a top lawyer for a husband. Husband.

The word shouldn't have seemed so alien to me, given that I was sitting in a mandap, getting ready to take seven rounds around the ceremonial fire that would bind me to Jai for seven births, but still it did. *Husband*. I could not believe it.

It was true; I had fallen in love with him. I had even wanted, in some fanciful sort of way, to spend my days with him. But I had never thought of the responsibilities and finality that the process involved. This wasn't supposed to happen for another three months. Our families were yet to meet and decide if we were suited. I thought I had time to make up my mind. We needed that time!

Jai didn't seem to share any of my trepidation. He had been quietly determined all through the signing of the marriage documents, the negotiations with the head priest of the temple and during the uttering of the prayers. Now, as he strung a mangalsutra around my neck, he looked at me with glorious relief, smiling for the first time on that awful day.

I found myself smiling, too. It was relieving to be a relief to him.

Perhaps three months is too short a time to make a decision about marrying someone. But, I wonder, if left to my own devices, I'd ever be ready. Jai is the most ready I think I'll ever be. He is the only man I can bind myself to and remain delighted with life. The fear of the unknown, of this adventure of sharing a life, will always exist, but now we can navigate it together, doubling each other's happiness and halving our sorrow.

At least that is what I am telling myself.

Husband.

Well, there is not much I can do about it now.

Forty years later, Gayatri shook her head with regret. She should have put her foot down and insisted on taking more time before committing herself to a marriage neither of them was ready for.

What a sentimental fool she had been. And what a sorrow-soaked life it had led to. Fortunately, Radhika hadn't got her hands on the rest of the pages of the diary, the ones after these, in which ink had been blotted out by tears so often that the print was barely legible. Gayatri had documented her life only till their honeymoon. After that, there had seemed to be no point in writing about her life with Jai anymore. It made no sense to her to chronicle unhappiness.

But then … without Jai she wouldn't have Mangala. Or Radhika. And that was a world Gayatri didn't want to imagine.

Still, Gayatri would rather die before she let her granddaughter's life turn out like her own—married to a stranger who thought of himself as her lord. Nor would she let it turn out like Mangala's—lonely and sterile, with no room for romance, a knee-jerk reaction to Gayatri's mistake.

No, Gayatri would do everything in her power to make sure Radhika married a well-brought-up young man who loved and respected her in equal measure. She would introduce her to the best families in India. Even if it meant sacrificing her own last joy.

7
Apology

'I have done nothing but disappoint you all our lives,' Gayatri said, looking down at her hands submissively folded in the soft, pink cotton of her lap.

Her eyes were red with the effort of reining in tears. She was determined not to let them spill down her cheeks, because that would only end up in Birdy consoling her once again, even though he was so clearly the wronged party. She wanted to be as stoic as possible, but her eyes moistened with every passing moment.

She had spent the last five minutes uttering apologies to Birdy in the newly furnished study of his large bungalow, taking back every promise she had made to him the night of her party. They could not get married right now. They may never be married. And she couldn't even tell him why without compromising her granddaughter. Birdy's only response so far had been to open a bottle of Scotch and offer her a glass.

He was being chivalrously calm so as not to upset her, but she saw a glint of helpless hurt in his eyes, which broke her heart. She longed to take him in her arms and comfort him, but soothing him was no longer her prerogative.

The sight of Jai's golden bangles on her feeble white arms began to sicken her. She looked away, her eyes focused on the sturdy wooden leg of the armchair Birdy was sitting on, focusing on the carvings to steady her mind and wobbling voice. The flower petals etched into the mahogany looked so familiar. Suddenly, she looked up at her friend in surprise.

'Is this … it can't be—'

'It is Professor Khurana's chair,' Birdy confirmed with a hint of a smile. 'I just tracked it down.'

'How? When?' Gayatri faltered, unsure what to ask.

Birdy cleared his throat, as though making an effort to speak. 'I thought it would be a good wedding present.'

'Oh.'

He rose to let her examine it, and perhaps to avoid her gaze.

Gayatri bent down to hide the tears that had managed to find a way down her face and traced the soft curve of the wooden petal with her thumb. *How many hours, how many years had she spent at the foot of this chair, her back resting against her father's strong legs as they read together in contented silence?* She had been a different woman then.

She had been Gayatri Khurana, a soon-to-be IAS officer. Gayatri Khurana, capable of anything a man could do, the pride and joy of her father.

She had lost that young girl in an abyss of marital responsibility. She had sacrificed her spirit to the requests of her husband. But in the last ten years, with his death, there had been a resurrection. She looked up at Birdy, unafraid of the tears streaming down her face now. He was always bringing her back to who she was. And all she did was reject him.

'Gayatri, Gayatri, please,' Birdy said, raising her up by the shoulders. 'It's all right.'

'Birdy, I'd marry you in a heartbeat,' she said finally. 'God knows it is what I should have done at the beginning.'

Birdy winced. 'Please don't apologize, Gayatri. I mean, you're Gayatri Khurana …' he faltered, embarrassed. 'I mean, I understand that—'

'No, Birdy, you don't,' she said. She had to tell him. He couldn't spend the rest of his life thinking that she had rejected him a second time.

'Birdy, Radhika wants an arranged marriage,' she blurted. 'And it's up to me to introduce her to respectable families. I can't do that if they don't consider me respectable, which they would if I remarried at my age.'

Birdy's mouth dropped open, as Gayatri had expected it would. His eyes grew concerned.

'Has Radhika asked you not to—'

'Of course not.' Gayatri shook her head. 'She has no idea about us, and I'd like to keep it that way. If she found out, she would insist that we get married, ruining her chances with the best families in Bombay.'

Gayatri knotted the end of her dupatta in her hands and then unknotted it. She had to look up at Birdy. She owed him that much. 'I will not compromise my granddaughter's chance at happiness for my own.'

'But do you really think Radhika will be happy in such a narrow-minded family?' Birdy asked.

'Most people are narrow-minded about a suitable marriage, Birdy. It doesn't mean that they're bad parents ... or even bad partners. Some of our oldest, most intelligent friends are limited in their thinking about matters such as these.'

'None of my friends would be critical of our marriage. Nor would their families,' Birdy said robustly.

Men, Gayatri thought, smiling, *are so blissfully oblivious.*

'*Her whole family is loose! The mother is divorced and living with some American, and the grandmother is still getting her jollies on in Bombay—that too with Anand Saab's best friend. No wonder Radhika's still unmarried at twenty-nine! The girl must be just as fast—*' Gayatri voiced out the things she expected to hear from people.

Birdy flinched. Gayatri stopped.

'I heard Mrs Sinha and Mrs Patel in the bathroom at the club on our first evening there,' she said. 'I found it amusing at the time, but since Radhika has told me that she wants to be married, it has become less comical and more catastrophic. If my own friends could react so cattily to our situation, other families are sure to be more critical.'

Birdy was silent for a while.

'I understand,' he said, letting out a long sigh of resignation. Gayatri could see that he believed her.

'I will help you in whatever way I can.'

A warmth spread through Gayatri's chest, starting in her heart and making her face burn with gratitude for having met such a wonderful man. It was incredible how, for the last forty years, he had been ready to help her, even at the expense of his own happiness.

Gayatri decided at that moment that she could not let go of him. She rose and kissed Birdy's cheek. He looked at her in surprise. She had never done that before.

'We don't have to stop seeing each other, Birdy. We will just have to be more discreet.'

Gayatri thought he would be pleased, but Birdy, to her surprise, seemed more upset than ever.

'Absolutely not,' he said.

Gayatri flinched. *Was he rejecting her now?*

'Why not?' she demanded, wounded.

'No, Gayatri,' he said in his firmest tone. 'I want you as a wife, or as my dearest friend. I refuse to make a mistress out of you.'

Gayatri looked at her friend in silent marvel, at the strength of his character and the resilience of his sentiment. If she stayed a minute longer, she would betray her granddaughter and marry him that afternoon.

'Will I see you tomorrow morning for breakfast?' she asked.

'As usual.' He nodded, looking down at his shoes, refusing to meet her eyes.

Gayatri turned and left her friend in the home that would never be theirs.

❧

Breakfast would never be a rushed, lonely affair again.

At Naani's, it was a ritual of milky coffee, scrambled eggs and hot toast, with the background hum of Birdy's rustling newspaper, the everlasting boil of the electric kettle and the koels chirping on an unseen branch. I hadn't expected both the older folk to be up as early as me, but Naani and Birdy had already finished their morning walk. They were showered and dressed by 8 a.m.

When I grow up, I decided, *I want to be like them.*

'What do you normally have for lunch?' Naani asked me as I stuffed a thermos of coffee in my bag. I had lingered over my second cup for too long and was on the verge of running late for my first day of work.

'Oh this and that,' I said, looking around for my laptop charger. Birdy and Naani exchanged a glance.

'What is "this"? Or "that"?' she asked.

I tapped at my phone, willing for the data to connect so that I had a GPS map to guide me to my new office.

Naani snatched my phone away. 'Radhika, I asked you a question.'

I kept forgetting what a disciplinarian Naani was. She could go from soft to strict in ten seconds. It was no wonder that Mum escaped and became such a nutcase for individualism. I, however, could deal with her better, because I was an adult and not a teenager like Mum when she lived here.

'I normally skip lunch,' I said, shrugging. 'You don't have to worry.' I gave her a kiss on the cheek and tried to snatch my phone back, but Naani had it out of reach.

'Excuse me?' she asked, her expression incredulous. 'You don't eat anything between 8 a.m. and dinner?'

'No, but I drink six cups of coffee,' I pleaded, making another unsuccessful swipe for my phone. 'And sometimes I have a pot of yoghurt.'

Naani and Birdy stared at me in shock.

'It's a low-calorie lunch,' I explained. 'I have a really rubbish metabolism—'

'No.' Naani's voice was stern. Birdy hid a smirk from behind his newspaper, clearly enjoying the performance.

'No?'

'You will give me your office address,' she said. 'And I will send you a tiffin.'

'Naani—' I started to protest, but she cut me off.

'It will be low-calorie, if you like, but it will be actual food,' she said. 'And you will finish it, or you will not come back home.'

I looked at Naani, bemused, but she wasn't smiling. She meant business.

'All right,' I agreed reluctantly. She placed my phone back in my palm.

So much for being an adult!

Rajni

Best of luck on your first day, love!

Thanks, Rajj <3

Everyone misses you like mad here.

Rich, especially. He's already having major battles with the new analysts on the soda company account.

LOL. I'm glad he's realizing that not everyone can put up with his deadlines.

Maybe he will treat me with a bit more respect when I'm back

You will be back, won't you?

Maybe I will, you know?

Yeah, maybe the guy you marry will be one of those America-mad people, dying to get out of India!

Yeah! Maybe!

I'll end up with one of those green-card hunters.

God! I really hope not.

Me too.

I MISS YOU!

You have no idea!

❧

I had made no friends in office yet.

All my fellow heads of divisions were balding men in their late forties, who discussed subjects that I had no opinions on, like last night's squash game and how exorbitantly expensive their children's international school fees was. The latter was the topic of choice when I arrived in the brightly lit conference room of McKinley India. There were no other women in this room, except for Anjali— my secretary—who immediately started to note down everyone's coffee order.

Mr Bhatia, the managing director, got up to shake my hand.

'Team, I'd like to introduce you all to Ms Anand, our new head of acceleration for North American accounts.'

I gave the men my most winsome smile, but it didn't work. Four dubious faces, wrinkled with confusion, stared back at me. The thought bubble was evident: *How did she get here?*

It was moments like these when I was eternally grateful that Mum raised me in New Haven, thousands of miles away from the disapproving scrutiny of discouraging uncles.

'How long are you here for?' Mr Gomes, the head of HR, asked.

'Six months. For now,' I replied, trying not to frown.

'For now?' Mr Gomes looked aghast at the possibility that I could be here long-term.

'But you're an American citizen?' Mr Maruti, the head of finance, asked, narrowing his eyes.

'Yes.'

'Then you will definitely go back,' pronounced Mr Thakkar, the head of analytics, with great confidence.

Mr Maruti and Mr Gomes breathed a collective sigh of relief. *Really. You would think I wasn't in the room.*

I thought my day could only improve after this not-so-warm welcome. I had specifically asked Anjali to put some female analysts on my team, so I was looking forward to seeing a few friendly faces that morning. Women in consulting have a universal sisterhood of sorts, since it is such a male-dominated industry. I had made friends with female analysts on work trips across the world, from South Korea to San Francisco. Unfortunately, that sisterhood was unheard of by the women on the sixth floor of McKinley India.

The two women who were in my cabin now hadn't smiled once throughout what I thought was a charming introduction speech, despite my three attempts at ice-breaking jokes. They simply stared at me with a mixture of deference and suspicion, their eyes flitting to my Steve Madden peep-toes every few minutes. Their expressions were impassive though, so I couldn't tell whether they liked the shoes or despised them.

The men on the team were more enthusiastic. Maybe a little too enthusiastic. One had already asked me to have a drink with him, and two others had asked if there were any openings in the New York office, and could I maybe take them along when I go back? Their tone was jocular, but their eyes were shrewd.

Some boundaries, obviously, needed to be set.

I smiled tightly and moved away from the male analysts to address the room at large. 'First, let's concentrate on making Ka-Ching Computers the market leader in India. Your reports are due day after morning. We have a conference call with Mr Goldenblatt and Rich on Wednesday night. We can talk about advancement opportunities once I've had a chance to evaluate your work.'

The analysts exchanged disappointed glances and shuffled out.

In fact, the whole office seemed to shuffle. Everyone ambled along, instead of striding forward with purpose. It made me ache for the bustle of my Manhattan office, where consultants talked and walked so fast that it felt like chaos, but really it was a whirlwind of well-directed energy buzzing through a high-rise on Lexington Avenue. I could hang out with Rajni during lunch breaks and kiss Siddhant in secret on the stairwell.

The thought of Siddhant jolted me out of nostalgia for New York.

Suddenly, I was very, very grateful to be in my office in Bandra Kurla Complex. I may not have any friends yet, my colleagues may resent my presence and my team may think of me as a disappointment, but at least I wouldn't run into my ex-boyfriend kissing someone younger in the stairwell.

There was a knock on the door and Anjali's eager, spectacled face appeared through the crack.

'Ma'am,' she said tentatively. 'Your grandmother sent this for you.'

She proffered a blush cloth bag, which had 'GRACE' emblazoned across it. I was surprised by the size. *How much food had Naani prepared?*

'Shall I have it heated up?'

'Heated up?' I had expected a salad. Nothing more. But I peered into the bag to see two large parathas, a container of yoghurt and a jar of pickled mangoes.

She had to be kidding me. I said low-calorie! There was no way I could eat this. *They must be five hundred calories each*, I thought as I looked at the large, round parathas, sitting so satisfied with themselves, stuffed to the brim with spiced cauliflower, chillies and potatoes, next to the fresh creamy yoghurt that Naani set herself at home.

I hadn't tasted full-fat yoghurt in years.

'Please heat it up,' I said to Anjali. She nodded and left.

Ten minutes later, I was tucking into lunch at work for the first time in my adult life. It was a gloriously gratifying feeling. In fact, it was so pleasurable that I didn't know how people got back to work after such a filling break. I would probably need a packet of sugar to hold on to the focus I would need to spend the rest of the day getting acquainted with the accounts, besides Ka-Ching Computers, that I was now in charge of.

Mr Maruti was supposed to meet me this afternoon, to brief me on the financials of all the other American accounts I'd be handling, but I had a feeling that he won't show up. Maruti and the other heads didn't want to help me understand the workings of this company. It was sad, but it was all right. It wasn't the first time I would have to wrest power away from jealous men in a corporate setting.

I was mulling over my next course of action, and mopping up the leftover pickle on my plate with the last bite of the doughy paratha, when I noticed a little list sticking out of the 'Grace' bag. It was in Naani's handwriting.

Dear Radhika,

Based on our discussion yesterday, I have compiled a list of things you will have to do before we start looking for boys. They are all necessary, I'm afraid, and will have to be made a priority.

I love you, sweetheart. Enjoy the parathas.

Arranged Marriage Adjustments:

1. Put on 5 kg (at least).
2. Clear skin. Yoghurt cleanse every other day.
3. Start taking care of your feet. Pedicure once a week.
4. Delete photos with ex-boyfriends on Facebook.
5. Delete photos with pimples/acne on Facebook.

6. Buy new dresses/get rid of black, unshapely clothes.
7. Join a yoga class.
8. Attend Design One exhibition.
9. Attend Ganpati celebrations and prayers.
10. Vitamin injections?

The list went on for two pages in a similar vein, but I stopped reading at vitamin injections, realizing that Naani had totally lost the plot. I had no idea that I had bargained for an appearance and personality overhaul when I had asked for an arranged marriage. Every time I looked at the list, I was offended. *What exactly was wrong with my feet?* I thought they were quite nice. Okay, perhaps they were slightly callused—but that was because of years of pedalling on a spin bike. And from years of kathak training before that. But there was no way I was putting on five kilograms (at least!). I had spent a fortune in money, time and effort trying to tone my stomach into feminine abs at SoulCycle. I was not going to give it up for love handles so soon.

Naani and I obviously needed to talk. But not right now. I had another task to tackle, with the fire of the pickles and defensiveness sitting in my belly.

I walked over to Mr Maruti's office and knocked on the door.

'Come in,' he called out. His face fell when he saw me. He rearranged it lowly into a more polite expression. 'Oh, Ms Anand.'

'Yes, Mr Maruti,' I beamed at him. 'I thought we had a meeting scheduled for an hour ago?'

'Did we?' his eyes flickered with guilt, but his face remained impassive. 'It must have slipped my mind because I ran into some trouble with my team, creating our quarterly review.'

He grinned unashamedly. That was when I knew that Mr Maruti wasn't busy at all. He wanted to teach me my place. To let me know that in the grand order of things my work was not important enough to be his priority.

'I will send the files you need to your assistant. Anjali, right?'

Both of us knew that Mr Maruti won't send me the files. He would delay it, so that I would be useless all day and in his office tomorrow, humbled and begging for the information I needed to do my job. The power games had begun.

Fortunately, I was good at them.

'No.' I smiled just as brightly at him. 'That won't do, Mr Maruti.'

His eyebrows shot up in surprise as I continued in my most formidable tone. 'Mr Bhatia entrusted you with the task of catching me up to speed on the American accounts today. I know you wouldn't want me to leave without fully understanding my responsibilities towards our clients.'

Mr Maruti looked startled. He obviously didn't expect the new girl to address him so directly, with barely veiled accusations. He nearly looked up at the camera in his cabin. I suppressed a smile.

'Can I meet you in an hour?' he asked. His smile had vanished completely.

'I'm afraid not. We've lost enough time because of your struggles with the quarterly review.' My language was inoffensive but the message was clear. *You messed up. I shouldn't have to pay for it.*

His mouth pressed into a hard line as he pressed the intercom on his desk to call his secretary. 'Rajiv, get the US files please.'

I settled down in the chair opposite him. He flicked an annoyed glance at me as the secretary placed the heavy folders on the table between us. I opened the first one with gusto.

'Apple Systems. Let's go.'

Mr Maruti's eyes glinted with anger at my commanding tone, but he began nonetheless. 'Apple came to us in 2000, to understand a way to penetrate the Indian market with its new laptops ...'

As I took notes, I started asking questions.

When I finally left his office, it was evening. I was up to speed on the eight American companies' current strategies, their products and deadlines, and the teams handling each of their portfolios. Over the four hours of talking, taking notes, questions and clarifications, I thought I had got through to Mr Maruti. *Surely, a colleague so invested in her work on the first day had to be impressive?* Once, I had even caught him looking at me in reluctant awe, when I showed him how to break down the risk strategy of the only fast-food company we were handling.

'Thank you, Mr Maruti,' I said, injecting warmth into my tone as I gathered the files and left.

'It was my pleasure,' he said with a smile that was sincere instead of flashing. *Yes! I had won him over*, I thought as I exited his office. *All it takes is time and inclination—*

But the door had hardly closed when I heard him mutter under his breath. 'Bitch.'

I stopped, shocked. *Should I go back in and give him a piece of my mind?*

I decided against it and walked back to my cabin, ready to leave. I' had had enough for the day.

❧

Zain Rajan was late for dinner with his football lads at Nara Thai in Bandra Kurla Complex. Fortunately, all of them understood the perils of working for the family business, so wouldn't even blink when he told them 'Sorry, cotton machine exploded' and pulled out the eleventh chair at the table. They knew better by now and would just pass him one of their Juuls in solidarity, continuing to chat about Kiara Khemnani's tiny, glittery shorts at the house party last weekend. Smoke would be puffed and sushi stuffed into their mouths till the evening ended. All of it underscored by inane and incessant banter about who was fucking whom between South Bombay and Juhu.

Zain had half a mind to turn the car around as he imagined the half-baked conversations, the snorting laughter and the constant stream of Instagram stories that the dinner was sure to be. He was not sure if he could be a frat boy again tonight. But then, going home wouldn't be fun either since the Rajan house was empty that evening. Zain knew that two Netflix episodes later he would be in danger of replying to Kiara's message, which had been sitting in his inbox for two days now.

'Hey. What are you up to?' The message was innocent enough. But it would invariably lead to her coming over, some pleasurable fumbling and then a vacuum of discomfort as they would struggle to make conversation at three in the morning.

Kiara, through no fault of her own, bored him to distraction. She had the face of an angel and the mind of a baby. Zain sometimes marvelled at how sheltered her life had been; she could only concern herself with clothes and Instagram and the lives of her friends. She had tried to ask questions about him, about his family in the UK, and his relationship with Birdy, but Zain could never answer her honestly. He was quite sure that her questions stemmed not from a genuine interest in his life, but from the curiosity of her mother.

'Ask him about his childhood,' he could imagine Mrs Khemnani instructing her pretty daughter while she combed her hair. 'And about his relationship with his uncle.

That is how we will know if he's the heir to Rajan Textiles or not!'

Despite this, Zain wouldn't have minded opening up to her a little more if Kiara had anything more to offer than 'mmm, that sucks', when he had told her that he had never met his father, and 'oh, that's great', when he had alluded to his ambitious plans for expanding Rajan Textiles globally.

After that, he had clammed up. In response, her questions had only become more pressing. He wouldn't be surprised if Mrs Khemnani demanded to know how much information she got out of Zain each day. A spa treatment for four questions answered. A new bag for discovering how much he was worth.

Zain kept on driving. At least with the boys he could redirect the conversation. The new FIFA game was out. They could talk about that for at least an hour. The longest signal in BKC flashed an angry red. Zain groaned, reluctantly stopping his car.

That was when he saw her, standing outside a volkswagen, kicking the tyre with her high heels.

Zain laughed and pulled over. He honked and she turned around, frightened. He didn't blame her. The road was deserted except for a few trucks filled with men, whizzing past with their nightly cargo. He rolled down his window and her expression cleared, relief evident.

'You're going to break your shoes,' he said.

'Stop talking and open the door,' Radhika said, laughing.

Zain unlocked the car and she slid into the passenger seat.

'Please, let's go,' she said. 'Far away from here.'

'What about your car?'

'The company gave me one with a faulty battery. I bet it was that asshole Maruti who assigned it to me,' she fumed. 'I'm going to call Rich up tonight and make sure they get the firing of their lives.'

Zain was amused by the aggression in her tone. He never expected this skinny girl to be capable of so much fire. 'So, should we just leave it here?'

'I'll get my assistant to deal with it in the morning,' she said. Then she closed her eyes, clearly exhausted, and looked at him. 'I just want to go home,' she pleaded.

It was such an honest, sweet request that Zain didn't think twice before saying, 'Just give me a second.'

He quickly whipped out his phone and texted the group: 'Sorry, guys. Something's come up. See you on the weekend for FIFA.'

A reply popped back within seconds: 'Lol. Say hi to Kiara.'

Zain shook his head and turned the car around. Radhika didn't know this, but he was as relieved as she was at that moment.

❧

'... I took a wrong turn and the car ran out of petrol and my battery died as well,' I explained, speaking into Zain's phone, seated in the passenger seat of his white BMW.

Naani was on the other end, her agitation calming now that I had been traced and was in the car of a man she trusted. I knew most twenty-somethings got irritated at having to tell their parents and grandparents their whereabouts, but I had always secretly loved this aspect of visiting Bombay. Naani was the only one who ever waited up for me. Mum went to bed at 10 p.m. every night and woke up at 5 a.m. to begin her research. And Siddhant had always stayed out much later than I had. Or hadn't cared enough to ask me when I'd be coming home.

'I'm sorry for worrying you, Naani,' I said. 'I'll make sure to keep my phone charged from now on.'

'Thank God you ran into Zain!' Naani said. 'I was about to send a search party out if you hadn't called by 10 p.m.'

I looked at Zain, confused. 'Didn't you send him?'

'No, no. But it's such good luck that he ran into you! You don't know what that area is like. You two are coming home, aren't you? Or are you going to meet his friends?'

I turned to look at Zain slowly, gulping guiltily. I had just assumed that he was there for me. I hadn't even paused to think it might be a coincidence. He might have been headed to one of those trendy BKC restaurants for a date. *Oh dear, he may even have been headed to one of the many hotels in the neighbourhood for a rendezvous.*

I felt like a fool as I put the phone down.

'Er, Zain?'

'Yes, Radhika,' he turned to me, amused. He had overheard the conversation and was enjoying my embarrassment.

'Were you going somewhere?'

He grinned suddenly and with such feeling that I felt like a headlight had been flashed at me.

'Nowhere special,' he said. 'This is more fun. I don't get to play knight-in-shining-car often.'

I snorted. 'I'm sure that's a lie.'

'What do you mean?' His face assumed a mask of innocence.

I rolled my eyes. Naani's words reverberated through my mind. *He's not the marrying kind.* I had deleted the Facebook friend request after that conversation, but I had done a little more stalking. There had been many girls tagged in his photographs, posting on his wall, all of them in Balenciaga and partying at exotic resorts; or in Dior, enjoying high tea at The Claridges, London. They were like beautiful models who were too rich to even be paid to model. I imagine he had played knight in shining BMW to them many times.

I wondered what perfect, airbrushed beauty I had deprived him of tonight. She probably didn't need Naani's list of adjustments.

'You're one of "The Guys", aren't you?'

'Who are "The Guys"?'

'You know the type. Rich, good-looking, always got a new, glamorous girl to take to a bar on Saturday night, and to Goa on a long weekend.'

Zain laughed. 'You stalked me some more?'

'No,' I lied.

He laughed some more. 'You're a terrible liar. You could just send me a follow request on Instagram and find out more about my life like a normal person, you know.'

Now, it was my turn to laugh. 'I don't think an Instagram follow request is how normal people form meaningful bonds, Zain.'

Zain looked at me, bemused. 'So, you want to form a meaningful bond?'

'Doesn't everyone?'

'No,' he looked at me for a moment and then added, 'Nobody I've met in Bombay at least. Most of us just want to have a good time. Enjoy our fleeting youth.'

'I am enjoying my youth,' I said, perhaps a tad defensively. 'But I'm about a little more than just instant gratification.'

'Really?' His voice had an odd note to it. I couldn't tell whether he was mocking me or not. 'What are you about then?'

I looked at him, cautious, wondering how much I could tell him. Every *Cosmopolitan* article I had read warned me to keep my mouth shut. A basic rule of dating was to never let a member of the opposite sex know how serious you wanted to get. The answer to 'Do you want to get married?' was always 'Maybe'. Even if you had a lehenga hanging in your closet and henna designs picked out on a Pinterest board.

But I didn't want to pretend anymore.

'I want a marriage with someone romantic,' I said. 'I want to come home to the same person every night, to know them a little better with every passing day. Both of us will keep growing, changing, discovering and encouraging each other. And we will take a bunch of holidays together across parts of the world that fascinate us, to make sure we keep growing together, too.'

Zain stared at me in shock. He looked like someone has splashed cold water on his face. I nearly laughed. He was used to the coquettish ways of the fun, young Bombay girls who dated and drank and pretended to dangle him. I, however, couldn't do it any more. I wanted what I wanted, and I was not afraid to ask for it.

'So, that's why you moved back to Bombay?' His voice sounded choked.

'Yep,' I nodded. Then, with a chuckle, I added, 'If you have any cute friends who want the same thing, hook me up.'

A strange expression crossed his face. He let out a hoarse laugh. 'I'd love to introduce you to my friends. If you want, we can head to Varun's house at midnight. That's when the poker and doob session begins.'

'Don't they have work in the morning?'

'You set the timings when you own the company,' Zain said casually, but I detected an edge to his tone that wasn't there before.

'What time do you go to work?'

He smiled. '9 a.m. But I'm up by seven to go to the gym.'

I grinned. 'That's my routine, too.'

He laughed. 'Fantastic, you can be my gym buddy.'

'Even if I don't follow you on Instagram?'

Zain picked up my phone and typed his number into it. 'We'll do this the old-fashioned way.'

Suddenly, I was looking forward to the next morning.

'Zain?' Birdy called out as soon as Zain handed his car keys to their housekeeper. He ventured into the living room, surprised. It wasn't like his uncle to be up later than midnight. Well, usually. He must have heard about the explosion at the factory.

'Don't worry, Mamu,' Zain began, sitting opposite his elderly uncle, already reaching for the laptop in his briefcase. 'The repair work has already begun and nobody was hurt. It shouldn't make a difference to production timelines at all—'

But Birdy was shaking his head, a look of grave concern on his face. 'I'm not talking about the factory, Zain. I'm sure you have that under control.' He paused and put his hand on his nephew's shoulder. 'I am talking about Radhika.'

Zain straightened up, surprised at the warning in his uncle's tone. He slid his laptop back into his bag and listened.

'She isn't just any girl, Zain. She's Gayatri's granddaughter. Professor Khurana's great-granddaughter.'

'I know that, Mamu,' Zain said in his most respectful tone.

But Birdy did not look reassured. He had not missed the glint of excitement in Zain's eyes from spending the evening in conversation with a girl … as unexpected as Radhika.

Radhika's bright grey eyes, as she had prattled on about marriage and partnership, had been a refreshing contrast to the shadowed lids and pouting coquetry of the other girls who had occupied the passenger seat of his car in the last couple of months. Zain did not share her views about marriage, but he respected the passionate honesty of her opinions.

'She wants to get married, Zain,' Birdy said threateningly, hoping the smile would vanish from his nephew's face. But it did not have the effect he wanted. If anything, it reignited the light in Zain's eyes.

'I'm aware,' Zain smiled.

Birdy looked surprised, but his tone did not lose its gravity.

'Gayatri told me that she was hurt badly by her last boyfriend. You are to protect her, not to hurt her further or toy with her in any way,' Birdy commanded.

'I wasn't going to hurt her, Mamu—'

'Zain, Gayatri has found three strapping young fellows from good families for Radhika, all of whom want to be married. Soon. This is not what you want, is it?'

Zain shook his head, but slowly. Birdy had expected a more eager, more definitive response from his nephew. Could it be that his nephew harboured strong feelings about Gayatri's granddaughter?

'Son,' Birdy's voice softened. 'If you've changed your mind about marriage, I'd be only too happy to propose the match to Gayatri—'

'I haven't changed my mind,' Zain said firmly. Birdy's smile died on his lips. He regarded his nephew seriously.

'In that case, you are not to trifle with her.'

Zain paused, unsure of how to respond. A hint of an idea had formed in his mind during his conversation with Radhika. He had felt a tug, a propelling towards some deeper, fuller possibility that he was yet to explore. But he had realized that his uncle was right. An exploration couldn't guarantee commitment. Instead, it could very likely lead him to hurt a close family friend.

'You're right. I'll be more careful,' he agreed.

'No more flirting.'

'No more flirting,' Zain echoed.

When Zain went up to his room, he looked at it dissatisfied. It was filled with all the gadgets his heart could desire, but still, it was mockingly empty. His phone beeped with a message: 'See you at 7 a.m. tomorrow? Radhika'

He decided not to open it. Instead, he moved to another message, the one he had permission to open.

He began to type: 'Hey K, come over if you're free.'

A reply dinged back, moments later: 'On my way. xxx'

Zain laid back on his bed and closed his eyes, letting the cool air from the split air conditioner caress his face. He reminded himself of how lucky he was to be here, in this large bungalow with a beautiful girl to spend the night with. He could have been lying on the moth-eaten couch of a dingy flat in east London, with his mother groaning in pleasure in the next bedroom. He owed his good fortune to Birdy, who owed his good fortune to Gayatri Anand's father.

He wouldn't betray them just to satisfy his curiosity about his fiery new neighbour.

8
Children

'So, these are the guys?' Rajni asked through a pixelated video screen.

Her almond eyes were currently a blurred squint. I couldn't tell whether she was smiling in appreciation or frowning in derision.

I didn't know why, but it seemed like FaceTime anywhere in my office building was of the same crappy quality. I had half a mind to take it up with Mr Gomes in HR and Admin. After all, the head of American accounts should be able to establish contact with legal representatives in the New York Headquarters. Even if the current conversation wasn't strictly about business matters.

I glanced over my shoulder to make sure that the door was closed and then pulled up the pictures Naani had sent me, which I had immediately forwarded to Rajni this morning.

Vikas, Anurag and Kabir. The triumvirate of thirty-something eligible bachelors. None of them divorced, none of them disfigured.

'Yep, these are the ones so far,' I said smiling. All three of them looked promising. Honestly, I should have moved to Bombay ages ago.

'The fourth one is the cutest,' Rajni grinned. 'He's got a great smile.'

I rolled my eyes. I wish I had never included that picture. I don't know what had got into me.

'Zain,' I said, gritting my teeth, 'is not an option.'

'Then why is his picture here?'

'Because—' I faltered. My cheeks flamed at the memory of waiting for Zain at the gym two weeks ago, only to have him show up an hour later with a pretty, young girl on his arm. He hadn't even had the decency to look ashamed. He had just given me a smile that he reserved for his buddies and said 'hi' in passing on his way to the juice bar with the girl. He hadn't even acknowledged the fact that he had stood me up.

'He isn't up to standard,' I shrugged to hide my disappointment. I would not waste precious energy pining over another commitment-phobe. That was not why I moved here.

'But he has grey eyes just like yours—'

'His are green.'

Rajni shrugged. 'Still, you two would look cute together. I think you should give him a—'

'He's another Siddhant,' I cut her off.

'Oh.' Rajni's nose wrinkled with disgust and she deleted the photograph. 'Good riddance then,' she said with a big, goofy grimace.

I smiled. I wanted to hug Rajj so bad. I wished she were here scouting men with me. It was a lot like what we had done through our late teens and twenties, except Naani was definitely a better wingwoman than her. Rajni always got lazy at the bars, preferring to sit and sip her drink instead of talking to the men. Naani, on the other hand, had spent two whole weeks preparing me to meet men, leaving no stray hair unplucked and no nail unpolished to ensure that I was the most appealing choice in a bevy of brides-to-be.

My release into the marriage market was as ordered and strategic a launch as that of a debut actress. All my old, unflattering photographs on Facebook had been deleted, my Instagram had been cleaned of any pictures with men (even the ones with my second cousins in Atlanta), and new, glamorous photographs had been taken to make my grid as gorgeously wholesome as it had ever been.

I should have put my foot down when the photoshoot was brought up. I should have been offended by the obviously negative connotations of dolling up to be chosen by a man. *Was I really going to alter my entire social media identity just to attract some fellow I didn't know?*

Yes. Yes, I was.

I knew it is wrong. I knew my mother would faint at the idea of new photos being taken to seduce strange men into believing that I was The Choice. But I had always had the haunting feeling that I was much better looking than my Instagram. And besides, here was the thing about photo shoots: they were fun! I had spent all of last Sunday being primped at Grace, and then I had sat on Naani's couch and smiled beatifically at the camera while her bridal photographer friend Asif had yelled fun directions at me.

'LOOK DREAMY. Look dreamy. You're the dream girl. That's right, Radhika! Now let's try shy but coy. COY. Just a hint of mischief,' he had said.

Priscilla, the lighting guy and Naani had watched on, yelling similarly encouraging things: 'oh beautiful!', 'that's perfect lighting!', 'what wonderful hair!'

It was all very glamorous and surreal. I had never been professionally photographed by anyone except the guy at the DMV before, and he had seemed determined to make me look my absolute worst on my driving licence. In contrast, everyone at the photoshoot wanted to make me look my most beautiful. It made me a little emotional, to think that Naani cared so deeply for me that she was willing to spend all this time, money and energy on fulfilling my ludicrous fantasies.

The shoot was worth every penny though. Asif had made me look dreamy, shy and coy, all at once. All I was doing in the photos was laughing on Naani's balcony at sunset or reading on the couch. I guessed that was the prescribed activity for good wives: laughing and reading. The guy who would see the photos would be prompted to think, 'Oh, this is the picture I could return to everyday. One of joy or serenity.'

The way it all worked was a fascinating exercise in marketing and distribution, really. As soon as Asif gave us the Photoshopped images, Naani WhatsApped them to a few close friends from the salon, who sent it to their friends, who sent it to their families of friends who had eligible sons looking for brides.

The Aunty Network was real, alive and determined to make matches of young men and women every day. I would never again make fun of my aunts. I may just owe my marriage to the employment of their leisure hours. Vikas was blow-dry enthusiast Payal aunty's nephew. Anurag was sourced by Mrs Choudhary, who swore by Priscilla's mani-pedi, and Kabir was cardio surgeon Dr Parineeti Sadanah's brother. (I had half a mind to cut him off the list. Imagine being related to someone as insufferable as her.)

'So, this is the guy you're meeting tomorrow?' Rajni pointed to the first picture.

'Yep,' I said.

Vikas. Consultant at a rival firm in Bombay. Dimples and glasses.

'He's cute, too,' Rajni nodded. Then she added, earnestly, 'Much cuter than that Za … other fellow.'

'He's also the only one who lives in Bombay,' I said. That made him the most eligible to me. I didn't really want to move anywhere else in India. Not even Goa, which was where the second guy, Anurag, lived with his dogs.

'And he's a consultant, so he understands your work,' Rajni nodded approvingly.

'Exactly,' I nodded back, already picturing our life together. We'd read the *Economic Times* together over breakfast every morning. I'd count out almonds for both of us as we would exclaim over the dismal decisions of the finance minister. Then we would kiss each other goodbye passionately, grateful to have someone steady in a world of falling growth rates and increasing economic inequality.

'Stop it,' Rajni said warningly, noticing my faraway expression.

'Stop what?' I blushed.

'Romanticizing him.'

I shrugged defensively. 'If I can't romanticize a potential husband, who can I romanticize?'

'Jesus, Radhika! Don't call him that!' Rajni yelled. 'It's the first date. Actually, it's not even a first date because your families will be around. Please don't agree to anything yet.'

I shook my head. The tragedy of my life was that I was surrounded by profoundly pragmatic women.

'Rajj, if he's the right guy, I don't see the point of looking any further. I'm not going to marry him tomorrow, obviously.' I said quickly, before she could start yelling again. 'I'm just saying that he seems to tick all the boxes—'

'You always do this,' she sounded exasperated. 'You fall too hard, too fast and then—'

Fortunately, Mr Gomes entered just then. I immediately switched the volume off.

'Ah, Ms Anand, how is the internet working out for you?'

'It could be better, Mr Gomes,' I said in my most commanding manner.

He peered at my laptop and smirked on seeing Rajni and the photographs of my suitors on the screen.

'A personal call?' he asked, his eyes glinting with malice.

I frowned and switched the sound back on. 'Mr Gomes, meet Ms Rajni Dutt. She is my legal point of contact at the New York headquarters.'

'We were discussing the recruitment of potential candidates to assist Ms Anand in her operations in India,' Rajni said in her most professional tone.

I stifled a laugh. She wasn't even lying. Mr Gomes didn't need to know that we were looking at potential candidates for me, not for McKinley.

Our ruse worked a little too well, however. Mr Gomes was looking at us, deeply offended.

'Are the employees here not good enough for you?' he sneered.

Oh no, I didn't mean to offend the head of HR.

'If you're thinking of replacing any of our employees with your new American recruits—'

'No, no. Nobody is being replaced,' I struggled to reassure him. Rajni shot me a worried glance. I couldn't risk Mr Gomes branding me as the American boss who hated her Indian employees, as he was sure to do if I didn't salvage the situation quickly.

'I love my team,' I said eagerly. 'In fact, their work has been so good that I think there is potential for growing this department by hiring new recruits.'

'Really?' Mr Gomes looked unconvinced. I didn't blame him. I hadn't thought this through myself. But I nodded eagerly anyway.

'Yes. I want to start pitching to more American businesses soon. Why stop at eight companies when there are a hundred operating in India?'

Mr Gomes looked surprised. 'I didn't realize you were thinking of acquiring new accounts in your short time here.'

I wasn't. But there was no turning back now.

'I think that we haven't fully exploited our potential as far as the North American market is concerned.'

'What is this? A mini conference?' Mr Bhatia, the MD, swung open the glass door of the conference room, his expression good-natured and curious. 'Oh hello,' he added, waving to Rajni on my laptop screen.

'Mr Gomes, I thought we had a meeting five minutes ago,' Mr Bhatia said, turning to the HR head.

'I was on my way there when I got distracted by Ms Anand's fascinating new proposition.'

Shit.

Mr Bhatia's expression brightened with intrigue. 'Oh, what is this fascinating new proposition?'

If it had just been Mr Gomes, I could have later gone back on the proposition, said I had thought it through and decided that he was right—expansion wasn't feasible in my short time here. I hadn't meant for the MD to hear this bucket of lies.

But I couldn't renege now, not without losing credibility, so I just smiled brightly as Mr Gomes said, 'Radhika and her legal team in Manhattan were brainstorming a strategy to help us gain the business of more American companies.'

'Really? You want to pitch to new accounts?' the MD asked, giving me a quizzical smile. 'In just six months? That's quite ambitious, isn't it?'

'I was hired for acceleration.' *What was I saying?* 'Being ambitious is in my job description.'

Oh dear.

'I'd love to hear what you've put together,' Mr Bhatia said, impressed. 'Let's meet at 6 p.m.? A meeting of mine just fell through.'

'Absolutely,' I nodded, confident as ever. Inwardly, I was crying. I had just under two hours to come up with an efficient and comprehensive strategy to win the business of companies we had never even looked at before this. I would have to rifle through years of data, analyse sales strategies and prepare an original pitch based on piles of market research.

'Best of luck,' Mr Gomes said with a grin. 'Not that you two need it.'

I wondered if he could tell that the armholes of my white Anthropologie shirt were now damp with sweat.

Once the two gentlemen left and the conference room door was locked (as it should have been all this while), Rajni looked at me with a woebegone expression.

'I think a little brown sugar is okay today.'

I was already ripping a packet open.

❧

I had to take back everything I said earlier about my female analysts. To paraphrase Yeats, they may be quiet, yet they were fierce.

Padmini and Mukti were somehow able to pull up the private data of Adobe, Sensodyne and Ford India's projected sales for the next five fiscal years, within thirty minutes of my explaining this random assignment to them. We had chosen these three companies because, despite having superior products, they were still not the market leaders in the country.

Closeted in my cabin, we worked out a preliminary plan for acquiring the business of these companies. What started as a false project grew before my eyes to become a near-reality. Ambitious as our task was, we could do this, I realized. A familiar adrenaline rush of productivity started to surge through me as we crafted pitches, hurled ideas at each other and added bullet points to slides as the sun dropped into the sea outside the glass window panes of McKinley India.

I was particularly confident about the pitch we had created for Adobe.

'Your eyes are shining,' Mr Bhatia said when I finished the pitches. I laughed, hoping he didn't look under the table of the conference room, which was currently littered with empty sachets of brown sugar. Six at the last count. (*I know.*)

'I'm excited about this,' I said truthfully. 'I have a good team.'

Padmini and Mukti looked up from their reports, a surprised smile spreading across their faces simultaneously. *I want to do this. I want to do this with them.*

'This strategy has the most merit,' Mr Bhatia pointed at the Adobe presentation. I nodded.

'If you're serious about it, I can arrange a meeting with the CEO of Adobe by the end of this month.'

'I'm serious,' I said, giving him my most assured grin.

It would be a mess of late nights and early mornings, of course. But it would be worth it, I knew. By the end of the month, when I saw the CEO of Adobe light up with the aggressive fire of our strategy, I would know that I had brought value to this company. It would feel glorious.

It already felt great as I drove home, humming to the beat of a pop Bollywood song on the radio. Nothing beat the triumph of a good pitch. My shirt was untucked, my hair was in disarray and my eyes were red with weariness, I noticed in the rear-view mirror, but I didn't care. I felt relevant again. This was a goal that I could control.

I alight from the car, briefcase swinging, unconcerned about looking horrendous, until a horn beeped and I turned around. Zain was behind the wheel of his car, looking perfectly dapper in a shirt and tie.

Suddenly, I didn't feel so blasé about my dishevelled state. I wondered if it was the private joke of the cosmos that I only ran into him in situations in which there were sweat patches under my arms.

'Long day?' he asked, taking in my appearance through his rolled-down window.

'*Good* day' I said, shrugging as I pointed to myself in what I hoped was a self-possessed manner. 'This is what hard work looks like.'

The effect was ruined, however, as I tripped over my own feet. So much for being self-possessed.

'Do you need help?' he asked, his mouth twitching as I steadied myself.

'No, it's just a sugar rush,' I retorted.

'What does that mean?' He looked bemused. And then his eyes widened in shock. 'Wait, is sugar code for … cocaine?'

'NO!' I said, shocked, and quickly pulled out the remaining Starbucks sachets from my pocket. 'Cane sugar. It helps me focus.'

Annoyingly, his face lit up with more glee than before. 'Wow,' he said, as though truly impressed. 'So, you're not as perfect as your Instagram suggests.'

'How would you know what my Instagram suggests?'

'That's right. You never accepted my follow request.'

'You never replied to my text.'

'I was busy,' he said with a frown. 'One of our cotton machines exploded at the factory.'

'Not busy enough to bring your girlfriend to the gym the next morning, though.'

'Are you jealous?' he laughed, surprised. 'I don't see why. I hear you already have a triumvirate of eligible bachelors coming to see you this month.'

'Zain,' I said, irritated beyond measure now. 'I'm going home. You have a good night, okay?'

'Okay.' He shrugged and drove away.

What an ass! A gentleman would have walked me in regardless.

'That's what I was doing,' he said, appearing out of nowhere, his eyes laughing.

I have to stop saying what I think out loud.

'I didn't want to park in the middle of the street and block parking for all your … suitors,' he explained, biting back laughter.

I blushed furiously but said nothing. I would *not* be embarrassed for wanting an arranged marriage.

'Gayatri aunty showed me your photographs. Nice,' he grinned. 'Very trophy wife.'

I walked on, ignoring him. But he took my bag and laptop from me, and swinging them on his shoulder with his own laptop bag, followed me into the house.

'Please don't feel obliged to do anything,' I said emphatically.

Zain smiled broadly. 'Don't worry. I don't do anything I don't want to do.'

'Sounds like a selfish way of living,' I said and rang the doorbell.

It's the only way of living,' he shrugged. 'Nobody wants a life of fulfilling someone else's desires. Except trophy wives, maybe.'

I looked at him, stung.

'Nobody wants a life of considering only their own desires,' I retorted. 'Except sociopaths, maybe.'

I bit my tongue immediately. Perhaps that was a step too far, but Zain had burst into laughter.

'Is that what you think I am?'

'No,' I sighed, tired. The day had exhausted me of banter and pretence. 'You're just an entitled Bombay brat. And I've had my fill of your kind.'

'Entitled?' His laughter came to an abrupt halt. Now he did look offended. He opened his mouth to ream me out, but fortunately Naani opened the door just then.

'Sweetheart,' she looked at me shocked. 'What happened?'

I had forgotten what a day of Diet Coke and brown sugar did to my face. I probably looked much worse than I realized.

'I'll leave you to get beautified for your un-entitled boy.' Zain's tone was suddenly hard. 'Goodnight, Gayatri aunty. Good luck, Radhika.'

With a mockingly polite nod of his head, he turned on his heel and left.

I fumed for a moment, looking at his retreating figure with his broad shoulders arrogantly drawn back together.

Impulsively, I yelled, 'He isn't even due today!'

But Zain didn't turn. Annoyed, I turned back to Naani, who looked at me pitifully.

'He isn't due at all, I'm afraid.'

'What?'

'I tried to call you earlier today—' Naani insisted.

'I'd switched my phone off.' I shook my head, feeling dizzy. 'To focus on a presentation.'

Naani put a hand gently on my shoulder. 'They asked me your salary, sweetheart. It's more than the boy's. They are no longer interested.'

❦

'I didn't like the family,' Gayatri said, as she handed her granddaughter a cup of masala chai and sat down on the edge of the bed.

Radhika took a sip of the hot, milky concoction, letting the sweet spices burn through her nose and distract her brain from the sting of rejection. She took another sip and laid her head down on Gayatri's lap. A whimper escaped and Gayatri's hand immediately went to her soft, silky hair.

'There is absolutely no reason to cry over a weak man.'

'I'm not crying,' Radhika sniffled. 'But I was wondering … perhaps … what if I quit my job?'

'Don't talk nonsense, Radhika!' Gayatri snapped, her hand dropping from her granddaughter's forehead. Radhika rose and faced Gayatri with a determined expression.

'It's not such a big deal, Naani,' she began. 'I would want to quit, or at least take a break, when I have children anyway. I wouldn't want them to grow up alone like I did—'

Gayatri got up, annoyed. She couldn't stomach Radhika's self-pity. It reminded her too sharply of her own failures as a mother. She needed to do something with her hands, so she began rifling through Radhika's lunch bag, taking out the tiffin boxes to put them in the sink for a wash.

'What are you doing?' Radhika asked as Gayatri removed her head from her lap abruptly and headed to the kitchen.

Gayatri opened the tap and let water flow over the plastic containers. She squeezed soap on to the sponge and began to scrub, enjoying the feeling of cleaning something. She took the next box and watched gratified as the red spots of mango pickle disappeared under the pressure of her expert fingers.

'Naani, the maid will do that in the morning—' Suddenly, Radhika closed her mouth, guilt flashing across her face as though she had been caught stealing Dairy Milk from her grandfather's cupboard again.

Gayatri pretended to keep washing the dishes, observing from the corner of her eye as Radhika coolly picked up the tiffin bag and began to saunter back to her room. She shut the tap abruptly and turned to her granddaughter.

'What is in the bag, Radhika?'

'Nothing.'

Gayatri held her hand out. Reluctantly, Radhika handed it over. As Gayatri peered in, she wondered what could it be that she hadn't already washed. Then, at the base of the cloth bag, she saw the offenders. Empty little paper packets from Starbucks.

She brought them out. Sugar crystals spilled on to the floor. Gayatri's eyes narrowed in disgust. Radhika winced, aware of what was coming.

'What is this?' she asked.

'Some days, I need a hit,' Radhika said, gathering the sugar packets from Gayatri's hands and dropping them in the trash. 'Of glucose. I need the energy to keep going.'

Gayatri inhaled, trying to quiet the scream that had been building up inside her all evening. She had spent an hour listening to Vikas's uneducated mother fumble through a rejection of her granddaughter—unless she was quitting her job. Then she had listened to Radhika whine about being thirty and unmarried. She had tolerated her talking about giving up her independence to attract a man and raise his children. All through this, Gayatri had quelled the urge to take her by the shoulders and *shake* her into seeing sense. But now that she was watching her granddaughter ruin her health, that urge was greater than ever.

'Don't worry, Naani. I won't put on weight. I gave my tiffin to the interns, so I'm well within my calorie limit.'

Gayatri nearly slapped Radhika.

'Calorie limit?' she spat out. 'You idiot girl. *Have you eaten anything today*? Anything not out of a packet?'

Radhika recoiled at the sharp tone her loving grandmother had taken. She hadn't heard Gayatri's voice raised in years. She didn't think it was possible for her grandmother to yell.

'Naani, I told you I had a presentation—'

'You say you want children, but you can barely take care of yourself!'

Radhika looked shocked by her grandmother's outburst. It took her a moment to make enough sense of it to form an apology. But by the time she had opened her mouth, Gayatri had turned around and started climbing the stairs to her room. Radhika didn't understand the vehemence of her grandmother's reaction.

It was all right. Gayatri would rather have Radhika confused than know the truth about her guilt. Gayatri couldn't speak to her granddaughter, not now, when her tongue was bitter with regret and self-reproach for not taking better care of her daughters.

She didn't know which secret she would betray in such a state.

Best to go to bed and forget it all. Tomorrow, they could try again.

Rajni

How did it go with the consultant boy?

He didn't show up.

WHAT

AN

ASS

I don't know how many more beatings my ego can take tbh.

Babe. Please don't let these idiots get to you. They're CLOWNS, the lot of them.

Yeah, but I'm dying to be part of the circus.

The next morning Gayatri watched, mesmerized, as her granddaughter's eyelids fluttered, battling wakefulness as a few rays of sunlight touched her pillow. She could sit there for hours watching Radhika sleep. The years seemed to fall off her face as she slept. She didn't look like the haggard woman who had stumbled into the bungalow the night before, her eyes and shoulders drooping with the tiredness of the work week. After their fight, Gayatri had warmed up some dal and rice, and the grateful child had eaten an entire bowl. When Gayatri had run her a hot bath before bed, Radhika had nearly cried with relief.

What sort of life had Radhika been leading that simple maternal kindness seemed like such an alien pleasure to her? Gayatri clicked her tongue in annoyance at herself, at Mangala, at Jai. This was what came of letting children live alone in strange cities. They started looking to strange men for comfort.

Gayatri blamed herself for Radhika's lacking upbringing.

She knew that Mangala wasn't much of a mother, and that was Gayatri's fault. After all, Gayatri had been the one to fill Mangala's head with feminism, her heart with independence, and her application to Boston University. She was the one to urge her daughter to study harder and harder till her scores were good enough for a graduate scholarship to an American college. She had all but kicked Mangala out of the house by twenty-one. But she had only done that to let Mangala escape Jai's constant criticism, to allow her room to study and grow and become her own person. Someone other than her father's resentful puppet.

Gayatri had never imagined that Mangala would never return. Nor that she would think herself independent enough to have a baby in her first year of graduate school.

Jai, the controlling fool that he was, had made matters worse by forcing Mangala to marry the fellow—a completely unsuitable Irishman who had moved to Europe for research soon after, never to be heard from again. Radhika had inherited her pink mouth and grey eyes from him, not that she knew. As far as Radhika, and the rest of the world, was concerned, her father was an Indian scientist who had left his family in America for the intellectual freedom of Europe. That was the fairy story Jai had concocted. It was more respectable than admitting the truth of 'having a whore for a daughter'. That was what he had told Mangala when she had called him in tears, begging his permission to divorce the husband she never wanted. Eventually, she had stopped asking for Jai's permission. Or for Gayatri's advice.

The entire episode had soured Mangala's relationship with her family. She had refused to return to Bombay, deciding to raise her daughter on her own on the modest income of a junior research assistant at Yale University. It would have been all right if Mangala hadn't been such a child herself, a child who dealt with trauma like her father—

by delving into work and ignoring her problems, such as the crying baby in the next room.

Mangala's tenacious study of psychology may have propelled her forward in the world of academia, but it had removed her completely from the realm of human relationships. She wasn't a mother. She was a hurt teenager in need of a mother herself. But she had refused to let Gayatri visit to help her, believing her to be complicit in Jai's plans to control her life again.

Incredibly, out of this tangle of hurt and confusion had come a perfect pink-mouthed little girl who never seemed to cry. At least not when she was in the crook of Gayatri's arms.

Mangala had finally acquiesced to allow Radhika to spend her summers in Bombay when she was offered a teaching assistantship in the second year of her doctorate at Yale. Gayatri was only too happy to host the toddler every summer since then.

Radhika was the happiest child Gayatri had encountered. But to Gayatri, her granddaughter's constant, rapturous delight during her summers in Bombay only betrayed the deep loneliness she experienced in New Haven. She was a little too elated by what young girls in Bandra took for granted—stories from her grandfather, long hugs from her grandmother and a glass of cold coffee waiting after her dance class. She looked so happy when she was putting on a little performance for them in their living room, such a stark contrast to the subdued photos Mangala had sent them from America, that Gayatri nearly asked Mangala to leave her behind in Bombay with them. The child would be happier for it, she knew. But she also knew that she didn't want Radhika growing up around Jai, as Mangala had. He may be able to rein in his temper and play the proud grandpa for the length of a summer holiday, but she knew what it would be like if Radhika were to live with them permanently.

No means no, Mangala!

Any particular reason?

Whose name is on the door? That is enough reason!

For a chief justice of a high court, your arguments are SPECTACULARLY mediocre.

Gayatri remembered Mangala's young, crumpling face the first time her father had struck her. Mangala had the same questioning spirit that Gayatri was born with.

Jai had thought Gayatri's banter alluring in courtship, but he didn't care for it much after their wedding. He had rigid, fixed ideas about the topics wives were allowed to broach with their husband. Gayatri had stopped asking questions six months into the marriage.

Gayatri wanted Radhika to be her own person, to be able to make her own decisions, instead of being dominated by her bully of a grandfather. So she held her tongue, even though her heart broke a little every time Radhika packed her little ghungroos and R.K. Narayan books and left for the airport.

After Jai's death, she could have insisted upon having Radhika stay with her. But by then, her granddaughter was already in her last year of college and spending the summer interning at a big business firm in New York.

She looked at Radhika's prone form now and felt a heaving sense of remorse. The truth was that she hadn't even been thinking about Radhika all these years. The girl was so capable that Gayatri just assumed she would be taking care of herself. She had been gallivanting with Birdy and running her beauty salon, not really worried about her efficient granddaughter.

God, she was as bad as Mangala! But she would take care of Radhika now. She would make sure she met the right man. That she didn't go to sleep hungry ever again. You couldn't have children and then just leave them to raise themselves. They weren't Americans for God's sake.

Trrrrrrrring.

Gayatri's eyes flew open to see Radhika blinking at her, her hand reaching out aimlessly for the alarm.

'Naani, what are you—' Radhika's sleep-filled eyes slipped down to Gayatri's joint hands, to the little book open on her lap.

'Were you praying?'

Gayatri smiled and kissed Radhika's forehead.

'For me?' Radhika's eyes grew wide with surprise.

'Always, my love,' she said. Then she added gently, 'Sweetheart, I have an idea.'

'What is it?' Radhika looked wary already.

'I thought we could take a bit of a break from the marriage hunt this weekend.'

Radhika sat up, anxious. 'Naani, we've barely begun. If I got rejected, that's all the more reason to try harder.'

Gayatri put a palm on her cheek, quieting her down. 'I think this will be good for you. For your self-esteem … just hear what I have to say, my love.'

'All right.'

'How would you like to dance again?'

9
The Court Dance

I twisted the ghungroos around my ankles and the bells clung to my calves, chiming in anticipation at the dancing to come.

It was only my second week of Kathak, the classical court dance, but I already felt graceful, more in control of my body and more confident of my femininity. I raised my elbows to my chest and let my palm rest lightly on the other, fingertips alive and delicately curved. The percussionist began tap-tapping at his drum and my feet began moving automatically, fifteen summers of training finding their rhythm back into my toes.

The beauty of Kathak wasn't that your white skirts flared into a floating parasol with every endless twirl, or that your feet made music of their own with four rows of ankle bells ringing out with every tap of my heel. The beauty was that every muscle in my body had the same intent, of graceful precision, of alluring everyone yet no one in particular. The music was mine. The dance was mine. Anyone may watch, but this wasn't about their spectatorship, it was about the grace I could produce, should I want to.

The other girls in the gharana watched me now as I flew across the floor, my loose braid whirling behind me. Gopiji, my new dance instructor, had asked them to observe this intricate choreography that he was counting out in time to the drums. He changed the beat at will, and it was my duty to keep in time with the rhythm, which was going faster and faster with the completion of every sixteen beats. Mercifully, Gopiji started slowing down his counts; I slowed down in response. He brought it to a sudden stop and I jolted, nearly falling on the marble floor, sweat trickling down my calves.

I looked at him quizzically, but he was speaking to someone else who had just entered the gharana. She was tying her dupatta around her waist.

'Go, join Radhika,' he said to her. She looked up and smiled at me.

It was the insufferable cardio surgeon from Grace. Dr Parineeti Sadanah.

She bent and touched her forehead to the marble floor, in respect, before joining me. I didn't have time to wonder what she was doing at the gharana on a Monday night, when she should have been at home to spend precious moments out of the operation theatre with her husband. The percussion had started, and we were dancing in perfect synchrony with the other.

I forgot what fun it was to have a dancing partner of similar skill and grace. The mirror afforded us a lovely picture of our coordinated chakkars and rhythmic tatkals[3] that I found my initial dislike of her fading, replaced by hope for a friendship, so that I may have someone to dance with whenever I liked.

When I glanced at Parineeti's shining eyes, I had a feeling that she was thinking the same thing.

❦

'We have to do this again,' Parineeti said, as I sipped from her water bottle.

'Absolutely.' I nodded, laughing. Endorphins were still coursing through my body from the two hours of dancing. It was late—nearly 10 p.m. I should have been exhausted. I should have been dying for a hit of sugar, but I was exhilarated.

'It's a wonderful feeling, isn't it?' Parineeti asked. 'When things get just a little bit too much, I come here—which is often.' She let out a short laugh.

'How do you find the time?' I asked, as we walked out of the gharana and on to the street, our dance bags swinging on our shoulders.

'My husband cooks dinner twice a week, so that I can dance after surgery.' Then, with a mischievous smile, she

---

3 One count of sixteen.

added, 'The deal is I put on a little private performance for
him later.'

I laughed. Their marriage already sounded lovely to me.
I hesitated, quelling the natural inquisitiveness that rose
within me on hearing about a successful couple.

I had taken a little break from looking for men and
thinking about marriage. I had given myself this time to
lick my wounds and repolish my armour before going back
to battle again. Living with Naani and not thinking about
boys had been so pleasant that I had even considered the
idea of giving up the battle altogether. But now, as I saw
Parineeti's shining face when she talked about her husband,
I felt a familiar tug in my gut.

I couldn't help but ask, 'How did you two meet?'

'We were in medical college together in Delhi. He
was my senior in college,' she said, blushing. 'And from
Bombay. The cool city.'

So that's how people here do it. They find partners
in college. *What was I doing in college?* Competing for
internships.

'Do you live by yourselves or with the in-laws?' I asked
lightly, trying not to sound overtly curious.

Fortunately, Parineeti was happily chatty. 'Alone.
Thank God,' she exhaled dramatically, dodging an auto
rickshaw as we turned on to a dimly lit street. What I had
misunderstood as insufferable cattiness earlier was actually
natural gregariousness. And I was grateful for her company
on the lonely walk home.

'Not that they aren't always over,' she continued good-naturedly, 'or summoning us over. Still, they're not as bad as my family in Delhi—' Parineeti stopped mid-sentence as a large jeep appeared from a side street and flashed its headlights directly at us. Both Parineeti and I stiffened, suddenly conscious of the fact that the street was deserted, except for us and the jeep.

'Just keep walking,' Parineeti whispered. 'We're not too far from my house.'

Surreptitiously, I glanced behind. The driver had got out of his jeep to follow us. Parineeti clutched at my hand, equally scared, as we sensed his footsteps approaching us. I was about to reach for the pepper spray in my pocket when the man closed in and touched Parineeti's shoulder.

I reacted immediately, shoving him hard in the chest. He slipped and fell backwards, but before hitting the ground he caught my shoulder in a futile attempt to break his fall. All of a sudden, I was falling with him. His shoulder landed on the pavement with a deafening crack; I crashed on top of him. I sat up quickly and was about to stick my fingers into his sockets to gouge his eyes out when Parineeti yelled, '*BHAIYA!*'

I looked at the groaning face to realize that the stranger was not a rapist. In fact, he wasn't a stranger at all. His photograph was in my Google Drive, as no doubt, mine was in his.

'Kabir?' I asked.

Thirty-two. Lives in Delhi. *Businessman?*

'I think you may have broken my clavicle.'

Ah, a doctor, I remembered. I tried not to smile as I got up, setting him free.

❦

Parineeti iced her brother's shoulder as her husband, Rajat, mixed us a drink. It wasn't broken according to Rajat, who was a doctor himself, but just a sprain, so I didn't need to feel too bad about it.

'I'm going to get an X-ray all the same,' Kabir said, grinning at his brother- in-law. 'You physios don't know your diagnosis.'

'Oh, go pop a pill. That's all you believe in now, isn't it?' Rajat shot back with a grin, handing Kabir a glass of Scotch.

'Please send me your bill,' I interjected. 'If you do get an X-ray, or for any painkillers—'

Parineeti and Rajat burst into laughter.

'My father won't accept payment from you,' Kabir said, grinning.

His father?

'You're looking at the drug prince of Delhi,' Rajat said, chuckling some more at my confusion.

Kabir shook his head at this unfavourable introduction. 'Don't listen to him. Our family is in pharmaceuticals. We manufacture most of your painkillers.'

The medicine business. Not a doctor. The dots finally connected and his biodata flashed clearly in my mind. Given the way he was looking at me, I could tell that he was also thinking about my pictures. A hint of a smile played on his lips.

Feminist or not, Asif and his photoshoot had been worth every penny.

'What are you doing so far from Delhi?' I asked lightly.

Parineeti answered before he could. 'We begged him to come.'

'I never visited Bombay before this,' Kabir said.

'What?' I asked, shocked.

Kabir shrugged. 'Our parents only took us abroad during school holidays.'

'And you're still waiting for them to choose your holiday destinations?'

Kabir grinned. 'Doctors don't travel too much. On the few holidays that I get from the hospital, I take my jeep and go to Manali with my dogs. We have a house in the hills.'

That sounded fabulous. 'I thought you were in pharmaceuticals.'

'I will be, now,' he explained. 'I just finished my residency at Apollo Hospital.'

'And you don't want to specialize?' I asked, surprised. 'Why go through the trouble of getting two medical degrees if you didn't want to do medicine?'

Kabir laughed. Rajat did too.

'Don't you love Americans?' Parineeti said. 'They're so straightforward. They'll ask anything that's on their mind!'

I coloured. I blamed the sugar withdrawal for making me forget my manners.

'I'm just curious,' I said, smiling in what I hoped was a winsome manner. 'Why, is it a secret?'

'No,' Kabir chuckled. 'It's no secret that I serve at the pleasure of my father, Dr Chander Sehgal.'

I was conscious of Parineeti and Rajat exchanging guarded glances over our heads, but it didn't dissuade Kabir from talking.

'My father had a very humble beginning. He was a surgeon himself before he saved up enough money to start his own pharma business. His one condition, when I turned eighteen, was that if I wanted to inherit the company, I had to first become an accomplished doctor myself to know the ins and outs of how drugs worked on the human body.'

'What if you had refused?'

Kabir grinned. 'Dad would have sold the company and kept me on an allowance for the rest of my life.'

My eyes widened in shock. I had never heard of an Indian father who would do anything like that.

Parineeti noticed my expression and chuckled. 'You have to meet my father to understand. Sehgal Pharma is his firstborn, even though Kabir is the oldest son on paper.'

'Daughters, of course, can get away with anything,' Kabir said, affectionately mussing his sister's hair. 'She could do fashion design or theatre or whatever she wanted.'

'She's a cardio surgeon, bro,' Rajat said with a laugh.

'Only because she spotted you in Dr Chaudhary's anatomy class when she came to drop me to campus,' Kabir retorted, grinning.

'Absolutely.' Parineeti laughed, kissing Rajat on his cheek. 'That is the reason.'

I hid a smile. I never thought, when I woke up this morning, that I'd be enjoying Parineeti and her husband's affectionate banter. For the first time since I had moved to Bombay, I felt as though I was in the company of friends.

'So, now you've finally proved worthy of joining the business?' I asked Kabir.

'Yes, after a lifetime of studying and interning.' Kabir laughed.

His eyes had a sleepy quality to them, I noticed. As though he was so focused throughout the day that in leisure he was at risk of falling into a deep slumber. I wondered what it would be like to take a nap with him.

Woah. Where did that come from?

'That's why we asked him to come to Bombay before he jumped into something else,' Rajat said. 'Kabir doesn't know how to take a break. And then there's the matter of finding a girl, too—'

Kabir shot him a look of warning. 'Rajat—'

'He's not wrong,' Parineeti jumped in, insistently. 'You have to meet someone on this trip, before Daddy starts monopolizing all your time. I know you'll lose interest once you start work, and then Ma will die of embarrassment.'

'Thirty-two years old, you're thirty-two years old! If you cross thirty-three, only the divorcees and widows will be left, mark my words. Or we'll have to go to WEST DELHI to find

someone. Is that what you want? A WEST DELHI girl having dinner with us every night?'

'Rajat!'

'Sorry,' Parineeti said to her brother and then turned to look at me. 'But it's true. We're looking for a beautiful, intelligent girl for him. Someone who'd like to be married before the year is out, preferably. If you know anyone who fits the description—'

'I'll keep my eyes open,' I said, avoiding Kabir's eyes, which were staring at me in chuckling delight.

So, Parineeti and Rajat weren't aware that our families had already assessed the possibility of a match between Kabir and myself. He, like me, probably didn't want too many people to know that he was already considering an arranged marriage and looking at potential brides' photographs.

This encounter was even more delicious, now that it was underlined by a shared secret.

'Falling in love on a timeline must seem odd to you,' Kabir said dryly. 'Nobody in New York does it, I imagine.'

I shrugged indifferently. 'New Yorkers are nothing if not adaptive.'

❧

I had never sat in a jeep before. It was enjoyable for the most part, since we were driving under the open night sky with Bombay's ocean breeze whistling in our ears, but it was also very high off the ground. So high that while clambering in, Kabir had to help me up. And I still tripped over the end of my dupatta. So much for my Kathak dancer's grace.

'You're making this a bit of a habit,' Kabir said, wincing as I clutched on to his hurt shoulder while getting into the jeep.

'Shit, sorry!'

'It's all right,' he said, slamming the door shut behind us and turning to look at me. I waited, wondering if he would say anything, perhaps make some allusion to the fact that our formal introduction had been pre-empted by this chance meeting, but his lips remained firmly pressed together, refusing to let his thoughts escape.

We didn't speak at all as he drove me to Naani's. I didn't know what he was thinking, but his expression remained collected and incomprehensible as he followed my directions, his steady hands turning the steering wheel with a surgeon's precision, carefully navigating the winding alleys and by-lanes of Bandra's barely lit streets.

I was silent and tense throughout, and trying not to say something silly—like how lethal a combination of being good-looking, hard-working and family-oriented was for a man. The sugar withdrawal didn't help. Once, I nearly brought up the fact that we were both considering the other for marriage, but then we hit a speed bump and the thought vanished, only to be replaced by itching worries such as: *Why hasn't he brought it up yet? Has he reconsidered the match after meeting me? Has he already rejected me?*

As this possibility presented itself, I haughtily turned my face the other way to pointedly look out of the jeep's large window. Again, I blamed the sugar withdrawal for the mood swings. My dopamine-reward circuit really was shot.

Now it was too late to attempt conversation, I thought. He was going to drive away, but he didn't. He looked at me, waiting wordlessly.

I was confused. Was he waiting to kiss me? Should I close my eyes in the shy but coy way that women in Hindi films do?

'Um, don't you want to go in?'

I looked at him surprised.

'Yes?' I said, confused again. Was this some roundabout way of inviting himself up?

Then realization dawned on me. 'Are you waiting to … watch me go in?'

'Of course.'

Oh no! He was a gentleman. Now, I had a full-blown crush. I stared at him, bewildered.

'I'd come in to drop you, but I figure your grandmother will be asleep.'

'How do you know that I live with my grandmother?' A slow smile spread across my face.

Kabir immediately looked sheepish. And then he chuckled, dropping the act.

'I know quite a bit, as you already know.'

'I'm glad you admitted it,' I said. 'I didn't know how much longer I could pretend.'

'You were doing a pretty good job of it at Rajat's,' he pointed out. 'I was worried that you may have reconsidered the idea of an arranged marriage.'

I almost laughed in relief. 'I had,' I said, suppressing a smile.

'Oh!' his face fell.

'But now I'm reconsidering my reconsideration.'

'Oh?' he raised an eyebrow. His eyes were bright now, no longer asleep. I liked that. I liked having that effect on someone. 'Any particular reason?'

I hesitated. I was all out of doublespeak.

'It's late,' I said, shrugging coyly. 'And I have work tomorrow. We can carry on this conversation later.'

The playfulness in his eyes disappeared immediately, replaced by respectful understanding.

'Of course,' he said, frowning slightly. 'Goodnight, then.'

This whole arranged marriage thing was a little too civilized. He didn't even kiss my cheek before I turned and walked into Naani's house.

I kept hoping that he would stop, ask me for my number, or my Instagram handle, or some way to stay in contact. But he didn't. And I didn't dare to dial the number that came with his photographs.

This was a first. I was raised by a woman who had told me that agency was power. So, all my life, if I liked a boy, I told him. I kissed him. I made sure to ask for his number.

There was no indignity in desire, according to Mum. She had said this to me when she had given me that awful talk about the birds and the bees in the tenth grade. 'Nobody can make you feel inferior without your consent,' she had said. Mum had even bought me a little Eleanor Roosevelt poster to hang in my college dorm.

I hadn't ever felt like a lesser person for approaching a man. Even now, it was not the fear of inferiority that stopped me from messaging Kabir. It was the fear of losing the bright curiosity in his eyes when he said goodbye to me. No, making the first move didn't cause you to lose power. But being pursued—that had a power of its own. One that I was yet to experience.

So I could not text, follow or DM him. I couldn't even stalk him on Facebook, because then I would show up as 'people you may know' the next day and he would know that I had viewed his profile. I may just have to sit on my hands to keep myself from reaching out first. The only way I could have some communication with him was if his parents called Naani. Or if he somehow wrangled my number from Parineeti and called, or perhaps he just showed up at our doorstep tomorrow …

My eyes refused to rest. They were closed but full of visions of all the wonderful possibilities that tomorrow might or might not bring. I didn't know how Naani did it, sleeping alone every night with no guarantee of whether Naanu would turn up at her doorstep or not. But if I wanted old-fashioned romance, I would have to embrace its methods of courtship.

❦

It was excruciating, this business of waiting.

It had been a week and a half and he still hadn't called, texted or followed me on Instagram. My only ghost of a link with Dr Kabir Sehgal was his sister, Parineeti, who didn't show up at the Kathak class this week.

Maybe I should have been looking at other men, but I couldn't help it. Something about Kabir had taken root in my imagination. His broad shoulders and sleepy eyes seemed to feature in every other dream of mine. Although with the way my hormones had been flip-flopping over the last month and a half, I doubted it would take very long for someone else's eyes to take over my mind. Zain Rajan's golden face still flitted through the stages of REM, along with disturbing guest appearances from Siddhant. I thought, at this point, it won't be healthy to let another man enter my consciousness. Best to pause the search for a while and wait.

It was a weirdly wonderful feeling really. Like we were in a private game of staring each other down, waiting for the other to blink. That was, if he was playing at all.

In any case, I didn't have time to consider anyone else immediately. The many holidays that had found a place in the August calendar—Independence Day, Ganpati visarjan, Parsee New Year, etc.—had cheated our office out of many productive working days, so it was up to me to keep the department running smoothly and meet the goals our American clients set for us.

There was nothing more unprofessional than telling the head of Ford's sales department in Delaware that I won't be able to send him his reports on time because my staff was at a religious festival. Again.

The men on my team despised me for making them work from home through the bank holidays to deliver Mr Goldenblatt's quarterlies on time. Fortunately, Padmini and Mukti were tireless and willing, even to come to Naani's house on the days that the office was shut to help put together this Adobe pitch. They had never been allowed to be in the room for client pitches before, so they were quite excited. It was infectious, their enthusiasm. I had never enjoyed putting together a pitch as much before.

We weren't friends yet, since both Padmini and Mukti had politely declined all my offers of buying them a drink after work, but I was happy that I had got the young women to open up a little over the last month. At least we were more of a team now. The girls shared information about themselves in confiding spurts, like an old car that would stop and start, and then apologetically fall silent for days. I had realized that their reticence had little to do with dislike for me and was more a result of their discomfort with English. Padmini and Mukti could provide intelligent and insightful analysis on paper, but they were too embarrassed of their Marathi accents to voice their perspectives. (An idea some anglicized man put in their heads, I was sure).

Still, so far, I had been able to glean this much: Padmini grew up in Pune, and her husband still lived there. She was only a year older than me and they had already been married seven years! And they were still deeply in love. They videocalled during every lunch break and discussed what they were eating now and what they would make on Sunday when she returned home for her weekly family lunch. I stumbled upon one of their phone calls in the conference room last Wednesday and was astounded to see my timid analyst chattering away with her husband in Marathi, with a confidence I'd never seen before. Their sweet back and forth twanged at my heartstrings a little and I almost pulled out my phone to text ... someone. But the fact that I couldn't decide whom to message—Kabir, Zain, or even Siddhant—made me slip the device back into my pocket and spend the lunch break getting to know my junior analyst instead.

Mukti was twenty-two years old and wanted nothing to do with men, as she announced while sharing Naani's methi parathas with me. She wanted a corner office like mine someday and a house of her own where she could wear whatever she liked. Not just shapeless kurtas, blouses and pants but dresses, tank tops and ... hot-shorts! She followed Bella Hadid. Just like I did.

As I watched her deliver her pitch, stumbling through some of the English, I found myself hoping that she got all the little freedoms that I took for granted. Mukti may flounder, but she tried, unlike Padmini who refused to speak in a meeting.

'Well done,' I said, as Mukti concluded. I turned to Padmini, who was smiling at her young friend, and said, 'You will deliver the rest of the pitch.'

Her smile vanished. 'I cannot—' she whispered.

'You can.'

Mukti nodded along. 'You have to!'

And then, I took my first chance with them. I bent down and pulled out the boxes that Anjali had hidden in my desk two weeks ago. The girls stared at me in shock as I lift the lid to reveal two pairs of black pumps from Steve Madden.

'I asked Anjali for your sizes, so they should fit,' I said.

Mukti reached out and then stopped. 'May I?' she asked.

'Of course,' I said. She immediately kicked her shoes off and was standing in my office, four inches taller, with her hands on her hips in a model-like pose. Padmini, too, grinned and reached for the shoes, but before she could slip them on, I stopped her.

'You will wear these when you deliver the pitch,' I said.

She paused for a moment and I thought she would refuse. But then she reached down to unclasp her clumpy Bata sandals. She clambered into the suede black pumps and nodded at me. 'I will try.'

'I know you will.' I smiled at her.

I was about to ask them to have lunch with me when my phone rang. It was an unknown number. I frowned, wondering whether I should let it go to voicemail. But curiosity got the better of me.

'Hello?'

The girls quickly gathered their things and left my office. I wondered if I should stop them, ask them to wait. This could be our chance to transcend the boss–employer relationship and become real friends.

'Hello, Radhika?' A deep voice rumbled sleepily through my phone. I could hardly believe it.

The last time I had heard this voice, it was asking me if I had reconsidered the idea of an arranged marriage for any particular reason. All intentions of breaking down the corporate hierarchy with Padmini and Mukti were wiped clean from my mind.

'Who is this?' I asked, as Padmini and Mukti left discreetly.

'I thought I had quite a memorable voice.'

'It has been a week and a half.'

'Not that you've been counting,' he said, laughing.

Damn. Caught me out. 'I'm not used to waiting.'

'I wouldn't have kept you waiting if I had a choice in the matter.'

'And what limited your choices?'

'Dr Sehgal summoned me to Delhi to sign some papers at the factory. I missed Parineeti's Ganpati celebrations, too.'

'That's too bad,' I said, my heart sinking. So he was back home, undoubtedly surrounded by beautiful, marriageable Delhi girls already.

'Why is it "too bad"?' I could hear the grin in his voice.

I was smiling too. 'What does it matter?' I challenged. 'You aren't here any more.'

'See, that's where you're wrong.'

'How so?'

'I'm downstairs.'

❦

He was probably waiting on Naani's doorstep, I thought, heart thumping even as I checked my reflection in the bathroom mirror. There was no way he knew where I worked. And no way that he could have known that I was working on a Saturday. Most consultancy firms were closed on Saturdays. In fact, it was just Padmini, Mukti, Anjali and I at the McKinley office today.

I asked Anjali to check the CCTV camera at the entrance before going downstairs and making a complete fool of myself after finding nobody there. I'd rather not have the guards think me ridiculous.

There was no way, I thought looking through the grainy footage of the basement parking lot, the second-level car park, the gym, the PizzaExpress in the lobby—

Oh. There he was.

❦

Kabir was leaning against a cobalt blue Audi with his arms folded across his broad chest. His eyes laughed in delight as I emerged from the foyer of my office building.

'I had a feeling you'd come.'

'What happened to the jeep?' I asked, nonchalantly.

'I realized it's not the most comfortable vehicle for you to get in and out of,' he said. 'So I asked Rajat to lend me his car for the day.'

'How thoughtful! But I'm afraid I can't go anywhere today.'

'Why not?'

I laughed, perplexed by his perplexedness. 'Kabir,' I said, pointing to the glass building behind us. 'I work here. In fact, I'm in charge at the moment.'

I half-expected him to take off like Vikas the no-show. But Kabir smiled.

'I know,' he nodded. 'You're head of American accounts. Very impressive.'

So he had done a little more digging,

'My managing director won't think it very impressive if I leave in the middle of the work day.'

'Ah.' He nodded. 'A good work ethic.'

'Yes.'

'Disciplined.'

'Yes.'

'Shall we go?'

I laughed and looked at the looming glass office building. It was a one-off, I told myself.

'Yes.'

He swung open the door of the car.

And I played truant for the first time in my life.

10
A Matter of Taste

'Baby? What do you think?'

Zain felt a little nauseous. Kiara stood in front of him, in swatches of baby pink and silk, expecting him to feel desire again. But he didn't. He couldn't explain the 'why' of it. Usually, the sight of her in one of these expensive camisole creations did it for him; provided him the excitement and relaxation that he needed after a long day at work. But this morning, on a rare Saturday off from work, even with the hottest girl on Bombay's Instagram in his bedroom, all he felt was a little sick.

'Is something wrong?' she asked, leaning close to him. He resisted the urge to recoil as her intensely sweet perfume overwhelmed him. Everything about her had been designed to draw him in, he realized. Bile filled his mouth. Normally, he enjoyed the seduction, but today … he couldn't stomach seeing a woman bend over backwards just to pleasure him.

'It's not you. I just—' he sat up in bed and held her hand, not wanting to hurt her. 'I'm not feeling too well. I need to sleep it off or something.'

'Baby,' she crooned. 'Is it because it's your mum's birthday?'

Zain's head snapped up at her in shock. 'How did you know?'

'Mamma told me,' Kiara batted her eyelashes at him innocently. 'Anu masi used to live in London and she told me all about your—'

'Kiara, babe,' Zain said, exhaling slightly, unable to bear the conversation or her perfume any longer. 'Let me drop you home, okay? I'm just not up to it today.'

'Are you sure?' she said, grinning mischievously as her hand disappeared beneath the sheets to pull at the waistband of his boxers.

'I'm sure,' Zain said, gathering her fair hands in his, gently but firmly.

❧

He had planned to go home and sleep the day off. Tomorrow, 11 September, would have passed. One annual pill of Xanax and he could relieve his brain of the haunting memories of their London flat, with lingerie casually strewn about. Yes, he just needed to make it home, play the dutiful son for an hour on FaceTime and then sleep till the ordeals of his past receded into the past.

But for some reason, twenty minutes after dropping Kiara home, he found himself outside Gayatri Anand's bungalow. If he was being honest with himself (a habit he had inculcated at a young age), he knew the reason that he was there. He wanted to talk to Radhika about his mother. He certainly couldn't broach the subject with his football lads, and he didn't want to talk about it with Kiara Khemani, for fear that she would carry tales back to her mother.

In their brief encounters, Zain had felt a comfort, a sense that in Radhika he could find a friend, one who would neither judge his past nor set a value on his future.

He wanted to apologize to her for brushing her off at the gym a few weeks ago and then dismissing her marital aspirations. He had been trying so hard to adhere to Birdy's rule of not flirting with Radhika that, in suppressing his obvious attraction to her, he had reverted to being like his friends: an aloof Bombay bastard.

He didn't want to be so withdrawn. Especially after he found out from his friends who exactly her ex-boyfriend was and how it had ended between them. Zain realized that he had met the creep at house parties in Bombay and thought him to be an entitled lech even then. He didn't want Radhika to think that he was made of the same stuff as Siddhant Lodha, because he wasn't. He was made of the same substance as Birdy. Just like she was made of the same substance as Mrs Anand. That is why Zain knew he could talk to her about 11 September. That's why he was on her doorstep that afternoon, he told himself.

'Zain beta!' Gayatri Anand opened the door, happy to see him as usual. But then her brow furrowed with concern. 'Shouldn't you be at home, beta? I know your uncle is waiting for you to—'

'Oh, of course,' Zain nodded, mentally kicking himself for forgetting. 'It's already breakfast time in London.'

'Yes,' Mrs Anand nodded. 'Would you like—I ordered a cake for—' she left the door open and scurried in. Zain followed her to the kitchen as she retrieved a brown box with cursive letters on it and handed it to him.

'I know it's a little unusual but, well, sixty is a milestone birthday—' She broke off as she noticed the pain shoot across Zain's face. He should have been in London with his mother, he knew. She shouldn't have to spend this day alone.

'Oh, sweetheart, I'm sorry,' Mrs Anand took the cake back. 'You obviously don't want to make a production out of it.'

'No,' Zain said, shaking his head. 'It was kind of you to think of this, Mrs Anand,' he took the cake from her. 'The least I can do is cut a cake with her at breakfast.'

Especially since I still can't bring myself to be in the same room as her.

Perceptive as always, Gayatri put a soft hand on Zain's arm. 'Are you all right, beta?'

Zain nodded. He was touched by her concern. Despite knowing the entire situation in all its gory details, her sympathy never felt false or condescending. It didn't make him want to recoil, as Kiara had that morning. It made him want to lay down on her sofa and rest.

'Let me know if you—if you … need anything, Zain,' Gayatri said, smiling at him, the concern still there.

'Is Radhika home?' he asked suddenly.

'No, beta. She is at work.'

'On a Saturday?'

'She's coaching her analysts to take on more responsibility,' Gayatri said proudly.

'Ah,' Zain smiled, but his eyes glazed over with disappointment. Gayatri could tell.

'Why don't you come back in the evening?' she trilled. 'She should be home by then.'

'I'll do that,' Zain smiled and left to wish his barely lucid mother a very happy birthday.

❧

11th September was turning out to be my luckiest day in the year. *Who would have thought that after a lifetime of tiptoeing around love, it would suddenly find me at the office at midday and sweep me off to the fanciest cocktail bar in Bombay for an afternoon aperitif?*

I had tried to design the adventure of the day, to show off my Bombay chops to Kabir, but I had discovered soon enough that Kabir wasn't the kind of man who liked being led about. To be fair, my planning had brought us to Colaba Causeway, one of the most crowded areas in town. Kabir had taken one look at the sweaty melange of hawkers, juice vendors and henna artists through the glass pane of the Audi and laughed at me in bafflement.

'You don't expect us to walk through that, do you?'

I had peered at the hordes of pedestrians jostling for space on the pavement, under the hot Bombay sun, as they tried to buy sugarcane juice or little trinkets from the market's many vendors. It didn't look very romantic, really, to brush shoulders or share air with that many people.

I suppose there were fewer people on the roads in Naani's time.

'Er,' I hesitated. 'We could get sugarcane juice. I know a vendor by the high court—'

But I broke off as I noticed that Kabir was staring at me, absolutely aghast. 'You want to drink juice … from the road?'

I rolled my eyes. 'This vendor is totally safe,' I assured him, although my confidence was based on my grandmother's diary from 1960.

'As a medical practitioner, I am vetoing this plan,' he said and put the car into gear quite decisively.

'You're rejecting my adventure?' I asked, disappointed, as he accelerated out of the neighbourhood without any further discussion.

'I'm saving you from dysentery,' he laughed, shaking his head. 'And I thought Americans were paranoid about this stuff.'

'I'm not American! That's just my passport.'

He shook his head and took my hand. 'No way, babe. The New York finish is why I'll marry you.'

I raised my eyebrows, confused by this compliment. But then he leaned close and whispered into my ear, 'From now on, you only go to places that are worthy of you, okay?'

I smiled, too drunk on how close he was to be bothered by the things he was saying. Instinctively, I kissed his cheek. He looked surprised but laughed.

We had slipped into a dynamic of comfort already, one where I didn't have to think too hard before being affectionate. Suddenly, I didn't care where we were going or who was driving the plans. If the journey was going to be so pleasant, I was happy to go along for the ride.

The destination was as pleasant as the drive, I realized as we stopped at Neel: Tote on the Turf a few minutes later, where a valet and a waiter shimmered to our side with a glass of chilled Chardonnay already bubbling lightly on a tray. Kabir refused his and made me drink it up for him.

'I'm a single malt man, honey, babe,' he said. I rolled my eyes but drank up anyway. The wine was cool and delicious and ever-so-slightly sweet.

Once we were inside, the bartender poured us another glass of Prosecco each as Kabir leaned against the wrought-iron bar. I was already a bit tipsy, but in a very pleasant way.

Kabir was sober, but his smile was wine-drunk. The last rays of Saturday's sun slanted across his face, highlighting his chiselled jaw. He looked much happier here, picking at roasted peanuts and sipping a glass of Scotch with Gucci-clad guests at a convenient distance from him.

'What are you thinking?' He smiled at me sleepily.

'That Delhi men don't like adventure, unless it comes with a fifteen-hundred-rupee cocktail.'

'Babe, I told you. I don't do cocktails.'

I rolled my eyes and he laughed.

'But isn't this much nicer than where we were?' he asked, tipping his glass towards the tree-lined, green lawns spread out before us. 'This is what our home in Delhi looks like, too.'

The bar, with its French windows and artfully potted plants, was undeniably beautiful, but it was also secluded from all of the life in the city. There was no noise or interruption or song here, just murmurs from models and businessmen over the hushed pouring of spirits. There was something false about it all. It was a bit too polished for my liking. Too forced. Too … arranged.

I quickly shoved that ungenerous thought to the back of my mind. I suppose I was uneasy because I was not used to being the arm candy at these affairs. I was used to being the businesswoman.

'Why are you so quiet?' Kabir examined my face curiously.

'Nothing, it's just—I don't usually do this, you know,' I confessed, laughing.

'What do you mean? Go on dates?'

'No, I've been on plenty of those.'

His eyebrows knitted together in disapproval, and I backtracked quickly. 'I mean, not plenty. A fair amount.' My cheeks were red as I continued. 'But only at night, never in the middle of a workday. I can't remember the last time I enjoyed a Saturday afternoon like this.'

Kabir took my hand in his. 'You can spend every afternoon like this if you marry me,' he chuckled.

I raised my eyebrows, surprised. *Was this a proposal? Or was it just bait?*

Kabir's eyes were watching me carefully as he sipped his whisky.

'You have a party every afternoon?' I asked, sipping my Prosecco, giving nothing away.

He grinned. 'Dad and I don't. We're the poor slobs locked away in the factory from breakfast till dinner, but Mom loves having these kinds of gatherings at home. She's always celebrating something to keep the family morale up: Dad's factory opening, reaching a new sales target, me clearing my MBBS exams. We make a fuss about it whenever she brings up guest lists and caterers, but it's good fun to return to a house filled with friends and family at night. And the food is great.'

'I can imagine,' I said. Kabir's eyes softened when he spoke of his mum. I could tell that if things were to progress for us, it was Mrs Sehgal's good opinion I would have to win.

'I'm surprised you didn't like anyone on one of the guest lists of your mother's parties.' I smiled cheekily.

Kabir looked at me with a curious expression and then, as though making a decision, shrugged and said, 'I did.'

Oh.

He must have noticed the crestfallen expression on my face because he immediately tried to reassure me. 'But it didn't work out. Evidently. Or I wouldn't be here, thinking about taking you home to meet my family.'

I looked at him quizzically, unsure how to feel about this. Was this all the information I was going to get?

It made sense, I reasoned. No urban, good-looking, well-to-do person entered the arranged marriage circuit without having first burnt his or her fingers in the forest fires of romantic relationships. Unfortunately, I couldn't ask about his past without risking him asking about mine.

And as he said, what difference did it make, now that we were here together, considering each other and nobody else.

'You do a lot of thinking behind those pretty grey eyes, don't you?'

I blinked. 'Doesn't everyone?'

'Not as much as you,' he laughed. 'It's like I can see the wheels turning in your analyst brain.'

'Let's do less analysis then,' I said as I tugged at his hand to follow me, through the bar, past the revellers and out the French doors on to the lush green lawn.

Surprised by my impulsiveness, he let me lead the way, but only until our shoes touched the grass, which was damp because of the sprays from the sprinklers.

'Wait,' he said, pulling me back. 'Where are we going?'

'Just off to the side,' I shrugged coyly. Realization dawned on his face, but I could tell that he was still hesitant. I stopped, a little hurt now.

'Do you not want to kiss me?'

Kabir burst into laughter. 'Of course, I do,' he said. 'It's just that my shoes, Radhika, are Gucci.'

'Take them off then,' I slid my own heels off and let my bare feet sink into the grass. It felt so wonderfully fresh that I took a deep breath, as though willing the pores of my toes to open up to the earth. Kabir looked at me, astonished, but then he slowly followed suit, taking his shoes and socks off, too.

'And what do I do with these?'

I took the shoes from his hand and dumped them into my work bag.

'Radhika!' he yelled, aghast. 'That's PRADA!'

'It's fake.'

His expression was so shocked that I couldn't help but laugh.

'I never carry anything real to the office, Kabir.'

He shook his head, obviously disturbed. I couldn't believe how much this doctor cared about brands. But then again, he was from designer-mad Delhi. We all had our quirks. I grew up obsessed with the idea of being the only woman on the *Forbes* '30 under 30' list.

'We'll get you a real one,' he said, shaking his head as he snaked his arm around my waist. I looked up at him, smiling. I liked that he was using 'we' for us. Like we were already a team.

'I don't care about this stuff,' I said, pointing to my bag and his shoes. 'It's not important.'

Kabir looked at me for a moment and then he pulled me closer and whispered into my ear. 'If you say any of this to Mum, we're going to have to elope.'

'All right,' I shrugged. 'But I'm having second thoughts now. You are into girls, aren't you?'

Kabir laughed, incredulous. 'Excuse me?'

'I'm just saying. You seem to know your Prada. And now that I think of it, you're very quiet behind those pretty brown eyes. Some could think of it as shy even—'

But before I could complete my sentence, he yanked me to the side. We were underneath a large gulmohar tree. I was pressed up against the bark, with Kabir's hands pinned on my shoulders. He wasn't laughing as he looked at me with a strange, urgent expression. It was as though all the feelings that had been lurking under his calm exterior this afternoon had finally been given permission by his brain to erupt on to his face.

We said nothing for a while.

'So, you are into girls.'

'I think so.'

❧

'Kabir Sehgal'

Zain typed the name into his Facebook search box that
afternoon, sitting in his cabin at Rajan Textile factory.
He wasn't doing it for himself, he repeated to himself
as he glugged his chocolate protein shake. He couldn't
care less.

This investigation was being carried out at Mamu's
special request. His uncle had returned from Mrs Anand's
house later than usual last night, with an uncharacteristically
careworn expression. It had prompted Zain to ask Birdy if
everything was all right.

'We just had dinner with Radhika's new man,' Birdy
said, taking a sip of Zain's coffee. 'He's from a wealthy
family in Delhi. Sehgals.'

Zain was gutted, but his face hadn't betrayed this.
Wasn't Radhika supposed to be working late that day? Or,
at least, that is what Mrs Anand had told him when he had
gone back again at sunset to check if Radhika had returned.
Had she just been sparing his feelings?

Of course, Zain didn't say this aloud. Instead, he let
Birdy continue, uninterrupted. 'The boy seems nice enough,
but he wants to get married before the year is out.'

What?

'Is that advisable?' Zain asked, his tone flat.

'Radhika is keen,' Birdy nodded. 'And Gayatri is not against it, even though it is a bit rushed. She said he was respectful and charming, but I think she mostly didn't want to burst Radhika's bubble. I didn't either, to be honest. She was radiant with joy when Kabir started talking about a December wedding.'

'That's wonderful,' Zain said dryly. Then he added with more honest feeling, 'At least this means that you and Mrs Anand will be able to formalize things soon, too.'

Birdy shook his head. 'Gayatri may be convinced, but I am not,' he said, blowing slightly on the coffee mug in his hand. 'I've dealt with his father back when I was still in the government. He's—'

'What is he?' Zain asked, eager.

'They've got different values. A little too class-conscious, if you ask me. I don't know if Radhika will fit in. But then she's spent time with the boy and seems to like him, so maybe he is different from his father.'

And then Birdy looked at Zain abruptly. 'Do me a favour. Find out all you can about the boy.'

'You want me to—what—snoop?' Zain was shocked.

Birdy despised any kind of deceit. Once, Zain had suggested collecting intelligence on one of their competitors' dust-resistant fabrics. He had received an hour-long lecture on standards of honest business practices that had concluded with Birdy challenging: 'Do you want to trade in a world where everyone sells their sense of fair play for a small spike in profits?'

Birdy's form stiffened. He seemed to be remembering this particular argument, too.

'This isn't the same as business, Zain,' he said, putting an arm on his nephew's shoulder. 'This is about the protection of the women of my family. It is far more important.'

Zain nodded and decided to spend the rest of his lunch break the next day stalking, with the blessings of his godfather. If he was being honest, he would have done it anyway.

The page loaded and Zain began scrolling through it. Fortunately, Kabir Sehgal had low privacy settings on his profile, so Zain could see all his photos, likes and friends. The only thing that was hidden was Kabir's timeline, but Zain could pay a detective to get the rest of the information. He was older than Zain by three years, and a doctor. Most of his photos were in the mountains, grinning at the camera with two golden Labradors next to him. A few photos were in his lab coat at a hospital, smiling with a fair, young girl who was pretending to choke him with a stethoscope. That could be trouble, Zain thought enthusiastically. But when he checked the tags, he realized that the girl was also a Sehgal and not a threat to the potential marriage in any way.

Marriage. It was all a bit bizarre, Zain thought, as he clicked through more pictures of Kabir at a poolside brunch party at his farmhouse. The girl he had sat with on top of a diving board a few weeks ago would soon be swimming in this fellow's pool. They would have a wonderful married life, most probably. If his profile was any indication, Kabir was an easy-going man who enjoyed spending time with his Dior-clad family at their large farmhouse.

Good for Radhika, Zain thought, aggressively clicking through more photographs till he had gone all the way up to the time Kabir had joined Facebook. Zain stopped, dissatisfied at having found nothing incriminating.

Nobody can be this perfect, he thought.

Some people are, a voice inside his head retorted.

Some people grow up loved by their families, in charming neighbourhoods. They attend private schools and know that they will run a company once they come of age. They make good partners to beautiful girls because they've all been brought up in the same world, with similar childhoods, incomes and expectations from the future. They aren't rejected by their mothers and indebted to their uncles.

I have nothing to complain about, Zain reminded himself. His beginning may have been different, but he had ended up in the same situation as men like Kabir. *Wasn't he sitting in the director's cabin of Rajan Textiles? Wasn't this entire factory and all of its one hundred and twenty-one outlets under his command?*

Zain was going to make sure that this number doubled soon. He may not have grown up in a mansion, expecting to lead a factory of men when he came of age, but ever since his uncle had found him floundering in London and given him a future to look forward to, Zain had devoted his life to two purposes: increasing the value of Rajan Textiles and improving the life of the Rajan family, of which Mrs Anand, and now Radhika, were an inextricable part.

Zain dialled the number he used for collecting intelligence on his competitors (yes, he had used a detective despite Birdy's warnings). The PI picked up on the second ring.

'Yes, Mr Rajan?' PI Seth's hoarse voice croaked.

'Mr Seth, I'd like some information as soon as possible.'

'Is it an individual or a company?'

'Individual. Delhi-based,' Zain said. 'Urgently.'

'It will be done.'

11
A Song for the Sehgals

'*H*as your son moved in with your son-in-law permanently?' Chander Sehgal asked his wife at dinner.

The comment was flung across their long dining table with such piercing provocation that Dolly Sehgal stopped in the middle of admonishing their houseboy for scratching yet another silver thali.

'One second, Chander,' she said to her husband of forty years, perplexing him. Before Chander could launch into a tantrum, she explained, 'This fellow has scratched the silver.'

Chander Sehgal quieted down immediately out of respect, as Dolly had known he would. After all, this silverware was the Sehgals' first piece of wealth: a lavish present from Dolly's mother at the time of their marriage. It was the only luxury in their little flat in Noida, before Chander made money, before the first factory or the fancy cars or the fabulous holidays abroad—a lacklustre era when they didn't even have a spare bedroom to put cousins in when they visited. Yet, they had these silver plates, and they dined like a king and queen every night, waiting for the riches to come.

Now the riches had come, and their houseboy had scratched the precious silverware. It was a pity that hitting the help was frowned upon these days. A good, tight slap was what this simpering idiot deserved.

Forget it, Dolly thought to herself as the houseboy finished blaming their cook of thirty years for the scratch. She'd simply throw him out tomorrow. Right now, she had to pay attention to what her husband was saying.

'What is it, darling?' she turned to Chander, agreeable again.

'Kabir is embarrassing us in Bombay,' Chander Sehgal grumbled. 'I knew we shouldn't have let him go back to visit your daughter—'

'He's not staying with Rajat, darling,' Dolly said, eyes softening as she thought of her prince of a son. 'He's booked into the Taj, of course.'

'Then why didn't the hotel reservation show on his credit card statement today?' Chander taunted.

Dolly hated it when he did things like this, hunting through documents like a detective trying to uncover some shameful secret about his own son. How could that possibly help their ascent in the world? What good did it do to lay out one's children's mistakes bare at dinner for the staff to snicker about later?

'He wouldn't stay at Rajat's house, Chander. Not after we explicitly asked him not to.'

'He wouldn't disobey me on purpose, I'm sure,' Chander Sehgal said, 'but your daughter might make him. She would think it a good joke!'

Dolly Sehgal flinched. Even five years after the wedding, Chander still blamed Dolly for his daughter's mésalliance with a middle-class doctor. Chander thought that Dolly hadn't done her best by Parineeti. She hadn't tried hard enough to introduce her to Delhi's best society. But that wasn't true.

The day Parineeti had turned eighteen, Dolly had started taking her to luncheons, bridge club parties, golf club parties and jewellery exhibitions. She had flung lakhs of rupees at her tailors to kit her daughter out in the best dresses. Dolly had ensured, through conversation and light flattery, that the boys and their mothers took note of what a well-brought-up, gentle, pretty girl Parineeti was. The old money matrons and their sons had all agreed that her daughter was an asset worth acquiring, a blooming rose in their Nehru coat pockets.

How happy Dolly had been when that first proposal had come, that too from the Tannas, who had wealth that could be traced back to the treasury of the Mughal empire. They were royalty, unlike the Sehgals, who had just made money as late as the twentieth century. It didn't matter that the Sehgals were as rich as the Tannas on paper, perhaps even richer. Delhi society was all about history and legacy, and one could not buy that. But one could marry into it.

Except Parineeti had refused and refused, till the offers stopped coming. She kept putting her mother off, giving her one more medical college deadline before she agreed to marry someone.

After the midterms, I'll have coffee with him, I promise.

After the finals, I promise!

My residency applications are due, Mamma. How can I meet Mrs Tanna's son now?

And Dolly, like the fool that she was, had believed her well-brought-up, gentle, pretty daughter. Till Chander had discovered Parineeti kissing that middle-class medical student in the back seat of her Mercedes, only to find out that they had been going around for the entire duration of her medical education.

Obviously Chander had commanded her to break it off immediately, but Parineeti had been adamant. She had not even shied away from telling Chander that she had slept with the boy. Dolly had been surprised that her husband had not had a stroke right then.

Chander, humbled and pale, had gone to Rajat's hostel in Delhi Medical University the very next day and requested that he marry his daughter. He had paid for the wedding and danced at the sangeet, but Dolly knew that a dream of his had been crushed. He may have made money and bought factories, but he wasn't one of Delhi's elite yet, and might never be now.

His beautiful daughter had been his only possible entry ticket into 'best society'. After all, she was the only one from the entire family who ever got invited to the affairs of her old money friends from school. She could have been their golden ticket into a different world, but what had she done!

She had sacrificed the chance of becoming a queen married to a king, only to be a surgeon married to a physiotherapist *in Bombay* of all places. Where space was at a premium and dirt was inescapable. The couple lived in an apartment after the wedding. *An apartment.* His princess went from a sprawling mansion in Sultanpur to two bedrooms, a hall and a kitchen in Bandra. Not even south Bombay, which had some history, some class. It brought tears to Dolly's eyes and acidity to Chander's gut, so they tried their best to never think of it.

Still, they told their son, in no uncertain terms, that he could not marry someone who didn't belong to the old money club. Kabir didn't protest. Unlike Parineeti, he had his mind set on the right things and was conscious of their position in society. He had even dated the Sahanis' lovely younger daughter, Aishwarya, for seven long years. But then they found out that she was having an affair with some richer fellow in London. And then there was that mess with her painkiller overdose—stolen from Chander's vault! The Mahabharata that had ensued between Chander and Kabir after the incident—gosh! Well. Best not to think of that either.

After Aishwarya, Dolly's son had spent the remainder of his twenties studying for his medical exams and rejecting girls.

Kabir was thirty-two now, and even Chander could see that he was lonely and dangerously set in his ways, in a manner reserved for bachelors in their fifties. The Sehgals knew that as he started to take over the family business, the days would only grow longer and lonelier. Kabir needed someone to enjoy his evenings with, so that he didn't feel cheated out of life with most of his day being spent in a grey office at the pill factory.

Already, after his medical exams, Kabir had gone a bit quiet. In fact, even Chander didn't balk at the idea of him having a few weeks off to go to Bombay to visit his sister and her husband.

But the weeks had turned into a whole month, and Chander now needed his son back to start work soon. Besides, he was uneasy about Kabir spending too much time with Parineeti and her middle-class husband. They would only introduce him to other middle-class people, and he couldn't risk having his heir married to some Bandra girl who wore overalls and refused to touch the feet of her elders.

As Chander turned his attention back to dinner, the bowl of mutton biryani in his silver plate glared at him mockingly. *Oh God! What if Kabir has found a Muslim girl?*

'Call Parineeti!' he erupted, suddenly. 'I want to know where Kabir's been sleeping every night!'

'All right, Chander, darling. Don't get your blood pressure up,' Dolly said, leaving her plate untouched to sit closer to her husband on his end of the dining table. The houseboy immediately appeared and shifted her plate.

Their daughter picked up on the second ring.

'Hello, Ma,' Parineeti said, her voice as bright as ever.

'Hello, beta,' Dolly Sehgal replied. 'Beta, is Kabir there right now? He's not answering his phone.'

Parineeti hesitated for a moment. 'No, Ma. He's not here.'

'So, he's staying at the Taj?' Dolly Sehgal smiled in relief at her husband. She knew her son wouldn't embarrass them.

'No, he's staying with us, of course.'

Dolly's face froze. Chander became alert. 'What, what did she say?'

'How come he's not home then?' Dolly asked slowly. 'It's nearly midnight.'

'He's not Cinderella, Ma,' Dolly could sense the restrained frustration in her independent daughter's voice. 'He's allowed to stay out past midnight.'

'Who is he with then? If you and Rajat are home?'

There was a long pause, during which Dolly could hear Rajat murmur something in the background.

'Parineeti!' Dolly said sharply. 'Where is Kabir?'

'Ma, I think you better ask him,' her daughter said apologetically. 'As you said, it's nearly midnight and I have an early shift. I'll speak to you tomorrow. Love you, love to Daddy! Bye!'

The line went cold. Dolly Sehgal couldn't believe it. Her daughter had absolutely no manners. She looked at her husband, expecting him to share in her dismay, but he was looking at her accusingly.

'What?' she asked, clearly annoyed.

Dolly wished he would just speak up and accuse her of being the reason Parineeti had ruined her life, so that she could defend herself. This silent offense was simply non-combatable.

'Nothing,' he said, pushing away his plate angrily.

Dolly's heart sank. She didn't want him to go to bed hungry.

'Darling, I'll call Kabir and get to the bottom of this if you take two bites of your curd.'

Chander Sehgal looked at her in disbelief. Here he was, the pharmaceutical baron of India, being told to eat his curd by his wife and being hung up on by his daughter. *What had his life come to?*

He considered arguing with her, but there was no point. Dolly never argued. She would just listen to all his abuse and then push the curd at him anyway.

He shook his head in annoyance and lifted the spoon to his mouth. 'One,' he said, swallowing the yogurt. 'Two. Now go.'

Dolly's trick had worked. The yogurt slipping down his throat had cooled his body and whetted his appetite. He was hungry again, and less frustrated. He pulled the silver thali of biryani towards him and took a mouthful as she lifted her phone to her ear, a smile playing on her mouth.

'You are ridiculous,' he said to his wife fondly. She patted his hand and took the first bite of her own dinner. Kabir picked up the phone and she swallowed immediately, putting him on speaker.

'Hi, Ma!' Kabir's voice sounded distant and hollow, as though he was outdoors in some windy area.

'Hi, Kabir rajje!' Dolly said. 'Where are you? Why is there so much interference?'

'Ma, I'm on a boat with … some friends,' Kabir said.

Chander Sehgal perked up instantly on hearing this. Middle-class people couldn't afford boats! This was a good sign. And he was with friends, plural. One of them could be a classy south Bombay girl from one of the industrialist families! It wasn't as coveted an alliance as an old Delhi family, but it wasn't the worst choice.

'What friends?' Dolly Sehgal asked, smiling at her husband, sharing in his train of thoughts.

'Do you remember the photos Payal aunty had sent us?' Kabir asked.

Dolly Sehgal was instantly alert. Payal was their old neighbour from middle-class Greater Kailash II. Dolly had only shown Kabir the photographs to boost his ego a little after they heard that Aishwarya Sahani was engaged to some musician in London. She had never thought he would actually consider any of those women, not even for a second.

'Ye-ee-s,' Dolly said, haltingly.

'I met the Anand girl. Radhika Anand. The one from New York? I'm with her, right now, actually!'

Dolly raised her eyebrows in worry at her husband. 'Okay, beta. Shall I talk to you later then?'

'All right, Ma. But I'd like you to meet her soon.'

'Okay, beta,' she managed to say before disconnecting the phone.

Dolly Sehgal was almost too worried to look at her husband. Fortunately, he didn't seem enraged. Instead, he kept chewing thoughtfully.

'Anand,' he said, trying to recollect the name. 'Justice Jairaj Anand's granddaughter?'

'Yes,' Dolly studied the light that had come into her husband's eyes, trying to guess what he was thinking.

'That's not a bad reputation at all,' Chander nodded and chewed. 'Not rich, of course. Not even close to us.'

'Not even close,' Dolly echoed, letting out a little laugh at the very idea.

'But well known. Very well respected. Even in Delhi.' Chander bobbed his head from side to side in consideration. 'It could be good.'

'It could?'

Chander nodded again, taking a bite out of the mutton with enthusiasm now.

'Yes, I think the justice was friends with Mr Tanna's father in London growing up. I think they went to Oxford together. They're not old money, but they're definitely old guard!'

He had another bite of the curd, enjoying the cool sensation. 'If we play it right, we could host the Tannas at Diwali this year!'

Dolly shook her head. She hated to burst her husband's bubble, but she had to give him complete information before he started planning the announcement of the wedding of his son, Kabir, to the granddaughter of late Justice Anand, Radhika.

'The girl's parents are divorced, Chander,' she said flatly.

Her husband's face fell immediately, and it fell further when Dolly added, grimacing, 'And her mother lives with some white college student. *In campus housing.*'

Chander Sehgal was quiet for a moment, absorbing this information. 'But maybe—'

'No,' Dolly stopped him short. 'Imagine sharing grandchildren with those grandparents. Do you want the third generation of Sehgals to grow up around hippies?'

The word 'hippies' drained all the colour from Chander Sehgal's face. He, who had worked so hard to clamber to the top of society, who could someday be playing golf with the Tannas or taking trips with the Sahanis, couldn't risk it all by becoming attached to outcasts.

'No, no,' Chander shook his head vigorously. 'You're right, Dolly. Please get on a flight to Bombay and break it up before they get serious.'

Dolly nodded, satisfied, as she and her husband ate their dinner from the slightly scratched plates. *Everything will be all right*, she thought. They had got to where they had by the grace of God, and lots of plotting. And they would reach where they ought to be by the same blessed methods. This American girl would not stop her family from claiming their rightful place in society.

Kabir and I were kissing like we had never kissed before. We were stumbling across the cool marble floor of my bedroom, the little bells of my payals tinkling. Thank God I took my ghungroos off at dance class, or Naani would definitely have come in to investigate the source of the ringing.

This had become a neat little routine of ours over the last couple of weeks. Kabir picking me up from dance class every evening and dropping me home, I mean. Not the kissing. This was new. Usually, we stop at a few swift pecks in the car before I ran into the house and watched Rajat's Audi disappear down the street from my balcony, sighing with longing and secretly wishing someone was filming me and my chaste romance. But today something was different about Kabir. He lingered for longer in the car, and I did too, hesitating, as I waited for him to unlock the door.

Finally, I had to ask, 'Do you want to come up?'

He looked at me, torn. I understood his confusion. We had talked about sex briefly in the first week or so, but the conversation had been strictly in the third person. He had intimated that he thought he would like to wait till the honeymoon, to do it with his wife. He wasn't a virgin, no. But his wife couldn't be had in some Bombay hotel room, or on the couch of some Airbnb. It had to be a celebration. It had to be right.

I had been swept up by the romance of the idea, of course. But I could tell that resisting was becoming harder for him, especially since I had started wearing my most form-fitting kurtas, with mischievously dipping necklines to dance class. (Not on purpose or anything.)

Today, the rose and white outfit had been too much for him, I thought gleefully as we settled down on my bed.

Unless. A thought panted across my mind as his hands moved to my back, looking for the zip.

Unless he wasn't planning on making me his wife.

ZZZZIP.

As soon as my kurti fell off, I pulled it back up and moved away slightly. He stiffened and immediately put his hands behind his back. I nearly laughed. We looked like a heroine and a villain in a clichéd Bollywood rape scene.

'Is something wrong?' Kabir asked.

'Kabir,' I said, not sure how to broach the wrought subject. How did one tell a boy that if he liked it then he should put a damn ring on it?

As I flailed for words, he reached for me and pulled me back on to the bed. He started to kiss my neck and I nearly gave in. He smelled so good. And it had been so long. He was lying on top of me now and I was about to give in. I was about to go with the flow for once, without analysing anything, but then his hands cupped my breasts and instinctively I yelled, 'WAIT!'

Kabir stopped. He sat up, the confused expression back. 'What's the problem, doll?'

I was ruining the moment, I knew. But I couldn't risk being used and left behind. Not again.

'Kabir, I think we should wait,' I said firmly. 'As we had decided.'

Understanding flooded his eyes and shaky laughter fell out of his red mouth. He nodded, looking at me fondly as I slid out from under him and hooked my bra back on.

I exhaled in relief. 'Good. Now help me zip this up—'

'Wait, I was thinking—'

'What?'

'I was thinking that … we shouldn't wait till the wedding.' A glint had come into his eyes, like a child who had been waiting to play a long-planned prank.

'Oh?'

'I think an engagement is enough of a formal celebration for a young couple to consummate.'

'That's an opinion,' I said, waiting and wondering where this was going.

'It's a well-founded opinion,' he said, pulling me back on to his lap and making little circles on my bare back. 'That way we're not fumbling and confused about each other on the honeymoon.'

'All right,' I said, trying to break free so I could zip myself up. 'An engagement is enough then.'

'Fantastic—'

He pulled a ring out of his pocket and slipped it on to my finger.

I stared at it in shock. The stone was large. Gaudily so. And set in a bright gold band that clashed with the colour of the diamond. But it didn't matter.

It was a ring!

And it was on my hand.

'What brought this on?'

'Goddamn ghungroos.'

I laughed as Kabir flipped me over and lay me back down on the bed. Perhaps I should have stopped and sat down to talk with him, but I didn't want to. His face was inches from mine. I just wanted to enjoy this heady hour of celebration with my fiancé.

Almost as soon as his hand moved to the zip of my kurta, Naani called out. 'RADHIKA? Is Kabir there!'

Both of us got up with such a start that Kabir nearly fell off the bed.

I jumped off the bed and tied my hair back in a bun, draping my dupatta modestly around my neck. Kabir sprung to the opposite side of the room, holding a book in his hands. *We're adults*, I thought, trying not to laugh at his expression of innocence when Naani swung open the door with the dramatic flourish of a TV detective.

She looked at Kabir, eyes narrowed. That was her general expression for him, even when he wasn't in my room. Naani says she likes him, but it was obvious that she was wary of him. He wasn't given free roaming rights around the house the way Zain was. And she never hugged him close or touched his forehead fondly the way she did with Zain after he touched her feet. Somehow, despite Zain's Casanova reputation, Naani had a soft spot for him. And despite all of Kabir's respectability, Naani remained on guard with him.

She was at her most doubtful now, as she took in his half-sheepish, half-defiant expression.

'Kabir was just leaving, Naani,' I said, trying to salvage the situation.

'He will have to. Now.' Naani's voice was tight.

Kabir and I exchanged a look. It wasn't like Naani to be cold.

'Mrs Anand, there's no reason to be worried,' he said, glancing at me with a smile, about to deliver the good news.

'I'm not worried at all, beta. Your mother is, however. She is downstairs, waiting to see you.'

Kabir's jaw dropped slightly.

'Please come down, when you're both decent.' Naani pursed her lips and disappeared with a swish of her chiffon sari.

The first thing I noticed about Dolly Sehgal were the solitaire earrings made of diamonds so large that her earlobes drooped with the painful weight. The second thing I noticed was that she wasn't sitting on the sofa, but standing and peering at the house with the imperious curiosity of a noblewoman who had wandered into the slums by error.

She gave me a disapproving once-over as I emerged from behind Kabir, but her look was not half as withering as the one Naani gave her when she hugged her son dramatically and asked, 'Are you okay, beta? Do you feel all right?'

I understood Naani's umbrage. Dolly Sehgal's entire comportment seemed to convey that we had been mistreating her son in some way.

'I'm fine, Ma,' Kabir said, confused. 'What brings you here?'

'Oh, beta, this evening I felt in my heart that something was wrong! That something terrible was going to happen to you, so I got on the first flight and came here.' Dolly shook her head, letting her gold ringlets flounce on her shoulders, as she looked at her son with watery eyes.

This was definitely not the time to tell her we were engaged.

'It's such a relief to see that you're okay! That nothing unexpected has happened.'

Kabir shot me a cautious look. I shook my head.

'You are all right, aren't you?' Dolly Sehgal asked again, tugging at Kabir's sleeve to turn his face back to her, even

as a tear escaped her eye and rolled down her face in slow
motion. I wondered if she had choreographed this.

Naani rolled her eyes at me from behind Kabir's back.
I stifled a giggle.

'I'm better than all right, Ma.' Kabir put one arm around
his mother and kissed her plump cheek in what I thought
was a very sweet manner. You could tell that he knew
his mum was ridiculous, but he loved her all the same. It
endeared him to me even more. *Loyal? Check.*

'I'm glad you're here, actually. I'd like you to meet
Radhika.'

'Namaste, aunty,' I smiled brightly and joined my hands
together in greeting.

'Namaste,' Dolly Sehgal nodded at me once before
turning back to her son. 'Beta, let's go? I have dinner
reservations at the Maratha, and I'm absolutely starving!'

'Why don't you join us for dinner, aunty?' I was
surprised that Naani hadn't suggested it already. She was
usually so particular about hospitality. I looked at the empty
coffee table and realized that Dolly hadn't even been offered
a glass of water!

Something very unpleasant must have passed between
the two women before we arrived.

'No, that's all right,' Dolly Sehgal said curtly and placed
a hand on her son's arm. 'Kabir, we really have to go.'

Kabir hesitated, tormented. I understood that he
couldn't refuse his mother when she was being so adamant,

but at the same time it would be hugely insulting to Naani and me if he left abruptly.

Naani, fortunately, came to his rescue. 'Kabir,' she said dryly, 'you should listen to your mother.'

Relief flooded Kabir's face. He gave me an apologetic glance and escorted his mother out of our home.

As soon as they left, I turned to Naani. 'What was that?'

'Wait.' Naani put a finger on her lips and walked to the window to watch as the chauffeur opened the car door for Dolly to clamber in. Once they had safely driven away, she turned to me and gently took both my hands in hers.

'Sweetheart, I think it's best if we forget about him.'

I flinched and removed my hands from hers. If she saw the ring, she didn't comment on it.

'Why would you say that?'

'He's not going to marry you,' she said, looking at me with concern. 'The mother won't let him.'

'But … didn't the mother send the proposal in the first place?'

'She didn't. Payal aunty got her wires crossed apparently,' Naani said, shaking her head. 'Dolly had no idea that you and Kabir had been spending time together.'

'And now that she knows—'

Naani's upper lip curled. 'Did she look happy to you?'

I fell silent. Dolly Sehgal did not seem to approve of me at all. A first, truly. Most Indian parents loved me. Well, Siddhant's parents certainly had the few times we had dinner together at their hotel in New York, when they came to visit last Christmas. As did Rajni's and the parents of all the other Indian kids I had met over the years. To be honest, I thrived on the appreciation of Indian elders through school and college. It was a motivating factor for top grades, a scholarship and a toned body. Aside from increasing my own self-esteem, it also increased the chances of getting to hear 'What a wonderful girl!' from the mouths of impressed parents at graduation. Well, other people's parents. Not mine. But that was only because Mum didn't believe in rooting one's sense of self in external validation.

Dolly Sehgal certainly couldn't have such psychological qualms about compliments, could she? I mean I had heard her tell Kabir that he was her handsome, perfect prince on speakerphone enough times during our drives around town.

'Am I not ... attractive enough?' I asked, silently hating myself for even asking the question.

Naani was clearly annoyed. 'I think it is because we aren't rich enough for them.'

I raised my eyebrows, shocked that this should be a factor. After all, Kabir and I drove the same car in Bombay and had equally prestigious jobs. We even split the bill on most of our dates (at least I tried to).

But Dolly Sehgal's diamonds and Armani-spritzed plump perfection had reminded me how different our worlds actually were. I worked for a multimillion-dollar company. He owned one.

Both Naani and I looked down at the large diamond that rested on my finger. It sparkled, as though mocking me.

✎

'NO!' Dolly Sehgal screamed at her son. She couldn't believe it.

'I knew something terrible was going to happen today. She dunked her butter naan in her bowl of dal makhani. The warm, rich lentil curry slipped down her throat in comforting contrast to the reality that her son and heir was relating to her that she took another bite. And another. And another, till her mouth was quite full and Kabir was staring at her with concern.

'Ma,' he said, slowly, watching her carefully as she swallowed the large morsels of bread with aggressive difficulty. 'Do you want water?'

'No, I don't want water,' she snapped. 'I didn't even drink water at that girl's house!'

'What?' Kabir asked, aghast.

'Yes,' Dolly Sehgal jutted out her chin. 'That Gayatri Anand asked me if I'd sit and have a cup of tea with her while her granddaughter … I don't know what she did to trap you, but I am not going to let it happen. I refused their tea and you will refuse their granddaughter, do you understand?'

Kabir groaned inwardly. He wasn't worried about convincing his mother of Radhika's virtues; Dolly could be persuaded easily enough. But Mrs Anand was proud and had a nearly unforgiving standard as far as her pride was concerned. Refusing her hospitality was the etiquette equivalent of slapping her face in her own home. The last thing Kabir wanted to do was to disrespect a lady he had come to admire so much. Mrs Anand may not be vastly wealthy like his father, or even her neighbour Birdy, but she embodied an old-world grace that Kabir, like his parents, was in awe of. And despite being raised in New York, Radhika exuded the same grace of the past, with her long hair and her careful manners, which Kabir loved. She was a refreshing contrast to Aishwarya Sahani, the bold, rich girl of his twenties, with whom he had done all the wild things that youth would be incomplete without. Kabir may have broken up with Aishwarya a few years ago, when she overdosed on his father's painkillers and confessed to cheating on him with every guy in her design class in London, but he hadn't been able to get his deliciously dangerous girlfriend out of his head. That was until he met someone who enchanted him in a way that was completely the opposite of the curvy, spontaneous, party girl that Aishwarya was.

Radhika was a real lady. She didn't smoke, she didn't drink anything but the finest wines, and Kabir was yet to hear her swear. She had a soft femininity about her that made him feel as though ghazals were playing around him. Aishwarya had been good fun when they went out, but Radhika was the one he imagined coming home to every evening. They could eat dinner together like his parents.

Just thinking of Radhika at their dining table in Delhi, her bangles tinkling as she laid a plate out for him relaxed a tension within him that he didn't know existed.

'Ma,' he began slowly. 'You will like Radhika once you get to know her—'

'I know everything that I need to know.' Dolly said truculently. She put her spoon down and demanded, 'Kabir, are you aware of what sort of mother she's grown up with?'

So that was the problem. Kabir nodded, confident and ready for a negotiation.

'She hasn't, Ma,' he said, smiling.

'What do you mean?'

'Radhika and her mother barely talk.' He shrugged, pleased at having solved the problem so quickly. 'By her own admission, she's nothing like her mother and wants to be as different from her as possible. She wants kids and a family and all of the Indian values.'

'All of them say that,' Dolly said. 'Then they go to bed with some druggy in London.'

Kabir winced, but he didn't lose his temper.

Dolly continued, 'How can we be sure that this girl won't turn out like—'

'Radhika is different, Ma,' Kabir snapped. 'She hasn't had everything handed to her on a platter like Aishwarya had. She had to work for it. Girls like that respect opportunities and elders. They don't compromise people for … spontaneous pleasures.'

'So, she is looking at you as an opportunity?' Dolly demanded. 'Do you want to end up with a gold-digger?'

'Ma, *anyone* I marry will be less wealthy than us,' Kabir said, noticing his mother's countenance soften. If there was one thing his parents loved being reminded of, it was their superior net worth amongst their peers.

'There are brackets of wealth, son.'

'Look, none of the Punjabi Forbes families have daughters as pretty as Radhika. And I'm certainly not marrying a Gujarati.'

'Of course not!' Dolly looked horrified at the idea. 'I'd rather have a gold-digger than a Gujarati in the house!'

Kabir suppressed a laugh. 'Radhika isn't a gold-digger, Ma. She's family-oriented. Why else would she move back to live with Mrs Anand, that too at a time when the whole world is moving to America to make money?'

Dolly Sehgal's expression softened further as she absorbed this new piece of information.

Sensing her pliancy, Kabir continued, 'And nobody can say that Mrs Anand isn't respectable.'

'No,' Dolly agreed, nodding. But she wasn't entirely convinced yet.

'Still, your mother-in-law won't be Mrs Anand. Imagine what Radhika's mother will look like in the wedding photographs, smiling with her college-student-boyfriend? I want your wedding featured in *Vogue*. At this rate, we may not even make it to *Hello*!'

Kabir laughed out loud. If they were fretting about wedding photographs, he knew he had won already.

'I'll make sure that her mother's boyfriend isn't at the wedding, all right?' he said, smiling, 'And just think, you and Radhika will look lovely together in *Vogue*. You two can easily be the mother–daughter pair of the year.'

Dolly's well-shaped eyebrows went up in surprise and her eyes began to gleam. She had wanted to be part of *Vogue*'s mother–daughter spread for years now. It would be a definite step towards getting into all the right circles. Once, years ago, the editor of the magazine had called her to ask if she and the beautiful twenty-two-year-old Parineeti would be part of the photoshoot, but her daughter had categorically refused, blighting her mother's dream in a very cruel fashion.

But perhaps it didn't have to be that way. Now that Dolly thought of it, she and Radhika had the same fair complexion. Dolly could dress them both in shades of rose and have their photographs taken next to the jasmine tree in her garden, by the new Japanese water fountain she was having installed this month. She would put the photos on Instagram and the phone would surely start ringing with invitations pouring in from every big magazine in the country. With Radhika's pretty face and her New York polish, Dolly and she may even make it to the *Vanity Fair* instagram. Like Mittal and her daughter.

'I'm not promising anything,' she said to her son, her eyes already alight with the possibility of fame. 'But I'll meet the girl.'

Kabir grinned. 'Is tomorrow too soon?'

The Atrium Lounge at Taj Lands End was where Dolly Sehgal had asked me to meet her for coffee that evening. I had expected Kabir to join us, but when he picked me up from work at 5 p.m. sharp, he just smiled and shook his head.

'I'm afraid it's just you two today,' he said with finality that made the impending encounter seem more sinister than just a chat. I wanted to ask Kabir what this meeting was about. *Was his mum about to pick out lehenga swatches with me, or was she about to politely, but definitively, ask for her ring back?* But Kabir kept his eyes focussed on the road, his conversation curt in a way that did not invite conversation.

What the hell happened last night?

I was contemplating how to gently ask him this when he did the funniest thing. He reached towards the back seat and took out a white anarkali for me. One that had lovely little golden flowers embroidered all over it and cotton petals blooming across the bodice. The outfit was understated and elegant in a way that only something very expensive could be.

'I thought you could wear it to meet Mum,' he said, smiling hesitantly.

Aww. Perhaps I should be offended that he didn't think my work clothes were good enough to meet his mother, but really, I was touched that he went to the trouble of thinking of this. It had been a long day, and truth be told, I looked rather like rubbish before I ran to the Taj Lands End bathroom, splashed water on my face and in my underarms and changed into my new outfit. Now, nobody could tell that I had been squinting at a screen all day.

Dolly Sehgal certainly couldn't. She seemed truly impressed to see me sashay into the Atrium, hips swinging slightly, so that the businessmen in their deep-seated chairs turned their heads a couple of degrees to glance at me. I saw Dolly Sehgal notice, and a smile spread across her face as she rose to air-kiss my cheeks, all the animosity of the day before forgotten.

'Oh, beta,' she said. 'Please sit. What would you like to have?'

'Actually, Mrs Sehgal, I've already asked for something special for us.'

'Oh?' her eyes lit up with curiosity. 'What do you mean?'

I smiled in the veiled way that I had to practise for the photoshoot and gestured to Arthur, the manager I had got on the phone with five minutes after Dolly Sehgal had called and asked me to meet her. He nodded and appeared at our table a moment later with a tray of MAC Cosmetics.

Dolly Sehgal looked at me confused, wondering why I was presenting her with a platter of make-up.

'Kabir said that you have quite a sweet tooth,' I said, still smiling coyly.

'Yes?'

'You have to try these,' I said, uncapping a lipstick and handing it to Dolly Sehgal. She took it tentatively and rolled it open to reveal a stick of red.

'Bon appétit.'

Confused, Dolly Sehgal brought the lipstick close to her nose and sniffed it. Then she giggled with the cheer of a child discovering a new toy.

'It isn't … it can't actually be …'

'It's chocolate,' I said, uncapping another lipstick and unrolling it. 'Raspberry-coated chocolate truffle sticks, to be precise.'

Dolly Sehgal watched me in wonder as I bit into the lipstick and chewed. Then, gathering courage, she bit into her own lipstick. I could see delight spread across her face as the rich milk chocolate and tangy fruit melted on her tongue.

'It's delicious!' she said. 'This is very clever! Where did you find these?'

'A friend of mine is a popular pâtissier,' I said, shrugging nonchalantly. 'It was no problem.'

Dolly Sehgal didn't need to know that I had been on the phone with Royce' Chocolate for an hour and a half, bribing them with money and corporate-gifting contracts to get their chef to make these special chocolates.

I had spent enough time working for the seriously wealthy in the corporate world to understand that if there was one thing that impressed the wives of rich men, it was studied effortlessness. While their husbands loved to boast about how hard they worked, the ladies of leisure, by definition, could not admit to any sort of exertion without risking their husbands' reputation. Doing something yourself was unheard of. The trick was to make everything look like a breeze. The trick seemed to have worked here.

Dolly Sehgal smiled at me appreciatively, as though I had learned and effectively spoken her code.

'You managed to combine two of my favourite things: lipstick and chocolate.' She looked at me with new-found respect.

'I think special meetings, such as this, are a gift,' I continued as Dolly snapped photos of the chocolates. 'I had to give you something memorable to commemorate the occasion.'

'It is certainly memorable,' Dolly Sehgal smiled at me with warmth now and picked her phone up.

'Shall we take a photo to remember it?'

Yes!

'Why not?' I said coolly.

A photograph was always a good sign. It meant that she was willing to publicly proclaim to friends and family that she met me. We put our heads together and smiled as

Arthur took her iPhone 12 and clicked the photograph. Within seconds, I was on Dolly Sehgal's Instagram story. My goal was to make it to her grid.

'Here, try this one,' I said, unrolling another lipstick. 'This one is Fiery Amber. It's orange and dark chocolate, with a little cinnamon.'

She laughed and took another bite. But now she looked at me curiously, a question playing under her heavily mascaraed lashes.

'Have you always wanted an arranged marriage?' she asked.

I inhaled. We were finally getting down to business.

'No, Mrs Sehgal,' I began my rehearsed speech. 'But the men I've met, I've found lacking. I wanted someone like Kabir. Someone serious and kind. You've raised him so well that it's impossible not to want to be his wife. I haven't met such a considerate man yet.'

Dolly's eyes softened and a proud pink tinge came into her fair cheeks. 'He is lovely, isn't he?'

'He is,' I agreed. And then, in a sudden burst of honesty, I confessed. 'He is so thoughtful that he bought me this anarkali to wear for this meeting.'

Dolly Sehgal looked shocked for a moment, and I thought I'd blown it. What if she thought I was a fortune hunter, after him for the outfits and the money?

But then, to my relief, she laughed. 'He must really want me to like you.'

I smiled. 'Both of us want that.'

She shook her head. 'Tell Kabir that he has nothing to worry about.'

I stopped myself from breaking into a wide grin. She had all but given us her blessing.

'So, beta, have you ever been to Switzerland?' she asked.

'Not yet.' I smiled.

'We will have to change that. You have to see the house in Zurich before we have the wedding there.'

Yes.

We spent the rest of the evening eating truffles, sipping green tea and discussing wedding details. Dolly Sehgal seemed more and more impressed by my knowledge of how rose mandaps held up against the snow. I didn't dare tell her that I had once dreamt of an outdoor December wedding in New Haven with Siddhant. Instead, I kept the conversation focussed on my wealth of information on winter flowers.

Naani, however, was not impressed when I arrived home in Dolly Sehgal's car, wearing a gold and white designer outfit I didn't own at the beginning of the day.

'You didn't leave the house in that, did you?' Naani asked, her eyes narrowed.

'No,' I said, choosing my words carefully. 'I changed after work.'

'Why?'

'I couldn't meet Kabir's mum for tea in my office shirt, could I?'

'Oh.' Naani's mouth pressed into a thin line. 'So, is Dolly Sehgal going to dictate how you dress in the evenings now?'

'Dictation implies reluctance,' I said. 'And why would I be reluctant to wear something so pretty?'

I did a little twirl, letting the white and gold skirt of the outfit flare, and waved my hands in a Kathak mudra. The drama of the gesture worked. Naani was too surprised to keep frowning. As I danced through the living room and came to rest in the Suchita pose, with my arm outstretched towards her, Naani chuckled, despite her best efforts, shaking her head.

I flung my arms around her neck and kissed her cheek.

'It's good to see you happy again' she said, shaking her head. 'Even if it is in borrowed clothes.'

'It has nothing to do with borrowed clothes,' I said. 'And everything to do with living with you.'

Naani patted my cheek affectionately. 'Flatterer. What do you want?'

'Nothing, Naani,' I said truthfully. I won't ask her to give me away tonight. I would save that for later, once the dates had been picked. If the last day and a half had taught me anything, it was that there were no certainties as far as weddings were concerned—not even if there was a ring on your finger.

12
Heat

$\mathcal{M}$rs Anand placed another steaming hot paratha on Zain's plate.

'Yours is without coriander,' she said, placing an affectionate hand on his cheek before spooning a thick pat of white butter on to the paratha. Normally, Zain would be conscious of his controlled diet, as advised by his personal trainer, but today he didn't care. He was in a celebratory mood. He had worked aggressively every day since his mother's birthday and had finally emerged victorious, winning two new contracts for Rajan Textiles in the Middle East.

'Give him another paratha,' Birdy said, laughing. 'He hasn't eaten properly in a month.'

Zain grinned and took a bite of the hot paratha bursting with cottage cheese and white butter. 'It's worth it if I can make you a little money.'

'A little money,' Mrs Anand scoffed, pouring him a glass of cold Coca-Cola. 'You've set up a whole wing of offices in Dubai, all on your own. You haven't just made him a fortune, you've created value. Labourers, weavers and clerks will have more employment because of you.'

Zain smiled. He had forgotten how pleasant it was to spend the evening at Mrs Anand's. He was glad that he had refused Kiara's invitation to go to her father's farmhouse again that night. Even though he had successfully broken up with her a couple of weeks ago, she didn't seem to have accepted it. She had showed up at his house anyway, ready and waiting. And Zain, tired as he was from a day of negotiations, hadn't been able to resist. After all, people his age were getting married! The least he could do was enjoy the company of a pretty girl who wanted to please him.

He wondered where the bride-to-be was tonight. He had received a packet of information from PI Seth that he wanted to share with her.

'Radhika and you have the same tireless ambition,' Mrs Anand said proudly. 'She's been going to work at 6 a.m. every day this week.'

Zain was surprised. 'Why is that?'

Mrs Anand's lips pressed into a tight smile. 'Oh, you know, Kabir's mother is in town,' she said, forcibly upbeat. 'She occupies all of Radhika's time in the evening. So, the poor girl makes up for lost time by getting up especially early to focus—'

'That's commendable,' Birdy said.

'And exhausting.' Mrs Anand broke off a piece of her paratha, still trying to restrain her irritation with Dolly Sehgal. 'Not that Radhika would admit to this, of course. She is only too happy to hop over to whatever dinner party or shopping excursion or social event Dolly Sehgal has planned.'

'Maybe she enjoys it,' Zain suggested. He didn't know why he was playing the devil's advocate. After what he had learned from PI Seth, he knew for sure that the Sehgals were not to be trusted.

'Maybe,' Mrs Anand said, unconvinced.

Zain wondered whether he should share the information with the elders. But he didn't want them to be agitated for no reason. An arranged marriage was such a delicate situation that any suspicious information could seem like a deal-breaker.

The photograph of the red-faced girl flashed through his memory.

Aishwarya Sahani. Small, swollen eyes. Red from crying. Coke lines laid out by Kabir.

Perhaps he should tell them.

He was about to pick out the photo from the email PI Seth had sent him when Radhika walked into the living room, labouring under the weight of a large tote bag.

'Hello, all!' she said, giving her grandmother and Birdy a kiss on the cheek and a quick wave of greeting to Zain before dumping her bag on the dining table with a thud.

'What is all this?' Birdy laughed, looking at her large leather tote, which was bursting at the seams.

'My whole world.' She began taking out items. 'Laptop, charger, gym shoes, work clothes—'

'Work clothes? You know you don't need an outfit change at work? Despite what *ForbesWomen* tells you.' Zain grinned.

'Radhika isn't allowed to meet her boyfriend's mother in anything that isn't a designer outfit,' Mrs Anand said dryly. 'The evening clothes are provided by the boyfriend.'

'Fiancé,' Radhika corrected. 'You used to call him Kabir,'

'Before he started insisting on dressing you,' Mrs Anand shot back.

Zain decided to give Radhika the information PI Seth had dug up when Mrs Anand wasn't around. *The fiancé* already seemed to be a source of tension between the two women. He didn't want to make Mrs Anand any more wary of Radhika's man, not unless it was absolutely necessary. Especially since older folk were easily alarmed by the mention of drugs and dramatic past relationships.

'I wouldn't wear anything I didn't like,' Radhika said, shrugging.

'Your colour palette just suddenly shrunk to two colours, white and pink, on its own?'

Zain shook his head. Already, they seemed ready to break into an argument, with their identical jaws jutting out defiantly. Birdy, he could tell, was on edge too, hoping that his two favourite ladies wouldn't start to battle each other and ruin a perfectly pleasant dinner.

But then Radhika exhaled suddenly and took her pale pink dupatta off to drape it around her grandmother's head, startling everyone. And then she burst into a popular Hindi song, singing at the top of her voice with feeling: *'Gulabi aankhen jo teri dekhi'*.

Birdy joined in and started singing with Radhika. Zain couldn't help but laugh as Mrs Anand's cheeks started to flame into a bright pink, looking very much like a rose under her creamy, softly wrinkled skin.

'All right, all right, settle down,' Mrs Anand shook her head, cutting Radhika and Birdy off before they launched into the second verse. But she was smiling and the argument was forgotten, at least for the moment.

'She's exactly like you, Gayatri,' Birdy said, laughing. 'God bless you, my girl!'

'I wasn't before,' Radhika said, shaking her head and sitting down next to Zain. 'But I am now. At least I hope I am.'

'Does Kabir know what a kook he's marrying?' Mrs Anand asked affectionately.

'Of course not,' Radhika laughed. 'But he has his whole life to find out.'

Mrs Anand grinned at her granddaughter. 'As long as he's the only one reeling from rude shocks.'

An uncomfortable pain pierced through Zain's gut. Now he wondered whether he should even tell Radhika about what he had learnt from the detective. *What if she accused him of having very sour grapes?*

But still, he could not put the photograph out of his mind. He looked at Radhika, her eyes shining with joy, and wondered if they too would end up small and swollen like Aishwarya Sahani's in the photograph he had received.

No, they wouldn't, a protective voice rose from somewhere within him.

I wouldn't let that happen to her, he decided.

He took a bite of his paratha, but it seemed to have lost all its flavour. He was about to excuse himself and return home when Radhika turned to him, her eyes still shining brightly.

'Zain, can I tell you a secret? You have to promise not to tell anyone. Not even Birdy. And definitely not Naani.'

Zain's eyes lit up with curiosity. He thought he was going to do the secret- spilling today.

'All right,' he said.

'Bring your ice cream and come up to my room.'

❦

I watched Zain nervously as he picked up the watch. It was a limited-edition Rolex, worth six months' salary. But it was worth it. *After all, how many times did one get to make an impression on one's father-in-law?*

'This is not for Kabir?'

'No,' I said. 'It's for his father.'

'Radhika,' Zain looked flummoxed. 'This is a white gold GMT. It costs—'

'I know, I know,' I said, shaking my head. I didn't want to hear the price pronounced out loud. It still gave me a fright. 'But they've invited me to Switzerland with them this month, on their family holiday, and I didn't want to bring a cheap gift the first time I met his father.'

Zain let out a low whistle. 'Well, it definitely isn't cheap.'

'Do you think it's nice though?'

'It's very nice.'

I exhaled, relieved, and sat back down on the bed. The layers of my anarkali settled on my thighs, damp from the sweat of walking through Bombay's dense traffic. The flowing skirt was undoubtedly beautiful, but I wished Kabir wouldn't buy such elaborate pieces. I was waiting to peel off my skin-tight leggings, and the dress above it, and take a cool shower once Zain left. But he showed no sign of moving. In fact, he was staring at me with a concerned expression.

'Does Mrs Anand know about this trip to Switzerland?'

'Not yet.'

'You should tell her.'

I shrugged, turning away from him to keep the gift in my bedside drawer, thinking that this was the end of the conversation. When I turned back, Zain was standing right behind me.

'Radhika,' he said, very seriously. 'You have to tell her.'

'I will, Zain,' I said, startled at how close he was.

'I thought you, of all people, would approve of a spontaneous vacation with a boyfriend,' I laughed slightly to lighten the mood.

Three months of observation had made it obvious to me that Zain was happily non-committal. He had a string of girlfriends and a bunch of best friends. An impulsive, illicit holiday should appeal to his instincts, if anything.

'If it was just a spontaneous vacation, I would. But this is different. You're going abroad with the family of a guy you've known only, for what, three months? It's not exactly safe.'

I laughed, surprised. 'They're not the Corleones and this isn't the *Godfather*, Zain. We'll be at a five-star resort in Zurich with Wi-Fi connection the entire time.'

He shook his head, looking more and more unsatisfied by my answers.

'Plus, he's not some random guy,' I added. 'I'm marrying him.'

'Radhika ...' he said, glancing at his work bag. 'I have something to tell you.'

I narrowed my eyes a bit defensively. I didn't like the expression on Zain's face. It was the one my mom had when she had told me that I had to give up the chocolate-coloured Cocker spaniel I had been gifted on my eighth birthday. 'Go on then.'

'It's about Kabir's ex-girlfriend,' he began hesitantly. My hackles rose immediately. 'Do you know how—'

'I don't want to know, Zain,' I said, annoyed. Was he really going to try and make me suspicious of my fiancé? That was low.

'Radhika,' Zain looked pained. 'I'm not saying this to hurt you, I promise.'

Something in his voice sounded true to me, which was the only reason why I didn't kick him out of my room for trying to mess with my marriage before it had even begun. I studied his face and concluded that he was genuinely concerned.

'Look, I hate butting into other people's relationships, but I owe a lot to Gayatri aunty. I can't help but look out for you. You need to know about Aishwa—'

I screwed my eyes shut and yelled, 'NO!'

Zain shut up, to my relief. I didn't want to fall down the wormhole of googling another girl, like I did with Jia K. and Zain's many girlfriends. It didn't help to know about the other women. It just drove you nuts.

'I don't want to know, Zain. I don't want to have her image in my mind when I'm talking to him. I don't want to wonder whether he is thinking of her. Especially since I don't need to worry. We're getting married, okay? We're not just dating. That means he is serious about me. Not her. So, I don't need to concern myself with his past and he doesn't need to concern himself with mine.'

'How can you be okay with spending the rest of your life with some guy you don't know properly?' Zain asked, flabbergasted.

'I know enough. And I'm going to trust him on the rest. That's marriage.'

Zain didn't look convinced. 'You're going to trust him for the next fifty years based on a relationship of three months?' he asked, incredulous.

I felt a nervous tug in my stomach. I wished he wasn't piercing my hard-won happiness with all this logic. Where had logic and analysis got me so far? Dumped at twenty-nine.

'Don't you think it's a bit soon?' Zain asked with an urgency in his tone. 'To make so many life-altering decisions?'

I stared at him, stung.

There was only one way to explain this to him.

'Would you like to hear a story?'

❧

I held up the black-and-white photograph for Zain to take a closer look. He'd spent the last thirty minutes quietly reading every page of Naani's diary. Finally, he held the photo of Naani and Naanu in London, on their wedding day, and stared at it in satisfactory awe.

'That's Gayatri and Jairaj Anand at Hyde Park,' I said, pointing to the one on the bench. 'And that's—'

'The Big Ben.' He smiled. 'I know. I grew up there.'

'Oh, right,' I said, blushing. 'Sorry, I forgot.'

'It's hard to remember facts when your brain is filled up with fantasies,' Zain said dryly.

'This is hardly a fantasy,' I pointed out. 'It actually happened. My grandparents knew each other for three months before they got married. And they had the greatest marriage I've ever known.'

'Except you didn't know it, Radhika,' Zain shook his head, annoyingly self-righteous. 'You were barely here. You have a romanticized idea of their marriage based on a couple of weeks of summer holidays.'

I snatched the diary back from him. 'There's nothing wrong with romance,' I said, a little defensively. 'You could do with some of it yourself.'

'No, thanks,' Zain shrugged. 'Romance is just something weak men made up to get women into bed. I'd rather just tell a girl what I want and then it's up to her to accept or refuse. Although to tell you the truth, I haven't been refused very often.'

I glared at him, annoyed. 'You have a very low opinion of your own sex.'

Zain grimaced. 'For good reason.'

I rolled my eyes. I didn't have the time or patience to figure out the meaning behind his cryptic remarks. I'd had it with boys who thought they were so deep that they needed to speak only half-truths all the time to guard themselves.

'Naanu called Naani his good-luck charm. He won all his biggest cases after he married Naani,' I continued, trying my best to drum up some sentiment within him. I saw a ghost of feeling in his eyes, while he was reading the diary. Where had it receded to now?

'Do you really want to be somebody else's good-luck charm?' Zain challenged.

I looked at him with a flash of anger and then said with a shrug, 'Maybe.'

He nodded stiffly. 'You're convincing yourself that you're ready.'

'I am ready.' I was annoyed. 'I don't need to convince myself.'

'RADHIKA?'

Naani's voice rang across the room, sharper than usual. I was surprised. Normally, she came up to say whatever she wanted. The only time I was summoned was for punishment. An infuriating smirk broke out on Zain's face.

'Get used to being yelled at,' he said. 'Delhi men. Delhi wives.'

'At least Delhi men are *men*.' I shrugged coolly. 'All Bombay has got are boys.'

'Ouch,' Zain said, clutching his chest dramatically. I ignored him and ran down to see what the commotion was about.

Naani was standing at the door with Birdy. Mrs Sehgal's chauffeur was there, holding a bouquet of heart-shaped Lindt chocolates and an apologetic look on his face.

'I just wanted you to know that I'm returning all this,' Naani said, holding up an envelope. She looked upset.

'The Sehgals have sent you a ticket to Switzerland,' Birdy said, shaking his head in disappointment.

'No, wait,' I yelled as the driver turned to go. 'Naani, you can't send it back—'

'Of course, I can. The impudence! What did they think? That they can just send a ticket for my granddaughter and she will follow along. Like what? Excess baggage?'

Oh dear. I never thought of it that way.

'Naani. I—' I hesitated. There was no way this was going to go well. And yet I could not risk the wrath of Dolly Sehgal if I returned her gift. The Rolex I had bought would hold no weight if I insulted them in this way. I gathered courage and faced my grandmother.

'Naani, I already … promised to go on the holiday.'

My grandmother looked horrified. Birdy seemed appalled.

'I don't see the problem,' I began. 'I mean, we are engaged—'

'Are you?' Naani snapped. 'Are you really? Because you may have a ring and the outfits, and they may cart you to parties when they need a pretty plus-one, but has Dolly Sehgal come back to this house and formally asked us for your hand? Have they discussed setting a date? Have you met his father, or are you going to meet him at the airport like some, some—'

'Gayatri,' Birdy put a placating arm on Naani's shoulder and she broke off, exhausted. I was burning with shame and quite out of my depth. I had no idea that there were so many formalities that the Sehgals had not completed, while I was blowing up a lot of money on gifts for them.

'Really, Radhika, for a smart girl, you can be quite stupid at times.'

I was too shocked to reply. I could not remember the last time Naani looked this disappointed in me.

Then she shocked us all further: she took the boarding pass and RIPPED it to pieces, letting the glossy paper fall on to the chauffeur's chocolate bouquet like scattered confetti.

There was complete silence for a moment, which was finally broken by a loud guffaw from Zain.

'Zain!' Birdy hissed. His nephew put one arm over his mouth, muffling his laughter into a strangled cough.

'We should go,' Birdy said to Naani, squeezing her arm slightly and moving past the stunned chauffeur.

The only thing Naani said to me before going to bed was this: 'You are nobody's carry-on, Radhika.'

❦

'Zain?' Birdy asked the next morning, before Zain left for the factory. 'Yes, Mamu?'

'Did you find out anything about Radhika's young man?'

Zain hesitated, biting on his buttered toast to pause for time. The folders were burning a hole in his briefcase, even as Birdy's discerning gaze bore through him. Yet, he couldn't tell his godfather the truth.

Radhika had trusted him with something personal the night before. And even though he had ridiculed her for irrationally staking her future on her grandparents' past, he knew he had been a bit of a hypocrite. Zain had held on to stories himself when he had felt lost. Hadn't he read every *Forbes* article about successful rags-to-riches Indian businessmen on his moth-eaten couch in London and hoped beyond hope that his trajectory would be the same?

And the miracle had happened for him. He was on his way to realizing his desires. Why should he stop his neighbour from doing the same?

'Zain?'

'Nothing out of the ordinary yet,' Zain said, shrugging. 'But I'll keep looking.'

Birdy's expression, however, did not lose its vigilance, as Zain had hoped. He stared at Zain, plainly aware that he was being kept in the dark.

Finally, he said, 'All right, son. I trust you to keep my girl safe.'

Zain nodded. The responsibility was his now.

13
Safety

I barely slept last night. I kept tossing and turning, anxious that my potential engagement with Kabir and the fragile relationship I had been able to string with Dolly Sehgal had been snipped by Naani's one impulsive action.

I didn't even have the courage to argue the point with Naani. She was so terrifyingly disappointed in me all through breakfast that I couldn't say much other than 'May I have the milk please?' in my most docile tone.

And even that was handed to me with an aggressive thwack. All of Naani's movements were aggressive this morning, as though she wanted to drill some sense into me.

As someone who had only ever been regarded as the most sensible girl in a room, it was very confusing to go to work feeling like a 'problem child'.

I stayed later than usual at McKinley, going over the internal strategies of Mr Goldenblatt's account, as well as the other accounts under my department. I stayed so late, in fact, that Mr Bhatia, our managing director, knocked on my door to ask if everything was all right.

'It is,' I assured him.

'Everyone else in the building has left,' Mr Bhatia said. 'I suggest you go home, too. It won't be safe to stay longer.'

'Really?'

I had pulled so many all-nighters alone in New York, without any problems, that it didn't even occur to me that Bombay may not afford the same kind of security. I wouldn't be roaming the streets alone after a certain time even in Manhattan, but I never imagined anything could happen to me within my own office.

'It's not as bad as it's for women in Delhi,' Mr Bhatia said, shaking his head, 'but we don't want to take a chance, do we?'

Delhi again, I thought, shaking my head. *What was it with Bombay men disparaging Delhi men's attitude to women?* I wondered how much truth there was to their statements, and how much of it was misplaced machismo. Still, I rose to leave, not wanting to get into an argument with my managing director.

As Mr Bhatia and I got into the elevator together, I started to see what he meant about safety here. I was the only woman in the building at 10 p.m. And definitely the only woman in form-fitting slacks and a blouse. The men who filed into the lift on the twelfth and fourth floors couldn't help but stare straight at my breasts for a moment before I shot them a look and they averted their eyes reluctantly to the tiled floor of the lift. Mr Bhatia noticed this exchange and grimaced apologetically at me.

'By the way,' he said, trying to lighten the mood. 'I've been meaning to tell you—your two women did a good job in the preliminary pitch for Adobe yesterday.'

I grinned. 'I know.'

'You were right about them,' Mr Bhatia said, nodding. 'I didn't think they would be able to do it, especially not the older one—'

'Padmini.'

'Yes, Padmini,' he said, his eyebrows raised slightly. 'She did a good job.'

Of course she did a good job. We had been practising the pitch for two hours every evening. She went home and practised it on her own, too, speaking into an iPad video recorder as I had instructed her to do, so we could review the tapes in the morning. Together, we had managed to massage the tremor out of Padmini's voice as she delivered the presentation.

'I feel like a proud parent,' I joked, as Mr Bhatia and I walked to our reserved parking spots.

'As you should,' he said before getting into his car. 'Before you came here, I didn't know their names. Now I'm thinking of giving the younger, sparky one a promotion.'

'Mukti?' I smiled.

'Yes, Mukti,' Mr Bhatia looked slightly sheepish. 'Get home safe,' he repeated before driving away.

On my way home, I mused over this parting remark. *How peculiar was it that here a wish for my safety had become a substitute for goodnight.* I noticed for the first time that there were few women in the drivers' seats at the BKC signal at 10 p.m. It hadn't struck me till tonight just how unsafe the city could be for a lone woman.

It explained so much of my female analysts' trepidation to speak up at work. When you were subconsciously worried for your physical safety for a large portion of the day, it was hard to feel confident enough to stand up in a meeting full of men, command attention and make your point.

The signal turned green. And something within me clicked just then, too. I had to do something about this. I didn't know what, but I had to do something.

A chauffeur tried to bully me into the left lane. I blared my horn at him and drove on home, firmly in the right.

❧

Dolly and Kabir Sehgal had been sitting on Gayatri Anand's sofa for the last half an hour, hoping for the frostiness to melt slightly before Dolly revealed her real reason for being there.

It wasn't easy. Gayatri wasn't forgiving of Dolly's last visit. She took every chance to allude to Dolly's former high-handedness, constantly asking her if the water was now 'up to her standards, or should she order the sparkling kind from the supermarket?', if 'the tea was okay? It wasn't the Taj but—'

Dolly had sheepishly uttered that everything was perfect, repeatedly. From the moment Gayatri had said 'yes?' to her in lieu of a 'hello' or 'welcome' on finding them at her door, Dolly had known that she would have to drink many cups of tea and pour lavish praise of Mrs Anand's upbringing of her granddaughter to wrangle Gayatri's blessings for this marriage. But she was ready to swallow all of Gayatri's taunts if it meant securing Radhika as her daughter-in-law. Dolly couldn't believe it herself, but over the last few weeks she had actually grown quite fond of Radhika, even boasting her latest acquisition to her husband.

'What about the mother and the student?' Chander had asked her the evening before, while Dolly had FaceTimed him from her hotel room at the Taj.

'Oh, she's such a perfect girl. It cancels everything out,' Dolly had said cheerfully. 'Real old-money class.'

Dolly really believed this. She was charmed by Radhika in the same way that Kabir was. She thought her to be soft, feminine and respectful in a way that the other entitled rich Delhi girls could not be. Dolly liked the way Radhika referred to her as Mrs Sehgal, and not the ageing 'aunty'. She liked the way Radhika rose when Dolly came into the room and that she always had a genuine compliment to pay her. Aishwarya Sahani had been a crass coke-sniffer in comparison to Radhika's grace and good manners.

It was for all these reasons that Dolly Sehgal had appeared before Gayatri that evening, despite the fact that her chauffeur had returned with tatters of the ticket she had sent Radhika the day before. Dolly drained her cup of tea and decided that it was time to broach the subject.

'Mrs Anand, we would like to request your permission to take Radhika on our family holiday to Switzerland,' Dolly Sehgal flashed her most winning smile.

'That is out of the question.' Mrs Anand smiled an equally pleasant smile. 'More tea, Kabir beta?'

Kabir frowned, irritated. 'But why not, Naani? We will take good care of her. You will have no cause for concern—'

Gayatri shot Kabir a look of such withering hostility that he stopped short. 'My granddaughter isn't some sort of toy that you may ask my permission and take her where you please. She's a respectable young woman, and she isn't going to travel abroad on the charity of a family that isn't hers.'

'It isn't charity—'

'You're right, Mrs Anand,' Dolly Sehgal said, cutting her son off. 'I am sorry. The children don't think about these things, but I should have thought about it. A girl's reputation is important. I should have said something to Kabir.'

'Kabir should have realized this on his own. If he's serious about Radhika, her reputation should be important to him, too. They aren't children any more.'

Kabir frowned. Gayatri Anand could see that he was biting his tongue. Something within her wanted to give him a good tongue-lashing to provoke his temper, so that he could burst and she could gauge the magnitude of his anger. Was it going to be to a degree that her granddaughter could withstand? Or was it an all-consuming fire like Jai's had been? Was it quick to burst into flames, or would it blaze in silence for weeks on end till both partners' mouths were bitter with cuss words unspoken.

But Gayatri didn't have a chance to test her potential son-in-law. Radhika appeared in the drawing room and Kabir's agitation vanished immediately, replaced by a fond smile as she entered, yelling out greetings. Gayatri suddenly didn't feel as hostile towards him or his mother. She watched the strangers hug and kiss her granddaughter, and the black anger in her heart receded.

'This is such a nice surprise!' Radhika exclaimed.

'What is a surprise is how late they keep you at work!' Dolly Sehgal said, clicking her tongue. 'How can you come back all alone, beta? Please take my chauffeur with you if you're going to stay that late.'

Radhika shot Gayatri a tentative glance. 'It's all right Dolly aunty,' she said, with a smile. 'I enjoy the drive.'

Gayatri smiled. Her granddaughter had finally realized that she wasn't to take favours from those who were still strangers.

'You need a holiday,' Kabir said, peering at her face.

'I do,' Radhika nodded. And then she added quickly, 'But, uh, not Switzerland. Not yet, at least.'

Kabir's lower lip jutted out and Gayatri braced herself for the argument that was going to come. Fortunately, before he could open his mouth, his mother intervened.

'Mrs Anand,' Dolly said, turning to Gayatri. 'Perhaps Switzerland was a far-fetched idea, but can we please invite both you and Radhika to spend Diwali at our home in Delhi this year?'

Gayatri was surprised. This was unexpected. Radhika's face, she saw, had lit up with excitement. As had Kabir's.

Gayatri sighed. She couldn't protest the idea any longer, not when the young couple was gazing at her so hopefully.

'Is this a formal proposal, Mrs Sehgal?' she asked. 'Because we don't stay at the homes of anyone but family members.'

Dolly Sehgal looked at her son with slight trepidation. The boys' side's biggest asset was that they could hold out for as long as they wanted. Most girls' families, especially upper middle-class families like the Anands, had been only too happy to wait, answering to the Sehgals' every invitation for high tea and dinner, jumping to attention at their slightest command. Making a formal proposal would mean giving up a significant portion of their power. She looked at Radhika, at her fair skin and her grey eyes. She was an unusual beauty, one that no other family in Delhi could boast.

'You have my word, Mrs Anand,' Dolly Sehgal said. 'We will announce the engagement at our Diwali party.'

Kabir grinned. A beaming smile broke out on Radhika's face.

My grandmother, ladies and gentlemen, is a badass!

Rajni

I know you're probably not going to be able to make it …

But I'm going to invite you anyway …

TO MY ENGAGEMENT IN DELHI THIS WEEK …

At the doctor's house.

OMG. WHAT?

HAPPY DIWALI TO US ALL!!!!!!

FaceTime tonight. I will wake up at 4 a.m. if you want.

Done.

14
Delhi

I wasn't sure what everyone had been on about. Delhi seemed perfectly lovely to me.

Parineeti had so far been very encouraging of Kabir and my romance, even inviting us to use her guest room if we needed to, but she had turned quickly pitiful when I told her that Naani and I were going to Delhi for Diwali.

'Better you than me,' she said, shaking her head, as we tied on our ghungroos on my last evening at Kathak.

'Why would you say that?'

Parineeti's expression became immediately guarded.

'Oh, it wasn't for me,' she said offhandedly. 'Too hot, too many people in my business. But it won't be like that for you, I'm sure.'

Parineeti didn't elaborate further, which had become part for the course for her ever since had I told her that I was engaged to her brother and soon to become a Sehgal.

Her response then, too, had been something along the lines of 'better you than me.'

I had tried to ask Kabir about it, but he hadn't been forthcoming with information either. His careful explanation was: 'Parineeti is just very independent. She doesn't like living in a big family.'

Personally, I didn't see what was not to like. The Sehgals really knew how to enjoy family life. Their palatial farmhouse was always bustling with relatives, especially this week, since there were two big occasions to be celebrated— Diwali and our engagement.

Ma (as I had been instructed to call Dolly Sehgal) and her sisters were always in some corner of the house, decorating it in some way with flowers or candles. The staff were carrying sacks of rice and sugar into the kitchen for our roka, smacking their lips in excitement at the feast to come. Cousins, aunts and uncles traipsed through the large mahogany doors in an endless parade of pink-cheeked relatives, blessing both Kabir and I, and wishing our families a very happy Diwali. I hadn't seen much of Mr Sehgal so far, but the little interaction we had had been appreciative, if not a little reserved, on his end.

I was eager, however, to win him over completely this evening.

I chose my moment perfectly. It was the day of Dhanteras, the most auspicious day as per the Hindu calendar to buy gold and silver. Chander Sehgal came home early, as per his wife's instructions, for the first puja of the Diwali season.

The Sehgals, Naani and I were in the large temple room of the farmhouse, waiting for the family priest to commence the ritual worship. Before the prayers began, I walked up to Chander Sehgal and smiled tentatively, taking care not to look at him directly, as though he was the sun and I was respectfully afraid of his great force.

'Mr Sehgal,' I said, taking the leather case out of my bag and handing it to him. 'This is a little gift from me.'

Everyone in the room was astonished. More still, when the heavy blue lid was lifted to reveal a limited-edition Rolex. Chander Sehgal stared at it in pleasant surprise. He opened his mouth to refuse, as I had anticipated, but before he could speak I said, 'Please, Mr Sehgal, you can't refuse this.'

Injecting warmth into my voice, I added, 'Today is Dhanteras. I had to buy something of value for our home. If you reject it, then our family risks bad luck.'

Out of the corner of my eye, I saw Dolly Sehgal smile.

'Your bahu isn't wrong,' the priest said.

Chander Sehgal let out a laugh and looked at his son. 'Was this your idea?'

But Kabir shook his head, both surprised and amused. 'I never know what she's up to.'

'All right, beta,' Chander Sehgal used the familial term for me for the first time. 'Help me put it on.'

I smiled and strapped the metal band around my new father-in-law's large wrist. As the clasp locked with a satisfying click, I knew that I had secured my own future with the Sehgals in one deft move.

And as I glanced at Naani's astonished expression, I saw that she had realized it, too.

❧

The festivities only increased in number and colour as Diwali dawned upon us.

My room overlooked the sprawling lawn of the farmhouse, upon which Dolly—I mean, Ma—had placed a hundred little floating candles in earthen pots. In the evening, they came alive like fireflies dancing through the grass. I tried to help with the preparations for the party, but Ma refused. She said I mustn't do anything that would tire me out, putting paid to Kabir's earlier plan of showing me around his city.

In fact, I was not allowed to leave the Sehgal mansion at all. The pollution levels in Delhi had risen to hazardous levels that were making global headlines. The salon girls and dressmakers were called home instead to beautify me for the evening. I felt like I was in a pretend game of playing princess. The only downside was that, trapped in the castle, I hadn't seen Kabir at all on the day of our engagement, ever since he left for the factory before I woke up. Nobody seemed too bothered about how his skin would react to the Delhi pollution.

'Because nobody is coming to see him tonight,' Dolly Sehgal said, shaking her head as she placed a string of Polki diamonds around my neck. Naani, who had been quietly observing from the corner, came forward now, her eye critical as ever.

'Not until the wedding,' Naani said and untied the diamonds.

Dolly Sehgal didn't even bother arguing. She had got so used to Naani admonishing her over the past week that she just nodded and left the room.

I turned to Naani, slightly annoyed. 'It was only a gift.'

'My jewellery is good enough for you,' Naani said, cutting off my defence of Dolly while taking out thick gold bangles from a black velvet pouch. I nearly gasped as I recognized them, from the description in Naani's diary.

'Jai's bangles!'

Naani raised her eyebrows at me in amazement.

'I mean, Naanu gave you these on the train, didn't he?'

'I never should have let you keep that diary,' she said, taking out a matching gold necklace and placing it around my neck. A dark emerald glistened in the centre, accentuating the light grey of my eyes.

'Where is this from?' I ask, surprised. 'Did Naanu give you this for an anniversary?'

'I bought it with my first earnings from Grace,' Naani said, drawing herself up to full height. Then her face fell slightly and she clicked her tongue, as though angry with herself. 'I should have made matching earrings for you, but I never thought this would happen so soon. We will have them by the time of the wedding, I promise.'

'Naani, you don't have to,' I began.

'I want to,' she cut short my protest and smiled at my reflection in the mirror. 'It would give me the greatest joy to have you decked up in *my* jewellery for your wedding day.'

I was so touched that I wrapped my arms around Naani's shoulders, inhaling her French perfume and trying not to sniffle as I thanked her.

'We are Khuranas, my dear girl. We take favours from no one.'

'You mean Anands,' I said, my voice thick with emotion. But Naani shook her head firmly.

'No, sweetheart. You are all Khurana. You are all me.'

I broke away from the embrace and nodded at Naani in agreement. There was nobody else I wanted to belong to.

When I emerged at the party later, I was glad I followed her advice.

As the heads of the Sehgals' overfed, over-decorated guests turned to look at me, I realized that Naani's elegant gold necklace stood out amongst the sea of diamonds and garishly heavy embroidery. Her light silk lehenga let me flit amongst the women, who were so weighed down by the burden of their densely embroidered sarees that they seemed like they were moving through soup. Everyone regarded me as an object of curiosity, wanting to get a closer look at the Sehgals' elegant young bahu.

It was great fun. Until I started interacting with Kabir's many extended relatives.

Nearly all the men owned businesses. Nearly all the women were housewives, raising children. They raised their eyebrows at each other when I told them that I worked at McKinley India. Their eyebrows shot up higher when I mentioned that I was a senior consultant in New York. After that, our conversation came to an end. I wished Kabir was there to help me out, but he was stuck at work with my father-in-law and refused to even answer my texts. I considered giving up with the uncles and aunties, but then I felt Dolly Sehgal's keen gaze on me. I knew I was still being tested. Gosh, would it ever end?

So, I persisted in making conversation with the relatives. Quickly, I became a sounding board for the uncles. If you chuckled enough at their pronouncements of economic doom and offered a clever statement or two about their industry, they were more than happy to climb on to their soapbox and prophesize for you all evening. It wasn't too different from the networking events I used to attend back in college, really.

Fortunately, Kabir and his father returned by 9 p.m., just in time for the ring ceremony. I hadn't spoken to him all day, but suddenly I was placing a ring on his finger and committing myself to him for life. It was a little nerve-wracking, to be honest.

Kabir smiled at me all through the ceremony and I was reassured for a while, but five minutes after the pictures were taken, he was whisked away by a phone call and I was alone, again, in a room full of strangers who I was also related to now.

It was all a bit strange. But nobody else, not even the Sehgals, seemed to think so. The outfits, the smiles and my ring kept shimmering.

I was trying my best to chat with Mrs Batra, my new second cousin, when Kabir suddenly appeared.

'Radhika, your grandmother wants to speak to you,' he said. I thought he would turn away and disappear again, but surprisingly he took my hand and pulled me out of the room with him.

I followed him as he led the way past his guests, putting one arm around my waist. The guests parted for us, smiling appreciatively at what a handsome couple we made. I immediately forgave him for being non-communicative all day.

Kabir pulled me through the kitchen and out on to a hidden balcony. Away from the guests and into the open smog of Delhi.

'Nobody will bother us here,' he said, pulling me close.

'And with good reason,' I said, laughing-coughing as the thick white fog of carbon dioxide enveloped us.

'Sorry, it's the only place your grandmother won't be breathing down my neck,' Kabir complained.

'Naani's just protective,' I explained. 'It comes from a place of love.'

'So does everything I do for you,' he pointed out.

I looked at him in shock. We hadn't used the word before. *Love.*

Jeez. He couldn't love me. Not in three months. *Could he?* We didn't know enough about each other yet.

A rocket whooshed up from somewhere on the main road, outside our gated community, and erupted in fiery stars in the shared sky above us.

Kabir put a hand on my cheek and caressed it lightly with his large thumb. 'Don't look so shocked,' he said. 'I love you, Radhika.'

Then why would you leave me alone to face your family? Why wouldn't you call to check up on me? Would a quick text kill you? Just to let me know when you're going to be back?

But I said none of this since Kabir was already looking at me, concerned. 'Did I say something wrong?'

I shook my head, rearranging my expression into a smile. Kabir smiled, too, his expression expectant.

I knew I should say it back to him, but my tongue couldn't form the words for some reason. It would be false if I forced it. And he would know. Nothing was worse than an insincere profession of love. As someone who had been on the receiving end of too many of the above, I could not, would not, bring myself to lie.

Kabir, however, was waiting. I settled, instead, for kissing him passionately, hoping that he would take it as a kind of promise from me, that I would make every effort to fall in love with him.

He didn't seem to mind.

15
Cards

Red boxes of mithai were placed on the table before Gayatri Anand. She wasn't sure where they had come from. She wasn't sure what she was doing there, in that large house in Delhi filled with strangers, some of whom were gambling away millions of rupees on the turn of a lucky card just two mattresses away.

Radhika had disappeared fifteen minutes after the ring ceremony. The Sehgals were busy playing host to their wealthy guests. To be fair, Dolly Sehgal had tried to introduce Gayatri to some of her friends, but the conversations had given Gayatri a splitting headache. They had so many questions about her late husband and her daughter in America that she had eventually excused herself to avoid speaking about her two least favourite subjects.

Her daughter had categorically refused to attend the engagement. On their last phone call, Mangala had simply said, 'I have no interest in seeing my daughter sold to the highest bidder.' She had implied, as usual, that Gayatri had a lower standard for women—one that encouraged their debasement.

'I've assessed the boy and the family,' Gayatri insisted. 'I wouldn't let her marry anyone who would hurt her.'

'You wouldn't even realize,' Mangala laughed, without humour.

Gayatri inhaled sharply. Her daughter always seemed to know exactly which scab to pick. Mangala had sighed and Gayatri could tell she felt some regret, not for the hurtful thought itself, but for articulating it.

'I'm sorry, Ma,' she had said tonelessly, as she had been saying for years. There was very little meaning left in the expression.

'It's all right,' Gayatri had said, equally meaninglessly. 'I didn't call to argue with you. I just thought that you would like to know that Radhika is doing well. She is much happier here than she was in America.'

Gayatri regretted the words as soon as she spoke them. She knew Mangala would take it as a personal affront—an attack on her parenting skills, or lack thereof.

'Of course, she thinks she is happy,' Mangala laughed acerbically. 'Weekly blow-dries blast one's capability of critical thinking, don't they?'

'Neither beauty nor love make a woman less capable of thought, Mangala.'

'I think you will find that what patriarchal Indian culture considers objective standards of beauty or love hamper a

woman's sense of self and the development of her identity.'
She sounded angry now. 'I refused to watch you murder
your personality to live with your husband and I refuse to
watch Radhika die a similar death. Tell me, Ma, how does
it feel to kill your own granddaughter?'

Gayatri couldn't listen to her daughter's bitterness any
longer. Especially since she blamed herself for Mangala's
cynical attitude towards life.

'I'll tell her you sent your blessings,' Gayatri had said
and cut the call.

Now, Gayatri sat alone on the Swarovski-studded white
sofa in the Sehgals' farmhouse, with a glass of champagne,
waiting for her watch to say it was 11 p.m., so she could
retire to bed without being rude. She had a piece of milk
chocolate and a Georgette Heyer novel waiting for her
upstairs. What more could she want?

Gayatri didn't notice that while she was dreaming of her
book and dessert, the red boxes of mithai in front of her had
turned into velvet boxes of jewellery. And they were being
piled up by staff she recognized from her home in Bombay.

She looked up surprised, only to see Birdy directing his
helper.

'Leave that one out. That one is for Mrs Anand,' he said
and held the box for his sweetheart.

'I didn't think you would be able to come,' Gayatri said,
waving the gift away and looking intently at her friend.

'I helped Zain set up the office in Dubai. He can handle
the rest,' Birdy said, smiling.

'I'm so glad to see you,' Gayatri said, with real feeling.

'I'm glad to make you glad.' Birdy took the box back out. 'Now, would you like to see what I've got for the bride?'

Gayatri's heart jumped. She nearly hugged Birdy. He was always lifting her out of loneliness and ensuring that her family was well-looked-after.

On an impulse, she held Birdy's hand. It fit warm and comfortably in hers. He looked at her, surprised. Gayatri allowed them a moment of intimacy in this party of strangers, where her granddaughter would ultimately be married. A love like theirs, one of friendship and depth, and knowing each other's soul like the back of your hand deserved a moment of intimacy, at the very least.

She only hoped her granddaughter was experiencing the same sensation with her fiancé. Anything less would never be enough for something as testing as marriage.

In another room, Dolly and Chander Sehgal were enjoying themselves, accepting jealous praise from their esteemed guests—the Sahanis and the Tannas—for their beautiful and sophisticated daughter-in-law.

'Your Radhika has the funniest stories about her business society at Yale,' Mr Tanna chortled. 'It's changed so much since I studied there in '72. But it's fantastic to hear. It's good to have fresh, young blood in the house, isn't it, Chander?'

Mr Tanna had never called Chander Sehgal by his first name before, nor had he ever thumped his back with such familiar gusto. Normally, the old money people maintained

a reserved silence, presented their gifts and left, leaving a
half-sipped glass of wine behind. But today, while talking to
Radhika, the Tannas had finished three glasses of Chander's
best Scotch, each!

No party of the Sehgals had ever been so successful. Not
even when Parineeti lived with them.

Pooja and Vijay Sahani had even gone so far as to invite
the Sehgals and their charming children on their cruise
through the Mediterranean for New Year's Eve, which was
an exclusive event that very few families were expected to
attend.

The Sehgals were so delighted by this attention being
paid to them that, before going to bed, Chander Sehgal
looked at his wife with more sentiment than he had exuded
in years and whispered, 'You did a beautiful job, Dolly. The
girl is perfect.'

Then he popped his two pills and slipped into a
satisfied sleep.

Dolly Sehgal could not have been more delighted. Now
all there was left to do was to ensure that Radhika and Kabir
were safely married and living in Delhi by 31 December.

❧

'What are you thinking about, Gayatri?'

They had taken Birdy's car all the way to Shri Ram
College of Commerce and were gazing at the home Gayatri
and Professor Khurana had once lived in. The spacious
bungalow had now been converted into a recreational

centre. Gayatri looked through the window, at the table tennis table that had once been the desk in her room, and shook her head.

'I'm wondering what it would have been like if—'

'If I had asked you to marry me?' Birdy offered hopefully. Gayatri smiled.

'I wouldn't have agreed, Birdy,' she said sadly. 'I wouldn't have said yes to anyone. There was too much I wanted to do at twenty-two.'

'You said yes to Jairaj.'

'I think …' she hesitated.

'I think if I had that month of engagement, if Bauji and I had the chance to meet Jai's family together, as we had planned, I would have never gone through with it. I would have understood a lot sooner what sort of man he was. What sort of upbringing he carried with him. In that very first meeting, when his father barked at me to touch his feet, I knew I had made a mistake. But by then it was too late.'

'But you did love him,' Birdy said drily. 'I saw the way you looked at him. You may have married him despite—'

Gayatri shook her head.

'The romance of him would have faded as soon as I realized that he would cost me my respect.'

❦

I gambled wildly that night. And cards were just one part of it.

The elders and children had gone to sleep, but the twenty-something crowd had stayed up, drunk on liquor and their own glamour as the young princes and princesses of Delhi. Everyone sitting on the mattress around me, I realized, was worth at least north of a million dollars, minimum. And they had all been born into it. As the kid of a psychology professor in New Haven, this wasn't the kind of company I normally kept.

But Kabir seemed perfectly at ease around them. *Of course he did*, I thought. He was an heir himself. It was just hard to think of him that way in Bombay, while he was living with his sister, driving his brother-in-law's car and spending all his time (all the time that he wasn't with me) reading up on pharmacogenomics to keep his information current. I realized, with a laugh, that somehow I had ended up as a part of the BGs (Brown Gang) that I had never interacted with at college. Rajni would be shocked if she saw me now.

'The buy-in is hundred, minimum,' Rohan, who was sitting to our left, said.

'Hundred? Rupees?' I asked.

Everyone laughed, thinking I had cracked a sarcastic joke. Kabir smiled and whispered in my ear. 'Hundred k, my love. One lakh.'

I was shocked. Both by the amount and by the easy endearment he used to address me. It came so naturally to him. *Did I have to say something similar back?*

'Don't worry about it,' he said, thinking that money was the reason for my confusion. 'Play; I'll cover if you lose.'

I tried to refuse, but he insisted. And now it was a matter of pride, so I had to play. Fortunately, it was late enough for the game to switch from Indian Flush to something I was familiar with. Texas Hold 'Em Poker.

I also realized that the young men and their girlfriends in the circle around us weren't as familiar with the game as they thought they were. They had played versions of it on Facebook, but bluffing in person, without a laptop screen, was an entirely different matter. They couldn't read people because they never had to. And they refused to fold even though their cards were crap. It was almost as though they preferred to lose their money with a carefree, defiant arrogance than make an effort to be prudent with their plays. After all, prudence was for the poor.

I won ten lakh in one night. About twelve thousand dollars.

Kabir looked at me in awe as I collected chips from the last round. His friends were laughing good-naturedly, congratulating me on my skills. I was one of the 'bros' now. I had been offered a Juul, an IOU and the keys to one guy's penthouse suite at the Oberoi.

'Are you always this lucky?' Kabir whispered.

'Fuck lucky,' I laughed. He raised his eyebrows. I couldn't blame him. I had made an active effort not to swear around him. But I was on a heady cocktail of winning and whisky. 'I've been playing Texas Hold 'Em for years.

After Naanu died, I spent a month working at a casino in Vegas—'

Perhaps that was too much truth for him. He looked less shocked and more horrified.

'Are you okay?' I asked.

'Yes,' he said slowly. 'Just don't mention this to anyone else. I'd rather not have to explain it to Ma and Dad.'

He let out an uneasy laugh, leaving me a bit unsettled. Would the Sehgals really care that much about what I did as a twenty-one-year-old to get over my grandfather's death?

'Why?' I asked, laughing slightly to lighten the tone. 'Playing cards in south Delhi is okay, but playing poker in Vegas isn't?'

Kabir just shrugged. 'I don't make the rules, babe.'

Before I could ask him what the other rules were, I was distracted. His hand was playing with the strings of my blouse. Suddenly, the argument didn't matter. We had the rest of our lives to figure out what our rules were. Right now, there was an opportunity, and a gleam in Kabir's eyes, that made me feel desired and powerful.

We disappeared into his room till dawn broke over Delhi again.

16
Home

I was back on an exercise bike after what seemed like years, pedalling with enthusiasm as I listened to a playlist of Bollywood wedding music. Any of these songs could be played at my wedding. MY WEDDING.

Thinking those words gave me a surge of energy and I pushed my legs down with even more force. The memory of Kabir, his face close to mine, laughing through the night, tumbled through my mind and propelled me forward. *He* definitely had fun. I wonder if everyone at the gym could read my thoughts, scrawled so plainly across my face and shining back at me from the large, sweaty mirror of the Otters Club.

'Having fun?'

I turned to see Zain, standing with a gorgeous young girl by his side who was dressed in a neon pink Lululemon jumpsuit.

I jumped off my bike and grinned at them both. I was in such a good mood that if I met myself, I'd want to punch me.

'Yes, living my absolute best life,' I said and then turned to the girl with my hand stuck out. 'Hi, I'm Radhika.'

'Kiara,' she said with a smile, giving me a quick once-over. She must have decided I was not a threat to her because she relaxed into a wider, more genuine smile. Normally, I bristled and tried to assert myself as worthy competition, but I was just too happy to care.

'You're getting married?'

Oh, her once-over took in my ring. Well done.

'I am,' I said, evenly.

'When is the blessed event?' Zain asked.

'12th December,' I said. 'A month before my birthday.'

'Two months from now!' Kiara squealed. 'That's so soon!'

'Suspiciously soon,' Zain glanced at my stomach, making my face colour.

'*Auspiciously* soon,' I corrected him, annoyed.

On our last day in Delhi, the family priest had visited again to match Kabir and my birth charts. He had chosen a holy date for the wedding, according to the Hindu calendar. The two options he and the planets had given us were either the first half of December this year or the second week of October, next year. Naani had wanted us to wait, but the Sehgals and I were keen to have it as quickly as possible. Too much could change in a year. I couldn't risk being unmarried and thirty. Kabir, fortunately, seemed just as keen as I was. While the priest and the elders were settling the particulars, he had leaned in and whispered, 'I'd marry you tomorrow if the gods allowed it.'

'The wedding will be in Bombay,' Naani had said firmly, as though expecting an argument. Birdy had stood behind her, nodding wordlessly. I had no idea when he had arrived the night before, but I suppose I shouldn't have been surprised. He was always around, hovering protectively like an eagle ready to swoop in should the slightest problem arise for Naani.

Naani needn't have worried though because the Sehgals were in complete agreement.

'Of course,' Dolly Sehgal had said. 'The wedding has to be at the bride's house. We're very traditional like that. None of this crass nouveau riche, destination-wedding-in-Thailand nonsense.'

Chander Sehgal had nodded, too, and my heart had started to sing at the vivid picture of my home being strung with garlands and scented with jasmine. Naani's house had never seen a wedding. Mine would be the first. That vision alone filled me with a unique excitement.

'And the reception will be at the Taj Mahal hotel,' Dolly Sehgal had continued. 'Nowhere else.'

The elders had nodded in agreement, and the conversation seemed to have come to an end. But then Chander Sehgal had cleared his throat, 'Mrs Anand,' he said, putting his cup of tea down. 'About the wedding costs.

We would like to take the responsibility of the entire thing.
We don't want to bother you with the hassle of budgeting
and whatnot at this stage of your life—'

Naani's expression had become stony with contempt.
Chander Sehgal had stopped mid-sentence, suddenly aware
that he had said something amiss.

'Mr Sehgal,' Naani had said, in a tone that could cut
glass. 'I am perfectly capable of affording the energy and the
expense of planning my granddaughter's wedding.'

'Oh, I only meant …' Chander Sehgal cleared his throat,
clearly embarrassed. 'Gayatriji, we don't want to discomfort
you in your retirement.'

'Chanderji, I'd thank you to be a gentleman and not
comment further on my age or my finances.'

I couldn't help but smirk at Chander Sehgal's chastised
expression and the quick apologies he had stuttered till we
left his house. Birdy had burst into laughter as soon as we
got into the car to get to the airport.

'You can still make a grown man blush, Gayatri,' he had
said, chuckling fondly.

'I had to provide you with some entertainment,' Naani
had said, smiling mischievously. 'You flew all the way from
Dubai.'

I turned to Zain now and asked, 'How was Dubai?' I had
remembered what Birdy had told us about his new office in
the UAE, on our way back home.

Zain smiled, glad to talk about his work as usual. 'It
was a really productive week. I'm glad I got away from

here. Diwali in Bombay would have slowed down our momentum.'

I was glad that he seemed happy and confident again. At least more so than the last time I saw him in my bedroom, while he was reading Naani's diary. There had been a pall hanging about him, a cynicism wearing down his usually laughing eyes. But that seemed to have disappeared now with the beginning of a new project. I knew what that felt like. I had filled many an emotional vacuum with productive work myself.

'Who chooses work over Diwali parties?' Kiara said, shaking her head and pouting prettily.

'My fiancé,' I laughed.

'Someone has to pay for the parties,' Zain shrugged.

'I offered to pay for the wedding,' I volunteered.

Kiara burst into laughter, but Zain looked at me, intrigued. 'Really?' There was a curious expression in his eyes.

'Don't be ridiculous,' Kiara scoffed. 'Do you know how much a wedding costs?'

'I do.'

'You can't possibly afford it.'

'I'd have to dip into my savings,' I said with a shrug, 'but I could afford it.'

'I don't mean a small "fifty people" thing—'

'I don't mean a small "fifty people" thing either,' I cut her off. Why was it so hard for her to believe the state of my finances?

Zain shook his head, interrupting us before we broke into an argument. 'It doesn't matter,' he said with finality. 'They won't let you pay for anything.'

And he was right. When I'd brought up the possibility with Naani on the plane, she hadn't even bothered dignifying the suggestion with a reply.

It was Birdy who had taken a sip of his English breakfast tea and said, 'Radhika, that is all very well, but it is out of the question.'

Our conversation had ended there, leaving me humbled at the good fortune of having such a strong and supportive family. And doubly grateful that I was going to become part of an equally strong and supportive family. The thought filled me with a joyous security that I'd never experienced before. As I looked out of the window of the plane, rising above the concrete and over the clouds and smoke of Delhi, I felt a matching, rising sensation in my gut, as though I had been sprung out of the orbit of my clutching anxieties and was now floating in a different stratosphere: one of rarefied air and unconditional love.

God, it felt good to be engaged!

It felt so good that I didn't even mind when Zain bent down to kiss Kiara goodbye as she left for Pilates.

❦

TO: radhikaanand@acceleration.mckinley.com
FROM: siddhantlodha@legal.mckinley.com
SUBJECT: Hey

Hi Rad,

Congratulations on the engagement! I saw the pictures on Facebook. You look great. Bombay's really done you good. I don't suppose you're coming back now, right?

Thanksgiving is coming up this week, and it's weird to celebrate without you. I bought those pumpkin-spiced candles you used to love. Trader Joe's has one-dollar deals again. But I'm sure you've got too much going on to care about Trader Joe's or Thanksgiving.

Well, I guess I'll see you at the next global corporate retreat now. Congrats again!

Siddhant.

There could not have been a better start to my day. It took all my maturity not to reply to Siddhant. I could have composed a disgustingly self-satisfied email to him. Something along the lines of 'Well, actually, I do have too much going on to think about Trader Joe's. Or you.'

Since I had risen above and was in the rarefied stratosphere of security, as I mentioned before, I didn't bother replying. Plus, Padmini and Mukti were in my cabin, sweating copiously despite the air conditioner running on full power. I forgot about the email and turned to their aggrieved faces.

'It's going to be fine,' Mukti said repeatedly to her older colleague who was exhaling frantically.

'I didn't think there'd be so many of them,' Padmini whimpered.

I didn't either, to be very honest. It was a bit of a shock to me to find twelve men and two women seated in our conference room, drinking bottles of Bisleri water and waiting for Padmini and Mukti to begin their pitch.

'Are you sure you don't want to present, Radhika?' Mukti looked dubiously at her partner, who was chugging from a bottle of water with a ferocity usually reserved for vodka.

'Or maybe if you could just be in the room?' Padmini pleaded, nervously mangling the plastic in her hand. I shook my head.

'I have a call with Mr Goldenblatt's accounts team today,' I lied.

'But that won't take all afternoon, will it?'

'Padmini,' I said firmly. 'This is a good strategy, and you've practised well. Do you agree with me?'

'Yes, eleven times,' she said, nodding. 'We practised it eleven times.'

'We can win them over,' Mukti added, working up her confidence. 'I know we can.'

'I don't want you to win them over.'

Mukti stopped speaking, shocked. Padmini moaned and picked up another water bottle to chug from. Both of them stared at me as though I had clipped the heels of their new Steve Maddens. I smiled at them in my most reassuring manner.

'I don't want you to charm them, or cajole them, or beg them to take you on as consultants, okay? I want you to walk into that room with this great strategy and behave as though you're doing them a favour by telling them how you plan to increase their profits.'

'You want us to tell them the entire strategy?' Mukti panicked. 'They'll just use it then. They won't hire us!'

'They will hire you for this project and the next,' I said. But the women looked unconvinced.

'They aren't buying the strategy, girls. They're buying your time, and your brains,' I insisted.

'I want you to be fearless when you walk into that conference room. You don't care about winning their business. You don't care about them stealing your strategies. There are enough strategies and ideas living in your brilliant brains. You're their geese with the golden eggs. If they're smart, they'll realize this and use your consulting services for the rest of their time in India.'

'If they don't,' I added after a pause, with a cool shrug, 'they aren't going to make the kind of money they could if only they had listened to you.'

My team didn't say much else, but as I finished speaking I saw that the panic on their faces had receded and a promising light had begun to glimmer in their eyes.

'You're ready,' I said, 'to expand their presence in the Indian market.'

The girls strode out of my cabin, heads held high atop their heels.

I drank a whole bottle of water. I was not afraid in the least.

❧

My phone buzzed with texts from Kabir, but I refused to touch it till I had completed the goals I'd set for the day. I knew that once I began replying, I would dissolve into daydreams of lehengas and honeymoons, completely sacrificing my productive hours. I was sure he would understand, since he never answered his phone during crucial business hours either.

I was doing so well as far as my to-do list was concerned that I could not stop now. I had met my analysts, gone over Mr Goldenblatt's reports and over the quarterlies of our other American holdings. But now, I was allowing myself the luxury of thinking. Of indulging in a train of thought that had nothing to do with work or the wedding.

Something Zain had said this morning was niggling at me: *someone has to pay for the parties.*

Kiara thought it absurd that she or I would ever be expected to pay for our indulgences. Yet men, like Zain and Birdy and even Chander Sehgal, thought it obvious that they were responsible for footing the bill because they had the greater access to earning the greatest amounts of wealth. I loved their confidence in their own capability to earn, and to pay, to keep society turning in a constant torque of commerce.

I wished I could inject some of that faith in Padmini, Mukti, and even Kiara.

If Padmini had Zain's confidence, she would quit her job as an analyst and move back to Poona with her husband to start their restaurant business. If Mukti had Chander Sehgal's ruthlessness, she would demand greater responsibility and a higher salary from Mr Bhatia. She would have ensured that he knew her name within a week of her working at McKinley. If Kiara had ever been told that she had to earn her own independence, like Birdy must have been told at a young age, perhaps she wouldn't think it so ridiculous that she could pay for her own wedding.

I realized how lucky I was to grow up in a household of independent women. Mum had fed me such a steady diet of female agency that I had never believed myself incapable of doing anything. Except, perhaps, getting married.

I wished I could feed the same diet to the women who hadn't tasted it here. I wished I could dissolve on their tongues every triumphant flavour of authority and ownership. I wanted to tell them what I had learnt from watching my mother and grandmother—that they already had within them the tools that they needed to soar in this unforgiving world.

I wondered if I could—

My train of thought was interrupted by Mr Bhatia, who swung open my door and said, 'Adobe signed the contracts on the spot. Congratulations.'

I jumped out of my swivel chair. Padmini and Mukti emerged from behind Mr Bhatia, their faces beaming. Mukti had sweat patches under her arms, but her face was radiant with success. I laughed as I realized that she looked a little like I did after a pitch.

'Congratulations!' I said, taking their hands in mine and shaking them with as much vigour as I was allowed in a professional setting. If Mr Bhatia wasn't here, I'd have hugged them and popped open cans of Diet Coke.

'Will you join us for lunch?' Mr Bhatia asked.

'Absolutely!' I said.

Nearly all the employees turned to look our way as we followed Mr Bhatia into his large cabin, which overlooked the Arabian Sea. I realized that here it was a rare privilege for employees, even heads of departments, to be asked to lunch with the MD. And for junior analysts like Padmini and Mukti, it was as unique a token of appreciation as the Pope inviting a common parishioner to the Vatican for tea.

Mr Bhatia, however, was as genial as ever. As his office staff set the table before us, with three types of salad and two rice dishes from the Chinese restaurant in our building, he praised my team for their original thinking with the Adobe pitch.

'Brilliant strategy,' he said. 'I would have never thought of giving free trials to Bollywood's editors as a viable option to get them all to switch from Apple's editing software to Adobe's.'

'It was Ms Anand's idea,' Padmini offered. 'We only collected the data from efficacy groups to corroborate her strategy.'

'But it was your presentation of the idea that closed the deal,' I pointed out.

Mr Bhatia regarded us with an expression of fascination. 'I love this team,' he said. 'Radhika, I may not be willing to let you go back to New York.'

I laughed. 'I may not be willing to go either, Mr Bhatia. I'm starting to enjoy myself here.'

As I said these words, I realized how true they were. Even through the excitement of the engagement, I'd been looking forward to coming back to Bombay. To my office and my analysts.

'You won't be going back now, will you?' Padmini asked, surprised. 'Or will he move to New York with you?'

'We haven't figured out the logistics yet,' I said, smiling coolly and trying to convey to them to hush.

'Really?' Mukti asked wide-eyed. 'You didn't discuss it before the engagement?'

I grimaced and Mukti stopped talking immediately. But it was too late.

'Engagement?' Mr Bhatia's eyes immediately dropped to my right hand. He did a double take when he saw the size of the diamond.

I must speak to Kabir about changing the ring to something less ugly.

'Congratulations! Did you meet him in Bombay?' Mr Bhatia asked.

'I did. But he lives in Delhi at the moment.'

Mr Bhatia's face fell suddenly. This is what I was afraid of. I wanted to break the news to Mr Bhatia myself. After Kabir and I had figured out our living arrangements.

'So you will be leaving us then?'

'No. I mean, I don't think so. We haven't discussed who's moving where yet,' I said. Personally, I would make a big push for Bombay. Chander Sehgal was thinking of opening a new export office in Panvel, only an hour from where I currently lived. Kabir could easily work from there. In fact, he would be glad to get out from under his father's thumb. It would be an ideal existence. We could buy an apartment of our own in the same building as Parineeti and Rajat, live only ten minutes away from Naani and Birdy, and visit the Sehgals every couple of months for one of Dolly Sehgal's big parties.

'Kabir loves Bombay,' I said. 'And he's very supportive of my work.'

Mr Bhatia shot me a pitiful smile.

'Of course,' Padmini said, nodding a little too vigorously. 'Here, have you tried this mango pickle?'

Mukti avoided looking at me.

I no longer had an appetite.

❧

Kabir

Hey! Where are you? Been trying to get thru all morning.

Everything okay?

Miss you, babe. Call me ASAP. Having a hell of a day with Dad.

Hi, sorry! Have been stuck in meetings all day!

Am so sorry you're having a tough day.

Wish I could do something to make it better.

> Won't be home for another 2 hours at least :(

> Call u at 10? After Kathak?

> Busy, busy girl.

> Can't wait till you're here.

What was I thinking? I turned and turned, letting my feet jangle and fill the gharana with the sound of bells. Of course, a family like the Sehgals would expect me to move to Delhi, to live close to them. After all, Kabir was the heir to the biggest pharmaceutical business in the country. He had to live close to the main factory. Mine wasn't a legacy; it was a job. I could find another one in Delhi. Perhaps it wouldn't be such a bad thing. We would work hard during the day and enjoy each other's company in our home every night. On Friday nights, we'd go out for dinner.

On Sundays, we'd have delicious biryani lunches with the Sehgals at their farmhouse.

I took another turn, but I had gone off beat now. I tried to catch the percussionist's rhythm, slowing my feet down to match my tatkal to his playing, but somehow my timing was off. My steps were too late or too quick, and the bells on my ankles became conspicuously cacophonous, ruining Parineeti's perfect melody and underlining each mistake of mine. She threw a confused glance at me. I stopped, ashamed. *Best to clear my head and begin again, instead of ruining the dance for her too*, I thought.

'Is everything okay?' Parineeti asked me, as I sat down to catch my breath.

'My mind is just ...' I made a waving motion with my hand. She nodded and sat next to me.

'I missed you in Delhi,' I said, smiling at her. But Parineeti didn't smile back.

'Rajat prefers spending Diwali in Bombay.'

'It wasn't just Diwali, Pari, it was your brother's engagement, too.'

'We'll be there for the wedding,' she shrugged.

The hurt showed on my face because Parineeti's expression softened.

'Oh, Radhika, I'm sorry,' she said, squeezing my hand. 'It's more complicated than you think. I just—I don't like going where Rajat isn't welcome.'

'What do you mean?' I asked, confused.

She sighs. 'Mum left his name off the invitation she sent us for your engagement. It was addressed only to me.' Parineeti scowled.

'Parineeti!' I looked at her, incredulous. 'It must have been an oversight. Everything about the engagement party was decided so last-minute. In fact, I WhatsApped most of my friends the news!'

'Were the Tannas there?' Parineeti's tone was sharp, nothing like I'd heard before.

'Yes,' I said.

'And the Khers? And the Bajajs? And, of course, the Sahanis?' She had a bitter smile on her face. 'All six of them?'

'They were,' I said slowly. 'But I don't see what that—'

'It's just surprising that not one member of the fancy families was forgotten, but her own son-in-law was too hard to remember for Mum.' Parineeti shook her head apologetically.

I was about to defend Dolly Sehgal, but her daughter won't let me.

'Rajat may not have cobwebs forming over his money, like the Tannas and all those people, but he does have self-respect, Radhika. And I would never make him visit a home where he is considered an "oversight".'

I stared at Parineeti, astonished. The Sehgals hadn't said anything to me so far, nothing that made it seem like their son-in-law wasn't welcome in their home. I realized then that I hadn't been initiated into the family as fully as I had thought. *What else didn't I know about the people I would be living with?*

'I'm sorry, Parineeti,' I floundered. 'I had no idea—'

She cut me off with a short, forgiving chuckle. 'It isn't anything to do with you, Radhika. I promise to be there for every function of the wedding. And even do a Kathak dance number at the sangeet.' She gave me a warm hug.

I smiled and hugged her back.

'Your husband will always be welcome in my home in Delhi,' I said. 'He will be the guest of honour.'

Parineeti broke away from the embrace and looked at me with a mixture of amusement and pity. 'Radhika, you're not going to have your own home till my parents are dead.'

17
Invitation

The Sehgals

**Request your presence at
the wedding of their son**

Kabir

with

Radhika

Granddaughter of

Mrs Gayatri Anand

And the late

Chief Justice Jairaj Anand

'What do you think, beta?' Dolly Sehgal asked me on a FaceTime call, as I turned over the invitation samples that had arrived at my home. They were not silver embossed, as I had always wanted, but gold embossed. Each of them came with a large box of home-made mithai with 18-carat gold dust on it. I picked the least ornate ones out. Well, at least bronze was better than shiny gold. I wondered if I could somehow make the band of my ring bronze.

'I like these,' I said, hoping she would give the phone back to Kabir. But it wasn't before another fifteen minutes of discussing lehenga versus sari options (also shiny gold) that I got to talk to my fiancé.

'Nice, aren't they?' he said, referring to the invitations. He looked so chuffed that I didn't want to tell him how garish they were. 'The coffee at the reception will also have 18-carat gold on it!'

I managed a weak smile.

'I don't think consuming that much metal can be good for our digestive systems.'

Kabir shrugged. 'Nobody's actually going to drink it. But it has to be served.'

'Why?'

'It's a status thing, my love. People expect to have gold coffee as a menu option.' Kabir laughed. 'You will get the hang of it soon enough.'

'When I move to Delhi, you mean?'

'Exactly,' Kabir nodded, a big grin spreading across his face. 'I can't wait!'

It was sweet, really, that he was looking forward to living with me. But it was also odd that we had never spoken about it. He had just taken it for granted that I would move to wherever he was, because I had agreed to an arranged marriage with a boy who lived in Delhi. I wished Naani had mentioned this on her list of adjustments.

'Mom will show you the ropes,' he said. 'She's really impressed with you, by the way. Apparently, Mr Sahani was raving about you at the engagement. So were the Tannas.'

'Who?' I asked, trying to recall the many, many people I had made small talk with that night.

Kabir chuckled at my ignorance. 'They're one of the oldest families in Delhi. A little like royalty. And they've invited us on their yacht for New Year's!'

'Oh,' I was surprised.

Kabir's grin faded. 'What's wrong? Aren't you excited?'

I hated to be the one to dampen his enthusiasm. Still, I had to say something. Suppressing my desires now would set a disastrous precedent for our marriage.

'Hadn't we decided to go on our honeymoon then?' I asked gently. 'I thought we could do a fun trip around North America—spend New Year's in New York, watch the ball drop at Times Square. And then take a trip to New Haven. You could see where I grew up!'

I hadn't thought this through before, but now that I had said it, I felt such a tug of nostalgia for the life I had left behind that I realized I wanted this very badly. I wanted

Kabir to see all of who I was, and how I came to be his wife, before we started our journey together.

But he just shook his head and all my ideas away. 'Babe, this is the Tannas' cruise. Everyone's going. We've already accepted.'

'We have?' *By 'we', he surely couldn't mean …*

'Mom and Dad have been invited, too, of course. It's for all the peer families of Delhi.'

I could no longer keep the horror out of my voice or expression. 'We're spending our honeymoon on a boat with your parents?'

'It's not like that, sweetheart,' he said, with a shake of his head. But he was unwilling to offer any other explanation.

I was getting tired of his condescension.

'Kabir, let's talk about this later,' I said, still trying to be diplomatic.

'Babe, there's nothing to talk about,' his jaw had jutted out in an annoyingly arrogant fashion. I did a double take. His voice reminded me too much of Mr Maruti and Mr Gomes. Of every idiot suit who had tried to shut me down in a meeting.

'You know what,' I snapped, 'let's talk about this now instead. And we will talk about it because I'm going to be your partner, not just some girl you can dictate to—'

Kabir looked surprised. I had never taken *a tone* with him before. 'I'm not dictating to you, Radhika! Jesus—'

Fortunately, before things could escalate, a familiar voice called out to me from downstairs. Both Kabir and I stopped to listen. The voice kept calling, rising up the stairs with accompanying footsteps treading closer to my room. Both our faces lost all hostility instantly.

I rearranged my expression into a pleasant smile to greet my grandmother, but it wasn't Naani who entered my room and shot a polite grimace at my fiancé.

It was my mother.

❧

Gayatri couldn't remember the last time she had seen her daughter and granddaughter in her house before Christmas. In the middle of the academic and financial year! It had seemed like a wonderful trick of light.

Even if they were currently being combative, as they reluctantly passed the cereal bowls and milk between each other, Gayatri's heart was full of gratitude. So full that she had even allowed them to eat the awful American muesli Mangala had brought back for dinner. It seemed to be the only thing the girls agreed upon.

'So,' Mangala said, scattering walnuts into her bowl before passing the jar to Radhika. 'The one on FaceTime, that was the boy?'

'That's my soon-to-be husband, yes,' Radhika replied, reluctantly taking her mother's trail mix of raisins and seeds.

'He's very—'

Radhika cut her mother off with a short laugh.

'You can't have an opinion on him after a two-minute chat!'

Mangala looked at her daughter with an infuriatingly patient expression. 'I was going to say that he is very tall.'

'Oh.' Radhika rolled her eyes. 'Sure, that's what you were going to say. But yes. He is very tall.'

'And very north Indian,' Mangala's voice rose slightly.

'You're generalizing, Professor Anand,' Radhika warned.

'Would anyone like a paratha?' Gayatri asked to cut the tension. Mangala shook her head, but Radhika nodded, enthusiastically shoving the bowl away.

'Yes please, Naani,' she shot a sharp glance at her mother. 'I've eaten cereal for dinner for too many years now.'

Mangala narrowed her eyes.

'So, you've turned your grandmother into your maid.'

'I have not.'

'Don't be ridiculous, Mangala,' Gayatri said. 'I like doing this.'

Gayatri gleefully took out the bowl of cold dough she had in her fridge for emergencies like these. She genuinely liked taking care of her granddaughter. She got to lavish on her the affection that her daughter had always refused. Gayatri rolled out a ball of dough and laid it flat on the stove. The scent of roasting ghee and spiced cauliflower filled the kitchen. Mangala's stomach groaned in response. Radhika looked at her mother and smirked.

'You can have one, too, you know,' she offered, but Mangala shook her head contemptuously.

'Don't get used to this, Radhika. Try and—'

'—be independent,' Radhika rolled her eyes and stubbornly stuck her plate out towards Gayatri for the paratha to be put on it. 'Mom, I doubt Gandhi rallied for independence as much as you.'

Gayatri couldn't help but snort. She should be concerned, she knew. She should stop them from fighting. But really, she was just so darned happy at having both her girls in her kitchen, trading banter, that all she wanted to do was sit down and drink in the scene before her.

'I'm just warning you not to get used to it,' Mangala said. 'Or adjusting to life will be tougher when you go back.'

'Who's going back?' Radhika asked with a shrug.

Mangala's lips went pale. Gayatri braced herself. Mangala had a blackened idea of India, one that was smothered in the tar of patriarchy. She didn't think that any Indian man, living in India, could be as liberal as she was. According to her, marrying an Indian man was bad enough, but living with him in India was suicide.

'What do you mean?' she asked slowly.

'Mom, I'm getting married. To a Delhi boy. So, I'll have to live with him. In Delhi.'

'What?' Gayatri turned to her granddaughter.

Radhika shrugged, her grey eyes steeled with defiance.

'But you're not quitting your job, are you?' Gayatri asked, concerned.

'I'll get another one,' Radhika shrugged again.

'Absolutely not!' Mangala yelled. Both Gayatri and Radhika were surprised. Losing her temper was not Mangala's way. She preferred cool-headed condescension as a tool to wear her opponent down. But now she yelled with a desperation that Gayatri hadn't heard in years.

'You can't be serious about this! You can't give up your income and move in with people you barely know in the rape capital of the country. Marital rape isn't even a criminal offence here! Radhika, do you know what Delhi is like? How unsafe the streets are for women—'

'I'm not going to be living on the streets,' Radhika cut her mother off. 'I'm going to live with my in-laws, the Sehgals. I'd like to see what it's like to have a proper family for a change. I think it will be fun.'

Gayatri shot a concerned glance at her daughter, expecting her to look stung, but Mangala only laughed.

'Ma,' she turned to Gayatri. 'Please tell her how much fun it is to be a housewife.'

Gayatri was shocked. They had an agreement. That Mangala would never tell Radhika about Gayatri's marriage.

'Tell her what fun living with your in-laws after marriage is.'

'*Enough,* Mangala.'

Gayatri's tone was so sharp that her fifty-year-old daughter looked ashamed of herself.

It would be delicate work, Gayatri realized, having both her girls together, with their different ideas about Gayatri's life driving their conversations into dangerously volatile territory.

First, she addressed the older one, whom she had robbed of her innocence much too soon. 'Mangala, Radhika has made her decision as an adult. We must respect it.'

Then she turned to the younger one, whose romanticism she had sheltered, perhaps a little too fiercely. 'Sweetheart, we only want the best for you. We will make suggestions when you ask for them. I only hope you are sure, in your heart and in your rational mind, that this decision, to live in Delhi with strangers, where you know nobody and have no network, is the best for you.'

Radhika looked appropriately hesitant.

'I want to meet him,' Mangala said, sitting down and sticking her spoon into her bowl with such force that the milk splashed on to the counter.

'Fine,' Radhika said, picking up her paratha and ripping off a piece with her teeth.

'Before the wedding,' Mangala insisted, shoving another spoon into her mouth.

'Fine,' Radhika said, her mouth full.

Gayatri bit her lip, trying to rein in laughter. It was going to be a long and lovely winter.

Kabir

My mum wants to meet you.

I'll fly down this week.

Because I love you

Nice try

Still not spending my honeymoon with your parents.

Lol! We'll see.

18
Business

A cup of creamy coffee was placed in my freshly manicured hand. I grinned as Padmini and Mukti took a sip from their mugs and licked their lips in satisfaction. I finally cottoned on to the fact that they were refusing my offers of a post-work drink not because they didn't like me, but because they didn't drink. So, I had decided to treat them for a job well done by bringing them to Grace after work. I thought the evening was more of a success than chugging alcohol at a noisy bar. Mukti looked like she was in heaven as Priscilla massaged oil into the roots of her hair. And Naani seemed only too happy to have my friends over, since it gave her an excuse to escape Mum's accusatory sniping at home, which went on well into last night, piercing my sleep through the thin walls of our adjoining rooms.

'I knew I should have never let her come here! Six months of living with you—'

'And she's *much* happier. Surely you can see that she's blooming—'

'In Bombay, Ma! She doesn't realize what she's in for in Delhi—'

'Nothing is going to happen to her!'

'Really, Ma? *Whose name is on the door?*'

There was silence, and then Naani's voice had sunk to a fierce whisper.

'Mangala. You will never, *ever*, speak to me that way again.'

At this point, I had put my headphones on, played 'Moonlight Sonata' as loud as I could and let Beethoven lull me to sleep.

'Show me your feet,' Naani said, coming over to Padmini now, who happily displayed her pink painted toes for inspection. Naani nodded, satisfied.

'Lovely. Would you girls like a blow-dry, too? You can waltz into your office with glamorous, straight hair tomorrow.'

Padmini and Mukti's faces lit up, but they shook their heads politely. 'No, no, thank you.'

'Nonsense,' Naani said. 'Radhika has to get it done for a special dinner tonight. You wouldn't leave now and let her go through it alone, would you?'

I smiled inwardly. There was no special dinner; just Birdy uncle coming over as usual, but I had to hand it to Naani. She had grace like nobody else I knew.

'She's lovely,' Mukti whispered, as Naani sashayed away to welcome another client.

'She is,' I agreed. 'She knows how to make women happy. That's why this salon is such a success.'

'She does more than just make women happy,' Priscilla chimed in as she kneaded my back. I looked at her surprised. Soft-spoken Priscilla rarely commented on the conversations of the clients.

'Mrs Anand took a chance on each of us,' Priscilla continued, a mildly strident note in her voice. 'I used to be a maid in her neighbour's bungalow. Anandi and Jiya are orphans. None of us had formal beauty training when we started here. Mrs Anand paid for styling lessons and English tuitions. She trained us and gave us a job with good pay and good hours. No girl who has joined has ever quit.'

I stared at her, surprised that this was the first time I was hearing about this. As I looked at Naani, speaking in gentle tones to a young girl with frizzy hair, I realized that I had never asked her about how she started her business. I always thought Grace was a distraction, something to keep her busy after Naanu died. But no, there was always a greater, well-thought-out purpose behind her actions. With this beauty salon, Naani had created a community all by herself.

That was the difference, I realized, between me and the two analysts sitting before me. I had inherited a legacy of agency from my fantastically brave grandmother, one that allowed me to believe myself to be capable of achieving anything I pledged my mind and discipline to. Padmini and Mukti would be their family's first generation of female bravery. Their granddaughters would benefit from the chances they were taking.

What a difference one woman's faith in herself could make, I thought, as I looked at the salon of securely employed women around me.

What lucky, lucky women we were, to be connected to Gayatri Anand.

Kabir

I should probably start looking for jobs in Delhi, right?

McKinley doesn't operate out of there, but PCC, and a couple of other consulting firms, are in Noida, I think ...

God! Noida is miles away, babe.

> In any case, there's no rush.

> You could also just take some time off if you like.

> Ah! Taking time off isn't really my thing TBH.

'Radhika, it's rude to text at the dining table,' Mangala scolded her daughter. Gayatri bit her tongue to stop herself from scolding her daughter. It was obvious that Mangala wasn't annoyed about Radhika texting. She was irritated that Radhika and Gayatri had spent the day at the salon without her; she had been spoiling for a fight ever since they had returned, pink-faced and polished.

'It's all right, Mangala,' Birdy said graciously. 'Tell me, my dear girl, how is your research going? I watched you on the child psychology panel in Boston—'

Mangala's frown faded immediately, replaced swiftly with sharp delight.

'Were you in Boston, Birdy?' she asked eagerly.

'Oh no. But Zain live ... what's it called? Oh yes. He live-streamed it for me. Isn't that a funny word for the thing?

Stream. As though a river of thought is running from you to me. Hah!'

'It is funny,' Mangala said, but Gayatri could see that her eyes had brightened with the spark of a child who had been starved for attention. Mentally, Gayatri kicked herself. Why hadn't she live-streamed Mangala's conference?

'Anyway, it was very enjoyable,' Birdy continued. 'Your paper was the most intelligently presented. You should think of turning it into another book—'

'I am,' Mangala nodded, squeezing Birdy's hand and scooping fresh fig ice cream into her bowl. *Bless Birdy*, Gayatri thought. He could induce a good mood even in her prickly daughter. Surprisingly, it was Radhika who was unusually sombre that evening. Perhaps she was just tired of being around the old folk.

'Is Zain still at work?' Gayatri asked Birdy.

'In a sense,' Birdy said. 'He's working from home tonight.'

'That's quite late,' Mangala said, but she had an approving look in her eye. *If Mangala had it her way, people would work till they were numb to every other sensation life had to offer,* Gayatri thought. *Did her daughter ever have fun?*

'He has a video call with some investors in Dubai. They want Zain to do a workshop with some of their younger entrepreneurs, those who have never headed a business before.'

'Wow,' Mangala looked impressed. 'So, Zain will be training people in leadership?'

'Something like that.' Birdy nodded, his cheeks pink with pride. *As they should be*, Gayatri thought. Zain, considering how he had grown up, had exceeded all their expectations with his tireless work ethic. He definitely had more Birdy in him than either of his layabout parents.

'He must be quite a leader himself then,' Mangala said with a smile. 'Is he excited?'

'He's doing it more as a favour to one of our investors. You may have heard of her ... Dipa Ghanshyamdas?'

'No way!' Radhika exclaimed suddenly. Gayatri, Birdy and Mangala turned to look at her. It was the first time the girl had spoken all evening.

'Really, Birdy uncle?' she asked, her eyes intent with excitement. 'Zain is working with Dipa Ghanshyamdas?'

'Uh, yes, my dear,' Birdy said, his expression slightly unnerved.

'Who is she?' Gayatri asked.

'How have you not heard of her?' Mangala laughed superiorly. 'She's a leadership icon.'

'Naani, she was awarded businesswoman of the year by *Forbes*,' Radhika said, slightly breathless. 'But in the acceptance speech, she asked *Forbes* to stuff it.'

'Why?' Gayatri was curious now.

Radhika immediately typed 'DIPA G BUSINESSWOMAN OF THE YEAR' into her phone. A video popped up and everyone at the dinner table watched the tiny screen as a silver-haired lady in a violet silk gown strode up to a podium. She raised the award in the air and spoke in a clear, commanding voice.

'While it is not untrue that I am a fantastic businesswoman, I cannot accept this award.' Dipa Ghanshyamdas's voice bellowed through Gayatri's dining room.

'I refuse to participate in this ceremony where business is gendered. I refuse to be seated at this consolatory children's table of awards. I have earned as much, if not a greater revenue in the last sixty years, than most *businessmen* of the year. And I have definitely broken more social barriers in my career in India, North America and the Middle East.'

The audience and the presenters, who had been politely chuckling, fell silent. Gayatri and Birdy exchanged glances. Radhika, however, was mouthing the words.

'Your magazine would do well to recognize the achievements of professionals, not men or women. If you want to invent a category, make it business*person* of the year. And for the love of God, have at least one woman on the jury.'

There was a stunned silence for a moment, and then the audience erupted into cheers and laughter. Radhika and Mangala also began chortling with glee.

Gayatri couldn't remember the last time she had seen them both laugh at the same thing. She wished she could open her eardrums wider and absorb every note of the lovely, chiming sound.

'I can't believe Zain gets to work with her,' Radhika said, her eyes sparkling. 'And on leadership training!'

Gayatri smiled at her granddaughter, at the ravenous look that had appeared on her face. She knew that expression from looking in the mirror all through her twenties. It was the bold determination of a leader.

Birdy must have noticed it too, because he looked at Radhika appreciatively and said, 'If you're interested, Radhika, you should speak to Zain about it. He may be able to connect you with Dipa and—'

Before any of them could react, Radhika got up from the table, kissed Birdy's cheek and ran out the door.

❧

Perhaps this qualified as stalking, but the thought didn't cross my mind as I knocked on Zain's bedroom door.

He opened the door, wearing an odd combination of a blazer and boxers.

'Just one second, Dipa,' he said into his AirPods casually before turning to me. 'Radhika? I'm on a call—'

'I know—'

'If this is Mamu asking about dinner, I'm not that hungry—'

'It's not dinner. It's about your call. Finish up and then can we talk about it?'

'Oh-k-aay?' he looked at me very confused for a moment and then chuckled, shaking his head. 'It's never a dull moment with you, is it?'

'I hope not.'

As Zain finished his Skype call, I waited on the sofa by his bed and began typing out the ideas I'd been mulling over all day. Ever since I had started working with Padmini and Mukti, I had been feeling a sense of purpose that I hadn't experienced before. My brain had never pulsated with so much excitement before as it did now, after getting my colleagues to take a chance on themselves.

At Grace today, I discovered where I got this from. Naani had been doing it for ages. She helped every woman who came to her salon, and all the women who were employed there, too. She didn't just decorate them from the outside, she encouraged them till they were proud, not just of their appearance but of their person, of their hopes and ambitions, which must once have felt so foolish and impossible.

Didn't Parineeti tell me that when she had first come to Bombay after her marriage, and was struggling to give her specialization examinations, Naani had insisted upon her coming in for a pedicure every day with her textbooks and get her toes painted while she studied? After Parineeti's pedicure, Naani would make her tell her why she wanted to be a cardio surgeon, every single day.

'It's almost like she forced me to want it more. She forced me not to give up on my dream, or myself,' Parineeti had said, grinning. 'I'd have been just another GP in a clinic without your Naani. That would have been fine. But it wouldn't have been this.'

It's funny how much a few kind words, consistently repeated, can actually manifest change, isn't it?

I wanted to do the same thing. I wanted to help the fantastic hard-working girls of Bombay who secretly harboured big dreams but were afraid of voicing them. I wanted to help them articulate these dreams to the right investors. I wanted to turn skilled Indian women into leaders.

A part of my brain was probably subconsciously working on this idea since the time I arrived in Bombay, because it lit up like a Christmas tree the minute Birdy mentioned what Zain was working on, and who he was working with. And even though it was late at night, and I hadn't fully realized my ideas yet, I had run over to his house. Some things were too important, and too exciting, to wait for business hours to commence.

Zain turned to me now, finally signing off from his call. I was grinning.

'I have an idea, and I need a favour,' I said. He looked at me, scratching his golden beard.

I half-expected him to laugh or to dismiss me. But he didn't.

'All right,' he said, his eyes dancing. 'Let's hear both.'

❦

An hour and a half later, we were both sitting at his work desk with the outlines we had made for the project. It was titled The Queen Network. 'Queen' was my idea. 'Network' was his.

I was hesitant while explaining the idea to him; I didn't know if he would see the business potential in creating a leadership workshop for Indian women. After all, most men didn't understand the internal limitations women possessed, the snarky voices in our head that kept telling us we were too stupid, too ugly and too inefficient to speak up in a meeting, or sign up for a scary exam, or start a business of our own.

But Zain listened patiently and passed no opinion as I rambled on. 'We could go to schools and colleges and tie up with the HR departments of different companies to train their female employees. Women would attend workshops with industry leaders; they could network with each other at social events. We could even help them improve their CVs and their public-speaking skills.'

When I finally ran out of steam, Zain smiled at me in a disarmingly kind way. It wasn't his usual guarded grin. It made him seem less like a player and more like a person.

'These are all big, interesting ideas, Radhika,' he said slowly. 'And it could be very lucrative if you manage to wrangle important businesswomen to speak at these events.'

'But?' I raised an eyebrow at him.

He cracked a slight smile. 'But how are you going to afford this? We don't have the network or infrastructure to make this happen.'

'I know,' I kept my gaze fixed on him as I said, 'but the friend you were just talking to does.'

Recognition dawned on Zain's face and something in his expression hardened.

'Oh,' he said. 'That's why you shared the idea with me. Because I can connect you to the MD of Ghanshyamdas Capital.'

'Yes,' I nodded, confused by the dryness of his tone. 'Is something wrong? If you'd like to be involved in the project, I'd love to offer you equity—'

'No,' Zain cut me off. 'I have too much on my plate as it is. I'll connect you with Dipa first thing tomorrow morning.'

His voice was friendly but flat. The initial warmth in his eyes had vanished, replaced by a guarded cynicism. I wondered what happened to make Zain spring from trusting to wary at just a moment's notice.

I rose to leave, thinking our conversation to be over, when he commanded in the same flat tone, 'Where do you think you're going? Get your laptop and Google slides out.'

I stared at him. 'Why?'

'Do you want to be unprepared while trying to persuade Dipa Ghanshyamdas that you can run a leadership workshop?'

He had a point.

'Wait,' I looked at him, shocked. 'You want to help me make this?'

'If I'm referring you, I have to make sure your work is of a certain standard, or it will damage my credibility.'

Patronizing as his tone was, there was a twitch in his mouth that let me know he was only teasing. I threw a pillow at him and disappeared home to return with my laptop and a box of Swiss Muesli I stole from Mum's suitcase while she was in the study.

'I brought snacks.'

'I don't snack—' Zain began, but then he stopped. His eyes lit up when he saw the red box of cereal in my hand. He watched, riveted, as I poured the toasted oats, raisins and walnuts into a bowl.

'Where did you get that from?' He sounded excited.

'Mum brought it from the States.'

Zain snatched the box and started pouring some for himself in a bowl.

'I thought you didn't snack,' I raised an eyebrow at him.

'This,' he lifted the bowl for dramatic effect, 'this isn't a snack. This is the food of the gods.'

I wanted to laugh, but I matched his deadpan expression. 'And why is that?'

'This cereal was my lunch and dinner for every day of high school,' Zain said, looking at the bowl with fond nostalgia, 'And I was a god then. Now I'm a mere mortal.'

I rolled my eyes. 'Your mum didn't cook either?'

Zain shot me a careful glance. 'No, not really.'

It was then that I realized that I knew nothing about Zain's parents, or his life before he came to live with Birdy.

'Was it just you and your mum?'

'Yep,' he said with a curt nod.

'Me too.'

He smiled briefly, but he didn't seem keen to elaborate on the subject. I didn't press further. I understood. I never really wanted to talk about Mum either. I just wanted to eat her cereal.

We spent the rest of the night snacking on toasted oats and bouncing ideas off each other to frame the mission and philosophy of my leadership workshops. Zain put on a jazz music playlist on Spotify that eased the work along. Soon, we were crafting slides to Ella Fitzgerald.

Zain was a good partner to collaborate with. His suggestions were gentle, his criticism wasn't ego-driven but always in service of the idea, and he took the time to listen to feedback without getting defensive. Every now and again, he looked up from his laptop and gave me a happy, warm smile, which made me feel as though we had both unlocked something special in this room.

It was nearly 2 a.m. by the time both the presentation and the cereal were finally finished. I closed my laptop and Zain yawned a little.

'I think we did well,' he said, stretching a little. 'Even though you chose that font—'

I stare at him, affronted. It was the only thing we disagreed upon. *The Queen Network* looked much better, in my opinion, than The Queen Network.

'It's about taste, Zain,' I said shrugging. 'You obviously have none.'

He laughed and threw a pillow at me. Perhaps it was the fact that we had been in one room for hours or the fact that it was 2 a.m., but a boundary had disintegrated between us. Before I knew what I was doing, I had picked up the pillow he threw at me and clambered on to the bed to thwack him with it. He picked up another pillow and defended himself. Before I know it, we had launched into a proper no-holds-barred, pillow fight, with little gasps of 'I can't believe you', punctuated by Billie Holiday's voice.

Finally, I fell back on the bed, exhausted from hitting him and spluttering with laughter. Zain laid back, too, chuckling. I was suddenly aware of the time and the fact that we were alone in his room, on a large bed.

It's all right, I told myself. It was innocent pillow-fighting. And his green-gold-brown eyes were far away from mine. Still, I sat up, putting some more distance between us and taking note, for the first time, of the room around me. It was large and white and plush, like a hotel room. It told you nothing about itself. Just like Zain.

There were no photographs, no posters, no cards. Nothing that could personalize it, except for a stack of books next to his bedside table. Unsurprisingly, they were all business-related books, the kind that all millennials (including me) read. The Silicon Valley book, the Indian start-up book, the classic business mantras book and then, something out of the ordinary—*Oliver Twist.*

I raised it questioningly, a smile playing on my face.

He shrugged and said, 'I dip into it now and again.'

The easy warmth of his tone had vanished again and resident mistrust had seeped back into his manner. He obviously didn't want to talk about this either. For some reason, I was ravenous for more information.

He couldn't just switch on and off. In my head, we were friends now. And friends chatted about their likes and dislikes.

'I never took you for a Dickens kind of guy,' I persisted.

He flicked a guarded glance at me, 'Oliver gets me.'

What? I laughed. Zain Rajan, with his abs and women and international businesses was closer to Batman than he was to Oliver Twist. But I stopped laughing as soon I saw his wounded expression.

'Sorry,' I said, a little confused. 'I just don't see it.'

'We're both from Britain,' Zain pointed out.

'And the resemblance ends there,' I laughed. 'I mean Oliver was born in a literal poorhouse and you—'

'Radhika, the only difference between me and Oliver is that Oliver didn't have a Birdy.'

For the first time, I noticed a sharp pain beneath his wry smile.

'What do you mea—'

'It is late. Let me walk you home.' Zain got off the bed and walked to the door in two quick strides. It was clear that I was no longer welcome.

'Zain,' I began, my voice soft and apologetic. 'I just want you to know that I'm around if you do feel like talking about—'

'Radhika,' his tone was sharp. 'It's none of your business.'

I recoiled as though he had slapped me.

'There's no need to be rude,' I said with all the dignity I could muster.

Zain's manner changed abruptly. The familiarity was gone. He was polite to the point of being cold. 'I'm sorry. I didn't mean to be rude. But it's late and I'd like to drop you home and go to sleep soon.'

What could I say to that? He had been generous enough with his time, expertise and network already. And he was right. It was late, and it was not my business.

Still, for some reason, I wanted to stay and fight. I wanted our conversation to rise back to a point of intensity where he burst out and told me all about himself. I wanted to fault him for … something. But he was faultless and uninterested.

All I could do now was say goodbye and leave, as he had requested.

Thank God for Kabir, I thought as I reached home. Thank God I didn't need to deal with strange men and their strange hang-ups any more.

Kabir

We can have our honeymoon wherever you want.

I knew you would come around!

How was work?

Did you give your notice yet?

Not yet.

Want to talk?

Can't. Exhausted.

Try and give your notice ASAP, so we don't have to play hookey again! :P

But I'll be there soon enough.

<3 <3 <3

Dipa Ghanshyamdas (72) is a UAE-based global venture capitalist who has stakes in companies such as BrandMi and popular food delivery brand Zoom. She was the vice president of E and Q Consultancy Services for the Asia division before she retired to pursue social impact entrepreneurship. Currently, she lives in Dubai with her dog, Bazooka, and runs a start-up incubation programme for Women in the Middle East. (WIMES)

'I've heard promising things about you,' Dipa Ghanshyamdas said as we began our Skype call. I was surprised. I hadn't realized that she would have managed a background search on me already, considering the fact that Zain had only spoken to her about me this morning and managed to wrangle a meeting for the same afternoon.

His voice had been curt on the phone while informing me of the good news. 'She seems interested in the idea. But she can only give you thirty minutes.' He could have come to the house to tell me this, seeing as he normally came by with Birdy for breakfast. But obviously, after my interrogation, he had decided that I must be kept at the safe distance of a phone line.

I felt like a fool when I thought about last night. *What had I been playing at? Why in God's name did I care so much about whether or not he opened up to me?* Zain and his life, as he had rightly put it, were none of my business.

I thanked him over the phone in my most official, businesslike manner, hoping that he would soon be convinced that I wasn't a nosy parker. I knew how to respect boundaries like a normal adult in a healthy friendship.

'I'm glad to hear there's a good opinion of me in the UAE,' I said confidently to Dipa Ghanshyamdas.

'There is no opinion of you in the UAE,' she said flatly, taking the wind out of my sails. 'But your friend, Mr Rajan, speaks highly of you. And our team is very impressed with him.'

'Ah,' I said, trying not to let the surprise show on my face. 'I'd be glad for a chance to show you that his praise is not unmerited.'

Ms Ghanshyamdas looked at me with a curious expression, as though she was trying to suss me out. I was slightly intimidated. She had the kind of enigmatic smile that only a seventy-year-old woman CEO could harbour. One that was achieved only after weathering and winning the most heartbreaking corporate battles.

'All right,' she said finally. 'Go on. Impress me.'

'Ms Ghanshyamdas,' I shook my head. 'I'm not going to impress you. I'm only going to tell you the truth. About my abilities, and about the inequality women professionals in this country face. And based on this truth, you can decide whether you want to invest in my business or not.'

Dipa Ghanshyamdas was silent and, for a moment, I thought I saw a spark in her eyes—*dare I hope it was respect?* But then she blinked and it was gone, replaced by her usual enigmatic expression.

Still, to me, that look was enough encouragement. Dipa gave me the briefest of nods. I propped open my laptop and began.

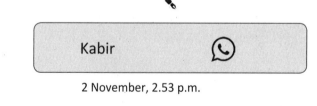

Kabir

2 November, 2.53 p.m.

Guess who's waiting downstairs?

Radhika? I can't get through to you.

2 November, 4.30 p.m.

Babe, I've been calling for an hour.
Call back, please.

I'm in Bombay.

2 November, 6.17 p.m.

Are you *still* at work?

November, 7.21 p.m.

Where are you??

19
Venture

Mangala didn't know what to make of the boy her daughter wanted to marry. It was obvious that he was very attracted to Radhika, which was a good sign, she supposed. But there was something in the way he touched her daughter that irked Mangala. It was too proprietorial, she thought, as though he was staking his claim when he settled his heavy, hairy arm on Radhika's narrow shoulders. Mangala had to stop herself from flinching every time she saw Kabir's big hands caress her daughter's fair arms, or watch him possessively kiss her cheek.

Radhika didn't seem to mind though. She laughed and fed her handsome fiancé fig ice cream from her own bowl. All through dinner, they had carried on this way, picking off each other's plates like a couple who had been together for longer than just a few months. He ate her tomatoes and she fiddled with his hair comfortably. Mangala kept glancing at her mother, expecting Gayatri to tell them off for being so nauseating at the dinner table. But nobody else seemed to mind all the romance.

Mangala thought that she probably shouldn't complain. Kabir had flown all the way from Delhi just to spend time with her. It was a sign of respect she didn't believe most men capable of. And to her pleasant surprise, Mangala had found him to be a responsible, intelligent adult— nothing like the entitled south Delhi man-child she had imagined. Kabir was politically informed, socially informed and laughed at all of Radhika's jokes. There was nothing inadvertently wrong with him. Still, Mangala couldn't stop searching his face, waiting for the polite inexpression of his eyes to give way to some real feeling. She was waiting for him to crack.

And then he did.

Radhika was talking about the wedding, about the flowers she wanted strung along the house. 'I'm going to have jasmines and lilies in every crevice of the bungalow. I don't care so much about the jewellery and clothes and make-up,' she said offhandedly, 'but I want the house to be filled with so many flowers that it would give Thumbelina a complex.'

'You do have to care about the jewellery and clothes though,' Kabir chuckled, but there was an edge to his tone.

Radhika shrugged and waved her hand vaguely. 'There's enough time to decide all that.'

Kabir caught her hand in his and pressed it insistently. 'Have you not thought about the outfits at all? You know a thousand people will be coming to see my bride.'

My bride. Mangala tried not to cringe.

'A thousand people?' Gayatri asked, shocked.

'At least.' Kabir shrugged and turned back to Radhika, his voice thick with accusation now. 'This should be a priority already. You should already have all this stuff picked out.'

Radhika laughed, a high-pitched and chirping laugh, an attempt to try and ease the tension. 'It is a priority, Kabir. Of course, it is. I promise to have it all decided soon.'

'And your notice?'

Mangala nearly slapped the boy. A pink tinge had appeared in Radhika's cheeks, too, but she averted her face from her mother's horrified gaze to smile prettily at her fiancé. 'This week. Okay?'

'Okay,' he kissed her face again, a little harder this time. Mangala could feel her own gums hurt from the pressure of his lips on her daughter's cheek.

The couple turned back to everyone else at the dinner table with too-bright smiles, as though nothing unusual had passed between them. *Was this sort of negotiation and reward par for the course for them?*

'More ice cream, Mum?' Radhika asked, smiling an unnaturally toothy and unnaturally dimpled grin at her.

Mangala shook her head. She felt sick to her stomach.

She was gratified to note that her concern was finally reflected on Gayatri's face as well.

I thought Kabir's annoyance with me had dulled over the evening. At least it had seemed that way as he praised my intelligence and beauty all through dinner with Mum and Naani. But as soon as we got into Rajat's car, his good-natured facade crumbled into explicit hostility.

'Do you want to tell me where the hell you've been all day?' he demanded. 'And don't say work, because I went there and they said you hadn't been in.'

How was I to know that Kabir would surprise me at work on the very day that I called in sick to meet with Dipa Ghanshyamdas?

It must have been tedious, I was sure, waiting for seven hours with no word from me all day. But I couldn't have helped it; my phone had been switched off for the meeting. It wasn't that different from what he had done to me on the day of our engagement.

'I'm waiting, Radhika,' he growled.

I inhaled. I didn't know where to begin.

At the end of our Skype call last week, Dipa had been intrigued and impressed by *The Queen Network*. As a woman who had worked in Bombay herself, she knew what it was like to feel small, alone and exposed all the time. She understood the business potential of offering Indian career women a mentorship network of successful career women, and she was willing to invest in developing the idea.

By the time I concluded the presentation I had made with Zain, Dipa's shrewdly assessing smile had vanished and an appreciative warmth had brightened her eyes. She had nodded and my heart began to beat quicker than ever before.

'Yes,' she had said.

'Yes?' I had asked, confused. Yes to the presentation? To the potential of the leadership series? To another call?

'Yes, all right,' she had said. 'We can work this out together.'

I had been shocked. All I had hoped from this thirty-minute call was a meeting sometime in the future. I certainly hadn't expected her to be nodding at me seriously and referring to the future of the project as though it were already a reality.

'So, you're interested in investing in this?' I had asked, suppressing the smile that wanted so badly to break out on my face.

'Of course,' she had looked confused by my question. 'I'll fly down to Bombay next week with my lawyers to set it all up. We can't lose another moment. Something like this should have been set up in the '90s. We're already late. Do you have a notepad? Get it out.'

I had complied, reining in laughter as she had continued to bark a stream of instructions at me.

'We will have to start dipping into our professional networks and your college network. You went to Yale, you said? Start looking up all your Indian classmates. And the professors. See what all the women are up to. See if they're interested in an all-expense paid trip to India—or in a webinar. We can get a back-end development team to set it up. I'll give you the number of my website guy. Use him; I'll settle the bill. I don't think a mobile app is necessary at this stage, but we could think of expanding eventually—'

'I'd like to eventually create a Tinder for women mentors and qualified girls,' I had blurted out. 'A non-romantic one, obviously. Strictly business networking.'

Dipa's eyes had lit up. 'I love that! Write that down! We have to patent it!'

It had been a torrent of activity on the first day itself. I could scarcely believe how quickly it was all happening. When I had returned to the office the next day, I had felt as though I was floating through McKinley. None of the accounts, none of the contracts, none of the Excel sheets held the same importance for me any more. It became instantly clear that I was going to do this. I was going to run a company of my own, very soon.

And Dipa Ghanshyamdas, global venture capitalist, businessperson of the year, wanted to help me.

And today, true to her word, she had flown down to Bombay to meet with me.

'Of course, I will help you,' she had said almost fiercely, putting down the cup of green tea she had ordered at the Taj Lands End. It felt so strange to think that just a month ago I had sat in the same café with Dolly Sehgal, trying to convince her of my viability as a daughter-in-law. A twinge of guilt rose in my stomach, but I suppressed it immediately.

I hadn't breathed a word about *The Queen Network* to anyone at home. Not even Kabir, despite the fact that I spoke to him every night. The lucky thing was that he never asked for too many details. He had so much to share about his father's tyrannical leadership at the factory that he was happy to hear just bullet-point descriptors of my day. 'Oh, just work' was an acceptable response to his 'How was your day'. 'Just', I had learned, was the best way to drain anything of its substance and instantly bore your listener into not asking more questions.

Just work, just business, just the expansion of my mind and horizons.

The Queen Network was still too raw, too much of a leap, and too deeply personal to share with anyone just then. But somehow, I knew in my bones that this was something I could make something of. This was something I was willing to shift careers for.

'It will be quite an investment, Mrs Ghanshyamdas,' I had said to Dipa today at her hotel, in the clearest tone I could manage as I placed the files I had worked on all week before her.

'I'm aware,' she had said, looking through my files. I had waited with bated breath as she had flipped, flipped and flipped, the wrinkles near her eyes contracting as she read. Finally, she had put the files down on the coffee table, where only a few months ago Dolly and I had eaten lipstick truffles. It was all hilariously surreal.

'I like it,' she had confirmed.

'You like it,' I had repeated, a bit dazed.

'I will get my lawyer to look over it, of course—'

'Of course.'

'But I think I can start you off at fifty lakh rupees of seed capital.'

I hadn't dared to speak.

'And then we can have a larger infusion of cash once the website and workshop series are up and running. When do you think that will be? Is January too soon?'

'January,' I had allowed myself to breathe, 'is perfect.'

'Fantastic. Now, where shall we have tea? This is rubbish.'

'… And so I took her to the Taj Mahal hotel in Colaba,' I said to Kabir, who was looking at me in complete confusion. To his credit, he did not interrupt me once as I narrated the entire haphazard series of events. 'For scones and five-hundred-rupee bun paos, where she told me about her special relationship with her golden retriever, Bazooka.'

Kabir stared at me in complete silence, his eyes still accusatory and hurt. I couldn't blame him. I had kept so much from him in the past week. I tried to reach out for his hand, which was on the steering wheel, but he moved it away defiantly.

'Is this a joke?' Kabir asked finally, his eyes narrowed.

'No,' I said, smiling a little. 'But I can barely believe it myself. I'm sorry I didn't call you back today, but my phone was on silent the entire time. Between the signing and the—'

'Show me a picture,' Kabir said suddenly.

'What?'

'Show me a picture of the research. Or of the scones, or the contracts. Something. Hell, show me a picture of Bazooka.'

I look at him, incredibly confused now. 'I didn't take a picture of the agreement, Kabir. It was only a draft agreement.'

'But you must have a PDF on your phone?'

I nodded.

'Show it to me.'

'You want to check my phone?'

'Is there something I'm not supposed to see?'

I handed it over to him, bewildered, and watched as he opened my inbox and rifled through it, his eyes intent and his jaw taut with tension. As he found the folder titled 'The Queen Network', and all the emails within it, his shoulders relaxed. The manic look in his eyes disappeared. He turned to me, visibly relieved.

'This is great, baby,' he said, kissing my forehead. 'Good for you!'

I took my phone back, feeling slightly sick.

I had signed up for a lifetime of discovering my partner but not one of being investigated by him.

'Don't you think she's old enough now? To know the truth about Daddy?'

'No.'

'Didn't you see them at dinner? Didn't you see how he—'

'How he *what*, Mangala?' Gayatri snapped, irritated beyond belief. 'Couples have arguments now and then. It's normal. It doesn't mean that people aren't meant to be together.'

'Is that what you call what Daddy and you had? Arguments?'

'It was … a different time. Different things were considered acceptable then.'

'So, what do you call the bruises, Ma? Decoration?'

Gayatri flinched, but Mangala remained relentless.

'I'm going to tell her the truth.'

'It's not your truth to tell.'

'She deserves to know.'

'Absolutely not.' Gayatri's eyes were fierce now. 'I won't make her as afraid of relationships as you are.'

Mangala's jaw became taut with anger. 'I am not afraid.'

'Why isn't Steve here then?'

Mangala fell silent.

Gayatri sighed, kissed her daughter's forehead and left the room.

TO: stevek@yale.edu
FROM: mangalaanand@yale.edu
SUBJECT: Hi

Hope everything is going well with you.

India is hot as usual. My mother is overbearing as usual. How are the classes going?

I hope McQueen isn't giving you a tough time with the citations!

Mangala

TO: mangalaanand@yale.edu
FROM: stevek@yale.edu
SUBJECT: Don't be ridiculous

Of course, things aren't going 'well' with me. I can't believe our entire association meant so little to you that, after ending it, you have the gall to ask me about goddamn McQueen's citations and the classes I'm subbing.

I'm sorry about your mum. Congratulations to Radhika.

Steve

TO: stevek@yale.edu
FROM: mangalaanand@yale.edu
SUBJECT: I'm sorry

I really am sorry.

Maybe someday, if you have a daughter, you will understand.

Mangala

20
Decoration

'Mangalaji,' Dolly Sehgal trilled as they alighted from her BMW at Rajputana Jewellers. 'Your daughter is like a machine, I tell you!'

Radhika, who had excused herself for a few moments to answer a work call, returned and grinned at Dolly Sehgal. 'I'm sorry, this was my boss in New York again, trying to convince me not to get married.'

'Tell him to match your salary to the price of the choker we just bought you,' Dolly said, laughing. 'He will never call again.'

Mangala smiled a thin-lipped smile at her daughter's new mother-in-law. Was this what Radhika wanted? This cloying, false woman who was decked in ugly diamonds and spoke of nothing more than her next purchase?

'I am so glad she's finally quitting that job,' Dolly prattled on as they walked up the marble stairs to the jewellery store. 'When she told me her hours, I nearly died of shock.'

If only, Mangala thought. Radhika shot her a knowing look, which cooled the sarcasm threatening to erupt from Mangala's tongue. Fortunately, Dolly Sehgal was always too involved in her own blustering monologues to notice her companions' subtle exchanges.

'We will spoil her in Delhi,' Dolly said, putting an affectionate palm on Radhika's cheek. 'She will never want for anything Mangalaji, I promise you.'

Except an identity, Mangala thought. She had fought battle after battle with Gayatri every day of the last fortnight that she had been in Bombay. Today, she was promising to keep an open mind, as Dolly Sehgal and she traipsed to jewellery stores to find wedding sets for Radhika. But biting her tongue was proving to be harder than expected. So far, they had been to six jewellery stores. At each, Dolly had made it a point to mention to every salesman that Radhika had to have 'the best' because she was 'the Sehgal bride'. As though Radhika was nothing else. As though becoming a Sehgal was the only reason she deserved the best.

It didn't help that Radhika seemed to be lapping up the attention, revelling in her new identity, not realizing that she was shedding the skin of her personality with every precious jewel rung up on the Sehgals' account.

'I can't wait to move,' Radhika chirped, squeezing Dolly's arm as the doorman of Rajputana Jewellers swung open an ornate, brass door for them. 'I think we're going to have a marvellous time together.'

Mangala fought the urge to roll her eyes. All morning, Radhika had carried on this way, putting on a bell-like laugh and a saleswoman's singing tone while conversing with Dolly Sehgal. Sometimes, she even looked straight at Mangala as though daring her mother to critique her, but Mangala had bit her tongue each time. She had promised Gayatri that she would be supportive.

'Oh absolutely,' Dolly Sehgal agreed. 'All of Delhi is going to sit up and take notice of you at the wedding. You're going to look like a real rajkumari, a princess, if I can help it. Then just wait and see the invitations that start pouring in. Kabir already told you about the Sahani cruise, didn't he?'

Radhika's smile dimmed slightly, but she nodded. 'He did.'

'What is this?' Mangala asked, sensing a point of tension.

Radhika turned to her brightly. 'Kabir and I have been invited on this beautiful Mediterranean cruise for New Year's. We will travel to Mykonos, Ibiza and San Sebastian. It will be a lovely time.'

'Your honeymoon is going to be a group holiday with strangers?'

Radhika bristled, but before she could say anything Dolly Sehgal interrupted. 'She won't be with strangers. Chander and I will be there, too!'

Mangala laughed in disbelief. Radhika scowled.

'That sounds lovely,' Mangala said, still snorting with laughter. 'What a marvellous start to your marriage.'

❧

TO: dipaG@ghanshyamdascaptial.com
FROM: radhikaanand@gmail.com
SUBJECT: The Queen Network Conference
Dear Dipa,

I'm happy to report that, so far, I have received a total of **sixteen** acceptances from the list of women speakers you shared with me! We even managed to wrangle some of our 'shots in the dark', such as MD of Tada group, **Arundhati Chibber** and **Lali Rai**, the only female steel industrialist I've heard of. (We've titled her talk 'Women of Steel' tentatively. Let me know if you think it is too cheesy.)

In more good news, the dates, which I thought would be a nightmare to coordinate, have come together serendipitously. It seems as though all the powerful women I spoke to are just as keen as us for a leadership series to exist for women in India. They are willing to alter their schedules to be able to speak at this event on **22–24 October 2021**, and the location is Taj Lands End's banquet hall.

Once our branding is in place, I will start contacting colleges and businesses to encourage their female students and employees to attend the conference and our workshops. A buzz seems to be spreading about us already—a couple of international business magazines have already called to ask if they can be official distribution partners for the event. I wouldn't be surprised if we become the **TED WOMEN** of South Asia very soon, with the names and attention we are attracting. I haven't lined up meetings with the various publications and sponsors yet because I'd like you to attend them with me, if your schedule allows it.

On a personal note, I would like to thank you once again for helping me in the realization of this project.

Look forward to hearing from you.

PS: Hello to Bazooka.

Radhika.

TO: radhikaanand@gmail.com

FROM: dipaG@ghanshyamdascaptial.com

SUBJECT: RE: The Queen Network Conference

Dear Radhika,

I'm glad to hear that so many of my friends and colleagues are proving useful to our work. I knew in my heart that those brilliant women wouldn't let us down, but one never knows for sure until a commitment has been made, isn't it? Go ahead and start making the relevant flight reservations and hotel bookings for each of them. **My accounts team will send you a credit card, for the same, this week.**

I'm afraid I won't be able to fly down for any of the meetings with brands or sponsors. But I trust that you will be able to handle it just fine. I'd suggest asking your friend Zain to accompany you if you're feeling unsure of clinching a negotiation on your own. Although I'm confident that a stalwart consultant like yourself can close deals with brand sponsors on her own, it helps to have an ally to back you up in a pitch.

You will, however, have to resign from your job before I can allow you to start making expenditures on the card and representing The Queen Network as the head of the organization. So make sure to get that done by the end of this month, at the latest.

PS: Bazooka responds with a friendly woof.
PPS: Hope the wedding planning is going well!
Warmly,
Dipa

❧

'Turn that off and show me what you bought with Mum today.'

I shut the laptop and turned my attention to Kabir. It had taken two days, but the tension between us had finally dissipated. After a lot of special attention and ego-stroking on my end, Kabir had let go off the fact that he was waiting outside my office in a hot car with flowers for an hour and a half, and then at my house with Naani for another five hours.

Now, he was sprawled lazily across his bed in Parineeti's guest room, his arms folded behind his head and his dark eyes staring at me hungrily. I loved this feeling, I've realized. I loved it so much that I refused to bring up the fact that I was disgusted by him rifling through my phone the other day.

But I had analysed the incident with my phone and decided that more than a violation of privacy, it was proof of how passionate Kabir was about me. So passionate that he couldn't bear the thought of sharing me with someone else. That he would break the rules of decency to make sure that he didn't have any reason to be jealous. It was a little strange, but it was also incredibly romantic, if you thought about it from his perspective.

In any case, it was much better than indifference. Much better than a guy shutting you out and dropping you home, because he no longer wanted to talk about *Oliver Twist* with you. I would never give up this feeling of knowing for sure that my boyfriend wanted me. I would hate to be kept guessing, to be wondering whether the man I slept next to at night would suddenly be unable to communicate in the morning.

Kabir would always be mad about me. I would ensure it.

'Where are you going?' he asked, as I got up from the bed and began undressing.

'You wanted to see what I bought, didn't you?' I asked, unbuttoning my shirt.

Kabir nodded, confused.

'Well, I bought jewellery,' I said, shrugging out of my shirt and putting the heavy diamond choker around my bare neck. The glittering stones matched nicely with my lace bra.

Kabir watched, mesmerized. 'What are you doing?'

'You spent a great deal of money on this,' I purred in a way that would infuriate my mother.

'I did?' his voice came out in a hoarse whisper, as his eyes roved over the glittering stones on my naked collarbones.

I nodded and slid out of my jeans, clasping the gold and silver anklets around my bare legs. 'So, I'd like you to appreciate it properly. You shouldn't be distracted by anything else I'm wearing.'

I unhooked my bra. Kabir got up and locked the door. 'That makes sense.'

I shrugged and my body jangled with the weight of the jewellery.

'I'm a sensible girl.'

'I'll say.'

✎

'Someone had a good night,' Parineeti laughed as I emerged from Kabir's room at dawn. *Crap!* I was hoping to sneak back home before anyone saw me. Technically, I wasn't supposed to be spending the night with him till our honeymoon. Neither the Sehgals nor the Anands were okay with turning a blind eye to that particular rule.

'Relax,' Parineeti said, handing me a carton of milk. 'I don't snitch. In fact, I'm surprised you haven't stayed over before.'

'Too risky,' I said, shaking my head to her offering of milk. 'I need to be home before Naani and Birdy get back from their morning walk, or all hell will break loose.'

'Loose? Like your character?' Parineeti teased.

'Funny,' I grimaced.

'Is my mother driving you crazy yet?' Parineeti asked, kissing my cheek as she opened the front door to allow me to leave.

'Not at all,' I shrugged and grabbed my car keys from her.

Kabir emerged from the room just then, rubbing his eyes sleepily. 'Radhika, your um … jewellery,' he said, glancing at his sister. I blushed slightly and quickly took the bags of Rajputana Jewellers. If Parineeti noticed the lingerie also stuffed in, she didn't comment.

'Mum asked me to send you a list of doctors you have to visit this week, by the way,' Kabir said, touching my hair lightly. 'If your Naani is busy, Mum will be happy to go to the appointments with you.'

'Doctors?'

'And so it begins,' Parineeti chuckled. Kabir shot her a look and she moved back to the kitchen counter with her cereal bowl and milk.

'It's routine for brides here,' Kabir explained. 'Dermatologist, nutritionist and a gynaecologist, of course. But the wedding planner will explain it all to you. I think you have an appointment with her tomorrow.'

I raised my eyebrows, incredulous. I even chuckled a little in disbelief.

'Was anyone ever going to ask me if I was available for this appointment?'

'Nope!' Parineeti called out from the kitchen. Kabir shot her another look, but she was defiant. 'You know it's true.'

Annoyed now, I turned to Kabir, whose hands were folded across his chest defensively.

'Kabir, just because I'm quitting my job doesn't mean that you get to design my day—'

'I'm not designing your day, Radhika,' he rolled his eyes. 'I was going to tell you on my first evening here, but it slipped my mind. Just like telling me about your new business slipped yours.'

I did a double take. I thought we had got past that.

'The Queen Network didn't slip my mind, Kabir. I chose not to tell anyone because nothing had materialized then.'

'You told Birdy's nephew, didn't you? That lady wrote about him in your email.'

'You went through my email again?' I asked, shocked.

Parineeti cleared her throat. 'Guys, relax,' she laughed lightly. 'You have your whole life to argue with each other. Right now, there is a wedding to plan and a beauty regimen to be started.'

Kabir exhaled and his arms dropped to his side. He put a hand on my shoulder and gave me a tight hug. 'Pari is right. I'm sorry. I should have set a reminder or something to tell you about the appointments. I did take it for granted that you would be free all week.'

I exhaled. I wanted to talk a little more about boundaries, about him checking my phone, but I couldn't, not with Parineeti in the room. Plus, it was hard to stay angry with Kabir when he was looking at me with such genuine affection.

'I would have told you last night, but you distracted me,' he planted a kiss on my lips.

I cracked a smile. He knew what to say to win me over, I had to give him that.

'It's not so bad, meeting a wedding planner, is it? She's there to help you. To make your work easier so you can concentrate on your project—'

'*The Queen Network*.'

'Exactly,' he sneaked out the big, warm smile that he knew was my favourite. When Kabir smiled like that, it was like standing under a hot shower after walking through a New York blizzard. But I could not grin back for some reason. I didn't want to fight with him any more, but I was unable to smile.

'Now go give your notice so you can plan our wedding properly,' he kissed me again.

He chuckled, as though we were just joking, but there was no answering laughter from me.

As I drove home, I was oddly relieved that Kabir was flying back to Delhi that day, leaving me in command of my life again.

❧

'Kabir?'

He didn't look up from his bowl of scrambled eggs. He was annoyed with his sister for mucking his goodbye with Radhika. Why did she always have to bring her problems with their mother into every family matter? And why could she never remember to put enough pepper in his eggs?

'KABIR.' Parineeti waved a fork before his eyes. He looked up reluctantly at his baby sister.

'What is it, Pari?'

'Have you told Radhika about the Sahanis?'

'Sure,' he shrugged. 'She's looking forward to the cruise.'

Parineeti narrowed her eyes. 'So, she knows that Aishwarya will probably be there, too?'

Kabir rolled his eyes. His sister was such a drama queen sometimes. She was more like Dolly Sehgal than she knew.

'Jesus, Pari,' Kabir laughed lightly. 'That's ancient history. I haven't even seen Aishwarya since last summer. And that was just in passing, with Mrs Sahani at Emporio.'

'Still. She's your ex-girlfriend, Kabir,' Parineeti insisted. 'And judging by Radhika's reaction today, she doesn't like being kept in the dark about things.'

Kabir got up, smiled at his sister in his infuriating older brother manner and kissed her on the forehead. 'Don't worry about it. We're all adults.'

Parineeti exhaled, giving up. 'All right. In any case, Aishwarya may not even come back this December. She's thinking of finally starting a fashion label in London.'

Kabir paused and sat back down across the kitchen counter. 'You two are still in touch?'

Parineeti shrugged. 'She DMs me on Instagram from time to time. I tried to ignore her at first ... but we have been friends since nursery.' Parineeti bit her lip, worried as she observed the change in her brother's expression. 'It isn't a problem, is it?'

'No, it isn't a problem,' Kabir said. A strange yet familiar disquiet began to rise within him. Parineeti was right. They had all been friends since nursery. And other than medical school, Aishwarya had been his entire adolescence. It was hard to cut off that kind of connection.

'I hope she comes for the wedding,' he said out loud.

'What?' Parineeti asked, her voice suspicious again. 'Why?'

'Because,' Kabir let out a laugh to ease his sister's tension. 'It will be better for Radhika to meet her before the honeymoon, don't you think?'

Parineeti's suspicion disappeared, replaced by surprise. She couldn't believe Kabir was actually being thoughtful. Perhaps he was actually in love with Radhika and this wasn't a delayed rebound, as she had started suspecting it to be.

'That's not a bad idea,' Parineeti said. 'I'll suggest it to her.'

'Thanks, Pari,' Kabir rose from the kitchen bar stool and hugged his sister. He was lucky to have Parineeti around. She was always such a help.

🖋

TO: radhikaanand@gmail.com
FROM: zainrajan@gmail.com
SUBJECT: Congratulations
I didn't think I'd hear the name Radhika as many times in Dubai as I did from Birdy in Bandra, but that is the hazard of introducing you to anyone I know, I guess.

Dipa and her entire team are raving about **The Queen Network**. Apparently, investing in you is like buying a marketing team and a finance team, all for the price of one, according to her very happy accounts department.

Dipa mentioned that you need someone to attend meetings with the brand partners. I'd be happy to come to a few, as long as you can arrange them for Tuesday or Thursday after 4 p.m., so it doesn't interfere with my work at the Bombay factory.

I've had some business cards printed for you. Will bring them with me.

Don't worry, it says **The Queen Network**, and not The Queen Network.

Love,

Zain

Love? Was Zain high?

TO: zainrajan@gmail.com
FROM: radhikaanand@gmail.com
SUBJECT: RE: Congratulations
Are you high?
Rad

TO: radhikaanand@gmail.com
FROM: zainrajan@gmail.com
SUBJECT: RE: RE: Congratulations
Yes.
Zain

TO: zainrajan@gmail.com
FROM: radhikaanand@gmail.com
SUBJECT: RE: RE: RE: Congratulations
Are you drunk *emailing* me?
Rad

TO: radhikaanand@gmail.com
FROM: zainrajan@gmail.com
SUBJECT: RE: RE: RE: Congratulations
Yes.
Zain

TO: zainrajan@gmail.com
FROM: radhikaanand@gmail.com
SUBJECT: RE: RE: RE: Congratulations
You're sorry, aren't you? For kicking me out of your room the other day?
Rad

TO: radhikaanand@gmail.com
FROM: zainrajan@gmail.com
SUBJECT: RE: RE: RE: Congratulations
They should cut us off after four whisky sours on a three-hour flight. The stewards should have the savvy of bartenders in Bombay. Only one drink per hour for well-tipping patrons.
Zain

TO: zainrajan@gmail.com
FROM: radhikaanand@gmail.com
SUBJECT: RE: RE: RE: Congratulations

I'm sorry too, Zain. I shouldn't have pried.

PS: Eat the bread rolls and the nuts that come with the in-flight meal. They will soak the alcohol, make you feel less gross when you land.

PPS: It is not too many carbs. You look fine.

Rad

21
Planning

Radhika Anand

Letter of Resignation

I placed the envelope on Mr Bhatia's mahogany desk. Astonishment crossed his face for a second, but then he shook his head and smirked, as though we were both in on a secret.

'It's too early, Radhika. Your wedding isn't for another month.'

'I'm afraid,' I cleared my throat, 'I'm afraid I will have to leave before that, sir.'

The easy humour fled his face. He ripped open my letter and read the three paragraphs in a quick minute. When he looked up at me again, his eyes held a cold, incredulous anger.

'You're starting your own company?' he seemed irritated.

I was surprised by the tone. Mr Bhatia had always politely encouraged me. My throat prickled with fear. Yet, I willed myself to continue.

'I need to quit now, so that I can start setting up my business. It will be a conflict of interest to be employed as a consultant and start my own consultancy—'

'Oh, come off it, Radhika,' Mr Bhatia laughed, glancing at my letter again with such swiftness that the paper made a *flick-flick* sound as he waved it through the air. I almost expected to feel a paper cut as he read from the letter in a derisive tone. '*The Queen Network*, really?

'What you're proposing isn't a consultancy, it's like group therapy sessions for women. It's not a real business when your product is feelings.'

I recoiled, taken aback by his reaction. So far, Mr Bhatia and I had shared a good, even friendly, rapport. I had expected this kind of negativity from Maruti or Gomes, but not from him.

'Maybe it will start out as that, something based on values and ideals. Maybe it will grow into something else,' I said.

'Don't hold your breath,' Mr Bhatia laughed.

I narrowed my eyes at him, suddenly no longer afraid. I didn't need the good opinion of anyone who was so regressive that they couldn't see the way forward.

'There was a young woman named Arianna, who wrote a blog based on her liberal values and ideals. One of them was a firm stance on gender equality,' I said. 'That blog is now called HuffPost and is valued at a billion dollars.'

Derision fled Mr Bhatia's face; he looked very annoyed. He said nothing for a minute, just stared at me intently as though trying to figure out my strategy.

'You can't leave now, Radhika,' he said finally, dropping my resignation on to a desk littered with old papers. 'For one thing, Mr Goldenblatt's contract in India holds you here as its supervisor for the next month and a half. So, I'm afraid—' his tone became sharp as he continued, 'it's out of the question.'

I couldn't help but bristle a little. I was not doing anything as criminal as he was making it out to be. If he was trying to scare me into staying, it wasn't going to work.

'I've already informed Rich and Mr Goldenblatt of my situation,' I asserted. 'They were very understanding. They will send a replacement by the end of the week, whom I will coach to take over all the accounts that I have been handling.'

But Mr Bhatia only seemed more annoyed by my reassurances. 'I'm afraid I can't be as understanding,' he snapped. 'For one thing, you should have informed me at the same time as you informed your boss in New York. I can't have my heads of departments changing every five months.'

I wanted to laugh. He was grasping at straws now. *Didn't he know it didn't do any good to lose one's temper in a negotiation?*

'With all due respect, sir,' I said evenly, 'you were aware of the possibility of your head of division changing in a short time. My contract in India was only for six months. I'm only ending it a few weeks earlier. And the headquarters that I respond to doesn't have a problem with it.'

'Yes, but you gave every impression of wanting to stay. Why else would you take on all that work? Why else would you help the company gain more business?'

Because it is my nature to grow. To improve things. To move on when a situation no longer serves me.

I said none of this out loud, however. I knew this explanation would not make any sense to Mr Bhatia. I was sacrificing a promising career, a large salary and the possibility of becoming a partner in my own right, on a gamble. And a gamble on women, no less.

But the minute Dipa Ghanshyamdas had agreed to invest in *The Queen Network*, it had become less of a gamble and more of a reality. It was already more real, more important, than any of my work at McKinley. I no longer had the same fiery motivation to improve the profit margins of American companies. It was not as gratifying as spending my time and energy on a business with a purpose I connected with—making leaders out of women professionals.

It was scary, thinking of the fact that next month I won't have a salary coming in. But it would be scarier still to spend the rest of my days hiding under the glossy umbrella of McKinley, only because I was too afraid of taking a chance on the work I wanted to do.

The fact that my boss was trying to command me into staying in a job that I didn't want to be in, the fact that I was very nearly cowed, that every bone in my body was begging to acquiesce, to say anything that would have him smile at me in approval again, only proved how badly I needed to leave. I needed to begin *The Queen Network* as soon as possible.

'I was never going to stay, sir,' I said out loud. 'But I think I've equipped your analysts with the skill and managerial expertise to take charge of the accounts they've won.'

Mr Bhatia scoffed. 'Padmini and Mukti aren't qualified enough to handle accounts on their own, not without your direction, Radhika.'

'Then perhaps you should consider sending them and your other employees to my leadership series soon.'

Mr Bhatia shot a dark look at me. I continued to smile brightly.

'If it even happens,' he muttered finally.

'I'm sorry?'

And then, finally, the real reason for his irritation was revealed to me.

'Radhika, we both know that you've started this little thing as a ruse to prepare for your wedding, as all you rich brides do these days. The least you can do is be upfront about it.'

I was about to open my mouth to defend myself, but I didn't have the time to argue with him any more. My phone was ringing with reminders to meet with my wedding planner this evening.

❧

'She quit her job today,' Mangala stopped by Gayatri's room that morning.

'I'm aware.'

'My daughter is unemployed.'

Gayatri refused to give her daughter the satisfaction of flinching or betraying in any manner that she was just as worried about Radhika. There was nothing to be worried about, Gayatri reassured herself. The Sehgals might be a little money-obsessed, but they really seemed to love Radhika. And if what her granddaughter wanted, more than anything else, was to be a wife to a loving partner, then there was no doubt that a marriage with the Sehgal boy was perfect for her.

Surprisingly, Gayatri was starting to believe that it wasn't necessary for every girl to be a career woman to have an identity of her own. Her granddaughter had arrived at her doorstep as the head of a department, but also as a ravaged mess of a human being. Gayatri shuddered when she thought about Radhika's first appearance in Mumbai: her hair stringy, her cheeks pale, her eyes twitching with pain and insecurity. In the last six months, Radhika had bloomed. Her hair had thickened to become black and glossy like Gayatri's at one time, her hips had filled out into a healthier shape and her entire person had expanded with a brightness that Gayatri hadn't seen in a long time. It was like someone had switched a light on in the young girl's body. If Kabir and a slowing down of her career had such a pleasant effect on her granddaughter's quality of life, Gayatri was more than happy for her to sacrifice her career completely and spend her time finding a new purpose—whatever that may be.

Gayatri turned to her daughter, who was gazing at her accusatorially as usual, her face scrunched up in irritation. How she wished that Mangala would bloom one day. Or at least unfurl a little.

'Technically,' she said to her daughter. 'You're unemployed, too.'

'I'm on a paid sabbatical,' Mangala rolled her eyes. 'I'm going to write another paper that contributes to research on marriage psychology across the world.'

I'm going to be the best pilot in the world, Ma. I will be the prettiest pilot, too. So pretty that the passengers won't even look at the air hostesses any more.

Gayatri nearly chuckled as eight-year-old Mangala's bluster erupted in her mind, back from the first time she had sat on a plane to visit Jai's father in London. Jai, of course, had snipped her dreams in one go by telling her that pilots were just celebrated chauffeurs and that only cheap women wanted to be looked at so desperately. Mangala had stopped wanting to be pretty overnight.

Gayatri's heart suddenly softened for her daughter. She was still, in so many ways, just a girl who wanted her parents to believe in her potential. But her father, the non-believer-in-chief, was gone. *So, whose approval was Mangala begging for now?*

'That sounds interesting, Mangala,' Gayatri said, smiling at her daughter. 'Is Steve helping with the research, too?'

Mangala flinched. 'No.'

'Oh!' Gayatri was confused. 'Why not?'

'I've—' Mangala inhaled sharply and her jaw tightened. 'We've parted ways.'

Gayatri stared at her daughter's brown eyes, trying to detect an emotion, but they remained opaque as ever.

'As colleagues?' Gayatri asked.

'Overall,' Mangala's jaw tightened further.

Gayatri didn't say anything. She had learned over the years that with Mangala it would never do to ask too many questions. The fact that she had shared this piece of information with Gayatri at all was a great breakthrough. Gayatri just had to wait, like she would if a butterfly landed on her arm when she was in Bauji's garden, and hope for it to flutter and show her the prism of colours that lay beneath the black frames of its wings.

Mangala fluttered. To Gayatri's great surprise, she dropped her head on her mother's shoulder and fluttered.

'He wanted to come for the wedding. I told him it was out of the question.'

'Why would you do that?' Gayatri asked, surprised.

Mangala shook her head, angrily wiping away the tears that were escaping her eyes and spilling on to her mother's cotton sari.

'Because,' her voice became fierce now, 'he isn't my husband. And he shouldn't pretend to be.'

Gayatri stifled a laugh. It was amazing that her daughter could research others' relationships and still remain oblivious to the particulars of her own.

'Mangala, you've known the man for over a decade now.'

'We never put a label on it—'

'He *lived* with you!' A chuckle finally escaped Gayatri.

'Only because it made research easier!' Mangala pressed her thumb into her mother's palm, like she used to do when she was younger and helplessly angry after a fight with Jai. The warmth and pressure of Gayatri's hand instantly calmed Mangala down. She spoke in a softer tone now, her voice thick because of the tears.

'I had told him. On our very first date, I had told him how complicated all of this was. That I'd never bring him, or any other man home to you or Daddy,' Mangala whispered. 'And he had understood. He had respected my decision. Just because Daddy was gone didn't mean it was okay to—'

'Mangala, sweetheart,' Gayatri whispered back to her daughter with urgency. 'It's not nearly as complicated as you would think.'

'He said he loved me.' Mangala shook her head defiantly. 'Then he left the minute I refused to bring him home. What does that say about him?'

'It says that he wants to be included in your family,' Gayatri said.

Mangala's thick black glasses were skewed to the left. Gayatri reached out and straightened them. To her complete surprise, Mangala didn't swat her hand away or bristle with irritation.

'It isn't fair to a man to expect him to be your lover, confidante and punching bag, but to never publicly acknowledge him as your partner.'

Mangala looked up at Gayatri, her freckled cheeks wet with tears like they used to be after a fight with Jai. Gayatri gently placed her fingers under the delicate skin of her eyes and wiped the tears away. She wondered if her daughter ever cried on her own in America.

Somehow, she couldn't imagine it. She couldn't imagine Mangala permitting tears to escape her eyes for Steve or Radhika or anyone else to see. Strangely, Gayatri was glad that her strong daughter was finally weeping, and that she was doing it on her shoulder.

'It's how we've been for the longest time,' Mangala stuttered. 'Why does anything have to change now?'

Gayatri patted her head. 'Maybe Steve wants to be a part of your daughter's wedding. Maybe he thinks of you as his family now and wants you to feel the same way about him.'

Mangala didn't say anything, but her ragged breathing became even as her mother spoke to her in soft, soothing tones.

'Labels are necessary, my dear. Lovers need them especially to know exactly how important they are to each other.'

'Like you and Birdy?'

Gayatri looked at her daughter, shocked. Perhaps Mangala wasn't as oblivious as she thought. Her daughter had pinned her down through wet eyelashes and a questioning glare.

'It isn't fair to Birdy either, is it, Mum?'

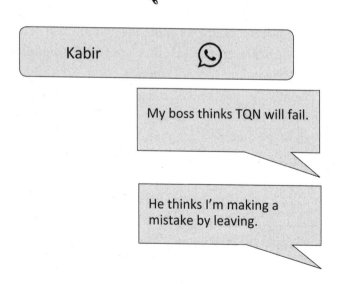

> Tell your boss that your husband can afford the failure.

> And still make sure that you live like a queen.

> I'd much rather tell him that TQN won't fail.

> Because I know what I'm doing.

'The house-blend coffee with clotted cream for Mrs Sehgal and I, and jasmine tea for the bride,' my wedding planner, Aashna Soonawalla, who was also Dolly Sehgal's friend, said in a bell-like voice to the waiter at The Champagne Lounge of the Oberoi, which was where Dolly Sehgal had insisted on having the meeting. The cafe was undoubtedly beautiful with its polished grand piano and floor-to-ceiling windows looking out at the Arabian Sea, but it was also all the way at Nariman Point, which involved an hour-and-a-half-long commute after my showdown with Mr Bhatia to get there.

It had been a long day, to say the least. I could have used a cup of coffee, too.

'Actually,' I stopped the waiter with my most graceful smile, 'I'd like the house blend, too.'

But both Dolly Sehgal and her Gucci-clad wedding planner narrowed their eyes at me.

'That is not a good idea, beta,' Dolly said warningly, while Aashna Soonawalla shook a pink acrylic nail at the waiter. 'She'll have the jasmine tea.'

I was about to argue, but before I could say anything the waiter had swiped the menus off the table and flitted away. It was obvious that my opinion on my choice of beverage held little importance.

I glared at Aashna Soonawalla. But Dolly Sehgal put a soothing arm on mine.

'Sweetheart, it's for your own good. Caffeine darkens the skin.'

'What?' I exclaimed, laughing with a derision that Mum would be proud of. 'That doesn't sound scientific at all.'

'Actually,' Aashna Soonawalla smiled brightly at me. 'Beyond a certain limit, caffeine inhibits the body's capacity to absorb vitamin E, which results in the darkening of skin.'

Oh.

'Well, a little darkness isn't so bad,' I shrugged. 'I'll have a lovely, tanned glow like a Spanish bride.'

'There is nothing lovely about a tan,' Dolly Sehgal said, aghast. 'In fact, you should stay out of the sun all together.

We can't risk any discolouration now. Aashna has designed the entire event around your fair skin.'

'What?' I was shocked. How does one plan an entire event around a complexion?

Aashna Soonawalla pulled out a leather-bound book that weighed a kilogram at least and placed it on her knees with a mysterious smile.

'Are you ready to see your wedding?' she whispered in what I was sure she thought was an 'enchanting voice'.

I nodded, barely suppressing laughter. 'Sure.'

But my sarcasm vanished when Aashna Soonawalla opened the book to reveal pages filled with gold and indigo and violet. I was appropriately enchanted. Photographs of an ornate royal court, like something out of an old Indian palace, adorned the page. There were exquisite sketches of a nautch girl's glittering shararas and men dressed in Mughal-era robes with bejewelled turbans. The images reminded me of a fairytale Naani would tell me, of an emperor and his queen. Mum had confiscated the picture book as soon as she had found it in my suitcase of special things, but I tried not to think of that now as my fingers traced the watercolour spread across this thick page of magic.

Dolly Sehgal and her wedding planner observed my quiet amazement with approval. But I was still unsure of what exactly they were trying to present to me.

They must have read my confusion, because Aashna Soonawalla proudly said, 'We will stage your wedding like a Mughal durbar. You will play Anarkali.'

Hold up. What?

'The, um, court dancer?' I asked, trying not to sound too judgemental.

Aashna Soonawalla smiled at me for the first time as she flipped to pictures of the iconic Hindi film *Mughal-E-Azam*.

'I was inspired by Kabir's story of how you two met!' Aashna said with four twitches of her eyebrow, the most excitement her Botoxed face could express. 'It was after your Kathak class, wasn't it?'

'It was,' I said slowly, unsure of where this was going.

'Well, we thought it would be romantic to make the whole thing like a little play—you starting out as a common dancer who catches the emperor's attention. Your entry song could be *"Pyaar kiya toh darna kya"* or something equally romantic. Then, after the marriage ceremony, you will be crowned queen and asked to sit on the throne with Kabir.'

I could no longer remain quiet. 'Excuse me?'

'You don't like it?' Dolly Sehgal's face fell.

I didn't even know where to begin. Dolly looked so enthused by this idea. You could tell that this was her idea of a perfect social statement, to have her son and daughter-in-law be crowned as modern-day king and queen at their wedding. It would cause the rest of Delhi to sit up and take notice, just as she wanted. At least those people who wouldn't be laughing at us for having such undemocratic fantasies in the twenty-first century. But I couldn't tell them that their need to flaunt their wealth had reached near-fascist proportions. At least not directly. I decided to recap the situation in my most gentle tone.

'So, the storyline is that I rise through the ranks? First, I perform a dance and then, because Kabir, the emperor, falls in love with me, I get to become a queen?'

I was hoping that the indignity of the situation would become obvious to them, but neither Dolly nor Aashna seemed perturbed. They were nodding at me, excitedly.

'Exactly!' they cheered, glad that I had understood the sequence of events.

'And for the entertainment,' Aashna Soonawalla continued with gusto, 'we will hire a mural painter to create a live painting of the entire scene, as though a historic marriage is taking place!'

I could not be gentle any more. 'It was historical because a prostitute had hooked a prince.' I then turned to my future mother-in-law accusatorially, 'Wasn't Anarkali a prostitute?'

Dolly Sehgal clicked her tongue in distaste. 'No, no.'

'She was a courtesan.' Aashna Soonawalla waved my concerns away with a flick of her bejewelled hand. 'It is very different.'

I guessed it was time to point out the obvious and biggest flaw of this plan. I turned to Dolly Sehgal, my expression softly worried, so that the blow of her plan falling through wouldn't hurt her too much.

'But Ma, if we're king and queen, won't that mean our guests would be subjects?'

I had expected Dolly Sehgal's face to crumble in delayed realization. After all, she wouldn't want the Tannas and the Sahanis and all her other important friends to feel disrespected, would she? But her expression didn't change at all. If anything, a glow flooded her cheeks.

'That's the best part!' Dolly squealed, her eyes glittering. She looked at her friend and both of them started giggling like schoolgirls planning an outlandish prank.

They recomposed themselves as the waiter arrived with our beverages. Aashna Soonawalla lifted my saucer for me.

'Jasmine tea for the bride,' she repeated. As I lifted my cup and took a long sip of the hot, flowery liquid, I tried not to think of the end of the original *Mughal-E-Azam*, where the prostitute who dared to fall in love with the prince was eventually entombed alive by his parents.

❦

TO: radhikaanand@gmail.com
FROM: zainrajan@gmail.com
SUBJECT: I Think That Went Well
Don't you?
Zain

TO: zainrajan@gmail.com
FROM: radhikaanand@gmail.com
SUBJECT: Yes

I think so, too! Thanks for coming along again. The lady from *Brand Quotient!* seemed to love you.

I won't be surprised if her offer letter includes her personal number with the explicit instruction to pass it on to you.

PS: Why don't we just text each other like normal people?

Rad

TO: radhikaanand@gmail.com
FROM: zainrajan@gmail.com
SUBJECT: Well …

You don't need to thank me, Radhika. Your sales pitch is strong. I like your attitude in meetings: passionate and no bullshit.

It's hard to pull off passionate without seeming like a fool, but you manage it fine.

I'd be happy to come to the other meetings, too, as an 'associate' of *The Queen Network*. It's good fun to be around this female start-up energy.

Also, the woman from *Brand Quotient!* already gave me her number. Not interested.

PS: Because emails are more interesting.

Zain

TO: zainrajan@gmail.com
FROM: radhikaanand@gmail.com
SUBJECT: I'm Not 'Pulling Off Passionate'

I *am* passionate.

And what the hell is 'female start-up energy'? If you say that in an interview about my leadership series, I will make sure that every latte at our future meetings is pumpkin spiced :)

PS: You're avoiding someone on WhatsApp, aren't you? Your last seen is yesterday at 2.13 p.m.!

Rad

TO: radhikaanand@gmail.com
FROM: zainrajan@gmail.com
SUBJECT: I Should Never Have Told You …

… About my thing with pumpkins. It's like Superman telling people about his aversion to kryptonite.

PS: You're a stalker, aren't you?

Zain

TO: zainrajan@gmail.com
FROM: radhikaanand@gmail.com
SUBJECT: I Hate to Break It to You …

… But you're not Superman.

You could pass for Tony Stark before he became Iron Man, if that's any consolation.

PS: Reply to Kiara, Zain.

Rad

TO: radhikaanand@gmail.com
FROM: zainrajan@gmail.com
SUBJECT: Tony Stark? Really?

A depraved, soulless businessman with no family, friends or morals? If I told Birdy Mamu, he'd tell you off.

Actually, he'd never tell you off. He'd probably tell me off for making that impression on you.

PS: Kiara and I broke up.

PPS: Not that we were ever dating.

Zain

TO: zainrajan@gmail.com
FROM: radhikaanand@gmail.com
SUBJECT: If It Helps ...

I hope you find your Pepper Potts soon. I hope you never say 'not that we were ever dating' about her.

PS: Stop being a drama queen! You aren't without family or friends. Birdy loves you like a son.

PPS: So does my grandmother, for some reason.

Rad

TO: radhikaanand@gmail.com
FROM: zainrajan@gmail.com
SUBJECT: It Doesn't Help ...

Because I wasn't looking for Pepper Potts or Lois Lane. Who wants a sidekick for a girlfriend?

Give me Wonder Woman, and then we'll talk. I would never say 'not that we were ever dating' about her.

PS: I love your grandmother, too.

Zain

TO: zainrajan@gmail.com
FROM: radhikaanand@gmail.com
SUBJECT: Are You Asking Me to Set You Up?
I've met quite a few Wonder Women over the last couple of weeks, setting up the TQN. I could introduce you if you wanted. Or I could invite them to the wedding and you could introduce yourself over a whisky sour or something.
Rad

TO: radhikaanand@gmail.com
FROM: zainrajan@gmail.com
SUBJECT: No Thanks
You don't find Wonder Woman. She finds you. That's the whole point.
Zain

TO: zainrajan@gmail.com
FROM: radhikaanand@gmail.com
SUBJECT: That's CONVENIENT
Sounds like a lazy man's argument.
Rad

TO: radhikaanand@gmail.com
FROM: zainrajan@gmail.com
SUBJECT: Are You Saying …
… That your fiancé is lazy?
If I remember correctly, you came here looking for him, didn't you?
PS: Btw, it's a bit weird that I haven't met him yet, don't you think?
Zain

I stopped typing at this point.

For some reason, I couldn't imagine Zain and Kabir in the same room. They seemed to inhabit such different spaces of the new life I had carved in India. Zain, with his laughing eyes, always carefully edited his thoughts before committing them to words. He wa s so different from Kabir who voiced every thought, letting all his information take up the space between us, so that I rarely got a word in—but at least I was never left wondering.

Watching them have a conversation would be like watching an uneven volley in a tennis match, I thought, smiling to myself. I didn't think they would get along at all. Kabir would think Zain too … focused, maybe. Not that Kabir wasn't focused. But in a different way. He wanted to do well for the sake of his family, for keeping up their lifestyle and improving it. Perhaps for, one day, becoming the pharmaceutical emperor of India. But he wouldn't want to chat about work at a dinner party. He'd much prefer talking about the car he wanted to buy or the house he would build in Italy, or Sehgal Pharmaceuticals's share price.

For Zain, being able to speak to someone about his work, or about anyone's work, was like a gift. He enjoyed it wholeheartedly, to be around industrious people and learn how exactly they were contributing to their industry. It was funny that he thought that I was passionate in a meeting, because he brought a whole other degree of reverence to every conversation we had about Rajan Textiles or **The Queen Network**.

I flipped over the business card Zain had printed for me in Dubai.

The Queen Network

CEO: Radhika Anand

Cell: 9818753327

Email: radhikaanand@gmail.com

I realized suddenly that he had combined two fonts. Mine and his. The title was written as per my taste, but my name was written as per his.

Before I knew what I was doing, I typed a quick email to him. Committing without thinking, even though he would never do it.

TO: zainrajan@gmail.com
FROM: radhikaanand@gmail.com
SUBJECT: Are You Free Next Week?
Kabir's coming to town for a fitting on Friday. We could have dinner maybe?
Rad

TO: radhikaanand@gmail.com
FROM: zainrajan@gmail.com
SUBJECT: RE: Are You Free Next Week?
I will look forward to it.
Zain

❧

'Good morning,' Birdy said as Gayatri slid into the car beside him. He already had a thermos of hot water with honey waiting in the armrest of his Mercedes for her. Gayatri smiled and kissed his cheek before sipping on it.

'Thank you for coming with me,' she whispered. 'I don't think I would have managed it alone, with this awful cold showing no sign of leaving my body—oh dear!' And then she moved away suddenly. 'I hope I haven't infected you.'

Birdy chuckled and took her hand back in his. 'Don't be silly, Gayatri,' he said. 'I would count myself lucky to be infected by you.'

Gayatri raised her eyebrows. This was the first overt sign of affection Birdy had displayed since their conversation in Delhi. So far, he had been behaving like an affectionate older brother, or an estranged husband; one who showed up for the family's dinners and brought mithai to the granddaughter's engagement, but who showed no feelings for her.

Gayatri had almost started to think that she had lost him. How ironic it would be if, after a lifetime of loving her, he stopped, just when she finally got around to liking him.

But here Birdy was, allowing her to kiss his cheek and saying he didn't mind her germs. Flirting with her like they were still in the IAS in Delhi and he was carrying her files home from Rashtrapati Bhavan.

'Thank you for coming flower shopping with me,' Gayatri said, a little tentatively, even though there were so many other things she wanted to say and ask. At the forefront of her mind was the conversation she had recently had with Mangala and the repressed hope for his easy company again. For the right to wander into his room and sit on the edge of the bed whenever she wanted. Or to drink a cup of tea (or warm water with honey) with him at the beginning of every day and the end of every night. Perhaps to rest her head against his broad, suited chest. She could say all this to him, and ask if he still felt the same way. Perhaps they could begin planning a future beyond Radhika's wedding ...

But it was impossible, Gayatri knew. The Sehgals were conservative folk, too obsessed with class and tradition, as this royal wedding extravaganza proved, to tolerate the idea of a grandmother remarrying. They would discredit

Radhika's character if the subject was even broached. They may hold it against her for the rest of her life.

Gayatri forced her most wonderful thoughts back into her chest and wittered on about flowers instead, rambling to keep herself from confessing.

'The Dadar flower market will have the jasmines she wants. Everything else is to Dolly Sehgal's taste, so I really want to make sure that at least the flowers are the ones Radhika wanted. She hasn't even been able to choose her own lehenga. I offered to speak to Dolly for her, but she kept saying that the wedding wasn't all that important to her, that it was the marriage with Kabir that counted. But still, if I can help it, I'm going to find her the freshest vendor of jasmines today.'

All the while, Gayatri was curiously aware of her hand in Birdy's. He nodded and lifted it to his lips now. Gayatri noticed for the first time that his eyes were moist from reining in emotion.

'Birdy?' she asked, surprised. But he did not lower her hand, keeping it secure at the level of the silk pocket handkerchief.

'Gayatri,' he said, his voice struggling against something. 'It will be as you want. It always is. But I do have one request.'

'Yes?'

'Will you help me tell Zain that ...' Birdy looked down at Gayatri's hand and kissed it again, as if for luck or courage. Gayatri understood then that something terrible had happened. Birdy wasn't a man to go back on his word and give in to impulsive temptation.

'What is it?' she whispered, trying to keep agitation out of her voice. 'You aren't ... sick, are you?'

To her relief, Birdy shook his head. But his eyes had a haunted look about them.

'Lali's in the ICU.'

Gayatri's mouth dropped open. 'What?'

'They moved her to London Bridge hospital last night,' Birdy nodded, unblinking. 'She had a cardiac arrest due to alcohol poisoning.'

His voice broke then. It was the first time since Zain had returned that Gayatri had heard her stoic friend indulge in emotion.

'Birdy,' Gayatri said his name softly, like a prayer. She gathered his hands in hers and held it to her chest, for warmth, so that even though she couldn't say the things she wanted to, he would know that she was here. She was his partner for all intents and purposes.

It seemed to work. Birdy managed to find his voice again.

'We moved her out of the rehabilitation centre at her request after her birthday. It seemed like a reasonable thing to do since she had been locked up there for nearly a decade now. Her therapists had said that she could be trusted, especially since we had employed a nurse from the centre to watch her around the clock,' Birdy looked down at his hands. 'I should never have listened. I should have known better—'

'This is not your fault,' Gayatri said emphatically. But Birdy was shaking his head, defeated by guilt.

'I should have known that Lali could bully the best of people into doing her bidding. I wouldn't be surprised if she got the nurse to buy her the vodka out of the cheques I sent her every month.'

Birdy laughed bitterly, but Gayatri could not join in. In her opinion, Lali Rajan had done nothing to deserve her older brother's generosity or regard. But she didn't say this out loud. Gayatri knew that despite his current anger towards her, Birdy cared very deeply about his younger sister. That was just Birdy's way. He loved unwaveringly without ever asking for anything in return.

Something twinged within Gayatri as she insisted again, 'This isn't your fault.'

Birdy closed his eyes and whispered, 'I could have visited more often. I knew Lali was lonely.'

'In that case,' Gayatri said steadily, 'I am to blame.'

It was true. Birdy was reluctant to leave Bombay because Gayatri needed him after Jairaj's death. It was part of the reason that he had given Zain all his business-related travel assignments. And, in return for his constant companionship, Gayatri had given him forty years of nothing.

Guilt ripped through her, acidic and burning. Like cheap vodka poured over an old wound.

'I'm sorry, Birdy,' Gayatri said, meaning it more than ever. 'I've wasted too much of your time.'

'Don't be ridiculous, Gayatri,' Birdy said, his eyes flashing with astonishing ferocity. 'I haven't thought of a second with you as wasted time. I never could. If anything, it has been my pleasure, one I believe I have earned.'

If Gayatri was blushing, Birdy ignored it. 'I only meant that I should have planned at least one trip a year to see my foolish sister.'

'And you didn't because of me. Because I've selfishly monopolized—'

'I didn't go because Zain would feel obligated to come.'

Gayatri quietened down. Birdy discussed everything under the sun with her, but he never ever spoke of his nephew's fraught relationship with his mother.

'Lali still has a terrible effect on him. She never did learn the trick of being maternal.'

'Even after all these years at the … centre?'

'Trust me. She's worse sober.'

'She doesn't still call him a …' Gayatri winced. She couldn't bring herself to say it.

'A mistake?' Birdy shook his head angrily. 'No, she calls him a fraud now. An impostor. The poor cousin playing dress up in rich Mamu's suits. And she says it with relish. Zain has to lock himself up at the office for a week after a call with her.'

'What an unhappy, poisonous woman!' Gayatri said in a rare burst of venom herself. She bit her tongue immediately on seeing Birdy's shocked expression. She couldn't help it. She had seen Zain arrive at Birdy's bungalow as a lanky, lost twenty-two-year-old with no belongings except a few T-shirts and a laptop. She had watched him grow, through sheer will and grit, into a self-possessed young businessman, whom other men turned to for leadership.

'Zain isn't an impostor,' Gayatri insisted. 'If anything, he is more deserving of his position than any of his rich friends who have inherited their CEO title.'

Birdy nodded in agreement.

'This incident got me thinking about my own estate,' Birdy said seriously. 'Lali cannot be trusted with money. I don't think she will ever be sane again. I am going to modify my will and divide the inheritance between Zain and you.'

'You will do nothing of the sort!' Gayatri exclaimed, her tone fiercer than before. Birdy's eyes dried up at her tone.

'For God's sake, Birdy! What do you take me for?'

'Have I said something untoward?'

Gayatri laughed, bemused. 'Aside from the fact that I despise speaking of your death with such frigid indifference, I understand on this, and only this, occasion why you might consider the subject worth broaching. But what I don't understand is how you could think so little of me as to think that I would take even one rupee of your wealth!'

Birdy stared at her, too surprised to speak.

'Zain has earned every penny of his inheritance, Birdy. I refuse to steal from him,' Gayatri said vehemently. 'Cut out Lali by all means, but don't you dare die and make a thief out of me!'

'I'm doing nothing of the sort,' Birdy said calmly. 'Knowing that you will be provided for will simply put my mind at rest.'

Gayatri's expression softened. She understood. He was trying, as she had a few minutes ago, to tell her that although they may never be recognized as each other's companions by the world, he was her partner in life and in death.

'I appreciate that, Birdy, but you needn't worry. I have all that I need,' Gayatri said, pressing his palm affectionately to cushion the blow.

'You want nothing from me then?' He seemed dejected.

'That isn't true,' Gayatri said softly.

Gayatri lifted the armrest with her free hand, the one that was separating them, and leaned her head against his chest. Birdy's hands wrapped around her for the first time ever, with such a natural warmth that Gayatri couldn't imagine why they had spent so much of their life not locked in a comforting embrace. In many ways, she had always been in his comforting embrace, but to physically get there had taken them too many years and too many deaths.

'Shh,' she said to comfort him. Gayatri put her arm softly on Birdy's cheek and patted it, letting his reluctant tears wet her fingers and letting her warmth remind his body that he wasn't alone. She would make sure that Zain felt similarly warm, similarly loved when she told him the truth that evening. And she would make him feel warm for the rest of his life, too, just as Birdy had kept Gayatri and Mangala warm even through Jai's iciest tantrums.

They drove to the flower market with the soft sunlight of the Sunday morning blanketing their bodies in more warmth.

❦

'You look fab,' Rajni said as soon as I signed into to our FaceTime call at 8 a.m. 'I know I say this all the time, but this time I really mean it.'

I laughed. 'Thanks for letting me know that all those other times were a lie.'

'They weren't a lie.' Rajni grinned. 'Fab just had a different standard then. Fab in New York means you don't look like you're about to pass out, as you should after a day of working out, working and surviving mostly on caffeine and sugar. But now …'

Rajni looked at me and let out a wolf whistle. 'Now you look fresher than you did when we were in college.'

I smiled. I missed Rajni's insistent, sass-laden voice so much that I wished I could pluck her out of my screen and hug her.

'Did I tell you that my wedding planner wants me to quit caffeine?'

'Did you tell her to go fuck herself?' Rajni asked, her face immediately indignant on my behalf. 'I mean, looking fresh ain't worth it if it means not enjoying your life.'

'Amen,' I said, solemnly raising my large cup of coffee in salutation.

This was why I needed to speak to Rajni, to cleanse my brain of Dolly Sehgal and Aashna Soonawalla's relentless stream of gossip with Rajni's straight talk and logic. The last few days of wedding planning had cluttered my mind with my mother-in-law's unkind opinions of the women of Delhi, their status symbols and appearances. If I had to hear *'Who does she think she is?'* one more time, and with no caffeine, I would scream.

'I wish you were here,' I said truthfully. 'I need my maid of honour to help me last the last two weeks of dealing with my mother-in-law and her wedding planner.'

'I know, babe,' Rajni's face squinted in apology. 'I'm going to take a flight out as soon as this soda deal is over. I can't wait to see the courtesan outfit you have for me, oh Queen!'

'Don't,' I said, shaking my head. I had Snapchatted Rajni pictures of the entire process so far. I needed someone else to make sense of this ridiculous wedding to keep me sane. Kabir didn't see any problem with the idea of being crowned emperor amongst his friends and family. And Naani and Mum were so embarrassed on my behalf that they didn't bring up the subject around me at all. Once, I heard them whispering about it in a concerned tone in Naani's room, but they fell silent as soon as I walked through the door.

It was my own fault that they won't tell me what they truly thought. I had been so adamant about all the Sehgals' choices, so goddamn defiant with my mother about the honeymoon, about living in Delhi, about quitting my job, that it was no wonder that she clammed up with fake excitement whenever I returned home to tell her of some new development about my wedding and marriage.

I felt ashamed to think back to the moment when I had told Mum and Naani that I would like a 'proper family' for a change. *What was I thinking? And what was a proper family anyway?* Mum had raised me, single-handedly, as a twenty-something graduate student trying to make her career to support us both. Maybe she didn't have a husband and all the time in the world to dress me up and tell me stories like Dolly Sehgal did with Parineeti, but at least she never asked me 'Who the hell do you think you are, Radhika?' when I told her I wanted to go to business school.

Dolly Sehgal never said this, of course. But her face did, when I told her that I wasn't going to be unemployed once I got to Delhi. I was going to run a business that helped women, and I was going to start running it as soon as 22 January. I wasn't going to tell her about *The Queen Network*, not until I had told Mum and Naani. But then it had become necessary to tell Dolly Sehgal the whole truth. She had wanted to know why I needed the morning hours to myself. Why I couldn't spend the entire day meeting florists and dermatologists and whatever other -ologists to ensure that I did, indeed, look like Anarkali on the day all her friends and foes came to see me.

'Is Dolly still insisting on the ridiculous dance performance?' Rajni asked. I grimaced, not wanting to get into it.

'On the bright side,' I said to Rajni, 'at least I get to marry a prince.'

'Absolutely,' Rajni said, 'I can't wait to meet him.'

I shook my head apologetically. 'I know. It's absurd that your schedules haven't been able to match up for a quick FaceTime call yet. But Kabir is even busier than we were at McKinley—'

'I find that hard to imagine,' Rajni challenged. But I was insistent.

'No, it's true.' I said. 'I think that's what happens when you live with your boss. Dolly says it's a lucky thing I'm going to live with them, actually. Then at least his dad will have to lay off him at home. From the way Kabir talks, I can tell that Chander Sehgal is really wringing him out at the factory in these first few months—'

I broke off as I noticed a funny look cross Rajni's face. 'What is it?'

'Nothing … it's just,' she said and let out a short, uncertain laugh. 'I keep forgetting that all of this stuff is really happening, that you're actually going to be the wife of some guy I don't know, and in Delhi of all places.'

I wrinkled my nose. I didn't like the way she spoke of Delhi, as though she was speaking of the Wild West.

'Yes, it's really happening,' I said. 'What's wrong with Delhi?'

'Nothing, it's just … ' Rajni shook her head as though trying to clear up some confusion. 'And it is probably too late to ask this, but I just have to. Once at least. As your maid of honour, I think it is my right—'

'What is it, Rajni?' I snapped, irritated now by the furtive, condescending manner everyone was taking with me.

'Do you love this guy?'

'Sure.'

'Radhika?'

And suddenly, for some reason I couldn't lie any more. Not to her. Not to the woman who had dissected every drunk call, every one-night stand and every 'potential man' with me over a bowl of cereal and a cup of coffee since we were nineteen.

'Not yet,' I said, letting my shoulders slump. My head suddenly felt lighter after finally admitting the truth.

To her credit, Rajni neither gasped nor did she say 'Aha! I knew it!' like anyone else would have done. Instead, she looked at me and nodded slowly.

'All right, love,' she said. 'That is fine.'

'Is it?' I asked, slightly fearful. For some ridiculous reason, tears started to well up in my eyes.

She nodded. 'As long as you know the truth and can live with it.'

I was touched by her acceptance. The tears spilt over. Before I knew it, I was bawling like a baby into my black coffee.

'Shh,' Rajni said, looking at me with understanding, like she had for the last decade.

'It's all right, babe. You've got this.'

'I do?' I asked through a stream of snot, tears and lashes.

Rajni smiled at me. 'Even if you don't,' she added, 'I've got you.'

I didn't know how she did it, but she made me feel better, that too from thousands of miles away.

If Kabir and I had half the understanding Rajj and I had within the first six weeks of freshman year, I would already love him with all my heart. But for some reason, beyond the romance, we were struggling to develop acceptance for each other. All I could do now was to hope that we would be able to build a loving relationship. That over the years, there would be trust and acceptance.

22
Conversation

Kabir

Afternoon :)

Guess who's playing truant today?

Lol! I know. Mom called me, freaking out, a little earlier.

Why was she freaking out?

She calculated the days to go for your next period and she's worried that you will be bloated at the wedding.

Please tell me you're joking.

She's just looking out for you, babe.

Wants you to look your best.

Which reminds me: how was the dermat appointment?

She asked if I wanted to clean out my colon for glowing 'movie-star' skin.

Do you?

Side effects include vomiting and possible renal failure.

How long does the glow last?

I'm not doing it, Kabir.

Alright, babe, whatever you want.

If you change your mind, I'm happy to pay for it.

You are joking, right?

Sure.

I was typing emails to graphic designers for *The Queen Network* website when Mum knocked on my door at noon. It was surprising to see her in her loose olive-coloured T-shirt and H&M jeans, holding a notebook and a mug of tea. I was suddenly transported back to the eighth grade, when she would emerge from her study on a random Sunday afternoon to ask me if I needed anything, as though suddenly remembering that she had a young daughter who may require a few minutes of her attention. Once she had decided that I was old enough to be left to my own capable devices, she had stopped showing up at all.

'Lunch?' she asked hesitantly. I nodded.

'I thought you were again eating in Naanu's study with your research.'

'I felt like a change,' she shrugged. 'I could make us sandwiches.'

I shook my head, chuckling. Soon, we were in the kitchen and I was breaking eggs into a frying pan, while Mum plucked coriander to add to the cold preparation of spiced potatoes Naani had left us for lunch. We hadn't been alone since Mum arrived in Bombay, I realized.

Now, as we sat opposite each other at the dining table, with steaming plates of fried eggs, hot potatoes and toast in front of us, I wondered what Mum was going to say to me with Naani out of scolding distance. *Was she going to lecture me on independence again? Or was she going to beg me to reconsider this wedding, and the Sehgals, as I knew she had been wanting to do since she met Dolly?* I wasn't sure if I could handle a feminist tirade after having a transatlantic emotional breakdown with Rajni.

But Mum surprised me. After she swallowed a forkful of her eggs, she said, 'I hope you and Kabir have a happy marriage, Radhika.'

I stared at her in shock. Mum had never wished me well in any of my romantic relationships before. Not that she had ever wished anything bad for me. But she had always been indifferent to the idea of my boyfriends, almost as though they were too superfluous to be worthy of comment.

'You do?' I was unable to keep the bewilderment out of my voice.

'Yes.' She nodded and nibbled at her toast. Then she cleared her throat and added in a soft voice. 'I'm impressed by you.'

My eyes widened. This had to be a trap. What had impressed her? How I had betrayed feminism, forgotten our values or become a slave to emotions?

I waited for her to deliver a bitter and dry punchline, but Mum continued to look at me as earnestly as ever. She even seemed a little … scared.

I had never thought that I would apply that word to my fearless mother.

'I could never … I don't know. Feel as deeply as you do, I suppose,' she said softly. 'I have hurt a lot of people as a result.'

'Mum?' I wanted to touch her hands, but they were clenched around her mug of tea tightly, as if depending on its warmth for strength. I felt as though she would break if I tried to loosen her grasp now.

'Are you … do you mean Steve?'

She barely nodded, as though too ashamed to be having this discussion but still plodding through anyway.

'All through it, I never gave him access. I told myself I was protecting you. But really, I was just protecting myself, wasn't I?'

Her eyes started to moisten. I had never seen my mother's eyes fill up. I didn't even think it was possible for her tear ducts to do that. Her voice choked as she spoke now.

'I never gave you access either, did I?'

Oh wow. I hadn't expect to have all this hashed out over a plate of afternoon eggs two weeks before my wedding.

'Well,' I laughed unkindly, but then I stopped as I saw her look up at me, eyes full of salt water and self-doubt.

I couldn't bring myself to be mean. It was easier when she was her usual cantankerous self, her tone always on the edge of condescension for my stupid need of a hug or a doll or a boyfriend. But I couldn't bring myself to feel the old angst when her voice was so soft and defeated, when she was just a girl who had strived and thrived but was still confused about love and loving.

I couldn't remember the last time I saw Dr Mangala Anand be so vulnerable. *It had something to do with being in a home full of women and warm meals*, I thought, *which gave us the confidence to be a little more naked*. I wouldn't have taken nearly half as many chances as I had in the past few months if I hadn't had Naani and some hot spiced potatoes to come home to every day.

'Mum,' I said, 'all that is done now. We're both in good places. You don't need to worry about me any more.'

Mum laughed, self-deprecating instead of sarcastic.

'I'm afraid that comes with the territory, sweetheart. I may not have given you access, but it doesn't mean that I don't love you with my whole being.'

Her voice dropped to a whisper and a few tears fell down her cheek.

'It doesn't mean that I don't love him either.'

I tried not to blush. It was a bit odd, to be discussing my mother's love life with her when we had such good practise pretending it didn't exist for the last fifteen years. A memory of her insisting that 'he is just a colleague' sprouted back from my adolescent memory. I pushed it away, embarrassed.

'I think it's great that you ... have someone like that in your life,' I said. 'That you're able to recognize it now.'

'Radhika, would you mind, if I—' she hesitated. It was weird to see my mother like this, tentative instead of commanding. I felt like there had been a shift in the space-time continuum. Dr Mangala Anand had finally put her textbook and glasses down and was daring to be a person, not a professional.

'Would you mind if I invited Steve to your wedding?'

I almost laughed. *Was that it?*

'Of course not, Mum,' I said, now freely reaching out to hold her hand, which had finally loosened its grasp on Naani's blue mug. 'You don't have to ask,' I added, although I was secretly glad that she did. 'He should be there. If he is a part of your life, he is automatically a part of mine.'

I could not remember the last time Mum and I had hugged, but we did so in that moment. It was not the kind of comfort that Naani's soft sari and French perfume afforded, but it was its own kind of warmth. Awkward and bespectacled and olive green in colour.

❧

Dolly Sehgal lifted her iPhone and let out a sob.

'The worst has happened.'

'Mom, calm down,' Kabir groaned from his little corner on the video call. Parineeti and Chander were barely listening as usual. Both their eyes were off the camera, probably focused on another window on their laptop screens.

'Don't tell me to calm down!' Dolly Sehgal yelled to get her family's attention. Her plump face was a beetroot red as she turned her phone sideways to yell at her son.

'Your precious fiancée wants her mother's underage boyfriend to come to the wedding. She wants Chander to put a mala on him! I wouldn't be surprised if she asks the white man to sit down and do the goddamn kanyadaan.'

'Dolly!' Chander Sehgal finally turned his attention to the family video call. He couldn't have his wife swearing while he was trying to draft an email to the head of Roxy Pharma.

'I'm sorry, Chander,' Dolly Sehgal shook her head, blinking back tears. 'I just don't understand how Radhika could be so ungrateful. Here we are, breaking our backs to give her a fairytale wedding, to crown her as a queen as she enters the best family in Delhi, and she can't even be bothered to come to all the wedding appointments. She's off running some blog all day.'

'Blog? What blog?' Chander Sehgal was immediately alert. He was suspicious of these blogger–activist types. They were always poking around his business, trying to ferret out another reason to levy CSR charges on him. They couldn't have one of those in the family.

'It's not a blog, Dad. God!' Parineeti, who had been half-listening all this while, had to weigh in now. 'It's a women's leadership organization, and it doesn't even start until *after* the wedding. So you have no reason to worry, Ma.'

'Oh God! Is Radhika going to start doing all that abla-naari nonsense?' Chander Sehgal was furious. 'We can't have one of those in the family.'

'No, Dad,' Kabir said, tired. He hated these family FaceTime calls. It was bad enough that he had to justify every business decision to his father; he didn't want to spend the rest of his life justifying his wife's business decisions to him, too. 'It's a proper business. Dipa

Ghanshyamdas is investing in it. There are not going to be any protests or any of that.'

'You should be proud, Papa!' Parineeti added. 'Radhika may even be featured in *Forbes* magazine by this time next year.'

Everyone stopped speaking for a moment, processing this.

'*Forbes*?' Dolly Sehgal was reluctantly impressed. 'Really?'

'I doubt *Forbes* would feature a partner of Dipa Ghanshyamdas's after that disgusting stunt she pulled at their awards ceremony—' Chander began.

'Yes, they will!' Parineeti laughed. 'Dipa G. is an icon and the controversy has made her an even bigger one. I wouldn't be surprised if Radhika becomes an icon, too.'

'Pari, don't be ridiculous,' Kabir said quickly.

'I don't know if we need an icon in the family,' Chander Sehgal pronounced.

'Yes, not unless she's a fashion icon,' Dolly Sehgal said. 'If only Radhika would focus on the wedding, she could be in *Vogue* by her birthday. Nobody here cares about *Forbes*.'

'That's the point,' Parineeti whispered. 'That's why what Radhika and Dipa are doing is so important.'

Kabir sighed. It was impossible to win an argument with his mother, he decided.

'All right, Ma,' he said. 'I'll speak to her.'

'About the wedding appointments and the gora.'

'Yes, yes,' he said. 'I'll have it sorted out.'

'Radhika?'

I was surprised to hear Kabir's voice on a Monday night. He preferred texting on weekdays. Talking to people all day at Sehgal Pharma drained him to the extent that he couldn't be chipper on the phone in the evening.

'This is a lovely surprise,' I said. 'How was your day?'

'Radhika,' he sounded tired. 'I called about something specific.'

His tone became terse around the word. 'Specific', as in 'I'm not going to chat'. *Fine.*

'What's up?'

'Mum called me, hysterical, earlier this evening.'

'Oh?' I felt indignation swell within me. 'What about?'

What could Dolly Sehgal possibly have to complain about? She had chosen my wedding jewellery, outfit, menu and honeymoon. Naani had had no say in anything but the flowers, and I had had no say in anything but the colour of the napkins the guests would wipe their mouths with after the à la carte dinner was served (also Dolly Sehgal's idea because 'buffets are so tacky!'). The Anands were paying for half this thing and still had absolutely no choice.

'It's about the guest list. She said you asked for an extra invitation?'

'Yes,' I said, trying to keep the defensiveness out of my voice. 'It's for Mum's partner. Steve. I told you about him, remember?'

'Yes, I remember,' Kabir hesitated and then lowered his voice.

'But I thought you said they weren't—as in, it wasn't official?'

'It is official, finally. They're together!' I was so pleased that Kabir was taking an interest in Mum and Steve that my irritation receded. Maybe this would lead to a conversation about our childhoods. Maybe I would find out a little about how he got that faint scar just below his hairline.

'Ah!' Kabir said in response.

All right, I will try a little harder.

'Isn't it fantastic that they are together? I had a real conversation with Mum yesterday. She opened up to me for the first time in, I don't know, my whole life. We even hugged. We haven't hugged since I was eight and had the flu.'

I smiled as I thought of the tentative but happy manner in which Mum had dialled Steve's number and whispered to him in an urgent, girlish tone I'd never heard before. It must have gone well, because Mum had joined Naani and I as we watched *Downton Abbey* on TV in the evening, instead of disappearing into her bedroom to work on her book some more. She had even hummed the theme song of the show with us. Zain and Birdy had joined us later for jelly.

'Yesterday was a good day. A great day, in fact,' I said, smiling. 'I wish you had been there, too. We felt like a family.'

'Oh,' Kabir cleared his throat. 'That's great, Radhika, but—'

'But?'

'But the guest list has already been decided, sweetheart. The caterers have been paid for a certain number of plates,' he said in a tense rush. 'I'm sure you understand that it's too last minute to get a place for your mother's friend.'

'Kabir,' I laughed in disbelief. 'We invited a thousand people. I'm sure not everyone is going to turn up.'

'Of course, they are.' Kabir sounded offended. 'It's the event of the season. Everyone wants to see the royal Sehgal wedding.'

I rolled my eyes.

'Fine,' I said. 'Then I won't eat. Steve can eat from my royal plate.'

'Don't be ridiculous, Radhika,' Kabir snapped. 'The plates aren't the point.'

'What is the point then, Kabir?' I was confused.

Kabir drew a sharp breath and then let it go. 'Never mind,' he said. 'Call your mother's underage boyfriend. I'll handle it.'

Underage? Steve was thirty-seven years old. But before I could point this out, before I could ask Kabir what the hell he meant or tell him to stop being a royal pain in the butt, the phone call ended.

I couldn't believe it. He hung up on me. So much for building trust and acceptance.

'Can I help you?' Gayatri asked the silver-haired lady who had appeared in her living room just as she was untying the laces of her much-abused pink trainers. In contrast, her visitor's feet were encased in midnight blue stilettos, with a brilliant crystal-studded barrette over the toes.

The lady smiled at Gayatri. Gayatri realized, from the crow's feet that appeared around her visitor's eyes, that she must be as old as her. Yet she didn't look a day over fifty because her skin had been surgically stretched into place unlike Gayatri's, which had wrinkled with softness and time.

'It's Botox and collagen,' the lady said with a matter-of-fact grin. 'Necessary, if you want to stay in business at seventy-two, I'm afraid.'

Gayatri was taken aback by her abrupt honesty. She blushed, embarrassed for staring. Immediately, she decided that she liked this woman and was willing to delay her cool shower after her sweaty morning walk to chat with her.

'It's a job well done,' Gayatri said. 'If I wasn't in the beauty business, I wouldn't be able to tell the difference.'

'You must be Radhika's grandmother, the legendary owner of Grace.' The lady held out her hand for Gayatri to shake it. 'I'm a fan of yours, Mrs Anand.'

Gayatri was surprised by the extent of the stranger's knowledge. She was about to ask her to introduce herself when Mangala emerged from her bedroom, murmuring 'morning' and rubbing her eyes with the back of her hand in the way that Gayatri had explicitly told her not to. She was about to tell her daughter off for ruining the delicate skin under her eyes when Mangala looked at her visitor and exclaimed, 'Oh. My. God.'

That was the first time in twenty years that Gayatri had seen her daughter look so impressed by anyone. It was nearly comical, the way she rushed forward, agitatedly tying her bathrobe with one hand and putting the other out to greet the lady.

'I cannot believe—' Mangala gushed, 'Ms Ghanshyamdas, it is so good to meet you. I'm Dr Anand! I've studied your case extensively for many of my reports on the "Agency of South Asian Women". I had no idea you were coming in today for an interview—although, as I told your assistant, a phone interview would be fine, too! Still, thank you so much. I'd love for your story to be the opening chapter of my book!'

Ms Ghanshyamdas's eyes twinkled as she shook Mangala's hand. 'That is a huge compliment, Dr Anand. I wish Radhika had told me I was a subject of academic interest. I thought I was only being covered by idiot journalists at *The Times* and *Forbes*.'

Mangala faltered.

'You mean,' she cleared her throat. 'You mean you haven't read my research?'

'Er, not yet,' Dipa said apologetically.

'So you ... aren't here for an interview with me?'

'I'm afraid not.'

To cover up for the awkwardness of Mangala's crestfallen expression, Gayatri asked, 'May I ask who you are please?'

'Ma, this is Dipa Ghanshyamdas,' Mangala said, piercing her mother with a 'please don't embarrass me' look.

This name, however, didn't ring any bells for Gayatri. Then, in a fortuitous flash, Gayatri recalled the video Radhika had shown them at the dinner table the other day!

'You're the woman who rejected the award!'

Mangala looked mortified. 'That's not all she is, Ma. Don't reduce her to a headline like that—'

But Dipa was laughing good-naturedly. 'Yes. I am the woman who rejected the award!'

Gayatri was immediately apologetic. 'I'm sorry,' she said. 'I didn't mean to—'

'No offense taken. I wear that title like a crown!' she said, grinning at Gayatri. 'But I'm also the principal investor in your granddaughter's new business.'

Gayatri and Mangala fell silent with surprise.

'And going by your expression,' Dipa continued, clearly enjoying herself, 'I'm guessing she hasn't shared her business plan with you yet. Or the fact that you two were the inspiration for this project.'

Mangala rose swiftly. 'I'll go wake her up.'

But Dipa Ghanshyamdas shook her head. 'Please don't. Our meeting isn't for another two hours. I simply jumped the gun because my flight got in early. And from what I gather about her wedding planning, it seems like she could use the rest.'

Mangala sat back down, but now it was Gayatri who rose.

'Tea,' Gayatri said definitively as she walked to the kitchen. 'If we're going to have revelations, we must have tea.'

❧

'You haven't quit your job then!'

I nearly screamed.

'Relax, Radhika. It's just me.'

I couldn't help but feel disoriented. I may have got used to seeing Naani's face hovering atop my bed early in the morning, but the last memory I had of Mum being in my bedroom was probably from the time I was in a cradle.

'Uh,' was my incredibly coherent answer. *What else would you expect at six in the morning, after an evening of debating silver spoons versus copper spoons with Dolly Sehgal?* (I had voted for copper. Silver had won. I had no idea why they dragged me along for these wedding shopping trips when my opinions were never taken into account.)

'I did quit my job,' I whined, pulling the blanket back over my head.

'Yes, but you're not unemployed,' Mum pulled the blanket away and laughed. It was lovely to see her laugh in this free, happy manner.

'What are you talking about?' I asked, propping myself up and rubbing the sleep from my eyes.

'Don't do that!' Naani's voice cut through the room as she entered with a mug of tea. Then, to make the morning even weirder, Dipa Ghanshyamdas appeared behind her, in an impeccable white pantsuit, holding a mug of tea herself, as though she were the jet-setting aunt of the family.

'Good morning,' Dipa said. 'I didn't know how much to tell them about *The Queen Network*, so I thought I'd let you explain.'

I laughed. Dipa G. might be the most eccentric investor I've met. Or she was the most intelligent, I realized. Even now, on the morning of our contract signing, she was testing my passion for this project in the most unusual way.

I turned to my family and grinned at their eager expressions.

'Mum, Naani,' I said, wide awake now. 'I'm starting an organization that gives women professionals leadership training to help them progress to the top in whichever industry they are in. Dipa G. here is my principal investor.' Then, turning to my partner, I added, 'Together we're going to revolutionize the way Indian women work, negotiate and network.'

Dipa nodded in approval. 'For a second I thought you had given up on it since your family didn't know anything about it. I was worried you might have become a full-time wife.'

'No chance,' I laughed. 'I was waiting till we signed the contract before I told my family the good news.'

Dipa smiled at me. 'Fair enough,' she said and then brought out the papers from her Goyard bag. 'Here they are.'

Naani and Mum looked at me in amazement. I didn't blame them. All of this was quite strange. I was half lying down, half sitting in my pink pyjamas with three feminist stalwarts in my bedroom, reading through the terms of partnership for my first business.

There couldn't have been a more perfect moment in my life. I signed the papers in my sure, cursive handwriting, ending with a flourish because a little drama seemed warranted.

'Congratulations!' Dipa said to me.

'Congratulations!' I replied.

'I was wrong,' Mum said to Naani.

'Thank you,' Naani said to the ceiling fan, her hands joined in prayer.

Kabir

You're really not going to talk to me?

I'm busy.

I'm not going to apologize about the Steve thing.

I never asked you to.

You're going to have to see me at the fitting, you know?

I know.

I'll talk to you then.

Fantastic.

On certain days, Kabir felt like his life was a prisoner to his family's wishes. He had spent the week driving to and from the factory at his father's command, and today, at his mother's request, he had taken a flight to Bombay for a sherwani fitting. As soon as he had landed, Radhika had told him that they were having dinner with that neighbour of hers.

Kabir tried not to growl at the army of cars boxing his Jaguar in at the car park of his mother's hotel. Now that Kabir's pursuit of Radhika had ended, all of Bombay's glaring irritations had come into focus. He thought it was a city of narrow roads filled with too many upstarts. Bombay didn't respect lineage. In Delhi, the managers of all the finest hotels knew his name and would probably park his car themselves if they knew he was in the line for valet. Nobody cared who your father was in Bombay, or which car you drove. People even took taxis to hotels sometimes—a fact that Kabir found absurd. *Why go to a five-star to eat if you obviously can't afford it?*

It didn't help that Radhika was being this different, snarky version of herself with him, stiffly presenting her cheek to be kissed at the airport and then maintaining an arm's distance from him at all times in Dolly's hotel room. So he hadn't picked up her calls for the past couple of days or replied to her texts. *What did it matter?* She didn't realize that he was avoiding her calls for her own good. If the white-hot rage that had been gathering in Kabir's stomach from his father's first 9 a.m. call were allowed to burst upon

Radhika in its raw form, she would be burnt to an ember.
She would not be able to handle his moods like Aishwarya
could. Then, Kabir would be sick with remorse but too
proud to apologize and it would raise a stink for days. So,
he had avoided her texts and waited instead to give her his
gift in person. The gift that would obliterate all his mistakes
and shortcomings.

Kabir's calm started to return as the designer's assistant
helped him into the princely gold sherwani tailored for him.
When he looked at himself in the mirror, with a sheathed
sword in one hand and a jewelled turban atop his head, his
irritation with Bombay, his mother and his fiancée began
to wear off.

'You look like Jehangir,' Dolly Sehgal crooned from
the plush velvet chair she was sitting in at the Sabyasachi
boutique.

Radhika emerged in an embroidered pink and blue
anarkali that shimmered as she floated to his side. The
designer's assistant flitted to her and hung an ornament
on the side of her head. Kabir grinned as he recognized
the jewel.

'What is this?' Radhika asked, in her adorable, faintly
American twang.

'It's a jhoomar.'

'All the nautch girls wear it,' Kabir said fondly.

Radhika's hand, which was lightly touching the pearls
in her hair, immediately fell to her side.

'We will exchange it for a crown once the wedding ceremony is over,' Aashna Soonawalla reassured her quickly.

Radhika frowned slightly but didn't say anything. Kabir gazed at their reflections in the mirror and felt a quiet triumph erupt in his chest. His earlier feelings of claustrophobia melted away completely.

He felt a deep gratitude for his parents. One parent was ensuring that he had an empire to run and the other had ensured that he would sit upon a throne with a princess by his side while the finest families of Delhi watched in awe.

Kabir left the boutique feeling very sure of himself, even though he was in Bombay, where nobody knew his last name.

❧

'I have a gift for you, babe,' Kabir said once we sat down to dinner with Zain at Joss, the Asian restaurant of his choosing.

I wondered why Kabir had waited till now to tell me this. Especially since we drove here alone and in complete silence. A silence that was stilted for me and self-satisfied for him. It was impossible to give Kabir the silent treatment, I had realized. He was too damn happy to be left alone.

'Give it to me later,' I said glancing at Zain apologetically.

'But I have it right here,' Kabir insisted.

'It's all right, you guys,' Zain laughed. 'I don't mind a little PDA.'

'It's not a big deal,' Kabir said.

I braced myself. *Was he being falsely humble again about an obscenely expensive wallet or watch or piece of jewellery?*

But Kabir didn't pull out a shopping bag, much to my relief. Instead, he brought out an invitation. Our wedding invitation.

I looked at it, confused. Zain looked bemused. Then I flipped the envelope over.

'To Mr Steve Smith,' I read out loud.

Kabir grinned at me, as if to say 'you're welcome.'

I glanced at Zain, but his face was a polite mask of inexpression—the kind you put on where you're deeply ashamed for your companion but don't want to embarrass them further with pity. My cheeks burned, but I didn't say anything. If Kabir was expecting a 'thank you' for a plus-one invitation for my mother to my own wedding, he was in for disappointment.

'Well?' he asked.

'Well,' I said brightly, ignoring him. 'Shall we order? What is good here? The Peking duck, I've heard?'

'Yes,' Zain said, signalling to a waiter. 'Let's order that. And a bottle of champagne. We're celebrating tonight.'

Kabir looked confused by this change in the conversation, but at least he caught our drift.

'What are we celebrating?' he asked politely, but his smile had become brittle. He was really smarting about not having his 'gift' acknowledged, I realized.

'The beginning of Radhika's new business!' Zain said. 'Dipa Ghanshyamdas flew into town herself to sign the contract for *The Queen Network*.'

Kabir's smile froze as the waiter appeared. 'I had no idea,' he said. 'Why didn't you say anything, babe?'

'I would have,' I shrugged, 'but you hung up on me. And stopped taking my calls.'

Kabir's eyes flashed at me in fury and I felt a twinge of satisfaction. *Good*, I thought. He should be a little angry. He should feel at least an iota of the furious shame I felt when he disconnected the phone on me, as though I was no longer worthy of his time, and let all my calls receive a busy tone. And then he showed up two days later in Bombay, expecting me to fawn all over him as his goddamn nautch girl.

We spent the rest of the dinner making polite conversation and fiddling with our chopsticks. Kabir and Zain talked about the football teams they supported and the charities they donated to. The three of us talked a little about an American sitcom we liked, and we made half-hearted plans to have a marathon session of it at some point in the future. But it was obvious to me, and perhaps even to Zain (I could tell from the way he glanced at me now and again), that everyone at the table was just surviving this dinner instead of enjoying it.

The bubbles in my champagne flute had long become flat and Kabir wasn't even tasting his as he guzzled glass after glass, always saying *'To Radhika!'* emphatically before pouring himself another drink.

By the time dessert was brought to us, my name had become a slur.

'Well,' Zain said, putting down his chocolate-coated spoon. 'I think I'm done for the evening, you guys. I have an early start tomorrow.'

'Same here,' Kabir said, making a little cheque signing motion in the air to the waiter. 'I have a 6 a.m. flight to Delhi and back-to-back meetings at the office right after.'

Zain nodded. 'I know what you mean, man. I have meetings till 9 p.m., then a flight to Dubai, and then another meeting at our office there.'

'The waiter is here,' I said, mostly to cut off this pissing contest of work hours. Kabir frowned at the waiter who had appeared empty-handed.

'I asked for the cheque?' he said.

'No. This is on me,' Zain said, flicking his platinum credit card on to the table.

The waiter, to my great satisfaction, shrugged at them both. 'Ma'am has already paid.'

I smiled at the two men as the waiter quickly cleared our table of the duck bones, the melted chocolate and the last dregs of champagne.

'When did you pay?' Zain asked.

'Sometime during Manchester versus Liverpool,' I smiled.

Zain started to laugh. Kabir, however, seemed like he was struggling to see the humour in the situation.

We didn't speak on the drive back home. But now, finally, the silence had unnerved Kabir. He sped, driving much quicker than I'd ever known him to. I wondered if it was the champagne or if he was trying to scare me with sharp, unexpected turns and rapid changing of gears. I refused to give him the satisfaction of a reaction, even though I was starting to feel a little nauseous. I sat there, teeth clenched and arms gripping the side of my seat till he stopped outside Naani's house abruptly, the tyres screeching to a halt.

I swung open the car door, glad to get out. But his hand was on my arm, pinning it into place with a vice-like grip. 'Wait.'

I narrowed my eyes. 'Let me go, Kabir.'

'I said, *wait*,' he growled. I looked on as he reached into his wallet. He counted out ten two-thousand-rupee notes.

'For dinner,' he said, dropping the money in my hand. Then he kissed me, hard on the mouth, and nodded for me to leave.

I was in shock, unable to move even though his hand was no longer holding mine.

'What the fuck, Kabir?'

'I can't let a girl pay for me,' he said, shaking his head furiously. 'Especially not my wife.'

There was a sharp churning, a rising in my stomach. I had to get out of the car immediately. He made sure that the pink notes were firmly clutched in my fists as I went, slamming the door behind me, unable to stay a second longer in his car or his company.

I vomited violently by the side of Naani's potted plants. Kabir had driven off obviously not interested in helping me throw up the dinner he paid for.

TO: radhikaanand@gmail.com
FROM: zainranjan@gmail.com
SUBJECT: Pick Up The Phone
Did you get home all right?????
Mamu was furious that I let Kabir drive you back. None of us should have been driving really after the bottle we put away.
Reply ASAP or I'm coming over to check on you.
Zain

TO: zainranjan@gmail.com
FROM: radhikaanand@gmail.com
SUBJECT: RE: Pick Up The Phone
Hey. I'm fine. No need to come over. Tell Birdy he has no need to worry. Kabir's an excellent driver, even when he's drunk! Must be a Delhi thing. LOL.
Not calling back because I sound funny; throat's sore from all the drinking.
Thanks for coming to dinner! We had a great time! Kabir especially! He loved meeting you.
Thanks for a fun evening! See you soon.
Rad

TO: radhikaanand@gmail.com
FROM: radhikaanand@gmail.com
SUBJECT: How Many Times Are You …

… Going to listen to 'Bad Guy' by Billi Eilish and cry your heart out?

Talk to him. He's your fiancé.

Gayatri would never have taken this kind of shit from Jairaj.

The difference was, of course, that Jairaj never hurt Gayatri.

23
Fabric

'*Ta* thai thai, tatth-aaa, tai tai tatth.'
'Sing it with your eyes, Radhika. You can't breathe without him. Your world makes no sense without him.'

I never thought I would despise Kathak, but ever since I started training with Aashna Soonawalla's wedding choreographer, the court dance had become less of an amusement for me and more of an aggravation.

So far, these dance practices had been only mildly annoying, but today, with Kabir's money burning a hole in my wallet, all the cloying lyrics I was asked to sing and all the coy expressions I was commanded to make started to infuriate me. Each time I heard 'Swoon, Radhika, swoon!' my face froze, refusing to comply.

Now, despite me being a romantic and knowing that music wasn't meant to be taken quite so seriously, there was something within me that just squirmed at the idea of singing these desperate lyrics and dancing for Kabir in a room filled with my family and all of his high-society friends from Delhi.

I couldn't imagine what my mother's expression would be like when she saw me dressed as a Mughal-era prostitute professing love to her king. Or my grandmother's face!

Oh God. Birdy would have a heart attack!

My feet stopped and my eyes stopped dancing. Rimi, the red-faced choreographer, turned to me, confused.

'What's wrong? There are still two verses left!'

'No,' I shook my head. 'I'm not doing this.'

Blood returned to my cheeks. I felt better. A release, coupled with relief, started to course through my body at this simple admission.

'No,' I repeated to myself, enjoying the sensation of refusal. 'Definitely not.' With that, I started to untie my dupatta from around my waist.

Aashna Soonawalla came forward immediately. 'Sweetheart, what do you mean you're not doing this? This is the main attraction of the event. You're a courtesan.'

'I am not a courtesan.'

Dolly Sehgal was baffled. I couldn't blame her. She had not seen me snap before. She probably thought I was incapable of snapping. Honestly, I didn't know what had got into me either. Perhaps it was nerves. Perhaps it was the fact that I had spent the last few days feeling as though I was straddling two completely different worlds. There was Dipa Ghanshyamdas and her marvellous women friends on the one hand, and on the other hand my future mother-in-law was commanding me to profess my love and loyalty to my kingly husband.

Somehow, I had expected planning my wedding to be more fun. It had been no fun at all, but I was getting through it because the thought of a married life made it all seem worth it. But suddenly I wasn't as sure any more.

And then I understood what was wrong. The realization rained down on me like the sound of percussion beats tapped across a drum.

I wanted to feel like a queen when I got married, not like a nautch girl. I wanted my husband to feel as though we were both lucky to have found each other, not as though I was lucky to find him.

'I don't want to do the dance.' I bent down to untie my ghungroos.

Dolly Sehgal came forward and leaned down towards me. 'Beta,' she said in a soothing tone, 'the dance is what ties the wedding together. Without it, the whole theme seems a bit foolish.'

She laughed lightly and looked around the room. Everyone nodded in agreement with her. She turned to look at me expectantly, as though hoping that the power of suggestion would pressure me into agreeing with her.

'Change the theme then,' I said with a shrug.

I untied the last knot around my feet and ripped off the ghungroos. The bells fell off with a sharp ringing, which to my ears resembled joyous laughter.

TO: zainranjan@gmail.com
FROM: radhikaanand@gmail.com
SUBJECT: Help

You wouldn't happen to know any graphic designers who could do logo/brand design for *The Queen Network*, would you?

I'm silently contemplating electrocuting myself with the fairy lights at WeCanWork, to feel some sort of creative spark after meetings with duds all afternoon.

What happened to the designers in Bombay? Everyone I met wants to do something '**e d g y**'?

Leadership is not edgy! It is dependable. It is classic, if anything.

Sigh.

Sorry for the rant.

Hope you're having a better day than I am.

Rad

TO: radhikaanand@gmail.com
FROM: zainranjan@gmail.com
SUBJECT: I can help

It's your lucky day. Your WeCanWork is ten minutes from my factory. Come through and I'll give you the spark you're looking for.

In terms of graphic designer options, I mean, obviously.

I like the rant. It's '**e d g y**'.

Zain

TO: radhikaanand@gmail.com
FROM: radhikaanand@gmail.com
SUBJECT: RE: I can help
Should i go should i go should i go?

❧

'Thanks, Zain! I really appreciate this,' Radhika said, as she sat down in his cabin at Rajan Textiles.

'It's no problem,' he said, taking out the portfolios he had dug up for her earlier that afternoon.

Of course, he could have emailed her this information. But he had invited her over because it was better to gauge a designer's work in person. It wasn't because he liked having her around, on his suede grey couch with her dangling gold earrings chiming against her cheek every time she smiled or nodded. It also wasn't because he had watched her disappear in a flash after Kabir's rash driving two nights ago and felt a sickly fear and a near-primal urge to slap the arrogance out of her husband-to-be.

She wanted help and he was providing it. That was it.

'I thought it would be better to show it to you in person,' he said, taking care not to touch her fingertips as he handed her the artwork of the first campaign he had issued when he had joined Rajan Textiles at the age of twenty-two.

Radhika seemed to understand the significance of it because she didn't flip through the file with off-handed interest. Instead, she held it in both hands with befitting reverence.

Zain was surprised to see how she had understood that the file was sacred to him. It was the first project Birdy had entrusted him to handle on his own. Zain had spent many hours working with the graphic designer, way more than he needed to. But it had been worth it. When the prints were finally out and the colourized fabric was spread into pixels on an advertisement that said 'RAJAN TEXTILES', Zain had felt a sense of ownership and pride he had never experienced.

He hadn't been able to share this enthusiasm for his work with anyone else before. He couldn't tell his friends about it. They would have thought it odd that he was making such a big deal about being given a project by his uncle. *After all, who else would the project be given to?* But Zain hadn't been used to a life of simply being given things, as they had. And now that he was one of them, he couldn't betray the fact that he had lived the majority of his life not as an heir, as they had, but as a charity case. That, to him, being able to work for a company that by some stroke of luck bore his last name was like being able to celebrate Diwali every day.

But for some reason, he felt like Radhika would understand. Her eyes sparkled with excitement in meetings, in the way he had trained his eyes not to. Just like they were sparkling now, as she touched the swirls of paint on the different mock-ups for Rajan Textile's moth-resistant fabrics that had been designed for him.

'Was the designer good at taking directions?' she asked him, suddenly looking up from the file.

'Yes. He's a pleasant fellow, very open to feedback,' Zain said. 'I was a bit hard on him though.'

'I think it's all right to be a little tough when it matters this much,' Radhika said, not taking her eyes off the poster in her hands. 'It's the face of your product, your ideology. It's everything.' She looked up at him, her eyes sharp, grey and sparkling again. Like freshly wrought metal.

'Exactly,' Zain allowed himself a smile.

'I'll use him,' Radhika said with a nod. 'I need someone who can handle a little heat.'

Zain was pleased that she would be using his contact. They would have things in common, a work relationship solidified, even after her surname and city changed in a week and a half. Zain could call her quite naturally and ask, 'So, how did it work out with Bharat, my design guy?'

They would, of course, always have a relationship because of Birdy Mamu and Mrs Anand, but this could be something of their own. An equation that had nothing to do with the friendship their families shared, but everything to do with the fact that he had once felt the possibility of something, something rare, blossoming with her while sitting on top of a diving board.

A possibility that had been prodded in his bedroom with a pillow fight, provoked further by a string of emails and finally put to rest in his cabin, in this moment while his whole world spun into cotton outside. A world that had been handed to him by fortune and the generosity of his uncle. A world that he had not dared to invite anyone else into.

'Radhika,' Zain said, suddenly aware of the fact that they had been sitting in silence for two minutes. 'Would you like a tour of the factory?'

Radhika nodded and her dimples deepened with a warmth and vitality that Zain had started to depend upon.

She rose and the two of them stepped out, into his factory to see everything material that he cared about.

❧

'We're the largest producers of long-staple and medium-staple cotton in India,' Zain said proudly as we walked through his factory.

I could not account for in any legitimate way what I was still doing there. I should have been at the hotel, arguing with Dolly Sehgal and Aashna Soonawalla about a new theme for the wedding; or at home, helping Naani with the decoration of the bungalow. The only way I could justify it to myself was that Zain had proven to be such an encouraging friend over the last couple of months that it only made sense for me to be curious and grateful to be invited a little deeper into his world, into the factory where his faith was formed. It was as I would feel about any good friend.

And with in-laws like the Sehgals, I was starting to realize that I would need all the encouraging friends I could get.

I watched him now as he looked at the rectangular bales of cotton being churned through rows upon rows of steel machines. All through this tour, he had tried to subdue the excitement in his voice. But now it broke forth despite himself.

'Look,' he said with quiet delight as we stopped at a section of machines that turned and spun the frothy little cotton balls into wires of thread so tight that it seemed like they could slice a man's neck. 'Look,' he said again, now taking my hand and pulling me forward to a new section of machines, one in which the threads were being spooled together over our heads and fabric was poured out like a white waterfall with ripples that would one day be worn.

'This is the best part,' he said to me. 'It's ridiculous, isn't it? Something hard and raw from the earth has been made into such a soft material.'

I laughed and held the fabric he offered me.

'It could go on your bed, or maybe your table,' he said.

'Or maybe I could give Dolly Sehgal a heart attack by making a wedding gown out of it,' I said, draping the cotton like a skirt. 'Imagine her expression if I asked for a white wedding instead of an Indian one.'

Zain smiled briefly, but he didn't laugh with me. 'You know, none of this would have been possible without your great-grandfather.' His voice was a low whisper.

I lowered the fabric, confused. 'Bauji?'

Zain nodded. 'He told Birdy Mamu that Bombay was the best place to start a cotton mill, because the soil in Maharashtra was rich for growing cotton.'

For some reason, my heart started to beat faster. 'He was a professor of geography,' I said.

'When your grandmother got married, he gave Mamu some money as a present and told him to finally start his textile mill with it.'

'Why would he give Birdy a present at Naani's wedding?' Zain glanced at me carefully.

'I think because Bauji felt a little sorry for him,' Zain smiled briefly. 'And I suppose he trusted him. He wanted Mamu to remain in Bombay to keep an eye on Mrs Anand, even after his IAS posting was recalled to Delhi.'

I gasped. Nobody had ever told me this bit of the story, not even Naani's diary.

'It can't be that much of a surprise to you?' he asked. 'You must know that Birdy—'

'Has always been in love with Naani?'

Zain nodded slowly. He looked like he was about to say something more, but then he seemed to decide against it.

'What is it?' I prompted, hungry for more details of my family's history, for whatever it was that he was going to say.

'You know what I love about this mill?' Zain asked abruptly. I shook my head.

'That it has materialized from intelligence, love and luck, and eventually come to me.' Zain laughed. I was thoroughly confused. 'I feel like I'm part of this fantastic cycle now.'

'What do you mean?'

Zain grinned. 'Mamu founded this mill with Bauji's intelligence. Love for your Naani kept him in Bombay as he worked hard to build it up. Then, by some stroke of luck, Mamu found me in London, a hungry teenager without anything to offer, but he offered the mill to me to run. Now, many, many years later, I'm showing it to … you.'

He said 'you' as though it wasn't a throwaway pronoun. He said it with … reverence, almost. As though I was part of the love or luck that had ruled the fate of this mill. I was quiet, and hyper aware of the danger of this moment.

'It's all a bit surreal,' Zain said.

'I thought you were too pragmatic to believe in surreal stories,' I laughed, drawing his attention to a lighter moment when he had mocked my obsession with Naani's diary.

'I thought so, too.'

The laughter was lost in my throat.

Zain looked at me as though I was good fortune. I was suddenly aware of the fact that my hand was still in his, since he had shown me the threads being spooled into fabric.

This was a kind of spooling of its own, I thought. *Or an unspooling, which I hadn't accounted for.*

'What,' I said, clearing my throat. 'What do you mean by you were a hungry teenager without anything?'

Zain didn't respond immediately, neither did he let go of my hand. He seemed to have decided that it was all right, even perfectly natural, for us to stand like this, hand in hand, close to each other, like the couple that owned this factory started by our families.

'Adnan bhai,' Zain called out to an old-looking worker. 'Two cups of chai, please. In my cabin. And some biscuits.'

Then he lifted my hand questioningly, as if to ask if it was all right. And for some gloriously foolish reason, I found myself nodding and following him back to the cabin.

Perhaps if it was just holding hands I could have still begged innocence. But as Zain spoke, the boundary of friendship, of formal physical distance, dissolved between us like a buttery biscuit crumbling in milky tea. We were sitting so close together on his sofa that I could feel the heat coming off his body.

'What did your grandmother tell you about my parents, Radhika?'

'Nothing,' I said truthfully. Naani always changed the subject when I asked. 'Just that your mother was an actress in London. She eloped with your father who was a playwright. But from Lahore, apparently.'

'I don't remember her acting, and I don't remember my father,' Zain said with a tense smile. 'But I do remember the unpaid bills, the whisky for breakfast and the margarine on toast. And the string of idiot boyfriends that stayed at our flat, of course.'

I winced a little. It wasn't easy, mums and boyfriends, I knew.

'She was all right in some respects though. She saved up enough money to send me to school, thank God! It wasn't Eton, but it was something. I studied my butt off and started working part-time the minute I was past the child labour age,' Zain grinned. 'I didn't have a phone to text my friends, or a driver, or a Game Boy, like you guys grew up with.'

'I didn't have any of that either,' I shrugged.

'But you had your mum. And your grandparents in Bombay,' he pointed out. 'I barely had a mother. And I didn't even know that I had Birdy Mamu.'

'Barely?' I began, unsure about how to ask the question.

'For now, let's just say that Lali preferred to pretend that I didn't exist. It meant that she didn't have to be a mother at sixteen.' Zain sighed, as though tired. I winced. 'She was more like a nutty older sister. I figured out quite early on that I'd have to fend for myself if I wanted to eat.'

Shocked as I was, I didn't dare utter a word of consolation. Zain's jaw was lifted at a sharp right angle to the ground, as though he was willing it not to droop. He would hate any kind of sympathy, I knew, because I had a similar expression. Rajni called it my warrior face. Apparently, it showed up whenever anyone asked me why I wasn't majoring in psych, like Mum, at college.

'And then?' I asked gently. I wondered if Zain was going to falter and fall silent now, maybe even ask me to leave as he did once before. But he closed his eyes and spoke softly.

'One day, a man knocked on our door. I had been eating cereal—your muesli, actually—straight from the box at our flat and studying for my A-level. We didn't have a penny saved, but I was still hoping to study at some decent university. King's and LSE had some pretty liberal funding plans, but they were competitive. I remembered being tense all the time because although my grades were good, I had no extracurriculars. Unless you counted making macchiatos at Pret A Manger in less than thirty seconds a talent.'

'I do, incidentally.'

Zain smiled and squeezed my hand.

'Anyway, here was this older man in a linen suit and polished shoes. He looked rich, so I thought he was one of my mum's latest blokes. But then he shook my hand and asked, "How are you Zain?"

'I was confused. What was this impressive man doing asking my name? Had Lali finally done something right and started dating a decent man? Even though I didn't know who he was, we began talking immediately. I showed him my books and told him about school. I even boasted a little about the A stars I'd got in my GCSEs. Especially math. For some reason, I wanted to win his approval. Something told me that this man, with his genial expression and Rolex watch, would make all the difference in my life.'

I waited as Zain's head flopped forward, his golden beard suddenly glistening with a tear. I could barely believe it. Zain Rajan was holding my hand and letting himself cry. Some answering tug in me wanted to cry, too.

'But then Lali appeared and ruined the morning with her usual snark,' he continued dryly.

'"Do you even know what GCSEs are, Birdy?" she asked, emerging from her room in her tattered nightgown. When Birdy Mamu shook his head, she said, "He's a swot, just like you were. It's about 95 per cent in the Indian system."

'He was impressed. "Going to college?" he had asked me.

'"I'm saving up for it," I had said. "I wait tables at the cafe downstairs."

'"I can help—"

'"We don't need your help, bhaiya, thanks," Lali had laughed. "My kid's not your charity project."

'I was furious and confused. I wanted to tell her to shut up. We definitely needed his help. She couldn't even remember to pay the electricity bill! But I remained quiet, because what could I say? I was seventeen and she was all the family I had. I didn't want to embarrass her in front of a stranger. Even one she was calling "bhaiya".

'He must have seen the desperation on my face though, because when he left, he slipped me his business card. What it said changed my life—RAJAN TEXTILES.

'Now, Rajan wasn't my surname at the time. But it was my mother's. So, I kind of thought it was my name, too. And there it was, on a business card. It had a business to its name. A little jolt went through me as I examined the rectangle of glossy paper over in my bed at night. It was just a business card, but to me it felt like Wonka's golden ticket or something. I already felt more normal. Less alone.

'The next morning, I swiped Lali's phone and rang my new uncle. By afternoon, I was sitting in his hotel room at The Savoy and drinking tea. Birdy Mamu was assessing me with an indecipherable expression on his face.

'"Zain," he had said finally. "As your uncle, I think it is my duty to set up a bank account for you." I literally spat out my scone, but Mamu continued, unaffected. "It will pay for your schooling, but you must promise me excellence. The minute your grades drop, I will cut the funding." I simply nodded, desperate to prove myself.

'"And then, you must pick a trade and excel at it," Mamu had said in a hard tone. "You must pay for yourself. It is important to know that, in this world, you cannot depend on anyone but yourself."

'"I already know that, Mr Rajan," I said in the deepest, most alpha tone I could manage at seventeen. And something within Mamu's expression yielded then. His tough demeanour vanished and he stood up and hugged me close.

'"Zain," he had said, "the next few years are going to be hard. For your mother and you. But I don't want it to distract you. We will get her the care that she needs—and then you must come away. With me, to India. To work. Would you like that?"

'I accepted immediately. He was offering me an education and a job. To someone who had no prospects at the time, it was a fortune.'

'I never thought to stop at that moment and question any of it. I never asked, why *now*, after all these years of radio silence, had my mother's successful brother turned up to help us?'

'The news came to me in September that year. They made sure I was safely enrolled in college, studying at King's, boarding in college housing and working towards a first class in business and economics, before telling me the truth.'

'My mother was a clinically diagnosed alcoholic. She had been operated upon for acute liver cirrhosis and then shifted to a rehabilitation centre by her brother, Mr Badrinath Rajan.'

24
Memory

They had received news that morning that Lali was out of danger. After a successful emergency bypass surgery and a week of being comatose, she was now conscious and coherent enough to call up her 'self-important' brother, minutes after the doctors had spoken to him, and berate him for 'thinking it was all right to throw money at your problems instead of doing the decent thing and showing up to see your sister on her deathbed.'

'Can't Gayatri Khurana spare her lapdog for a week?' Lali Rajan barked and banged the phone down.

Birdy looked at Gayatri, shamefaced. She had obviously overheard and was feeling stung by this last drop of venom, but she quelled the answering rage that rose within her. She was secure in the knowledge that it wasn't because of her that Birdy had refrained from visiting his awful sister. His doctor had advised him against travelling alone and Birdy had refused to take Zain along. Or to even inform him of his mother's condition, no matter how much Gayatri had implored him to.

Where initially Birdy was seeking Gayatri's help to break the news about Lali to his nephew, he was now looking for ways to sidestep it altogether. Ever since the doctors had conveyed the news that Lali was recovering, Birdy thought it unnecessary to tell Zain that his mother was ill and leave him feeling unsettled without cause. After all, Zain had just hit his stride helming the operations of Rajan Textiles in Dubai. Birdy had never seen him happier. Instead of seeming tired and overwhelmed, as he used to, the various projects Zain had undertaken—the enterprise in Dubai, the old factory in Bombay and now this project with Radhika (especially this project with Radhika)—had filled his nephew with a bright vigour at thirty-two that he lacked at twenty-two.

Lali would bring all of that crumbling down. She could puncture her son's hard-earned self-confidence with one poisonous remark.

'You have to go,' Gayatri concluded after the bitter phone call.

Birdy nodded. He knew she was right. Now that Lali was awake, he could no longer leave her to his associates in London. 'I'll ask my travel agent to book me on the British Airways flight tomorrow night. What Doctor Saab doesn't know, won't kill him. Or me.'

Birdy laughed lightly, but Gayatri narrowed her eyes at him.

'You will ask Zain to go,' she commanded. 'And you will take him with you.'

'Gayatri—'

'Birdy, this is not up for discussion. I have never contradicted you before this, but I will happily do so now if it means telling the poor boy that his mother nearly died.'

Birdy was quiet. 'You've never seen them together. You don't understand.'

'I understand that Zain is old enough to know the truth, Birdy. He can't be blindsided again. God forbid, if this turns out to be one of his last chances to see Lali—'

Gayatri broke off mid-sentence as Birdy flinched. She mellowed her voice so it was no longer lambasting.

'Their relationship may not be as it should be, Birdy, but he is still her son. He will resent you if he is kept in the dark about her health.'

And so, even though Birdy was reluctant, Gayatri had his tea served in the study and waited for Zain to return from work.

What she didn't expect, however, was for Radhika to return with him. The young pair reminded her of children returning from school, clinging to each other for innocent comfort after the harrowing adventures of a school day.

That was also why Gayatri didn't ask Radhika to leave. *Perhaps, for Zain's sake, it would be better to have a friend whose hand he could hold*, she thought. She glanced at Birdy meaningfully. He shrugged his acceptance of her granddaughter being in the room.

And so, Gayatri began.

'Zain beta,' she said, handing him a cup of tea. 'You know how proud we are of you.'

'I do, Mrs Anand.'

'Especially your uncle,' she continued. 'You haven't proven yourself to be just a good businessman but also an exemplary gentleman.'

Gayatri took the liberty of handing Zain the file Birdy's lawyers had prepared that afternoon. They had decided, together, that this would be the best way.

Zain read the documents briefly and then looked at his uncle. 'What is this about?'

'You're the son I never had,' Birdy said simply

Gayatri thought Zain's face would be filled with delight, but his gaze remained steady and careful as usual. Gayatri's heart went out to him. The boy had experienced so many chaotic twists of fate that he couldn't help but be suspicious of yet another change in his fortune. It was no wonder that he didn't want to be married, Gayatri realized. He probably thought it another unwelcome disruption to the calm life he had finally managed to craft for himself.

'Why are you doing this, Mamu?' Zain looked at his godfather.

'I don't think you've understood, Zain. I'd like to officially transfer the ownership of Rajan Textiles to you. My entire estate is now yours.'

Radhika's eyes instantly filled with happiness.

'Zain, this is fantastic!'

But Zain laid the file down and shook his head at her sadly. 'This is the cycle I was telling you about. Of love and luck. I'm on the wrong turn of it now.'

Gayatri was confused and Radhika's expression had darkened.

Zain turned to his uncle and asked, matter-of-factly. 'Mum's sick, isn't she?'

Birdy stared at his intelligent nephew, unable to say anything.

'Every time she's sick, I get a windfall from you,' Zain said flatly.

Birdy's face was clouded with guilt. His eyes met Gayatri's and he realized that she had been right. There was a trace of resentment, of the faintest sort, that lived under Zain's devotion to him.

'I didn't mean it badly, Mamu,' Zain said, looking at his hands now. 'I am very grateful to you for all that you've done for me, but—' his voice suddenly dropped to a whisper.

'But I'd much rather you tell me this time.'

Gayatri couldn't bear the silence any more. 'Zain, Lali had a heart attack last week, but she's *fine* now.'

A small gasp escaped Radhika, but Zain made no noise. His eyes darkened slightly, but other than that his manner remained the same. Stiff and solid, just like his uncle's.

'Alcohol poisoning?'

'Yes,' Birdy did not avoid his nephew's gaze any more.

'We should never have moved her out of rehab. Especially after all that garbage she said about cutting herself.'

Radhika's hand, Gayatri noticed, was firmly intertwined with Zain's.

Birdy cleared his throat. 'I'll be going there this week to ensure that she's transferred back to the centre and ... and comfortable. You're welcome to join me, but—'

'I won't be joining you.'

Birdy nodded. He understood. Zain seemed to be struggling to maintain his expression. He took a deep, shivering breath to steady himself. Radhika seemed shocked by the haunted sound of it. She had never seen Zain on the edge before. She was just beginning to realize that it didn't come naturally to him.

'How bad is she?' he asked softly.

Birdy couldn't answer his nephew truthfully. Not without shoving the boy back into the sewer of self-doubt and anxiety that Lali had raised him in.

'Dr Stewart said she's recuperating very well,' Gayatri jumped at the opportunity to reassure Zain. 'The surgery went off very smoothly. In his words, "Her heart is surprisingly resilient."'

Zain smiled, but the smile did not reach his eyes.

'Anyway. All this has made me realize the temporality of our situations. We're all getting on in age and I'd like to have my affairs sorted out before I leave for London. Zain, I need you to sign here—'

'Mamu, stop.' Zain's voice was low. 'Please.'

'Oh, come now,' Birdy growled. 'Don't be silly about this. I could kick the bucket tomorrow—'

'Will you stop saying that?' Gayatri clicked her tongue at him, annoyed.

Zain looked at them for a long moment, taking in the pale peach fall of Gayatri's sari and the matching colour of Birdy's tie. It must have been a coincidence, but to Zain that only made the match sweeter. He let out a low laugh.

'It's about time you two got married, don't you think?'

Gayatri's mouth fell open in shock. Birdy, too, seemed astounded. Nobody had expected this turn in the conversation. Least of all Radhika, who was now staring at Gayatri and Birdy as they stood beside each other, her eyes wide with amazement, the light of realization brightening up her innocent grey irises.

'Zain,' Birdy began warningly, with a furtive glance at Radhika, but his nephew was beyond reproach. He was in a place of deep despair, struggling to keep his face propped up with dry humour.

'You two have spent too much of your life apart,' Zain said. 'I suggest you stick to the earlier plan and get married now. I'd like to see one set of parents happy.'

Radhika turned to Gayatri, astonished. 'What earlier plan?'

Gayatri blushed and Radhika's grey eyes widened further. 'Naani … were you going to *marry* Birdy?'

Zain squeezed her hand one last time, rose and disappeared from the study.

Nobody expected that he would disappear completely.

❧

TO: zainrajan@gmail.com
FROM: radhikaanand@gmail.com
SUBJECT: Listen

Zain, I spoke to Naani after you left. I told her that I think she and Birdy should get married. But she refuses to speak to me about it. I don't understand what is stopping them. He did propose, didn't he? It is clear as day that she wants to marry him, yet she won't.

Shall we plot to bring these two star-crossed lovers together?

PS: I'm here for a chat whenever you feel ready.

Love Rad

TO: radhikaanand@gmail.com
FROM: zainrajan@gmail.com
SUBJECT: RE: Listen

They won't marry till you get married.

No 'good' family would accept you if they did.

Congrats! On my way to the airport atm. Probably won't see you till the big day now.

Zain

TO: zainrajan@gmail.com
FROM: radhikaanand@gmail.com
SUBJECT: RE: RE: Listen
You're leaving?
For London?
Rad

TO: radhikaanand@gmail.com
FROM: zainrajan@gmail.com
SUBJECT: RE: RE: RE: Listen
Yes. And no.
Zain

'Radhika?'

'Hi Kabir,' I said.

'It's good to hear your voice.' He sounded relieved. His voice was soft, almost pliant, now. Nothing like the arrogant barking from his last visit to Bombay.

'I know you must be quite upset,' I began.

'Radhika,' he cut me off, 'I just don't understand what the problem is. Why are you fighting with everyone? Me, Mom, Aashna aunty …'

'There is no problem.'

'Really?' Kabir sounded relieved. 'Look, if you're still angry about … that last drive. Radhika—'

'There is no problem,' I repeated. 'Tell your mother I'll do the wedding, the theme, the dance, all of it.'

Kabir laughed, triumphant. Previously, that sound would have erupted within me like a firecracker; it would have caused my own dimples to explode in an answering joy. But now his laughter was muted to me, overwhelmed by the ringing that had been throbbing through my head since this afternoon. The Sehgals' silly dramas had paled in comparison to the fact that I had nearly deprived my grandmother and Birdy uncle of their last chance at happiness together.

Who would have thought that Naani had actually grown to love Birdy uncle in return? That the man she had once described as a 'stringbean', whom she had named Birdy for his hovering nature, would one day be her solace and her sweetheart? But once it had been said, I couldn't unsee it. It made perfect sense.

This evening, when she reluctantly confessed that my wedding was what had stopped them from getting married, I wanted to kick myself. *How selfish had I been? Had I even once asked Naani about her hopes and desires?* No, I had just assumed that they had died with Naanu.

I lived with Naani, benefitting from her appetite for life, getting head massages at her salon and going on dates with the sons of her friends, yet I had not spared a thought for her happiness. Never thought that Gayatri Khurana, the spirit I knew so well, still lived in the body of my grandmother. That she still dreamed and loved and hoped, like I did.

Well, I was not going to be standing in her or anyone else's way any longer. I would get this wedding over with as soon as possible so that Naani could have hers.

'Babe, you know, you had me worried there for a moment. I thought you would postpone the wedding!'

'I was going to,' I confessed. His chuckling faded. 'But I took some time to think and decided against it.'

'Oh? What changed your mind?' Kabir's tone was wary now.

'I need to be married to you as soon as possible.'

'That is so sweet, babe.' The smile, I could tell, had returned to his voice. He had misunderstood my urgency. And I hadn't bother correcting him.

25
Tangled

TO: stevek@yale.edu
FROM: mangalaanand@yale.edu
SUBJECT: I'm at the Airport!

Waiting outside Arrivals Gate 3 with a welcome basket of chocolate almond milk and vegan baked goods. It was Radhika's idea, not mine!

Don't stop to buy anything at Duty Free. Come straight out. It's been too long.

See you soon.

Mangala

TO: mangalaanand@yale.edu
FROM: stevek@yale.edu
SUBJECT: If This Is the Side Effect ...

... India has on you, I suggest we move here. Can't wait to see you.

I bought you an early edition of Pande and Moore's latest research study.

Love you.

Steve

Zain had spent an hour pretending to tour the facilities of La Clinique at Windsor Park, trying not to seem suspicious of their facilities. He couldn't help it. He was naturally predisposed to be suspicious of all things associated with Lali Rajan. It didn't help that the rehabilitation centre she was 'recuperating' at looked less like a clinic and more like a Swiss spa set in the hills of Surrey. It seemed to him that all his mother had to do was hurt herself and the people around her to keep getting upgraded to the nicer things life had to offer.

He wondered idly how much acid she had flung at Birdy during his visit this time for him to have paid for those maraschino cherries he saw at their buffet lunch.

He repressed, yet again, the surge of ungenerous thoughts that rose within him whenever he remembered his mother. Such a line of thinking would not bring him closer to doing what he had come there to do.

Zain tried to focus as Nancy, the receptionist, continued to point out the state-of-the-art gym, complete with a smoothie bar and spin classes, the 'social centre' that was modest nomenclature for a grand ballroom—'for spirited gatherings without spirits!'—and a heated indoor infinity pool that would make Otters Club cry tears of salt.

Zain instantly shoved all thought of Otters Club and its pool to the back of his head. The girl he had shared a diving board with would be married in seventy-two hours. She was ready to be married. He wasn't even ready to say hello to his sick mother.

She nearly died, he reminded himself, while Nancy went off to fetch him a brochure.

If only she had … but he caught himself just in time.

He was there because he didn't want to think that way anymore. He was there because he wanted to be someone, anyone other than the angry, wary person she had forced him to become. He had caught a glimpse of that person in the last few months. The hopeful, open version of himself. The roaring version of himself. It wasn't impossible. It was within reach. It was real. All he had to do was reach for the door of room number 612 and suck it up.

He took out his phone for a minute and glanced at the last email he had received.

❧

TO: zainrajan@gmail.com
FROM: radhikaanand@gmail.com
SUBJECT: Website Goes Live Today

thequeennetwork.com is alive and kicking. Just thought you'd like to be in the loop. Your graphic designer made the home page with Dipa's UI/UX guy.

In other news, Mum's man, Steve, arrived from the States today with a supply of muesli that could last us a lifetime.

Hope everything's okay with you. Call me when you get the chance.

Radhika

❧

He felt like he had been fading as he walked through the clinic in Surrey, imagining his mother living amongst strangers for the last decade, probably bittering their smoothie bowls with her well-aimed sarcasm, so that they remained strangers instead of becoming friends. He came back to life after rereading Radhika's email. It was like mouth-to-mouth resuscitation, with Radhika breathing confidence back into him through correspondence.

Her simple gratitude reminded him that he was able. That he was dependable. He came through for people and brought their ideas to fruition. Her familiar tone signified that he had friends. Real ones who trusted his capabilities and respected him for them.

There was no charade, no falsehood, nothing fraudulent there.

No matter what his mother said, he'd always have this email as a reminder of the countless other contracts, deals and projects that had been executed thanks to him. He, Zain Rajan, was a person. A businessman. A real one. And a friend to someone of the same stature.

He began typing a reply to his friend with a sudden burst of feeling.

'Here you go.' Nancy placed a little teacup on the table, along with the brochure. 'Let me know if you have any questions about the therapy sessions. Or if you like, we can schedule another visit for your wife, the patient.'

Zain put his phone down, mid-typing, and made a decision. 'Actually, Nancy,' he said, rising, 'are visiting hours still on?'

❧

'Well, if it isn't the golden boy himself.'

Lali Rajan propped herself up on one elbow and looked at her son with her usual disdain. Zain, for his part, was shocked. Not by her greeting, but by her appearance. The Skype screen hadn't done justice to the state of Lali's deteriorating health. Once so beautiful that she played Olivia in *Twelfth Night* on the London stage before Zain's birth, her fair skin was now yellow and wrinkled with the strain of alcohol abuse. There was a milky film clouding her eyes, giving her the appearance of being on the brink of tears or blindness. She may be twenty-five years younger than Gayatri Anand, but she looked ten years older.

Noticing his expression, her eyes narrowed immediately. 'Don't you dare feel sorry for me,' she rasped. 'Do you think that just because you went off and started licking a rich man's boots, you're better than me?'

Zain's sympathy for his mother vanished. Obviously, her eyes were still as sharp as her tongue.

'If you knew your brother at all, you'd know that he would kick anyone who tried to lick his boots.'

'I know my brother better than you ever will, son,' Lali snorted. 'A fine suit doesn't camouflage a snivelling bootlicker, even if it's pulled wool over your eyes.'

Zain had to remind himself that she was in terrible pain. That the doctors had said that the withdrawal period was the worst part of recovery that often led to oscillating mood swings. Still, it was hard not to yell back, especially since she was obviously taking so much pleasure in hurting him.

'You know how your precious uncle made his money?' she flicked words at him, grinning to herself as they landed. 'Sucking up. Snivelling. Bending over for—'

'What does that make you?' he snapped suddenly. 'A freeloader or a hypocrite?'

'What?'

Zain was shaking with anger at this point, struggling to keep his voice calm.

'You berate your brother for the way he earned his money, but you have had no problem living off his earnings,' his voice was cold and incisive like the relentless slashing of a knife. 'I don't expect someone as entitled as you to express gratitude. But the least you can do is speak of Badrinath Rajan with respect.'

Lali was shocked into speechlessness. She had bred her son to endure her acrimony, not to counter it. Usually, he did. He listened to her tirades in sullen silence and then disappeared into his room for days to lick his wounds. But something seemed to have changed within him. There was a solidity in his demeanour that she had never seen before. She knew, instantly, that he was no longer going to indulge her bad behaviour.

It scared her. She felt powerless for a moment. More alone than ever. But then, to cover up her weakness, she laughed. A nasty nasal sound that grated on her son's ears, at once chiding him for his insolence and insulting him for his pretence.

'So, you've become the sort of man who would abuse his own mother for a rich uncle,' she sniped. 'That's the way of the world, isn't it? You spend your life raising a child and then, just because someone richer comes along, he gives you a kick and runs off with him, never to be seen again.'

Zain's eyes flashed with guilt. Lali realized, gleefully, that she had got to him yet again.

'Our visits didn't seem to be pleasant for you,' he said, but his voice had lost its fire. He was fading. Slipping again into the subdued boy he used to be.

'Because I could tell that you were bucking at the heels,' she retorted. 'Just like you are now. Just dying to get back to your life of lapdog luxury, aren't you? God, I should have known that a lapdog like my brother would raise my son to be one, too.'

Lali sneered with satisfaction, relishing the pain that contorted her son's face. 'Let me tell you something about your dear Birdy, Zain. He may have made the money, but at least I lived on my own terms! At least I didn't spend my life bowing and scraping down to a professor and his cunning daughter because they spoke English like the English!'

To her surprise, Zain's face cleared. The hurt left his face and a calm settled upon it. The mention of the Khuranas seemed to have grounded him.

He did not reply, but he did sit down by her bed. Confused, she continued, still trying to get a rise out of him.

'I heard you refused Birdy's offer for his inheritance. What's wrong? Got used to a life of living on handouts? Don't like the idea of being responsible for the money?'

Little did she know that she could no longer hurt Zain. He was thinking of Gayatri and Birdy standing beside each other through forty years of life—an enduring, unspoken companionship in which a peach tie matched a peach sari without planning. He thought of Radhika, who was probably having dinner with them at that very moment, her mother and the faceless Steve also gathered around Mrs Anand's mahogany dining table, spooning cereal into their bowls while the others helped themselves to *ghar ka khaana*. He thought of how pleased they would all be if he entered the house just then, ready to scarf down the aloo parathas with them. He had a family. One that loved and appreciated him. Lali didn't.

This comforting vision allowed him to take Lali's frail hand in his. To kiss it, taking care not to touch the jutting veins and the needle marks.

Lali looked more surprised than ever. But before she could make any remark, there was a knock on the door. A nurse appeared. 'Pumpkin soup for Ms Rajan?'

'Take it away!' Lali barked at her.

'I'll take it. Thank you,' Zain said politely, discreetly slipping a twenty-pound note into the frightened nurse's palm.

'I don't need you to play nurse for me,' Lali said, but her tone was less combative now. 'I know you'd rather be in Bombay pretending to belong to someone else's family.'

The snark had lost its bite. Zain was starting to realize that his mother didn't hate him. She was just jealous.

'They are my family, Mum,' Zain said, gently tucking the table napkin into Lali's clinic gown, like a bib. 'But that doesn't make you any less of my family.'

Lali looked at him, wide-eyed. She didn't fight him off as he had expected. Zain took a breath and told her the things he knew she needed to hear.

'Mum,' Zain said softly. 'I don't judge you for your decisions.'

'That's bullshit,' Lali chuckled. 'You escaped, like your father, the minute—'

'Because I didn't want to live with your decisions any more. But I understand why you made them. You were only nineteen. You felt like I'd stolen your girlhood from you. It didn't help, I suppose, that I looked exactly like my father.'

He lifted a spoon of the pumpkin soup to her lips. She opened her mouth distractedly, like a child, listening to a story while eating her vegetables.

'I appreciate that you saved up to send me to school. I appreciate that you called Mamu for help when you realized that your addiction had got the better of you. In many ways, you improved my life by recognizing your faults. That was brave. And I'm grateful for it.'

'I thought I was going to die,' Lali whispered as Zain broke off a piece of the baguette and buttered it for her. 'They had said it was impossible for someone like me to qualify for a liver transplant. Since, I'd ruined my own body.'

Lali's milky eyes welled up with tears. Zain lifted the bottom of the napkin tucked under her chin and wiped her cheek. 'But Birdy managed to help me through it,' she continued, sticking her jaw out.

'It was a year of hell, but once I got through it, I thought you and I could start over. That was the only thought that kept me going through the months of pain in that awful rehab centre in London with its white walls and bitchy doctors. I thought I could finally begin to do right by you. I thought we could finally be a family.'

'But I left to live with Birdy.'

Lali stared at him and nodded. Zain met her gaze, unapologetic but considerate. He half-expected her to yell at him again, to throw a tantrum and ask him to leave.

To her credit, she didn't.

'I'm sorry that I left. I hope you see now, why I had to.' Zain lifted another spoonful of soup to her lips. 'I hope you will let me make it up to you.'

'Why now?' Lali asked.

Because nobody wants a life of considering only their own desires. Except sociopaths, maybe.

Zain smiled as the memory of his feisty neighbour crossed his mind. Out loud, he said, 'Because if we don't stop warring, I may never be at peace.'

Lali let out a rattling, tired breath. Zain knew then that she had become exhausted of sniping to retain power, too. Anger took energy and Lali Rajan was obviously running out of breath.

'At least war means you're facing me,' she confessed. 'Even if it's on the other side of a Skype screen.'

Zain considered this for a moment. 'What if I promise to visit every month?'

Lali's face cleared. She didn't smile, but she didn't refuse the slice of buttered bread Zain presented to her.

'Will you be able to keep that promise?' she asked, chewing.

'I'm a man of my word,' Zain smiled.

'Just like your uncle,' Lali laughed, but this time there was no malice. Zain smiled and lifted another spoonful of soup to her mouth.

'I hate pumpkins, you know,' Lali said, wrinkling her nose.

Zain laughed. 'Me too.'

They grinned at each other and set the soup aside.

A few hours later, when Zain was in the back of the Uber driving him to his hotel in London, he took out his phone and began typing the reply he had begun to write to Radhika. Then he stopped and decided against it. *Best to tell her in person*, he thought.

'Excuse me,' he asked the chauffeur. 'Do you think we could go to Heathrow airport instead, please?'

Radhika stared at her phone, willing herself not to cry.

TO: radhikaanand@gmail.com
FROM: zainrajan@gmail.com
SUBJECT: RE: Website Goes Live Today
Congrats. Glad I could help.
Zain

TO: radhikaanand@gmail.com
FROM: radhikaanand@gmail.com
SUBJECT: Fuck
That hurt.

26
Fortune

Kabir

Where did you run off to this morning?

Sorry! Had to do bride stuff.

Haldi, mehendi, etc.

Will lie in next time.

LOL, you won't have a choice.

Come over in the afternoon? After the haldi, mehendi, etc.?

Let's see. This may take a while.

✦

Strange women crowded around me all morning, brushing my hair, cleansing my skin with turmeric and soaking my feet in honey and milk. These were Kabir's aunts, whom I barely knew. Yet they could mould my body as they saw fit, because in a day they would be my family.

My own family hadn't had much of a chance to see me in this last week leading up to the wedding because my every waking hour was spent with Dolly Sehgal in beauty appointments and dance rehearsals. Naani tried to accompany me to some of these, but as chieftain of the bridal party she had her hands full tending to the scores of the Sehgals' guests who poured in from north India in the last week. Mum was not cut out for traditional mother-of-the-bride duties, but she had been a help in her own way, by taking charge of Swiggy-ing food for the Sehgals' hungry cousins who had become a permanent fixture on our couch. Even Steve, who had arrived the day before yesterday, had been useful as chief chauffeur for the Chandigarh aunts who liked to be driven to the mall every afternoon for their 'evening walk'. Shopping was the best cardio apparently.

I was glad that Mum had Steve and Naani had Birdy. This week had been stressful for both of them, but their partners had been supportive and loving all through the wedding preparations, easing their tension and halving their duties without even being asked to. Mum looked especially in love, a fact that had already been remarked upon by my mother-in-law so many times ('your mother really likes that gora, haan?') that I had to bite my tongue to restrain myself from telling her to mind her own business.

But Dolly Sehgal was not wrong. My mother really did like Steve, and she demonstrated it with an affection that was surprising to us all, including Steve. Mum had finally permitted herself to be in love. She held Steve's hand and even smiled at him from across the room when they were apart, entertaining different factions of the Punjabi wedding party. Steve, who—poor thing—had been starved of such affection for years, seemed to be a new man, basking in the light of Mum's adoration. Not unlike Birdy, who had returned from London last week (sans Zain), more devoted to Naani than ever. He was only too happy to be welcoming guests with Naani and making sure she sat down and had a piece of mithai herself, taking a break from the uninterrupted stream of hospitality and 'hello jis'. I suppose, from all that I had heard of Lali Rajan, Naani by comparison seemed like a fount of affection.

Now, more than ever, I realized that I had to get married. I could not go back to my sterile life in New York, and I could not remain here, crowding Naani and Birdy in their last chance to be together after a lifetime of being across the room from each other.

'Come, come,' Bulbul aunty said, lifting my feet out of the bowl of milk. 'It's time to start your henna. Stretch now if you want. You're going to be sitting for ages.'

Good, I thought, as the aunts chivvied me to the henna designer. That would mean I won't have to reply to Kabir's probing texts.

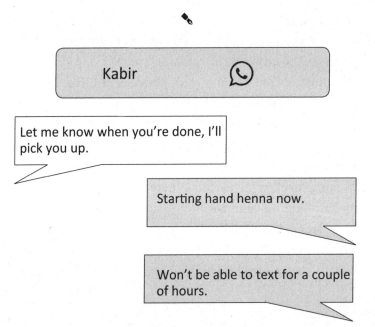

The designer tilted her cone on to the palm of my hand and began squeezing the cool henna out in intricate little petals at the crook of my elbows. I watched, focused, as she embroidered my arm with patterns of birds, flowers and letters. I wondered whether I would flinch again when Kabir inspected my body tomorrow night.

I would have to find some way to get over the physical repulsion I had developed for my fiancé ever since our evening together in his car. Where once I had been eager and waiting for his hands to encircle my waist, now my body seemed to recoil of its own accord, trying to escape his tight grip and grabbing fingers. Kabir has sensed this, but his ego had led him to think that my lack of attraction towards him was some sort of bedroom tease leading up to the honeymoon.

My henna designer suddenly gave me a knowing look, making me blush.

'Don't worry,' she said. 'I won't make his name too hard to find on your hands. You two will have plenty of time together to enjoy yourselves.'

I smiled at her glassily and ignored her lewd expression, just as I had been ignoring the cackle and chatter of Kabir's aunts all morning, when they described their honeymoons in unnecessary detail. I shoved away the thought of Kabir alone in a room with me.

I'll get over it, I thought, *this need to be around someone else. A particular someone else. Zain.*

I said the name into my phone and Siri searched through the inbox to reveal our many email threads, all of them warm, funny and encouraging. Like a cup of hot coffee in the lull of a winter evening. Such a contrast to his chilly tone in the last email, typed with a forced economy of words.

I never replied to him, or asked where he had gone, or asked him to stay with me to help me bear this last week in Bombay. Naani and Birdy had been tight-lipped about his whereabouts, too. I refused to beg.

I thought Zain would blame me for delaying Birdy's happiness by preventing Naani from marrying him. *Well, at least I won't be obstructing anyone's happiness any longer*, I thought. And I won't pry either. If Zain wasn't ready to speak to me about his mother's current condition, as openly as he had about her past, then I wasn't going to force correspondence and try to probe information out of him.

Still, I could not help but think of him, of the smell of cottonseed oil, coffee and cologne that wafted from his linen suit and enveloped me that day in his cabin. I could not help but hope that wherever he was, be it in Dubai or London or someplace else, he was all right and that he was talking to someone. That he was opening up in some sense, instead of closing himself up and suffering alone as he had for so many years.

Maybe he was with Kiara again, I thought. Well, good for him if he was. I hoped he enjoyed himself. He deserved to.

'Siri, Instagram Zain Rajan.'

Immediately, I was scrolling through his photos. And then Kiara's.

Laughter erupted from the centre of the room and I saw Steve waving a Chinese takeout menu in the air like a flag. Mum laughed again and snatched the menu from him to hand it to a chubby aunty who looked at them both in confusion and admiration.

Mum noticed me watching and called out, 'Radhika, sweetheart, would you like momos? We're ordering the pork ones.'

'Paneer ones,' Steve quipped, but Mum elbowed him.

'Pork,' she repeated definitively. 'I saw you scarf down the butter chicken yesterday, vegan.'

I shook my head at them, smiling. When I turned back to my phone and saw Kiara's life splashed across it, I wanted to scratch my eyes out. This was shameful.

What was I doing, stalking Zain's girlfriend, when I was marrying Kabir? Why the hell couldn't I love who I was with, like Mum and Steve?

'Done,' my henna designer said. I looked at her in surprise. It had only been two hours and both my arms were filled with intricate patterns of henna.

'That was quick.' I smiled at her.

'Only four letters. It was easy,' she said with a shrug. 'Hiding the letters is the hardest part—'

'Four letters?'

'The boy's name!' she clicked her tongue at me. 'See, here.'

And then slowly, to my horror, she pointed out the letters scattered across my palm in henna, camouflaged amongst leaves and petals and patterns.

Z on the tip of my index finger,
A on the centre of my palm,
I on the corner of my little finger,
N nestled at the base of my wrist.
Zain. Shit.

The henna artist looked at me with concern. 'I asked you the name, you said—'

'What?' I was confused. 'When?'

Then realization dawned on me. I hadn't even heard her. I had been speaking to Siri, searching through my phone for any evidence of Zain I could find, like an obsessive stalker.

Well, serves me right, I thought. My emotional infidelity was painted across my hand. Maybe it would serve as a reminder to be faithful to my husband. I would have to distract Kabir to keep him from spotting it.

'We are back in business!' Rajni Dutt, Radhika's friend exclaimed, putting bottles of whisky, rum and wine on Gayatri's coffee table with a triumphant thud.

Gayatri gazed at the wide-hipped, big-lipped young girl and marvelled at her vivaciousness. The minute she met Rajni, she understood how Radhika had survived all those years alone in New York City. Her thin granddaughter had obviously been drinking from the pool of this wonderful, full-figured girl's infinite energy. Even today, Radhika, whose form had started to slump with defeat, had perked back up with a vivacity of her own after meeting her friend after months.

'Did you leave anything at the liquor store, Rajj?' Radhika asked, looking at the accompaniments of syrups and soft drinks Rajni was placing on the table.

'I forgot how cheap everything was here,' Rajni laughed. 'All of this for under two hundred dollars.'

'Must be nice to earn in dollars,' Padmini whispered to Mukti as she poured herself a glass of wine. Even the conservative colleagues were letting their hair down tonight.

'Join *The Queen Network* and I'll get you there,' Radhika joked, pouring Mangala a glass of rum.

'No work talk at your bachelorette!' Rajni commanded.

'Radhika isn't allowed more than half a glass of wine,' Aashna Soonawalla chimed in. 'We can't risk any bloating tomorrow.'

Gayatri tried not to roll her eyes. 'We won't give her more than a glass, Ms Soonawalla.' *What was the wedding planner still doing here anyway?* 'You have nothing to worry about.'

Aashna Soonawalla, however, didn't look convinced. She turned to her client with a piercing glare.

'You promise, Radhika?'

'Yes,' Radhika sighed. 'I promise.'

'And please go to bed by 10 p.m. We can't risk under-eye bags.'

Gayatri resisted the urge to cheer as Aashna Soonawalla left. All this emphasis on looking a certain way! Gayatri ran a beauty salon and even she didn't see the point. One glass of wine, a little bit of a bloat and half a shadow under her eye wouldn't kill Radhika. It may rob her of the untarnished beauty the Sehgals wanted to show off, but it would make her happier and perhaps a more interesting kind of beautiful.

'Pour me another glass, please,' Gayatri held her gold goblet out to Rajni. *Gold goblets!* It was ridiculous and unnecessarily expensive, but Dolly Sehgal had insisted. Radhika had glanced at Gayatri furtively and Birdy had paid before any discussion could commence.

'Yes, Mrs Anand! Would you like rum or wine?'

Gayatri looked at the drops of wine settled at the bottom of her goblet. She chuckled. *Why not?*

'Rum, please, Rajni.'

'With soda, water, coke?'

'Nothing. Just the drink.'

'All right, Ma!' Mangala, who was already on her third glass of wine, laughed.

'Sure thing, Mrs Anand,' Rajni grinned and handed Gayatri the goblet of rum.

'Gayatri, please.'

Radhika turned to her grandmother, stunned. 'Naani?'

'I don't want to be Mrs Anand any more,' Gayatri shrugged and took a sip from her goblet. Bitter warmth flowed through her mouth and lit her throat aflame. 'Enjoy it. The name belongs to you tonight.'

'And to Mum,' Radhika said, pointing her glass of water at her mother.

'I don't want it either,' Mangala said, shaking her head emphatically. A little too emphatically. 'It's all yours.'

Gayatri had forgotten what a lightweight her daughter was. She laughed and took a large gulp from her own goblet.

'Goblets!' she said again. *Or was it the first time?* 'Ridiculous!'

'Really?' Radhika looked at her grandmother's glass, worried. 'Was it very expensive?'

'Yes. But it's all right.' Gayatri shook her head. 'You're only going to get married once. Or at least I hope so. Can I have another goblet of rum please, Rajni?'

Rajni looked at her with an amused expression. 'Are you sure, Gayatri? That was a bit quick.'

Gayatri nodded vigorously. 'Absolutely sure. I haven't had anything but wine since I married my husband. He didn't like me drinking spirits. Or having a spirit, really. But he isn't here any more, so I may as well have some fun!'

Mangala spluttered with laughter and raised her glass in salutation.

Radhika looked alarmed. 'Naani?'

'Call her Gayatri,' Rajni whispered.

'No, sweetheart. For you, Naani is fine,' Gayatri spoke in a heartfelt rush. 'It is the finest thing I could be called.'

Gayatri rose and kissed her granddaughter's forehead with a hot, intense pressure, as though planting an amulet to ward off bad fortune. Everyone fell silent, aware of the tears slipping down Gayatri and Radhika's cheeks.

Rajni stood up and started waving her hand around, trying to lighten the atmosphere.

'All right,' Rajni said, trying to steer the bachelorette back on to track. 'Radhika can't drink, but she can still have fun.'

'How exactly?' Radhika asked.

'Like this,' Rajni said, taking out her phone. 'I have all these bachelorette ideas that I looked up on the plane. I have an entire Pinterest board for you.'

'Classic overcompensation by a delayed maid of honour,' Radhika laughed.

'Shh! I'm here now,' Rajni said in a gruff voice. 'That's all that matters, baby doll.'

Gayatri laughed. She liked this girl. 'What are the ideas?'

Rajni looked at her phone and then at the women before her. Her face flickered as she looked at Gayatri. 'Well, er ...' she hesitated.

'Tell us!' Padmini urged.

'Yes, go on!' Mangala, who was properly tipsy, prodded.

'We could ... er ... eat some of these,' Rajni pulled out a bag of marshmallows shaped like penises: pink, purple and white in colour. Radhika looked at Rajni, aghast, as she sheepishly dropped the bag on to the table.

'Or exchange dirty stories of best sex and ... um ... weirdest fetishes.' Rajni stopped at this point, looking at Radhika's mother, grandmother and former colleagues.

'Well, it's ... er ... more suited for a group of girlfriends, I guess,' Rajni put her phone down, embarrassed. 'Stupid American nonsense.'

'I have a dirty story!' Mukti piped up, batting her eyes becomingly.

Radhika shook her head. 'No, no. No sexy story session with my family. Just no.'

'Sorry,' Rajni said, miffed. But then she turned to Gayatri, to whom things were starting to seem more musical than before. The girl's chatter sounded like a rhythm to her. She laughed, because it seemed to fit into the melody of Radhika's friend's questions.

'So, you will do it?' Rajni asked eagerly. Radhika was nodding, too, with such hopeful fervour that Gayatri didn't have the heart to refuse, even though she had no idea what she was agreeing to.

'Of course,' she said, slightly aware that her words were bubbling out of her instead of emerging with their usual crisp articulation.

'Fantastic,' Rajni said. 'That's the perfect story to tell tonight. You guys are in for a real treat. This is the love story that brought Radhu all the way from New York to Mumbai.'

'Er ... what?' Gayatri asked, smiling at Radhika's smiling friend.

'Mum,' Mangala said, wary now. 'They want you to tell them about Dad.'

Gayatri's laughter vanished. She waited for the knot of fear and anger to tighten within her and hurt in her chest. But the pain didn't come. Perhaps it was the spirits, or perhaps it was Birdy's loving or Radhika's living with her, but something had loosened within Gayatri. The tense regret she felt at the mention of her husband had disappeared in the last year.

She was no longer afraid or imprisoned by the mention of Jairaj. She didn't have to bury their life deep within her anymore, afraid that if she took it out she would hurt her children.

She looked at her daughter and granddaughter's shining, beautiful faces. She had lived with knives within her and still managed to create two fantastic women. *What did she have to fear now?* Certainly not memories. Definitely not ghosts.

She held Radhika's hand and began to speak.

✤

'My marriage was a foolish, foolish mistake.'

If the eager faces of the girls before Gayatri grew darker or confused, it didn't register with her. Strengthened by the rum, she was finally telling the truth out.

'From the very first day, it was awful. The minute I got to London, Jai's father and sister began bossing me around. There were a million things to be done and the daughter-in-law had to do them all. I called relatives, wrote letters and served the mourners who lived with us through the fourteen days of the Hindu funeral. And I did it without any qualms because my husband had lost his mother.

'I spent a fortune telegraphing India, trying to stay on top of work, making provisions for the state partitioning of the state. But I received no reply. When the reply finally came, it was as devastating as death. Jairaj had resigned on my behalf. Someone else was appointed as head of operations to execute my work. He had retained his position as the head legal administrator of the partition. His name can still be found on historic documents. Mine was struck out. The biggest moment in my career was sucked out of being, without my knowledge or consent.

'By the time we got to Bombay, we were no longer speaking. I had decided to go back to Delhi to live with Bauji. I could not be with a man who respected me so little that he thought he could make my decisions for me. Bauji supported me, of course, but only until we discovered that I was pregnant. I don't blame Bauji. He was an old-fashioned man. Progressive for his time, but even he had his limits. Jai was sent for and I was sent back to raise a child I didn't want with a man I didn't trust.'

Radhika's mouth had dropped open in a pink O. Her friends stared at Gayatri, shell-shocked and embarrassed. Mangala, however, didn't flinch. She had already lived through the truth; it couldn't hurt her any more. Gayatri put her hand on her daughter's by way of apology and continued, in a voice filled with regret.

'Once Mangala came, working was out of the question. I begrudged Jai every second he spent using his mind and earning a career for himself, while I talked twaddle to a two-year-old in the anonymity of the house. We spent nearly all our time together in argument or in bitter silence. He managed to find amusements ... outside our marriage, but I wasn't allowed to leave the house without his knowledge. And I wasn't allowed to wear anything too attractive either.

A lot of my youth was wasted in beige saris and reluctant motherhood.'

Gayatri closed her eyes. The next part would be difficult, but it had to be said out loud.

'I didn't enjoy raising Mangala. Not as I should have. Not until she was a teenager at least, able to answer me with intelligence. And then I filled her head with a hard kind of liberalism, one that drained her of humour and replaced it with hardiness. It didn't help that Jai was the worst father. He was afraid of her beauty and irritated by her wit.'

'You were a good mother, Ma,' Mangala whispered. 'Much better than I was, at least.'

But Gayatri shook her head, unwilling to accept this consolation.

'I owe you an apology, Radhika. If you felt Mangala neglected you while growing up, it was mostly due to my idiotic parenting. I didn't realize that instead of teaching her to fear love, I should have taught her to develop the courage it requires. I only discovered this courage in myself—to love, to appreciate my marriage and family for what they were—after Mangala was gone. I thought she would never return and I would regret never having enjoyed my daughter all my life.

'But then, you were born, Radhika. Like a gift. Like a reprieve. And I got a second chance at being a mother. Raising you during our few summers together gave me a joy that I never expected to have, at least not since I married your grandfather. All my joy has been delayed, sweetheart.

And it was because I was foolish. I was too quick to trust and then too slow to forgive. Love is something that requires courage, time and respect. That is the meat and bones of it. The dresses, songs and dinners are all superfluous.

'But you're more sensible than I was. You have chosen a partner, not a prince. You have made a rational, not just a romantic, choice.' Gayatri laughed nervously before allowing her most fearful thought to finally escape. 'Kabir is nothing like Jai, no?'

❦

It was 2 a.m. and I was still awake, sitting on the floor of my balcony with a box of laddoos, watching the dead street spread out in front of me, in desperate hope. Aashna Soonawalla was going to be furious when she would notice my under-eye bags tomorrow.

I was sober, but everyone else had fallen asleep fortified with their drinks. Naani, who I had thought would stay up for a little bit with me and parse out the wild, wild story she had told us, had fallen asleep, as though exhausted from living out the life that she had spoken about. The story hadn't seemed to affect anyone else either, drunk as they were by the time it ended. Mukti had fallen asleep on the sofa halfway through Naani's marriage, and Rajni was listening like enraptured children do with witches' tales. None of them, not even Mum, seemed to realize the consequence of these memories. If Mum did, she chose not to think about it tonight. She simply ran off to find Steve, like a child who had woken up from a nightmare.

It wasn't love then.

I look at the tattered remains of Naani's diary, the pages I had pored over for the last two years, and confronted the rest of the bitter history, despite myself.

What Naani and Naanu had wasn't love at all. It was infatuation and a rushed marriage and, finally, a forty-year-long struggle for control.

WHOSE NAME WAS ON THE DOOR?

I finally understood my mother's age-old taunt. Naani had lost all her power in the marriage once she lost her income. And I could see now that, with Naanu, power was everything. He always had to have things just so, and his wife, Gayatri, was to be yelled at if his morning tea didn't arrive on time, or if his files suddenly went missing. Files that she should have been writing, reading, carrying herself.

God! I couldn't imagine how angry she must have felt, making tea for a husband she didn't love, when she should have been presiding over the partition of her state! She could have gone on to become an IFS officer. She could have lived in Paris, London or Buenos Aires as the Indian ambassador!

She could have been a Dipa Ghanshyamdas in her own right. She could have married Birdy, had a loving, equal partnership and enjoyed raising her children instead of wishing at every moment to be elsewhere, far away from jealous and controlling Naanu.

Love requires courage, time and respect.
You have chosen a partner, not a prince.

Kabir literally wanted to be crowned king and have me dance for him. I could not think of Kabir now. I would scream if I thought about the wedding. Or of the life I was going to lead with him in Delhi.

A light flashed directly on to my balcony and distracted me from my unfortunate thoughts. I shielded my eyes and blinked through the glare, only to see a white BMW disappearing down the road. It was a car that hadn't been spotted in the neighbourhood for a few weeks now. But I didn't dare get my hopes up again. Too many white BMWs had played havoc with my feelings in the last few days, slowing down as though to stop at my home but then speeding up again, on their way, far away from me without so much as a honk.

Maybe it was the wine or wishful thinking, but this car stopped. Moments later, a man emerged with a suitcase. Minutes later, he was in my room.

'Shouldn't you be asleep?' Zain asked, sitting down across from me, perfectly naturally, as though he had never left. I stared at him like he was an apparition.

'Hello?' He waved a hand in front of my face. 'Has insomnia robbed you of speech?'

'How was your flight?' I managed finally, tearing my eyes away from his suitcase's baggage tag. Emirates.

He shrugged, non-committal. 'It was all right. Long.'

Long?

'It's only three hours to Dubai,' I ventured, my voice as nonchalant as his.

'I wasn't in Dubai.'

'Your baggage tag says Emirates.'

'You do know that they fly to other countries, too, right?' he chuckled. And then he realized that I was not in the mood to laugh. 'I was in Dubai first. But that's not where I'm coming from.'

I stared at him, wondering if he was with Kiara. If they had taken off to some exotic beach locale to help him process the pain of possibly losing Birdy, one pina colada at a time.

'Radhika,' Zain said. 'Do you want to know where I was?'

'No,' I shook my head firmly. 'It's none of my business.'

He sighed, obviously tired.

'I was in London. I met my mum at her clinic in Surrey. You'd love it there, by the way. They have spin classes at the gym and a garden that looks like it's out of one of your Jane Austen novels,' he smiled as he spoke.

'And how's—how's your mum?' I ventured, quite tentative. Zain, to my surprise, nodded instead of stiffening.

'She's not too well, but I think we made some progress. She and I.'

My anger vanished once I detected the truthful note in his voice. He was the good Zain again. The one unafraid to share what he thought with me. Trusting and warm. He must have noticed the shift in my expression because he used this opportunity to ask again.

'So, what's up? Why are you awake?'

'I'm just having a … bad feeling.'

'What about?'

I took a deep breath. 'I'm thinking about all this … marriage stuff … and realizing that, well, Kabir and I met only three months ago. And we don't really know much about each other. I thought we'd be closer by now, but we haven't talked properly in a while. It's almost as though—' I laughed flippantly to offset my words. 'As though I'm marrying a stranger.'

'Well,' Zain paused. 'You are.'

I looked at him, suddenly sick with fear. He scrambled to reassure me. 'But, like you said, your grandparents didn't know each other too well either, did they?'

I fell silent. 'Their marriage was a disaster.'

'What?'

'I found out tonight.' I was on the verge of breaking down.

'Ah,' Zain exhaled, looking out of my balcony, at his house. At Birdy's window. But he didn't seem surprised, I realized.

'You knew?'

'No,' Zain shook his head. 'But I did suspect it. Birdy was too honourable to have waited around for another man's wife. But if he knew she was unhappy … I see why he founded the factory in Bombay.'

I laughed dryly. 'I'm glad I'm not the only one reeling from revelations tonight.'

'It's hardly a revelation to me. Just interesting.' Zain looked at me concerned. 'Are you reeling?

'A little bit,' I grimaced. 'I'm teetering for sure.'

'All right, let's see if we can steady you,' Zain held his hand out and I placed mine in it hesitantly, and then I surrendered fully. The warmth of his large palm sent a surge of assurance through mine.

'You have no reason to be afraid,' he said with confidence. 'You love and understand each other. That's a great foundation for a marriage.'

I didn't say anything. *Did I ever tell him that I 'love' Kabir?* I probably did, being the idiot that I was. How ridiculous of me to say that I loved a man I barely knew! And to the man that I actually—

Not love. Not yet.

—to the man I trusted. The man who held my hand through a career shift and the founding of a new business, despite the fact that neither had anything to do with him.

Zain looked at me, worried. 'Hey.' He took my other hand in his. 'You're not scared.'

'Are you kidding?' I asked. 'There's a reason I'm sitting in my balcony, eating all the laddoos that are meant as party favours for guests. It isn't because I have a hankering for besan at two in the morning.'

'That's just nerves,' Zain said. His eyes were looking into mine so steadily that I turned away, at his arms upon which the moonlight was glinting, rendering his hair golden. Zain continued, his deep voice rumbling through my dark room, scaring off my self-doubt.

'Nothing scares you, Radhika. You go out there and take risks for your own happiness. You don't sit on your butt like everyone else in this entitled city and wait for things to be handed to you. You wanted to go to business school, so you earned your scholarship. You wanted to get married, so you moved to Bombay. You wanted to make a difference for women here, so you quit your job and started something new, something bold.

'You're always moving forward, and with good, calculated risk. Honestly, if you were a company, you would have the highest gearing ratio. I'd definitely invest in you for some massive gains.'

I put my box of laddoos down, shocked. 'That's the nicest thing you've ever said to me.'

It's the nicest thing any man has ever said to me.

Zain shrugged. 'It's not a line. I mean it.'

It's not a line? Why can't it be though?

Do you not like me? Do you not like me? Do you not like me?

Why am I thinking about my neighbour one day before my wedding? Why am I staring at his beard and wondering how it could be so golden under the amber glow of the street lamps?

I'm wondering if he might lean in … but Zain didn't move. Instead, he was looking at my palm curiously, as though studying it. As though he was reading something.

Immediately, I snatched my hand back. But it was too late. He looked at me now, his eyes dancing.

'Radhika,' he said, guffawing with laughter. 'Is that … my name?'

✎

Zain's lips crushed mine and, for a moment, I felt joy, triumphant and warm, pressed on to the little crinkles of my mouth. It would be easy to surrender to this feeling of elusive, fleeting delight. It would also be wrong. To Kabir, who had accepted me, who had made a commitment to me, who had said he loved me.

Immediately, I broke away, nearly falling backwards as I freed myself from Zain's body. He looked at me, confused.

'What's wrong? Didn't you want me to kiss you?'

God, if he only knew.

'Zain, this isn't fair. You know it isn't—' I said, his recently spoken words reverberating through my mind. 'It isn't honourable. To want another man's wife. You said so yourself.'

Zain immediately straightened up and dropped his arms from my shoulders.

'It isn't honourable if you're still intending to marry the guy. Are you? Are you really going to marry him with my name on your hands?'

'Well,' I said, pausing to reorder my thoughts. 'Are *you* going to marry me?'

Zain's mocking smile faded. The dancing light in his eyes dulled. And as I realized what his answer was going to be. A pit opened in my gut. A hollowness that I hadn't felt since Siddhant swirled around my stomach like a cyclone gathering force, drowning the butterflies that rose from Zain's sweet speech.

Until then, I suppose, I had been nurturing some silly hope, borne out of emails and fairy tales. But now it was dashed, dissipated and done.

'Radhika,' he cleared his throat. 'I would need time for such a … such a big commitment.'

I chuckled because I already knew that the dream was dead.

'Take all the time you need. But do you intend, someday, to marry me?'

'I haven't ever thought of that,' he coughed, his expression pained. 'But hypothetically, if we were to be together for a very long time,' Zain paused again, grappling for words, 'and if everything were to work out … then perhaps at some later date in the future, I could explore the possibility of … marriage with you. Someday.'

There were more conditional clauses in that sentence than in my exit contract with McKinley India.

He took a step forward, but I shook my head firmly. It was not good enough. Explorations aren't good enough anymore.

'I'm sorry, Zain,' I said. 'I'm going to be thirty in a month's time. I can't play these games anymore.'

'Radhika,' Zain looked tired now, as though I was the one being unreasonable. 'Don't be a fool. We can be happy together. Do you think you would be happy being married to someone who didn't understand you?'

'I think, if he's willing to marry me, he's willing to spend the rest of his life understanding me, Zain. He isn't just interested in exploring the possibility.'

'He could also spend the rest of his life misunderstanding you, Radhika.'

I stopped short. 'I'm willing to take that risk,' I said. 'But I refuse to risk being alone.'

Zain looked as though he wanted to say something more, but he rose, picked up his suitcase and left.

27
The Wedding

Gayatri woke up anticipating a roaring headache. She had even put a pillow over her eyelids, waiting for the inevitable throbbing to begin. One could not down half a bottle of rum after nearly fifty years of abstinence without experiencing some discomfort. But, funnily enough, the throbbing did not come. In fact, as she untucked herself from her sunflower-patterned blanket, she found that she was feeling curiously light, as though her head and body were unburdened of some terrible weight. As if she had within her a freshness she hadn't experienced in years.

Suddenly, she remembered why. Her words, her voice from the evening before came tumbling through her mind.

My marriage was a foolish, foolish mistake. Radhika's voice quivering as she said 'Naani?'

Immediately, Gayatri was on her feet, running to her granddaughter's room. Radhika, fortunately, was already awake, and dancing.

She can't be devastated if she's dancing? A familiar, old Bollywood song began to play. Gayatri was surprised. She knew Radhika was playing a courtesan in the Mughal durbar that Dolly Sehgal had staged, but she didn't think Radhika would be dancing to this song.

Gayatri immediately took a step back and hid behind the door to watch her granddaughter dance, unobserved. To her shock, Radhika was singing, too.

I am nothing, nothing without you. What is my heart,
You, my master, can take my life.
Just do, once, as I ask you.
I beg of you. Just once—

Gayatri's entire form began to shake with anger as she watched her granddaughter prostrate before an imaginary king.

How dare they? HOW DARE THEY.

❦

'Kabir! Kabir!'

Dolly Sehgal burst into her son's room in her furry La Perla bathrobe and bright blue rollers in her hair. To Kabir, she looked like an agitated polar bear.

'Yes, Ma?'

'Mrs Anand just called me in a state,' Dolly Sehgal said, close to tears. 'She … she …'

'Mum?' Kabir tried to control his own headache as he rose to hug his blubbering mother. 'What did she say?'

'She said I was a … a disgrace to women!' Dolly Sehgal cried. She didn't want to embarrass herself by weeping in front of her son, but Chander was still asleep after the whisky-drinking bender he had been out for with Kabir and his good-for-nothing nephews the night before. Dolly had tried to prod him awake when Gayatri Anand had called, but Chander had just mumbled unhelpfully.

'She accused me of disrespecting her granddaughter and her family. She asked me if I was going to be a mother-in-law or the madam of a whorehouse!'

With this, Dolly Sehgal burst into loud, vehement sobbing that amplified the throbbing in Kabir's head. He could do little more than pat the rollers on his mother's head and assure her that he would have everything under control.

After three cups of coffee and a shower, when Kabir went to Radhika's house, his intention was to set things straight with his fiancée and to demand an apology from her grandmother, whom he had been itching to fight with ever since she had torn up the tickets to Switzerland and scolded him for having crude intentions.

But when he entered the bridal home, Kabir could neither spot Radhika nor Mrs Anand amongst the riot of revellers milling about the living room of the bungalow— many of whom were his own cousins and aunts from Chandigarh. The house was a celebratory mess of activity, with orange- and mango-coloured garlands being strung and boxes of laddoos being exchanged amongst guests.

Kabir hoped to reach Radhika's room quickly, before his outrage on behalf of his mother faded, but one of the guests spotted him, the groom, in the bride's house before the baraat. All of them erupted in exclamations and jokes.

Oh ho! Couldn't wait till the baraat, Kabir Baba?
It's bad luck, don't you know?
Send for the bride. Send for the bride!
Make sure she isn't in her wedding clothes already.
Yes, yes, that would be very bad luck.

Kabir smiled like a prince, touched people's feet and kissed cheeks to make his way through his aunts and their peals of laughter, but it took him ten long minutes of inane conversation and false cheerfulness to reach Radhika's bedroom, in which he had lost to the environment some of the anger he planned to unleash on her.

Finally, just as he was about to knock on the door and have it out with his bride, he was accosted by a familiar syrupy and sweet voice.

'Kabir?'

He nearly didn't turn, paralysed as he was by that sound—the one that had whispered, crooned and screamed his name for much of his adolescence.

'Aishwarya?'

Kabir was shocked to see his ex-girlfriend at his bride's house. He had known she was going to be at the wedding, obviously. Her parents were the Sahanis after all. He had, in fact, personally ensured that the invitation included her name and that the wedding was on a date during her annual winter visit from London.

He was prepared to greet her as a guest in his royal durbar, with his beautiful wife on his arm.

What was she doing here?

Parineeti joined them then to clear up matters for Kabir. 'Aishwarya called me as soon as she got off the plane this morning. She wanted to meet Radhika.'

'Oh?' Kabir asked, slightly wary.

Parineeti gave her brother a reassuring look, as though to say she had the situation under control, but it didn't help Kabir in the slightest. And who could blame him? The last time he had seen Aishwarya properly, she had been sobbing big fat tears after swallowing too many of his dad's painkillers and confessing that she had fucked Aryaman Batra, the high-end drug dealer, before all their friends in London. Multiple times.

'Relax, Kabir,' Aishwarya laughed at his expression. She raised her hand and showed him a set of black numbers tattooed on the inside of her pretty wrist. 'I'm sober,' she said, pointing at the tattoo that said 'Since 18 January 2017'.

Kabir's eyes widened in amazement. 'January 2017? That's a month after …'

'We broke up,' she said with a nod. 'Yep.'

Kabir couldn't help but smile a little. It was impossible not to when Aishwarya was beaming at him with her sparkly green eyes boring into his face, like they had for so many years in so many countries. God, like that morning they woke up in Rome after—

'Look, I hope this isn't awkward,' Aishwarya said, laughing again. 'But I thought it might be nice for me to meet the bride before we spend two weeks together on Daddy's boat.' Then she added more seriously, 'I don't want to fuck things up for you any more.'

'No, don't worry,' Kabir laughed breezily, as though the idea that Aishwarya may have the power to hurt him was laughable. He was about to be crowned a king, after all. 'It shouldn't be awkward at all. Radhika is a great girl. Come, let me introduce you.'

Taking care not to put his hand on the small of Aishwarya's narrow back, he guided her into his fiancée's room.

*

My marriage makes more sense to me now, Radhika thought.

Aishwarya Sahani was a sexy, curvy thing. I'd be devastated and rush into an arranged marriage, too, if she broke up with me. Unlike Zain's pretty but passive ex-girlfriend, Kabir's ex had a fiery quality to her, an ownership of her identity, reflected in her nose piercing, her love handles and her laughing '*hai na*', which was tacked on to the end of every sentence, making foot-thumping bhangra music out of her otherwise British accent.

'List-en!' she said to me with earnestness now, 'I'll tell Daddy that I'm not coming out on the yacht this year if it's odd for you. I'm more than happy to chill with Pari in Bombay. *Hai na?*'

'Absolutely,' Parineeti nodded. 'Rajat, Aish and I have partied all over Asia. We can do Bangkok this time. Or, oh, Seoul!'

Kabir didn't say anything, but it was obvious from the many, many times he sneaked a look at Aishwarya's pierced belly button that he was dying for her to come on our honeymoon.

'I wouldn't want you to third-wheel with Pari and Rajat,' I said half-heartedly.

'Don't worry. I always find someone to kiss on New Year's, baby,' Aishwarya laughed.

Kabir all but keeled over in pain. 'Don't be silly, Aishwarya,' he said. 'It's your boat. You have to come.'

He then looked at me pleadingly, urging me to agree.

Wasn't this bizarre? I was getting married to this man in less than three hours, and he was concerned about his ex-girlfriend's feelings, that too over our honeymoon. That too an ex-girlfriend he never cared about enough to mention.

I'm surprised you didn't like anyone on one of the guest lists of your mother's parties.

I did.

Oh.

But it didn't work out. Evidently. Or I wouldn't be here, thinking about taking you home to meet my family.

'How long were you two together?' I asked, the past conversation playing as clear as day in my head. Aishwarya glanced at Kabir and grinned.

'Seven years if you don't count school,' she shrugged.

Of course, they were childhood sweethearts!

Kabir looked at Aishwarya with a frown. 'Five years, really, if you don't count your masters in London.'

'I count that,' Aishwarya said.

Kabir shook his head, but it was evident from their faces that they were thinking of some fraught, intense memory.

God, I bet that story was wildly passionate. Childhood sweethearts from Delhi, whose relationship started to fray once she left for London. They must have had at least one fight at the airport and three bouts of make-up sex. Was I supposed to compete with this?

Parineeti looked at me, worried. 'Aishwarya,' she said. 'Why don't I take you home to get ready?'

Aishwarya, catching her drift, said, 'Oh, of course! I didn't mean to stay and interrupt your tête-à-tête. I just wanted to say hello.'

'I'm glad you did,' I said, meaning it.

Once Aishwarya left the room, I looked at Kabir expectantly, waiting for him to say something reassuring, or at least something that explained what just transpired in my room. But Kabir remained speechless.

'So,' I prompted.

'So,' he looked down. 'You aren't doing the dance?'

I shook my head. Naani had made that abundantly clear this morning.

Kabir nodded.

'Right.'

'Are you disappointed?'

He nodded again.

'Yes, but at least,' he breathed in, 'at least you're here.'

He then kissed my forehead and left.

Gold dangled from my earlobes, nose and neck. Naani placed the golden dupatta, shimmering with zardozi petals and a silver border, around my head. My costume was complete.

'You look majestic,' Rajni said, her eyes wide as she gazed at my reflection and let out a low laugh. 'God, maybe I should have moved to Bombay and become a queen, too.'

I smiled at her weakly. I could not bring myself to confess, even to Rajni, how far from majestic I felt just then. Ideally, I should have been filled with triumph. After all, Naani had won us a victory this afternoon by returning the pink and blue courtesan's outfit to Dolly Sehgal and demanding, in no uncertain terms, that the entire narrative of the Mughal durbar be altered. Now, I would enter the Taj Mahal hotel that evening not as a performing commoner waiting in courtesan's dress, to be looked upon favourably by the king, but as a queen in my own right, resplendent in regal attire even before my marriage.

After so many weeks of conforming to Dolly Sehgal's wishes and whims, this had been a victory for Naani. I was glad.

Yet, I had noticed that she was not wearing an expression of satisfied triumph. In fact, beneath her kind smile lurked a disquietude not too different from my own. I longed for a moment to talk to her alone, to ask her what was bothering her, but there were too many people crowding the room. There was Mum, who peered at herself and adjusted the silver sari Naani had lent her for the occasion, and there was Rajni, who scrolled through Instagram stories of guests who were already at the durbar, providing us with a running commentary of my wedding. And as much as I loved these two women, I was too ashamed to voice any complaint in front of them. Especially not after I had been such a vocal advocate for arranged marriages and finding love in Bombay.

'Look at your throne!' Rajni said, showing me a picture of a gold and velvet chair, decorated with jasmine flowers and Swarovski crystals. 'God, it's gorgeous!'

Mum peered at the picture before it disappeared. 'Kabir's is higher than yours,' she noted.

I shrugged, tired. 'The Sehgals are sticklers for convention.'

'Those conventions were abolished for good reasons,' Naani clicked her tongue.

'Well, at least the cocktails look like fun,' Rajni showed us a picture of goblets lined up on a brass bar. 'Strawberry

Anarkalis for the women and rum-based tamarind Shahenshahs for the men.'

'Those weren't on the menu yesterday,' I said, surprised.

I caught Naani's eye and knew that we were thinking the same thing. Gendered cocktails were Dolly Sehgal's desperate attempt at winning back control. Weak, pink drinks for women and strong, spicy ones for the men.

I wondered if I was going to be expected to sip cosmos with Dolly Sehgal for the rest of my life. I could see her handing me a pink Martini glass on a boat a few weeks from now, while Kabir disappeared to have a stronger, more delicious drink with Aishwarya Sahani.

My heart began to thud violently. *How could I have agreed to this marriage without discovering more about my future husband?* I had been so grateful for his commitment, so pleased by his eagerness to wed, that I had not once questioned the reason behind the rush. My wounded ego had been only too happy to believe that he loved me, within a month of knowing me.

'Oh, the baraat is leaving now!' Rajni squealed, looking at another Instagram story. 'If you're done, shall we go downstairs and wait?'

My head started to throb. *What choice did I have?* I had quit my job in New York. And I had begun a business I believed in, here in India. There was no going back now. I didn't even want to go back now. Not to a life of sugar packets, spin classes and a sterile routine.

I would just have to marry Kabir and hope for the best.

As I rose to walk out of the room with Mum, Rajni and Naani, the conversation from last night came back to sting me.

Do you think you will be happy being married to someone who doesn't understand you?

I think, if he's willing to marry me, he's willing to spend the rest of his life understanding me, Zain.

God, this couldn't be. So far, Kabir had made no attempt to understand me better. He hadn't even thought it necessary to consult me before committing us to a honeymoon with his ex and her parents, nor had he thought it necessary to stand up for me when his mother had suggested that I perform as a prostitute at our wedding. He had not even asked about my day or called me when I needed to hear his voice.

Shit. No wonder those emails proved so effective. My entire flirtation with Zain was borne out of the fact that I had no real relationship with my husband-to-be.

The only thing holding this marriage together was the ceremony itself. Kabir may be willing to commit to me legally, but he wasn't committing to me at all.

He was committing to a girl who could play a devoted Anarkali to His Royal Highness Salim for the rest of his life.

But I couldn't waste all this, could I? We had spent so much money. I had spent so much time. I couldn't start over with someone new ... or could I? I wanted to be married ... didn't I?

Mum began to drape the dupatta over my forehead like a veil, so that Kabir could lift it according to tradition, as though seeing his bride for the first time. As she dropped the golden cloth before my eyes, a panic rose through my body.

It kept rising as we walked out of my bedroom and down the stairs. A collective gasp went through the cousins in the living room as they saw me. The aunts burst into exclamations and blessings. As I descended, they rushed forward to get a better look.

I stopped on the stairs, quite abruptly, and clutched at my grandmother's arm. She was the only person who would understand, who loved me to such distraction that she would forgive.

'Naani,' I said, breathing heavily. 'I need a minute.'

She held my hand firmly. 'Take all the time you need, sweetheart.'

I threw off my veil and ran back up the stairs, straight to my grandmother's bedroom.

❧

Zain watched as the baraat approached the Anand bungalow. The drums were deafening and the trumpets were exhausting. If he hadn't promised Birdy that he would be there that evening to help him welcome the groom's family, Zain would have been on a flight to Dubai, far away from the unhappiness that this wedding was bringing to him. Yet, he stood and watched as Kabir, astride a large white stallion, rode forward, while his family danced in celebration on the road, throwing wads of money at the pedestrians and passers-by to express the wealth of their happiness to the world.

This was the difference, Zain thought as he gazed at the approaching groom and his family, and their music. Kabir was the type of guy who could give a woman like Radhika the domestic experience she was looking for. He had the family, the set-up, the assured business structure. Zain, however, was all over the place. He had an ageing Mamu, a fledgling relationship with his sick mother and a cotton business that was growing all over the world like an incessantly spun web. Zain couldn't stop for marriage. He couldn't stop to start a new family. He liked the family he had now. After a lifetime of adjustments to new people and contexts, he finally liked the routine his life had settled into with Birdy and his business, and Gayatri Aunty and Radhika next door. *But Radhika wouldn't be next door anymore, would she?* No matter, he steeled himself. He had survived more than a loss of a friend. And there would always be a string of girls, more than happy to—

Zain abandoned his chain of thought and straightened up, alert as he watched the groom carefully now. Something about Kabir's expression had changed. He was grinning differently at someone dancing very close to his horse. At first, he thought Kabir was smiling at his sister, Parineeti, because the girl looked so familiar to Zain. But then, as they got closer, Zain realized it wasn't Parineeti!

It was the girl whose photograph was in his briefcase. The only difference was that in those photographs the girl's eyes had been small and swollen. Now they were bright with promise and lined with kohl. And they were looking directly at Kabir as the rest of her danced, with vigour—bouncing vigour—to the hectic beat of the drums.

What the hell was Aishwarya Sahani doing here?

❧

'Sweetheart? Is everything okay?'

Naani sat down next to me, and I was unsure how to respond to her. Even now, with her sweet face furrowed in concern, she looked lovely. Despite all the frustration of the wedding planning, she looked much younger than her seventy years.

'Naani,' I whispered. I knew what I needed to hear from her.

'Yes, my love?'

'You love Birdy uncle, don't you?'

Naani was startled. She blushed violently, but her voice was steady as she said 'yes'.

'And you can't marry him till I'm married?'

Naani inhaled sharply. 'Who told you that?'

'Never mind that,' I said. 'You would like to be with him. You have wanted to be with him all this time. But you haven't. Because of me?'

'Radhika,' Naani began, 'don't be ridiculous—'

'Is it not true then?'

Naani looked flustered. 'It is not important,' she insisted. 'Your baraat is at the door. Is there a reason we're discussing my marriage?'

Before I could respond, Zain burst into the room.

'Radhika, listen—' he almost yelled, but he stopped after seeing Naani. Then, as though abandoning courtesy, he strode towards me. 'Please don't marry Kabir.'

'Zain?' Naani was shocked. 'Beta, is everything all right?'

'I think he's still carrying on with his ex-girlfriend. They had a messy relationship, Radhika.' He knelt before me and said, 'Look, if you give me a few more days, I'll find out for sure.'

'Zain,' I said, looking at him perturbed. 'Why are you kneeling?'

'Because if you have to marry someone tonight,' he took out a gold ring and continued, 'then I'd rather it be me.'

Naani looked as though she was torn between laughter and tears. 'Zain!' she exclaimed, trying hard to steady her voice. 'Beta, get up.'

But Zain shook his head vehemently. 'You don't understand, Mrs Anand. I had a private investigator find out details of their relationship. It was long and very intense. The girl, Aishwarya, was wild and into drugs and other things, but Kabir kept going back to her. I'm certain that if she's come back, it's not a good sign.'

Naani was concerned as she looked at me, as though expecting me to burst into tears or to have an emotional reaction of some sort. But I was eerily calm. I was more surprised to hear that Zain had hired a detective to investigate Kabir than I was about Kabir's relationship with Aishwarya.

'Zain,' I said slowly. 'Please get up.'

'Radhika,' he said insistently, 'don't marry him.'

'I won't.'

All of a sudden, everything was clear. Relief flooded through me, pure and uplifting as a cool glass of water on a very warm night.

'Really?' Naani looked equally relieved.

I nodded. 'Really.'

Zain, however, seemed worried. 'Does this mean, we're—?'

'No, it doesn't.' I laughed. 'I'm not going to make you marry me. Now get up.'

As he stood up, I quelled the urge to wipe the sweat that had collected over his brow. I was touched that he even made an offer like that—one that had obviously caused him so much strain. All to protect me from making a bad decision.

Birdy entered then. 'The groom is here!' he yelled happily.

Naani, Zain and I looked at each other with a mixture of dread and hilarity.

Kabir strode through the house looking every bit the emperor with his majestic turban and the pointed gold mojaris encasing his feet.

Aishwarya trailed behind him, along with the rest of the Sehgal clan. He walked towards me, his grin as victorious as ever. For a moment I trembled, overwhelmed by the largeness of what I was about to do, at the number of people I was about to disappoint. But then I glanced at my grandmother and mother, standing next to each other, holding hands after years of tension and mistrust. It gave me courage. The Sehgals would never be content with me as I was and I would chafe against what they would try to make of me. It was better to recognize and acknowledge that now than to spend our lives in a relentless negotiation of values.

I stopped as Kabir took my hand to lead me to his horse. 'Kabir, can we speak in private please?'

Anger flared across his face and his dark eyes blackened. It seemed as if he was about to refuse, or maybe drag me to his horse, with the same force that he had used in his car. But this time our families were watching. My family was watching.

'All right.'

'Is everything okay, Radhika beta?' Dolly Sehgal asked, smiling as Kabir and I headed towards my room. Kabir nodded to her to indicate that he had the situation under control. She turned to the curious guests and laughed breezily, saying, 'Must be a little wedding surprise. She gave Chander a Rolex for Dhanteras, you know.'

'She did,' Chander Sehgal started showing off his watch to the aunts and uncles, but as I shut the door to my room, I could see that Mr Sehgal's expression was as wary as his son's.

'What the hell is this about?' Kabir snapped. 'Don't you think you've embarrassed my mother enough for one day, Radhika? Are you purposely trying to hurt our family?'

'I'm not, Kabir,' I said. 'I think we should stop this now, before anyone gets hurt.'

The anger drained out of Kabir's face. Only shocked horror remained.

'Have you lost it, Radhika!' he yelled. 'Do you know how it will look if we call it off now?'

'Kabir,' I glanced at the door and his voice dropped to an urgent whisper.

'Radhika, please.' His expression was pleading now. 'You can't do this, love. Everyone is here.'

'Aishwarya is here?' I asked. Kabir gave me a sharp look.

'I haven't touched Aishwarya—'

'Kabir,' I moved closer to him and held his hand. The indignation remained on his face, but he allowed the gesture.

'I'm not accusing you of anything,' I continued. 'I just don't think we love each other. Not enough to see this marriage through.'

I expected him to protest, to yell, perhaps even to shake sense into me—but he didn't. He sat down on the edge of my bed, where not long ago he had traced circles on my naked back.

He looked exhausted, defeated and … relieved. He took his turban off and the tension on his face eased out.

'You're right,' he said. 'Radhika, I wanted this to work out so badly. I've been without anyone for too long.'

'Me too, Kabir,' I sat down next to him and held both his hands. 'But it's better to acknowledge that we aren't right for each other now than to waste years being bad partners to each other.'

'I tried to stay away from her,' he confessed, finally looking up at me.

Wait, what?

'You … you slept with her already?'

Kabir nodded. 'This afternoon. I told myself it was the last time, but … I just …' he looked down at his hands remorsefully. 'I just can't stop myself. Even though I know she doesn't want to be married to anyone.'

I should have been hurt or enraged or betrayed, but all I felt was relief. I even laughed a little as I realized what a near-miss this had been. *God, to think I almost went through with this sham of a wedding.*

'What's so funny?' Kabir asked.

'Nothing … just,' I shook my head. 'Don't write off your relationship with Aishwarya just yet. If she flew all this way just to fuck you before your wedding, she may have changed her mind about marriage.'

'You think so?' he asked, his eyes full of hope. I nearly laughed again. I couldn't believe that I was sitting in my wedding lehenga with my groom, discussing his chances with his ex-girlfriend. It was almost cute, the pharma prince of Delhi and his favourite client.

'Definitely,' I nodded. 'I think this cruise will be good for both of you.'

'That's what I thought, too,' Kabir said and then looked at me sheepishly.

I chuckled and placed my hand on his shoulder. *Who was I to judge really? I had another man's name in my mehendi.*

'Mum and Dad are going to be so disappointed,' he said, getting up.

'They won't be. They may have a Sahani in the family now.'

Kabir smiled weakly, kissed my cheek and left with his turban in his hand.

28
Marriage

*G*ayatri pulled a cotton scarf lightly over her head before entering the gurudwara. As she stepped on to the soft green carpet, the hymns her father used to sing rose in her heart and came to rest on her lips. Soon, she was humming. Birdy, with an orange handkerchief covering his head, started to hum along. They were followed by the rest of their family—Zain, Radhika, Mangala and the new addition, Steve.

Gayatri knelt before the holy scripture. A turbaned old priest approached them.

'Is this the couple?' he asked, looking at Zain and Radhika.

The two of them smiled at each other in embarrassment. Radhika shook her head firmly. 'No. It is my grandmother. Gayatri Anand.'

'And my uncle,' Zain said. 'Badrinath Rajan.'

Surprise crossed the priest's face for a moment, and Gayatri felt fear dart through her body. *Was he offended?* She was about to suggest that they leave and go straight to the court for a legal marriage when the priest smiled with sanguine acceptance.

'Those who have loved are those who have found God,' he said in Punjabi.

'Guru Nanak,' Gayatri whispered, naming the founder of Sikhism and the first of its ten gurus.

The priest nodded and began the ceremony.

As he uttered the invocations and prayers that bound Gayatri to Birdy, she felt a peace grow within her, the kind that one felt on returning home after a long and weary travel. Birdy, however, grinned with a grander, almost inappropriate, joy that made Gayatri bite back a laugh.

As the priest paused in his muttering, Gayatri whispered, 'Birdy, you can't smile so much. It isn't decent.'

'Why not?'

'We're in the house of God.'

To her surprise, her reserved friend let out a belly laugh that rang through the Darbar Sahib as he took her hand.

'Gayatri, trust me, God *knows*.'

Gayatri coloured, but then she found herself joining in his laughter, giggling with mirth and some reverence. Radhika and Zain smiled at them bashfully. Gayatri hoped that someday they would understand what it meant to be as fully in love.

'And now, please kneel in front of the holy book,' the priest instructed. 'In acknowledgement that you are attached by divinity and love, in the eyes of God, till as far as he can see.'

As the couple touched their foreheads to the cool floor of the gurudwara, Gayatri did not close her eyes. Instead, she watched the heads of her children and husband similarly bent in prayer. Tears that hadn't surfaced for nearly a decade began to roll down her face of their own volition, like a river that flowed without needing anyone's permission.

✎

'What did you say to her?' Zain asked as we drove back home from the airport after dropping Mum and Steve off. I didn't catch the meaning behind his question the first time, since I was still processing Mum's departing words.

'Sweetheart, I have never been as proud of anyone as I am of you, for breaking off the wedding so close to your birthday.' Then she kissed my forehead, waved at Zain and was gone. Back to her world of books and a boyfriend.

How did I feel about my upcoming thirtieth birthday?

'Earth to Radhika?'

'Oh sorry,' I said, snapping out of my daydream. 'What were you saying?'

'What did you say to Mrs Anand to change her mind about marrying Birdy Mamu?'

'Oh,' I grinned. 'I told her I would never consider marrying anyone who had a problem with her and Birdy Uncle's relationship. In fact, it would be a good litmus test for the kind of man I needed to stay away from.'

Zain raised his eyebrows. 'It may take some time to find someone so progressive here.'

'I'm in no rush.'

My response was reflexive, not arrived at after reasoning, but I knew it was truthful. The anxiety in my gut had disappeared. I didn't feel the gnawing need for a companion anymore. *Almost marrying a man who was hung up on his coke-sniffing ex-girlfriend would do that to you.*

'Thirty, thirty-one, forty,' I continued, unperturbed. 'I'm willing to wait till I find what Naani and Birdy have. Although I do hope it doesn't take till seventy.'

Zain laughed.

'In the meantime, I've got work I love to fill my days, Naani and Birdy to dine with in the evenings and even Parineeti as a dancing partner on the weekends.'

I smiled as I remembered how Kabir's younger sister had come to me and whispered 'you did the right thing', right after the Sehgals had yelled at me and Naani and stormed out of the house, the Sahanis by their side, muttering consolations.

If nothing else, at least a mutual disrespect for me had helped the Sehgals bond with the friends they had aspired to have for so long. I hoped it would ease the path for Aishwarya and Kabir. Maybe she and Dolly Sehgal could do detoxes together at the chic rehab centre for movie stars in Switzerland. I, on the other hand, could spend my time building *The Queen Network* right here in Bandra, taking frequent trips to Dubai to meet with Dipa G. and less frequent ones to New York to cuddle with Rajni.

'A good life,' Zain said, glancing at me as he turned the steering wheel.

'A good life,' I agreed, meaning it, as we turned on to our street, where both our homes would be devoid of the elders for the period of their honeymoon.

Zain stopped his car in front of Naani's gate, but he did not unlock the doors. I waited for him to say goodbye, but he remained silent. I unfastened my seatbelt and got ready to leave, but I could sense his hesitation.

'Radhika, wait!'

I almost left. I didn't want knee-jerk emotions from Zain again. After witnessing Naani's wedding in the gurudwara this morning, and Steve and Mum's sweet departure, I thought I finally understood what love looked like. And I was not going to settle for a cheap imitation any longer.

'I'm going to London tomorrow,' he said.

'Okay?' I said, confused as to why he was telling me this.

'I may miss your birthday.'

'Oh.'

'I won't be back for a couple of weeks but—'

I waited as he hesitated again.

'But I want you to call me if you need anything. At all. Even a chat. Or a rant. Or a graphic designer.'

I smiled. 'I'm fine, Zain. You don't have to worry about me.'

Zain let out his characteristic quiet laugh. 'I don't think that's an option anymore.'

I turned my face away. I didn't want him to see my delight. Truth be told, I was glad he was leaving. If there was one thing I knew for sure, it was that I didn't want to feel anything more than platonic love for my new relative and old neighbour.

'Bye, Zain. Have a safe flight,' I said before I walked through the gates of our bungalow.

Ms Gayatri and Radhika Anand

The new nameplate greeted me as I turned the key in the lock. As it clicked, I felt a sense of 'rightness'. As though things had fallen into place for me. As though, after a lifetime of searching and working and adjusting and longing, I was finally in the right place at the right time.

I was home.

✎

TO: radhikaanand@gmail.com
FROM: dipaG@ghanshyamdascapital.com
SUBJECT: Happy Birthday!
Hi Radhika,
Many, many happy returns of the day. I wish you all the very best for the upcoming year. I am sure you are

going to make a lot of women very proud in the next few months, including me.

Congratulations on being fully booked for the conference! We may even have to add a couple of chairs because I have employees at Ghanshyamdas Capital begging me for tickets.

PS: A certain business tabloid emailed me, asking if they could do a magazine spread on you. Should I pass on your contact information? They're despicable, of course, but a high profile is good for business.

Again, I hope you have a lovely day, dear girl!

Warmly,

Dipa

TO: radhikaanand@gmail.com
FROM: siddhantlodha@legal.mckinley.com
SUBJECT: Hey!

Happy birthday! I hope you're having a great day. I'm sure you are. It's so weird that I can't wish you in person. I kind of thought you would come back after things with the wedding didn't pan out.

Sorry about that, by the way. But I'm sure you're fine. You're great at bouncing back from things.

I may be in Bombay in the next few weeks. Want to get a cup of coffee? No special reason. Just felt like visiting home for a bit. Haven't seen the fam in too long.

Anyway, let me know.

Siddhant

TO: radhikaanand@gmail.com
FROM: zainrajan@gmail.com
SUBJECT: Why Is Your Phone On Silent?

Pick up, so I can say 'happy birthday'.

TO: zainrajan@gmail.com
FROM: radhikaanand@gmail.com
SUBJECT: I'm Avoiding People, Including You.
Especially you.
Rad

TO: radhikaanand@gmail.com
FROM: zainrajan@gmail.com
SUBJECT: You Can't Avoid Family
You're going to have to deal with me for the rest of your life, whether you like it or not.
My mum wants to say happy birthday, too.
Zain

TO: zainrajan@gmail.com
FROM: radhikaanand@gmail.com
SUBJECT: I Don't Have to Do Anything
I can spend the rest of my life not speaking to you at family dinners, if I want.
Say hello to your mum though.
Rad

TO: radhikaanand@gmail.com
FROM: zainrajan@gmail.com
SUBJECT: She Says Hello Back
She could use the conversation, to be honest. She hasn't had anyone except me and Nancy at the clinic reception to chat with all month.

It would be nice if she got to see the new niece I've been telling her so much about.
Zain

TO: zainrajan@gmail.com
FROM: radhikaanand@gmail.com
SUBJECT: Now I Have to Call
You played the 'sick mum' card.
Rad

TO: radhikaanand@gmail.com
FROM: zainrajan@gmail.com
SUBJECT: I Have a Better Card
I love you.
Now pick up the goddamn phone.
Zain

About the Author

Riva Razdan is an author based in Mumbai. Her work has been featured in *The Hindu Business Line*, *Grazia India* and *The Telegraph*. Her debut novel, *Arzu*, was published by Hachette India in February 2021.

30 Years *of*

 HarperCollins *Publishers* India

At HarperCollins, we believe in telling the best stories and finding the widest possible readership for our books in every format possible. We started publishing 30 years ago; a great deal has changed since then, but what has remained constant is the passion with which our authors write their books, the love with which readers receive them, and the sheer joy and excitement that we as publishers feel in being a part of the publishing process.

Over the years, we've had the pleasure of publishing some of the finest writing from the subcontinent and around the world, and some of the biggest bestsellers in India's publishing history. Our books and authors have won a phenomenal range of awards, and we ourselves have been named Publisher of the Year the greatest number of times. But nothing has meant more to us than the fact that millions of people have read the books we published, and somewhere, a book of ours might have made a difference.

As we step into our fourth decade, we go back to that one word – a word which has been a driving force for us all these years.

Read.

Harper
Collins

HARPER
PERENNIAL

HARPER
BUSINESS

HARPER
BLACK

हार्पर
हिन्दी

HarperCollins
Children'sBooks

HARPER
DESIGN

HARPER
VANTAGE

Harper
Sport